PENGUIN BOOKS

The Tuscan Contessa

The Tuscan Contessa

DINAH JEFFERIES

PENGUIN BOOKS

PENGUIN BOOKS

UK | USA | Canada | Ireland | Australia
India | New Zealand | South Africa

Penguin Books is part of the Penguin Random House group of companies
whose addresses can be found at global.penguinrandomhouse.com.

First published 2020
001

Copyright © Dinah Jefferies, 2020

The moral right of the author has been asserted

Set in 11/13 pt Dante MT Std
Typeset by Jouve (UK), Milton Keynes
Printed and bound in Great Britain by Clays Ltd, Elcograf S.p.A.

A CIP catalogue record for this book is available from the British Library

ISBN: 978-0-241-98731-5

www.greenpenguin.co.uk

In memory of the Italian people whose bravery and courage inspired this book

Brief Timeline of World War II in Italy

July 1943 A few weeks after the Allied invasion of Sicily and bombing of Rome, the Mussolini regime collapses. Vittorio Emanuele III, the King of Italy, appoints Field Marshal Pietro Badoglio to be the new Prime Minister of Italy. Mussolini is imprisoned. Meanwhile, the Germans contact Badoglio, who confirms Italy's continuing loyalty to Germany. But the Germans are suspicious, so the Wehrmacht makes plans to take control of Italy if the Italian government switches allegiance to the Allies.

8 September 1943 An armistice between Italy and the Allies is publicly declared. The King and Badoglio flee from Rome, taking shelter on the Allied side. As the Italians surrender to the Allies, the Germans rapidly occupy Italy, including Rome. Italy officially changes sides, making peace with the Allies against Nazi Germany.

9 September 1943 The Allies arrive by sea to land on the beaches of Salerno. Shot and mortared by the enemy troops hidden in the mountains, it takes ten days to push the Germans back. Two thousand British soldiers die.

12 September 1943 On Hitler's orders, Mussolini is rescued by German paratroopers.

23 September 1943 The Italian Social Republic is proclaimed with Mussolini as leader. Although he prefers to return to Rome, the Germans establish his capital in a villa at Salò on Lake Garda, in the north. However, he has already lost control of most of

Italy and governs a puppet state dependent entirely upon Berlin. Much of the country is under German martial law.

1 October 1943 After fierce fighting, Allied tanks liberate the city of Naples. The Allies then head for Rome, but the enemy is using Italy's natural defences to stop them – impassable rivers, fortress-like mountains. Progress is slow.

13 October 1943 Liberated Italy declares war on Germany. The country is effectively caught up not only in WWII but also in a civil war between Fascists and anti-Fascists.

16 and 17 October 1943 Reinforcements from Commonwealth armies leave for Italy. There follow numerous brutal battles as the Allies slowly drive the German army back. German resistance is strong.

November 1943 This story, *The Tuscan Contessa*, begins. At this stage the Italian partisans are not organized and are mainly involved in random acts of sabotage.

5 June 1944 The Allies enter and liberate Rome. They head towards and then through Tuscany. By now the partisan units have grown in number, become better armed and are better organized.

6 June 1944 Elsewhere in Europe, the Normandy landings – referred to as D-Day – take place, the operation which begins the liberation of German-occupied France. Despite the symbolic and strategic importance of the fall of Rome, D-Day takes precedence in the popular imagination and the Italian campaign is largely ignored.

29 June 1944 Retreating German SS troops storm through Tuscany. In the villages of San Pancrazio and Civitella a massacre takes place in reprisal for the partisan shooting of four German soldiers.

June/July 1944 Part of the Allied advance, French North African troops, known as Goums, allegedly rape and loot their way through Tuscany.

4 August 1944 The Allies reach the southern parts of Florence and the battle for Florence commences, with enormous help from the Italian partisans. The German army retreats, looting and burning. Florence is left filthy, with no electricity, little water, no transport and almost no food. The fighting moves north.

12 August 1944 In Sant'Anna di Stazzema the reprisal massacre by Waffen-SS of 560 local villagers and refugees, including more than a hundred children, takes place. During the retreat, other massacres follow.

21 April 1945 Bologna is taken by the Allies.

28 April 1945 Mussolini is shot dead by partisans and hanged upside down in Milan's Piazzale Loreto.

29 April 1945 The German command in Italy signs the surrender.

2 May 1945 The surrender of the German Armed Forces in Italy becomes effective, two days after the collapse of Berlin. Fifty thousand Italian partisans are dead; 300,000 American and British have been injured during the Italian campaign, 47,000 are dead. American casualties at Anzio alone are 59,000. German casualties are approximately 434,000.

The Walled Village of Castello de' Corsi, Tuscany

29 June 1944 – 7.15 p.m.

In the small piazza overlooked by shuttered windows, balconies and terracotta roofs, the heat hangs heavily, the air smells of smoke, and the inhabitants are either asleep or hiding. The only voices are those of tiny swallows, but when a large black-winged crow takes flight from the top of the crenellated tower, an ear-splitting screeching starts up. Another crow follows. And another. Three crows, the old lady thinks. Three means death. She counts them off on her fingers before sipping her watered-down wine where she sits on a chair in the doorway of what had once been her son's house. Despite the warmth of the evening, she wraps a frayed woollen shawl around her shoulders and stifles a yawn. 'Old bones,' she mutters.

The ancient stone buildings surrounding the square gleam in the golden sunlight: homes, a couple of shops, the manor house with its large casement windows and the deep eaves from which water drips in the winter. Plus, a single archway into the village, wide and high enough for a horse and carriage. Blowsy crimson roses planted in a clay tub climb as far as the first floor of the manor, their heady scent drifting in the early-evening air. Before long, the sun – at present a mellow ball shining in the azure sky – will begin to sink and the sky will be threaded with red.

It is a rare peaceful hour, but the tranquillity is disturbed when a shriek echoes around the square. A few dark shutters rattle. One flies wide open and a startled young woman looks out from her window, eyes fixed on the piazza. *What now? What can it be now?* And the old lady glances up as if she might already know *what now* although there's nothing to see but for a few pigeons fluttering to the cistern in the centre.

A breeze rustles the flat leaves of a fig tree and a young boy races through the huge curved archway, shrieking again as he chases after a white three-legged dog, the child's crust of bread clamped between its jaws. They circle the cistern until the child slips on a fig and the old lady laughs as the dog escapes. *Good for you, little three-legged*, she whispers, though she knows the child and his grandmother, Carla, too.

A woman in blue walks into the square and stops in view of the tower. She signals to another woman and points to her right. 'Try that way.' After the other one slips through a doorway into the darkness, the woman in blue heads towards the tower, only pausing momentarily when she hears an engine. Surely not the Germans, not now. Allies then? She takes a second to cross herself and then carries on.

But, at that moment, a moment that will go on forever in her memory, she hears a strangled cry. She stares up at the tower, shading her eyes, disbelief flooding her whole being. A woman is perched on the crenellated battlement at the top with her back to the square. Head bowed, she is just sitting, not moving, not looking around. A few seconds pass. There's a gust of wind and, with a further glance up, the woman in blue frowns in puzzlement, uncertain of what she's seen. She calls out, 'Be careful!' There's no reply. Had it been a shadow or were there two people up there? The woman in blue shouts out again but everything is happening too quickly now, and the woman at the top of the tower is tipping back dangerously. Something falls, billowing, drifting, floating in the breeze. The woman in blue is running, faster than she's ever run before, tripping over her own feet as she does. She sees the silk scarf lying on the ground and, heart thumping, she races for the tower door.

2.

Castello de' Corsi

Seven months earlier – November 1943

With a mixture of longing and hope, Sofia stared out at the Val d'Orcia where the deep-brown slopes folded into valley after valley and the sky, purple and backlit by the setting sun, appeared to hold its breath. In the distance, the brooding, lonely Monte Amiata watched over them, while the golden-red vines, and the oak trees blazing defiantly in their final moments, only heightened Sofia's hunger to recapture what they had lost. Winter was skirting closer, but she still longed for those hazy summer nights when she'd wriggle her bare toes in the dry grass as they lay gazing at fireflies and drinking red wine from the bottle.

She used to love these liminal times when for those few moments the world became misty, magical, impossible; loved the minutes between sleep and wakefulness because neither one nor the other could claim her. She could believe they were still walking hand in hand in the dusty olive groves, dreaming up plans for their future with no foreknowledge of what lay in wait.

As the night slowly turned black and began to seep into the small salon, she yanked the creaking shutters so hard the window frames shook, then she closed the window itself and spun round to scan the scene. She smelt the rich comforting aroma of Lorenzo's cigars as she squatted by the hearth to throw another log on the fire, before glancing back at him where he sat on their faded blue-velvet sofa, both dogs snoring at his feet. With the house at its quietest, it was at its darkest too, and it was then that her fears pursued her. The shadows in the room altered with the flickering flames, alive and monstrous as they flared almost to the ceiling, then waning as the flames subsided. But she could still see the glitter of them in his gentle grey eyes. She had no idea what he was thinking or feeling. Grief, yes, but that edge he had was new. He patted the space next to him on the sofa and she stretched before going to nestle up close.

Even as he ran his fingers through her hair at either side of her head and lifted it away from her face, she felt as if she were losing parts of herself; parts of him too.

'There, I can see you now,' he said.

'You have always seen me,' she replied, and then she told him she'd been thinking about the poppy fields.

'Oh?'

'I wish it were May and then all this would be over.'

He pulled a noncommittal face. 'It may not be.'

'I had a dream about them. The poppies.' But she didn't add that the red of the poppies had spoilt and the flower heads had been dripping with blood.

His voice was gentle as he lifted her hand and examined her broken nails. 'That's not paint under what's left of your nails, is it?'

'Gardening.'

'Ah, yes. Well, *I* was thinking of Florence.'

'You mean before?'

'When you were at the Art Institute and I was in the Agrarian Faculty.'

She smiled at the memory of her carefree nineteen-year-old self.

'Nineteen twenty,' he added. 'And you are still the same.'

'Small? Pale? Wrinkled?'

'Hardly.' His eyes danced with amusement. 'Elegant. Beautiful as ever. But I'm going grey and you are not.' He ran a hand over his pepper-and-salt hair.

'I like it.'

'But you don't paint as much these days, do you?'

4

'Not since the war began, but I have started again.'

They slipped into silence, both with separate reflections. She longed to reminisce about the early days, remind herself of who he really was, of who she was too, but couldn't find the words. She watched him closely, but he only smiled, and she wondered if they were thinking the same thing. In the hush she heard the ticking of the grandfather clock above the sound of the fire, marking the seconds, separating them still further as the silence lengthened.

'Do you . . .' he eventually said, as if he were reading her mind.

'What?'

'It doesn't matter.' He shook his head. 'I was just . . . thinking.'

'About?'

'Well . . . you know . . .'

She frowned, unsure. Did she know?

'About us,' he said.

'Oh yes . . .'

They left it, this odd little snippet of conversation, and she hoped they were headed for safer ground. In the end it was he who spoke.

'Sofia, I've been wanting to say . . . well, I've been waiting for the right moment to say. But . . . really, there isn't one, so I'll just come out with it.'

'Go on.' She heard the touch of anxiety in her own voice as he, meanwhile, absently rubbed his chin.

'The thing is, I'm going to have to be away,' he went on.

She pulled back and moved across to the chintz sofa opposite, curling up her legs and trying not to look wounded. 'So, what's different? You're always *away*.'

He grimaced. 'And I always come back.'

'You mean this time you won't?' she said, alarmed at the notion of coping with the whole estate alone.

5

'No, I mean this may be for longer.'

'Considerably longer?'

He nodded. 'But it's not going to be straight away.'

'What will you be doing?'

'Nothing very difficult. No need to worry.'

But the tone of his voice was too breezy, and she was sure he was lying. 'Tell me,' she insisted.

He sighed. 'I've recently been asked to pass on information that the Allies may find useful.'

'Isn't that terribly dangerous?'

He held her gaze and she knew that of course it was dangerous. 'You'll still be doing your job at the ministry?'

'Certainly.'

He got up and she watched him from the corner of her eye as he took a small but bulky brown package from his pocket and held it up. She tilted her head, indicating he should put it on the coffee table.

'Aren't you going to look at it?' he asked.

'Later.'

'You'll be safe here at the Castello?' he asked, and she registered the raw emotion in his eyes.

The question was a serious one. He was picturing their high walls, and their home, not quite a castle but the manor house of their small, fortified, thirteenth-century village with only one archway in, or out, and walls which no enemy could ever break through. Until now.

'Safe? Us? Maybe.'

But not our pigs, she thought. *Nor our turkeys, chickens, ducks, guinea fowl, wild boar, cattle*. She resented the stealing from their thirty-two farms and reflected on the isolation of each one, below and beyond the village. Easy prey.

'There'll be no sausages this year.' And if her voice was bitter, she didn't care.

'But you have hidden food supplies?'

6

'Some, but there will be little meat for us or for the farmers. Why do you think we keep eating rabbit?'

He smiled, trying to make light of it. 'I like rabbit.'

'Just as well then.'

She gazed at her hands for a moment.

'What is it?' he asked.

'Nothing.' And knowing she still hadn't told him about the letter, she changed the subject. After all, it probably wouldn't happen and then she would be glad not to have worried him. 'What will you do about your card?'

After a sharp intake of breath, he gave her a disappointed look. 'Not this again?'

She bristled. 'Well, since the armistice with the Allies . . .'

Another silence followed, brief this time.

She carried on. 'But things *are* different, aren't they?'

He tilted his head from side to side as if easing his neck. 'It's complicated.'

He was right. Here, where they lived under German martial law, he had to carry the Fascist card, for safety's sake.

'In the south, in Allied-held territory, it's different,' he added. 'But you know what it's been like since the Nazis occupied most of the country. You're either with them or against them, there's no middle ground.'

'So, they will go on thinking you're with them.'

She hoped he'd carry the card inconspicuously. And she understood. She really did. He didn't want to talk about this, a sore point between them since 1932, when all state employees had had to sign the Fascist card or lose their jobs. She never really understood because he hadn't needed a job, not with the income from the estate and their investments. But he worked in the Ministry of Agriculture and his passion for the land drove him. He'd been riveted by Mussolini's *bonifica integrale*, the reclamation and salvage of previously derelict or unusable land. You only had to look at the Val d'Orcia, the visionary way in which

7

it had been cultivated when Lorenzo had been vice president of the local consortium. It had transformed from a dull, dusty landscape into fertile land, with abundant crops and flowering orchards.

Still, she couldn't help thinking of her cultured and terribly clever father who had refused to sign the card, and who now lived with her mother in a lofty apartment in a Renaissance palazzo in Rome with barely enough to survive on.

'I know what you're thinking,' Lorenzo said with a sad little smile.

She smiled back. 'You do?'

He stood and reached his arms out to her. She went to him and they rocked together in an embrace.

'So, what *is* in that packet?' She glanced at it lying on the coffee table.

He blinked and then stared at her. 'It's just a small pistol.'

'*Cristo!*' She felt more than a little shocked. 'And you need one now?'

'Actually, I already have one – the package contains yours.'

'You think I need it?'

'You might.'

'And you were just going to hand it to me as if it were a box of chocolates?'

He didn't reply. A pistol, for heaven's sake! She decided to think about it later.

He leant back a little to gaze into her eyes. 'You have the darkest eyes and the loveliest of voices.'

She laughed. 'You're changing the subject . . . and, anyway, you always say that.'

'And I always say I could spend my whole life trying to fathom them and listening to you.'

He loosened the combs from her hair and it tumbled sheet-like to her waist. 'Your parents could come here. I wouldn't object. It's getting worse in Rome.'

'You know they won't.'

She was right, of course. They didn't tell her everything, but she knew they were involved in something. And to be *involved in something* in Rome was becoming riskier every day.

'Is Carla still here?' he whispered in her ear, then nibbled the lobe.

She felt the usual tingle. At least they hadn't lost that. 'She's gone to her daughter's, to tuck in little Alberto. She'll be hours. Who knows what she gets up to?' she said, although she knew.

For a moment she pictured Carla hunched up against the rain as she hurried along one of the narrow, cobbled alleys to the row of little stone houses resting in the shadow of the tall bell tower. The wall compressed the houses together as if they were holding each other up, as they all had to do now.

'Giulia?' Lorenzo asked.

'Left for home. We have the place to ourselves.'

She saw his eyes soften.

'In that case, I'll put another log on the fire while you take off your dress. I need to feel your skin.'

She laughed. 'In front of the fire?'

And more than anything, more than war, more than survival, more than winning or losing, or wondering what on earth they were going to eat, she wanted him too. It was the only thing making this bearable because she dreaded the morning when she might sit across from her husband while they sipped their barley coffee and not be able to see who he was or know who he had become.

She removed two cushions from the velvet sofa plus the old chenille blanket from where it covered a bald patch. Then she undressed and lay on the rug that covered the ancient encaustic tiled floor from where she studied Lorenzo as he took off his clothes. Tall and lean, his shoulders glowed in the firelight.

'Socks too.' She pointed at his feet.

He laughed but gave in, then slid under the blanket. She

9

shivered. Outside the fortified walls the ghosts of this war were gathering and growing in number. Were they watching them now, jealous, aching to find a way back into the warmth of their lives? Or did she shiver because of the cold? It was a November night and the warmth of the fire heated only one side of her body.

Lorenzo rubbed her back vigorously and she laughed again.

'I'm not one of the dogs, you know.'

He kissed her on the forehead and then on the tip of her nose. 'I had noticed.'

Once they were warm, their love-making was fiery. It always had been. They had not succumbed to the dangers of habit, or the careless disinterest that could lead to infidelity. Instead the spark between them had grown, was still growing, into a deeper more reflective bond. And they both knew that human contact, connection, love, whatever you wanted to call it, was the one thing that would pull them through. She sighed and with each touch of his lips her thoughts began to fade until she surrendered to the sensation of their bodies moving together, as they were meant to do. It would be all right. It had to be.

Rome

Maxine Caprioni picked up her bag of clothes and left the drab room in Via dei Cappellari, where she'd been staying. Outside, she pulled her woollen collar up against the cold. Her coat, a dowdy brown colour, was a man's coat with large pockets, so she'd wrapped it around her tightly and belted it. She hurried down the unlit street, eyes peeled, avoiding the puddles of rain-water. At the sound of scratching she glanced behind her. Stinking heaps of uncollected rubbish littered the street, and she grimaced at the sight of a family of rats weaving through the filth. She moved on, passing through the neighbourhood of narrow streets, small piazzas and ancient churches of Campo de' Fiori. Then she made her way towards Via del Biscione, not far from the now ghostly Jewish ghetto. A shout somewhere near the corner ahead rooted her to the spot. She took a deep breath but then, without thinking further, hid her bag in the darkness of an alleyway and hurried towards the sound. A nose for trouble? Maybe – but more likely, and as her mother would say, her instinct to rescue a trapped kitten or a bullied child.

As she rounded the corner, she came to a halt just in time to avoid tripping over two men whose jackets were peppered with badges on the sleeves, collars and fronts. Underneath were the tell-tale black polo necks. Blackshirts, kicking an old man whose walking stick lay on the road out of reach. Her heart thumped in anger as they taunted the defenceless man with each vicious kick, then one of them lifted his head and smashed a fist into the side of his face. A third man – like the others, no more than about seventeen – picked the walking stick up and, laughing, snapped it across his knee. The old man, now in the gutter, bleeding profusely and whimpering as he attempted to protect his head with his arms, was pleading for his life. Maxine calculated the odds. If she intervened, she might get the same treatment but if she didn't the man could certainly die from his injuries.

These bullies had free rein to roam the streets before and during curfew, picking on whoever they wanted. She checked her watch. Still fifteen minutes to go before curfew.

'Hey, boys,' she called out, undoing her coat, throwing back her head and shaking her long curly chestnut hair so that it fell seductively over one shoulder. 'Fancy a drink?'

The young men stopped to stare.

'You're out late,' one of them said curtly.

'No worries, there's still time.' She was Italian by birth, and with her olive complexion and expressive amber eyes, she looked it. She only had to hope the influence of her New York upbringing wouldn't let her Tuscan accent down. She sauntered up to one and undid the top two buttons of her blouse. 'Look, that bar's still open.' She pointed at the opposite corner.

They hesitated, then one of them held out his hand. 'Papers?'

She burrowed in her handbag and came out with her new identity card and a ration book. Her American passport she'd had to leave with the British liaison officer.

'Drinks on me,' she said and started to move away, hips swaying as she looked back over her shoulder to smile at them, glad she'd worn her red lipstick. At twenty-nine and having grown up in Little Italy and then East Harlem, Maxine had come across thugs like these before.

One, perhaps the leader, gave a nod and, with a last kick at the now silent man, began to come after her, the other two trailing behind.

All three followed her into the bar and ordered wine. Now

what? She cracked a joke and made them laugh, taking the measure of them as she did.

Her mother's voice came again. *You're too impulsive, Maxine. You never stop to think.*

Her mother was right. One of the boys had an arm wrapped around her shoulder, pulling her into him as he fondled her neck, while his other hand lay heavily on her thigh. They probably thought she was a whore. *Get out of that*, her mother whispered.

She ordered a second round of drinks accompanied by large brandy chasers and glanced at the clock on the wall. The minutes passed slowly.

She would soon be leaving Rome to make her way to Tuscany, where she would be put in touch with key resistance groups – if reliable partisan divisions even existed. Nobody in England had been sure. If her verdict was that it – or they – did, she would liaise between the Allies and the resistance networks. It was a high-risk operation and the British had found it virtually impossible to locate Italians willing to go back to Italy as SOE agents to assist in espionage, sabotage or reconnaissance. She, however, had jumped at the chance to locate and ascertain strategic features of the *resistenza*.

Her training was minimal, her liaison officer, Ronald, had been at pains to point out, unlike the training given to SOE operatives sent to France. After all, Italy had only been an occupied country since early September and she had been interviewed by Ronald just a few short weeks later, in October. Admittedly, it was rushed, but they needed people on the ground at breakneck speed.

The boy was squeezing her thigh. She wriggled out of his clutches, chatting about some inconsequential thing, then smiled as warmly as she could. The image of the old man lying on the ground and her rage at his treatment spurred her on. An idea crystallized; it could work, and it might be her only opportunity.

She saw the boy staring at her, so gathered her courage and stroked his cheek. 'Just going to the washroom.'

He gave her a wary look.

She made it her business to know the back entrances to every bar – you might need a quick route out at any moment. And she was shrewd enough to avoid the area around Via Tasso where the Nazi SS and Gestapo headquarters were located. Here, she must be at least forty-five minutes away. She slipped out to the yard, bypassing the toilet, grazing her hands as she scaled the low wall into the next-door yard, then over a broken fence and into the alley running parallel to the street. She picked up her bag from its hiding place, raced back to the old man, helped him struggle to his feet and found out which palazzo he lived in. Luckily, it was close to where she was headed.

'We must move quickly,' she whispered urgently. 'They'll come for us.'

They began to move but, on such weak legs, he could only shuffle, groaning all the way. She tried to quieten him, but they made excruciatingly slow progress as they rounded the corner into the next street, thankfully the one she was heading for. A shout came from somewhere behind them, echoing into the emptiness. Oh God! The boys. Could it be them already?

They passed several buildings and arrived at a palazzo with the usual heavily carved and studded wooden door but a little grander than most. Was this the one? She didn't know but it had to be near. With the boys now on their trail, she pushed the door. Thank God, it opened. She half carried, half dragged the whimpering man through. In the internal courtyard she leant against the door and clamped a hand over his mouth. His breath was too fast and too noisy, and he looked at her with huge pleading brown eyes, obviously unsure if *she* was about to hurt him too. She shook her head then pressed her lips tight at the sound of booted footsteps. Nerves on fire, she listened and overheard them arguing, the three thugs at each other's throats as they approached the palazzo. One insisted they retrace their steps, while the leader declared she had definitely come this way. She clenched her teeth, hearing the vile acts they were going to force upon her when they caught her. But how long could she keep the old man quiet? She smelt smoke – not just the noxious smoke Rome was never without – and held her breath. The boys had lit cigarettes and were loitering until more 'fun' came their way. Or did they know she was there? She wouldn't be able to hold the old man upright much longer nor prevent him from crying out. She dared not move him. The street was too silent, and they'd be heard.

Maxine's head pounded from the tension of waiting but she fought to keep her breath long and slow. After another five minutes or so the boys finally decided to head off elsewhere. Inside the courtyard, Maxine quickly dragged the man to the ground-floor door he indicated was his own. A woman opened up and stifled a cry when she saw the blood on his shabby overcoat and the cuts and bruises on his face.

'*Mio Dio!* I always tell him not to go out after dark, but he's a stubborn old fool. Thank you for bringing him back.'

Maxine muttered that it was nothing then asked, 'Do you know where Roberto and Elsa Romano live?'

'Next door. Top floor.'

Maxine slipped out cautiously and into the next-door building, then up the marble staircase to the top floor.

Rome had been held by the Germans since 11 September. They had taken over the telephone exchange and the radio station, and with petrol already scarce, people feared there'd be no electricity before long. Although an announcement had declared it an 'open city', promising that troops would not flood the centre, Maxine had seen it wasn't true. She'd watched them marching up and down the Via del Corso with no purpose other than to intimidate.

Now, when the door opened a crack, she whispered the

password and was given entry into a dark hall by an older woman with greying hair who beckoned her down a corridor. The woman told her she was Elsa as she led her into a room lit only by candles and oil lamps. They had made the place look cosy despite the high ceiling and the cold. Maxine shivered. This had once been a grand room and, although the furniture looked shabby, she was sure there had once been money here. She glanced around and saw five pairs of narrowed eyes staring up at her. Naturally, their first instinct would be to distrust her.

'Hello,' she said, putting down her bag and then tying back her hair as she sat in the one spare seat at a large dining table where sheets of paper stapled together had been scattered randomly.

The woman was studying her grazes. 'Your hands?'

Maxine wiped them on her trousers. 'It's nothing. Sorry I'm late. Just managed to escape a spot of bother. I'm Maxine. I . . .' She was about to explain but recognized she'd better stay quiet and say no more about what had happened.

A couple of the assembled men and women nodded.

A distinguished-looking man smiled at her, although when he spoke and offered his hand, she noticed a tremor. 'I'm Roberto, Elsa's husband,' he said. 'This is our apartment. You come highly recommended. I'm assuming you weren't seen?'

Maxine gave him a noncommittal response. Elsa appeared to be quietly confident, but her husband's hands shook again as he picked up a sheaf of the papers. As the sound of machine-gun fire penetrated the room, they all exchanged anxious glances.

Elsa shook her head. 'It's not close.'

Maybe not, but Maxine told herself it was a damn good job she'd be heading for Tuscany in the morning.

The sheets of paper, Roberto explained, were the finished pages of a locally organized clandestine pamphlet produced by members of the Committee of National Liberation of whom he, Roberto Romano, was one.

'When the Germans crushed our troops defending the city at

Porta San Paolo,' he said, 'and then imposed Nazi martial law, we formed the committee.'

'Now,' Elsa added, 'we spread news from Radio London. You know it's banned?'

Maxine confirmed that she did.

'And we send out partisan information using underground press like *L'Unità* and *L'Italia Libera*.'

'And the printing press?'

'Few are given that information.'

Maxine glanced around at the assembled people, most of whom looked like intellectuals but for one man. His longish dark hair and slightly unshaven appearance identified him as a partisan except for the formal suit he was wearing. Maybe he'd been a soldier? The man spotted her staring, raised his brows and winked. She held his gaze. His eyes were extraordinary, with caramel-coloured irises shining with intelligence and life. Dangerous, exciting eyes, she thought. His face was angular, and she noticed a walking stick resting beside his chair. So many lost souls were hiding in Rome, including British prisoners of war who'd escaped or been let go by Italian soldiers who were no longer fighting on the German side. The man was now studying her. He didn't look like an escaped Britisher.

After a moment she noticed Roberto was waiting for a reply or maybe waiting for her to do something. She hadn't even heeded the question, if there had been one.

'Sorry,' she said, and picked up a pamphlet, read part of it and then looked at Roberto. 'You'd like me to take these?'

'Well, you might as well, as you'll be going north anyway.'

'Rather than a *staffetta*?'

'It's complicated for our ordinary couriers at present. Pass the leaflets on to partisans to disperse wherever they can. You know where to go?'

'Not yet. My liaison officer gave me your address, told me when to be here and that you'd give me further instructions.'

She didn't mention the British radio operative she'd been ordered to contact in Tuscany. That information was on a strictly need-to-know basis. And she'd been told in no uncertain terms that Italy was not France, that the resistance was extremely scattered, which meant that the ultimate goal of figuring out where and how to supply them with arms and ammunition would be extremely difficult.

'We need you to go to Castello de' Corsi in Tuscany,' Roberto said. 'At the manor house ask for Sofia de' Corsi. If you tell her we sent you, she will accommodate you. Her husband could be there too, Lorenzo de' Corsi. You may talk to him but speak to Sofia first if possible.'

'She doesn't know I'm coming?'

'Not exactly. Explain what you are really there to do, but away from the Castello keep quiet. You can tell *her* your real name but otherwise use your cover. You have your story worked out?'

'I do. I had been thinking of telling people I was there to write a piece on how the war was affecting ordinary men and women. I used to be a journalist, you see. But my liaison talked me out of the whole idea.'

'Just as well, I'd say, especially if you were to "bump into" any Germans. They'd think you were a spy,' Roberto said and then continued, 'From Marco here, we know the partisans in Tuscany are something of a ragbag – untrained, reckless, angry.'

She noticed that Marco, the young man with the caramel eyes, was nodding vigorously and she smiled at him. So, he *was* a partisan.

'You will work with Marco and he will give you all the help you need,' Roberto continued. 'Once it's clear how viable the groups really are, how many men there are, where they are, who their leaders are, *we* can relay the information on to your Allied liaison officer or, if you can make contact, just radio direct to him at SOE's subsidiary headquarters in the south.'

'We believe British radio engineers and radios will be dropped in several locations,' Marco said. 'We need to rapidly expand our partisan communications network because the Allies need us to be ready.'

She nodded. 'I'll do my best.'

'And your family originally came from?' Roberto asked.

'Tuscany. We always spoke Italian at home, English at school.'

'Your accent isn't bad. No German will be able to detect you're from New York, though the locals might.'

She gave him a smile. She didn't tell him her heart ached for her mother whenever she thought of Tuscany. She sighed deeply, hoping she'd made the right decision to come. Against her entire family's objections, she'd gone ahead and sailed for England as an accredited United States correspondent. Then, in a drab hotel room in Bloomsbury, it had all changed. A letter had been left at the news agency where she worked, mentioning just the time and place, and the name of the person she was expected to see. One Ronald Carter. The letter had been headed with the British Governmental official stamp of the Inter Services Research Bureau. It meant nothing to her, and during her first interview with the tall, dark-eyed and rather nattily dressed Ronald, she had remained just as mystified. He told her he had received her details from the Immigration Office, who controlled the waves of displaced people, screened refugees, enforced rules on exit permits and so on.

He had narrowed his eyes and said, 'I want to know more about you.'

She had thought maybe her permit to work in Britain was being revoked and she would soon be sent home. But in the long second exploratory meeting with Ronald, when he'd grilled her about her personality, her allegiances and her grasp of Italian, she found out what he really wanted. He was bilingual himself and they had carried out half the interview in Italian.

'We're casting the net for young Italian nationals both in

America and in London with the right attitude and personality to be recruited, trained and swiftly deployed under cover in Italy,' he'd said in a serious voice.

He then explained that if she agreed, she'd arrive with British troops by ship, disembarking in southern Italy, as would he. After that, she'd be dropped by parachute close to Rome. Partisans would take her to the city but then she was on her own.

Following that meeting with Ronald, she'd been sent to train in a kind of parachute academy for two weeks where she'd passed with flying colours after three real jumps. It had been terrifying but exhilarating. More training followed during which she had to carry out practice covert assignments. She'd held her nerve and now here she was and her parents didn't know anything about it.

'By the way,' Roberto was saying, interrupting her thoughts again and bringing her back to the present. 'You'll have to wear a dress.'

'Why? I *am* going up on a motorcycle.'

'Nevertheless, you'll blend in with the women in Tuscany if you wear a dress,' he said. 'Elsa?'

As Elsa got up and walked out of the room, Maxine struggled to control her irritation. Despite being tall and leggy, with a figure any girl would die for, she had a flair for slipping under the radar and felt most comfortable doing it in trousers.

Elsa returned with a pile of clothes.

Roberto stuffed a battered satchel with pamphlets.

When he was done, Maxine took it along with the clothes. Elsa indicated she should change in the bedroom and, as Maxine pulled on a dress, she could hear the assembled men and women whispering. She edged closer to the door but couldn't make out what they were saying. As she tied on a headscarf, the stamp of hobnail boots rose from the floors below. Then came the ear-splitting sound of gunfire and loud thumping on apartment doors.

'Jesus. What in God's name?'

Elsa flew into the room. 'Quick. Use the fire escape and please give this box to Sofia de' Corsi; she's our daughter and she lives in the villa – the manor, that is – at Castello de' Corsi. Say that her father and mother remind her about the sweets. It's important.'

'Sure. But will you be all right?'

Elsa gave a noncommittal wave of her hands. 'I think the Nazis are requisitioning our building.'

'You knew about this?'

'We had warning.'

'Christ, why didn't you go?'

'I didn't want to believe it. None of us ever want to believe it.'

They could both hear strident German voices barking orders and women wailing as their doors gave way.

'Jump over the rail to the terrace below this room and there you will find the fire escape.' She thrust the satchel into Maxine's arms. 'There's money in there too.'

'And the motorcycle?'

'It's rather battered but is where we agreed. Go to the Castello first, but remember you need to be in Caffè Poliziano, in Montepulciano, in ten days' time to meet with Marco, who you saw earlier. Make sure to arrive by ten in the morning.' She then whispered a new password in Maxine's ear and Maxine gave her the thumbs-up.

'Petrol?' Maxine asked.

'Yes. Go!'

Maxine threw the satchel and her bag over her shoulder then made for the railings as a rush of excitement rose up alongside the nerves. This whole thing was strangely thrilling, and her entire body had begun to tingle.

4.

Castello de' Corsi

While Sofia was spending the evening with her husband, their cook, Carla, was busy arranging her shawl to keep the draught from her neck and settling her body into the chair by the door on this darkest of nights. Eight of them had secretly gathered in her daughter's house in one of only two chilly upstairs rooms. With three-year-old Alberto finally asleep, the women were busy. Sara spinning wool in the corner, Federica unwinding the wool from the spindle, and the rest grouped around the table knitting socks and blankets. One oil lamp lit the room and a blanket draped over the window ensured no light could leak through the slats of the shutters.

Gradually the rhythm of clacking needles and the spin of the wheel merged with Sara's voice as she began to sing very softly. Because they were lonely, husbands and sons gone to war and nobody knowing where anyone might be, this time together warmed their hearts. This knitting, this sitting, bound them in solidarity as they worked, despite the curfew, for if they did not, the men hiding in the woods would freeze in the hard winter ahead.

Once the armistice had been signed, the soldiers, no longer fighting the Allies, had deserted their posts in the Italian army, risking everything to get home. But then, when Germany occupied Italy, she wanted the men as *her* soldiers, as her labourers, as her slaves, here or in camps in Germany. Many men had made for the wooded hills and joined the partisans. Some had never wanted to fight on the German side but had been conscripted.

22

Some didn't want to fight for anyone, and many had simply had enough of fascism. Hordes of rural men were supporting the communist movement in growing numbers. So now, as well as the world war, there was also a civil war between those who supported the Fascists and those who did not.

Carla glanced across at Anna, her elder daughter, twenty-five, tall and strong, slim too, unlike Carla herself, nearly fifty and showing it. But poor Anna's husband, Luigi, was already gone, drowned when his ship, the *Zara*, sank in 1941. Anna had been told that Luigi had taken part in sorties to catch British convoys in the Mediterranean. The *Zara*, a heavy cruiser built for the Italian *Regia Marina*, had been disabled by a British airstrike. Later, in a fierce night of fighting, it had been sunk by the British Mediterranean Fleet.

'Gabriella is in place?' one of the more nervous women asked.

Carla pictured her pretty, curvaceous, sixteen-year-old daughter curled up in the kitchen with Beni, her little three-legged dog, both hogging the only fire in the house. Gabriella had pestered to be allowed to act as their watch-out and, with her whistle so shrill it would wake the dead, Carla had given in.

'Do you have any new messages from the men?' one of the women asked Anna.

Those in the room knew Anna was a *staffetta*, a courier, for the partisans, though Carla and Anna rarely spoke of it. Even though the village women were friends you never could be completely sure. Take Maria, the old biddy who lived on the corner of the square, the one whose grandson, Paolo, had recently gone off to be one of Mussolini's Blackshirts. They were the voluntary militia for national security, not the army, and now nobody had a clue where Paolo was. At the start of the war, many local men had signed up for the regular army or navy and people had more or less accepted the call to arms, but the brutality of the Fascist Blackshirts against their own people was a different thing. They were loathed by much of the rural Tuscan population.

'No messages,' Carla said before Anna could reply, her rough country-woman's voice hushed and low.

'Who do you hate the most?' Federica asked. 'Germans or Blackshirts?'

The room went silent for a few moments.

'Blackshirts,' Sara said. 'I've seen them in the town pushing anyone they don't like the look of into the gutter. Even pregnant women. Old, young, they don't care.'

'They think they can do whatever they want.'

'Because they *can* do whatever they want. But, mark my words, we've not seen the worst of the Nazis yet.'

As the women whispered, Carla's thoughts settled on food, as they so often did. She'd pick wild mushrooms the next day and make a risotto of mushrooms and chestnuts. Foraging for wild onions, herbs, even berries, kept the farmworkers going in lean times. And her curly-haired son, Aldo, would soon be out hunting what was left of the wild boar.

There was a loud knock on the front door and then a piercing whistle.

'Quick, blow out the lamp,' someone said.

Carla sensed every woman's fear as, in complete darkness, they listened, mouths dry, throats tightening, as rough male voices rose from the street. Blackshirts, no doubt, out for a bit of fun. The Germans didn't run the risk of dark alleys in a Tuscan village at night.

But if the Blackshirts came in and you were caught aiding the partisans . . .

Carla heard the front door open and then close, after which, from outside, came a male guffaw followed by female laughter. Gabriella's laughter? Surely not.

A few days had passed and now, with Lorenzo likely to be away for a night or two, Sofia waved him off, then whistled for the dogs – both of them lovely chestnut-and-white Italian pointers, sometimes known as Bracco gun dogs, although theirs were rather too old for hunting now. They'd only just heard that the ancient village of Chiusi, on the border with Umbria, had been bombed by the Allies and it left an unshakeable feeling of doom. South of Montepulciano, it was a good fifty kilometres away, but still.

It was crisp and cool, with a sky so bright it almost hurt her eyes. The ground crunched beneath her feet as she left behind the village walls where the pigeons squabbled, and then wound her way into the woods. In the valleys below her a white ocean of mist drowned out the view so all she could see were the trees sticking up like islands on the tops of the hills.

In the chestnut woods the harvesters were at work. Ripe pickings when the branches of the trees were weighed down by tons of chestnuts, now a staple food. The women dried them and ground them to make flour for bread, *pane d'albero*, tree bread, made from water, yeast and chestnuts. And they roasted them to add flavour to ground barley coffee. *Caffè d'orzo*. Sofia preferred it to chicory. No one had real coffee since the government had done their best to eliminate all imports, though some said the scarcity of coffee was really a result of the embargo the League of Nations had imposed on Italy. Either way, they fed the chestnut leaves to the pigs and chickens, at least those of them who still had animals did.

She and Carla had hidden some of their supplies, not only to serve the manor, but to help the villagers too. This they'd kept secret. After Sofia had received the letter from Commandant

Schmidt, she'd asked Carla's son, Aldo, to build a thin wall at one end of their large larder. Since leaving school, Aldo had been their odd-job man. So now, behind the false wall they stored dried beans, bottled fruit, home-made *salame* and cheese, along with dried wild boar and grain. If German troops were billeted here, they would *not* consume everything.

Sofia thought back to their bottling week in the summer, the only time Carla allowed her to work in the kitchen alongside her daughters, Anna and Gabriella. It was a chance to contribute in a practical way for what could be better than providing food for them all? Position and status suspended, she became one of the women, and although the rest of the time she tried her best to be 'Contessa', she loved dropping her guard. She enjoyed the comradeship as they prepared figs, peaches, cherries and tomatoes ready for preserving. Lorenzo didn't know. His family had been noble landowners for hundreds of years and he'd been brought up to believe each must know their place. Although not one to stand on ceremony, and a thoroughly good man besides, he was nevertheless a little more aware of status than she. Not brought up to be a lady, it was different for her.

They had bottled peppers, carrots and cabbages too, the kitchen bursting with steam and colour and the rich scents of harvest, and for those few days they laughed and sang and very nearly forgot about the war.

Now, as she reached the chestnut woods, the women were hard at work. With the men gone, the work was in their hands, with the help of old men and young boys. One of the farmers' wives, Sara, beckoned her over and asked if she would carry a bag of chestnuts up to the house for Carla. Sofia knew the woman well. She had received two letters informing her of two separate losses, a brother and a son. It was unimaginable how much pain she must be in and yet she carried on. Sometimes there were benefits to being childless, Sofia thought grimly, then she grasped Sara's hand momentarily, took the bag and left.

Back up at the Castello, she slipped round the side of the house and walked through the part of the garden lined with citrus trees, oleander bushes and a sweet little pomegranate tree guarding the kitchen door. From there the aroma of baking bread met her. She never used to enter the kitchen that way but now, working at tending vegetables – cabbages, onions, spinach and fennel – she used it more frequently. Carla had seemed unsettled for the last few days and Sofia hoped the new supply of chestnuts would cheer her up.

The kitchen, cavernous with a great oak-beamed ceiling, ancient flagstone floor, walls lined with pale-green cupboards and a large scrubbed table in the centre, had always been a relaxed, comforting place. Twin leather armchairs nestled in alcoves either side of the range and, because the shutters were not fully open, she failed at first to see someone leaning back in one of them.

Carla, standing by the range, hair tied back and wearing her usual white apron over one of her shapeless grey woollen dresses, was scowling.

Seeing a batch of dough rising on the grilled shelf above the stove, Sofia guessed the cook would be itching to get on with kneading it. A large woman who made her feelings known without many words, Carla's firmly folded arms said it all and, at Sofia's questioning look, she rolled her eyes.

Aldo, meanwhile, stood by the door, scratching his head. 'I found him just outside the village. All he said was "Castello", and after that went on like a crazy man, before he passed out.'

'Castello? Us? You think us?'

Carla wrinkled her nose. 'Who else?'

Sofia gazed at Aldo and thought, as she always did these days, that he'd turned into a real heartbreaker. A handsome lad, with black eyes, long lashes, full lips and dark brows. He was eager and cheerful too, and Sofia always felt energized whenever she saw him.

He pushed the curling brown hair from his eyes. 'I thought he must be meaning the village, here.'

Sofia walked over to the man in the chair for a closer look at his face. The dogs, one step ahead, sniffed around him cautiously, but when he didn't respond they lost interest and sloped away. The man's eyes remained closed, his hair was matted, and an angry-looking gash had made his right cheek swell. Then she noticed his jacket caked in blood. When she asked him who he was, his eyelashes fluttered for a moment, after which he opened the bluest eyes she'd ever seen.

'Who are you?' she repeated.

He touched his throat.

'Water, Carla. Get him some water.'

Carla grudgingly filled a glass and brought it across to put to his cracked lips. As he swallowed, her thoughts spun. What if he was a German deserter? But then he surprised her by speaking in good unaccented English.

'James,' he said, his voice weak. 'My name.'

'Can you tell us what happened to you?'

He closed his eyes. Had he fallen asleep?

'I think he must be English,' she told Carla.

'That's all we need. Like I said, he was mumbling when Aldo found him in the woodstore beyond the walls. Didn't sound like German, Aldo said, but he couldn't be sure.'

'He needs a doctor.'

Carla pulled a face.

'I know. I know.'

She stared at Sofia obstinately but then relented. 'I suppose we can put him in Gabriella's room for now. And she can come in with me. The door has a lock, so he won't be able to hurt anyone. Aldo will sleep at Anna's as usual. She likes the company.'

Sofia smiled at her, understanding. At the beginning Carla had been a farmer's wife, a *massaia*, who later came up daily to cook for them at the manor. But when her husband, Enrico, had taken ill and could no longer work, Sofia brought them both to live in four good-sized rooms, one on the ground floor which was now Gabriella's room and three on the first floor of the partly unused side of the manor house with its own staircase. They'd been their previous housekeeper's quarters, but she had married and moved into the village and her rooms had remained empty. All three children had come with Carla, of course, and Anna now worked as their part-time housekeeper, living out. Enrico had been a large, jovial man who hadn't deserved to die young and for the year he was ill Sofia had helped nurse him. Then afterwards, because she and Lorenzo had been unable to have children of their own, she'd poured all her mothering instincts into Carla's children, especially Aldo who had been devastated by his father's death.

Despite her sometimes-gruff exterior, the Carla they all knew was a kind and generous soul who could let her hair down when she wanted. The images from their celebration supper in September came rushing back. Lorenzo and Sofia had pitched in before the black clouds rolled over and at the end of the week, aching with exhaustion from the grape picking, they'd crawled back up to the house. Aldo, wearing a brilliant white shirt which emphasized the beauty of his olive skin, had laid out tables in the square and Carla had washed and ironed blue chequered tablecloths. In September, just before the Germans came, they still had plentiful prosciutto, mortadella, salami and sheep's cheese to accompany the bread and wine. When someone began to play the violin, tiredness fell away and they danced beneath the star-strewn sky. Even Lorenzo, who, beaming with pleasure and heat and love, had twirled her round and round until she was dizzy. Carla, her laughter loud and free, danced longer than anyone, until Aldo had to scrape her from the ground and ease her indoors, the gentle charm of him enough to melt your heart.

The memories dissolved and now Sofia glanced at the man in the armchair again. 'He doesn't look as if he's likely to be hurting anyone or going anywhere.' She ran through the options in her head but could tell that without help there was a chance he might die. Lorenzo would be in Florence for a couple of days so if they could find somewhere for the man within the next forty-eight hours it should be fine. She didn't want to involve Lorenzo in this. He had enough on his plate and might not approve of her intervention.

Carla gave her a wry smile.

'About Gabriella's room. Are you sure?'

Carla nodded. 'Aldo will help move him, won't you, son?'

Aldo nodded and Sofia studied the man again. His hair, beneath the grime, looked fair so he certainly could be German. Large enough too. Funny how they were all so large. A race of giants. On the other hand, if he really was English, and not German, maybe he was an escaped prisoner of war. He looked so lost. Where did he come from? Did he have family? A wife? Children? She couldn't help comparing this well-built man with her tall, fine-boned, aristocratic husband. This man's clothing was so nondescript and filthy, it was impossible to see the colour, though probably it was a grey jacket and dark-green trousers. When she gingerly opened his jacket, his saturated shirt revealed such awful blood loss that she gasped.

Sofia snapped into action, explaining what they needed to do. Carla tutted and muttered but Aldo, although only seventeen and not beefy, was strong and between the three of them they managed to carry or rather drag the groaning man across the main hall and through to the little bedroom at the side of the house.

Carla pulled off her daughter's bedclothes and spread an old blanket on the mattress and then Aldo and Sofia lifted the man on to the bed. He moaned but didn't open his eyes.

'Will Gabriella be all right with this?'

She was puzzled when Carla didn't reply but instead gazed down at the floor. Aldo gave her one of his sweet, apologetic smiles, the kind that had got him out of trouble as a child. How vibrantly the life shone out of those dark eyes, she thought. It always had. Then she saw him nudge Carla.

'Tell the Contessa what happened,' he said. 'Tell her.'

Sofia looked from one to the other. 'Tell me what?'

'It's Gabriella,' he said, concern and worry clouding his eyes. 'We think she spent an hour with one of the Blackshirts who disturbed the women at Anna's house the other night.'

Carla glanced up at Sofia as if deciding before she spoke. 'Now is not the time.'

'Well, tell me later, but now, Carla, a bowl of hot water, please, and some clean rags,' Sofia said as she knelt by the bed. 'Aldo, can you help me undress the man?'

'Contessa!' Carla objected.

Sofia twisted her head to look at her. 'Don't be so strait-laced, I have to know where he's injured.' Carla still looked affronted by the idea of her mistress doing the undressing and Sofia couldn't help laughing.

'I shall undress him,' Carla said. 'If you don't mind fetching the water, Contessa. Clean rags are in the cupboard on the right of the sink.'

By the time the water was heated, and Sofia had carried a jug of it through to Carla, the man was ready for her.

'There's bruising around his shoulder,' Aldo said.

'Only his shoulder?'

He nodded. 'Yes. And a gunshot wound at the top of his arm.'

Carla had covered his legs and private parts with another blanket that she now pulled a little further up his torso.

Sofia laughed again. 'So, you've checked?'

'Nothing much to see,' Carla muttered and then let out a cackle.

Sofia examined the man. Carla fetched the brandy bottle and, when he opened his eyes a fraction, they attempted to help him drink. The bullet was still inside the wound so once he'd swallowed a little brandy, which Sofia hoped would dull the pain, she gritted her teeth and, with her heart in her mouth, made a start at removing it and then cleaning up the mess. Carla had offered to do it, but Sofia felt it had to be her. It had been her custom to help patch up their workers when injured, though nothing had been as bad as this. The man screwed up his face as she worked. 'I'm sorry,' she whispered, 'I'm sorry,' and worried about his increasing pallor. She wasn't exactly sure what she was doing but instinct told her they had to get the wound clean. When it was done, Carla fetched some antiseptic and bandaged his arm to halt the bleeding.

'He really needs stitches,' Sofia told them as she straightened up.

'You can't ask the doctor.'

'No.'

They were in a difficult position. Their local doctor at Buonconvento, known to have Fascist sympathies, couldn't be trusted.

'What about the nuns at Sant'Anna?' Aldo said. 'Don't they consult a doctor from Trequanda?'

Sofia thought of the beautiful frescoed refectory of the convent and the kindly Mother Superior there. Convents were especially useful nowadays as their hidden passages were rarely discovered during a Nazi raid. And, because the Germans tended to ignore nuns, their habit sometimes served as a handy disguise. The last time she had seen the Mother Superior they had discussed a rebellious village girl who'd run away from her family and had been found hiding in the convent's garden. The two of them had sat on the terrace, eating sheep's cheese and drinking a little Montalcino wine while gazing west to the Crete Senesi hills, and together worked out what to do. She would surely help them again.

Carla looked worried. 'What if she asks who he is? We don't want to get the nuns into hot water. I mean, it's dangerous to harbour an Englishman.'

'We don't need to move him yet. I will pop in and out, and if he speaks again I should be able to tell.'

'You understand the English, Contessa?' Aldo asked.

'Certainly, my parents insisted I learn English, German and French, and I spent nearly a year studying in London.'

Aldo dipped his head and reached into his trouser pocket then held out something. 'I found this inside his jacket.'

Sofia glanced at the booklet and flicked its few pages, but none of it made sense, so she decided to hide it for now and leave them to it.

It was too cold to paint outside, especially at the crenellated top of the tower where the wind could be furious, but Sofia had completed a few new sketches over the summer. She'd drawn the tower so many times in the past, from a seat on the wall surrounding the cistern in the middle of the square and from the windows of her home. She'd also drawn the view from the very top of the tower, which you accessed by a steep inner staircase. Before the war she'd envisaged transforming the top room of the tower into a studio, but Lorenzo insisted it stood a greater chance of being bombed so she never had. Maybe later. For now, she made her way through their large hall where several of her own small canvasses were displayed, and into a little studio with French windows overlooking the rose garden. Roses still flowered, even this late in the year, and the sight of those few blooms lifted her heart. Sofia favoured working on landscapes in soft muted colours but instead of painting the tower she would carry on with her latest canvas, a portrait of her mother, Elsa.

Whoever the injured man was, she hoped to find out for certain before they needed to move him and before Lorenzo discovered he was there. If not, she'd have a lot of explaining to do. Lorenzo wouldn't condone her putting herself at risk or placing anyone in the village in the path of danger.

6.

That night Sofia dreamt of spring, of voluptuous pastures so newly green they shone as if lit from within, and she dreamt of vivid red poppies again and silver olive trees and the beautiful, curving Senesi craters and the tall, dark cypress trees marching across her eyeline in the Val d'Orcia. She saw the verges of the tracks lined with swathes of purple iris, yellow field marigolds, pink rock roses, white daisies and blue hyacinths. And, as she dreamt of long lunches spent in Pienza eating stuffed artichoke hearts and roast lamb, she could smell the fragrance of fresh rosemary and wild mint and see the common blue butterflies floating in the air. Occasionally she dreamt of eating Tuscan flatbread and home-made cheese while sitting on a rug on the grassy lawns of the gardens of San Quirico d'Orcia. Hunger drove her dreams. Hunger, for good food, yes, for variety, but it was more hunger for their lives to be whole again. Sometimes she dreamt of long afternoons of love-making and carefree happiness where there were no sides to choose between and life was less complicated, but it was an illusion because for the last twenty years there had been Mussolini.

She half woke, hearing someone in her bedroom. She heard them moving about and instantly thought of the blue-eyed man. Had he been pretending to be asleep? But no, he was locked in, wasn't he? She reached for the light switch.

'Leave the light.'

It was Lorenzo, back sooner than expected.

She shifted over in the bed and reached for him lazily as he climbed in beside her. Her beautiful, complicated husband wrapped his arms around her, and she felt his heart thumping against her own. The occasionally distant figure her husband

34

had become vanished when they made love. As they embraced, they became whole again and not the uncomfortable versions of themselves they'd lately adopted. He kissed her neck and, still half in dreams of spring and sex and love, she arched her back, cat-like. He ran his hands over her breasts, her stomach, her legs, ending at the top of her thighs. He rubbed, searching for the right spot, and in her sleepy, defenceless state, she orgasmed quickly. He rolled on top of her, spreading her legs, and holding her arms above her head, he entered her body.

When Sofia woke to the sun streaming through the window, she reached out, but Lorenzo's side of the bed was empty. She patted the sheet. Cold. Had she dreamt him? But then she saw his clothes thrown across the sides of a wing-backed chair. Not a dream then.

Lorenzo believed Sofia should be like his mother and her mother before her. The stately Corsi ladies of the manor. He liked her to maintain dignity while showing gracious concern for the families who relied upon them. He didn't have the same easy-going ways as she, nor did he openly endorse her sympathy for the partisans. He believed it would be safer for her to remain neutral and her safety was what most troubled him. So, she didn't tell him everything. He had fallen in love with the way she embraced life, her *joie de vivre* he used to call it during their honeymoon in Paris. He said he loved her grace, her elegance, and the way she'd been brought up to have beautiful manners. He loved that she smiled, that she radiated happiness. She smiled less these days.

She hated having to be cautious around him but knew he'd worry, and, really, she wasn't doing much herself, although she knew what was going on and didn't say. She knew about the women knitting for the partisans and said nothing. She knew where the partisans were and said nothing. She knew Carla was cooking for them in their kitchen and said nothing. And now she knew about the injured blue-eyed man, who could be anyone. And still she said nothing.

Lorenzo was watchful, observant. He went along with what couldn't be avoided and, at the start, like others, he had truly believed Mussolini would be good for the country. Mussolini built roads, got the trains to run on time. But when he gagged the free press, tolerated Fascist squad violence and otherwise consolidated his grip on the country . . . things worsened. And then, after he declared himself dictator of Italy in 1925 and built up the secret police, they all began to understand what was really happening. As the power of the judges and the courts weakened, and political opponents were arrested and frequently given the death penalty, they learnt the full truth. Too late. Far too late. Friends in England asked how they could have let it happen and they said because people were fooled and manipulated, and they needed someone or something to believe in. And they warned the English to beware. For if populism, division and hatred could happen in Italy and in Germany, it could happen anywhere.

So, now Lorenzo had been recruited to pass information to the Allies – an incredibly dangerous undertaking as the ministry he worked for was controlled by the Nazis. She and Lorenzo didn't talk as frequently as they used to, so she didn't know much. It was no one's fault, but the war got in the way. She felt each of them had been forced to dive down into their deepest soul, something you could only do alone. When you didn't know if the person you loved above all others in the world would even be alive the next day, it made you love them more, made you want to hold on even more tightly, but you could not. It also made you want to protect them, but to do *that* you had to let them go just a little bit. Close off a little bit. Give them space to do whatever they had to do. Clutching too tightly to Lorenzo would only cause him pain when he had to go. Better he should believe she was all right, that she was safe.

7

As Sofia unlocked the little bedroom door and pushed it open the pervasive smell of illness overpowered her, and when she examined the man and felt the back of his neck, she realized his fever had worsened. She pulled the blanket away and instructed Aldo to soak a cloth in cool water, then she wrung it out and dabbed repeatedly at the man's face, neck and head. Finally, she told Aldo to lay two damp cloths across his chest. Despite James's grave condition, if that really was his name, they had to find a way to take him to the convent. And, unless she wanted to include Lorenzo in the plan, it had to be right away.

When they returned to the kitchen Aldo watched Giulia, the maid, preparing the coffee and cake for breakfast. Giulia had not worked for them for long. She was a village girl who used to live with her grandmother in Pisa, but since the war she had come back to be with her mother. Sofia wasn't convinced by her reliability but had given her the benefit of the doubt.

Aldo shot Sofia a confused look. 'Two coffee cups. You have a visitor?'

'No. Lorenzo is home.'

He couldn't prevent his surprise. 'Ah.'

'I was the one who saw him,' Giulia boasted. 'He rang for breakfast.'

'Will Conte Lorenzo be staying?' Carla asked as she entered the kitchen from the garden.

'I don't know,' Sofia replied then moved across to whisper to Aldo. 'Can you wait for me here? I could do with a hand to move the man.'

'Of course,' he said and sat down at the table to drink his coffee.

As she gazed at him, she couldn't help thinking of him as a toddler and then as the four-year-old cherub he'd been when his uncle Gino, a carpenter, had built him a little cart. How quickly the time had flown. It seemed like only yesterday when Aldo had raced around the Castello, getting under everyone's feet, and yet the sweetest of apologies had meant he was always forgiven. And she had loved it when he came to curl up in her lap, hair falling in his eyes, while he sucked his thumb contentedly without a care in the world. Then, later, how he'd enjoyed climbing the olive trees at harvest time, shaking the branches as he climbed higher and higher until the grey-green olives lay in piles on the net below. 'I got the most!' he used to shout while the older boys and the men were doing their best with long hooks. He'd always have a place in her heart.

As Sofia took a deep breath and returned to the present, she saw Carla looking as if she wanted to speak. The cook's eyes flickered away and then back again, and Sofia knew she was waiting for the maid to leave the room.

'What is it?' Sofia hissed once the girl had slipped into the pantry. 'I have to join Lorenzo. I haven't got much time.'

Carla bent over and, when she raised her head again, Sofia saw the worry etched in the lines of her face.

'Carla, what is it? You're scaring me. Is it to do with Gabriella?' She twisted round to face Aldo. 'You said something about the Blackshirts and Gabriella, didn't you? Said Carla should tell me.'

As Aldo pushed back his chair and rose to his feet, Carla's face fell.

'Carla?'

'Well, the other night, we were . . . you know . . . knitting . . .'

'I know about the knitting. For goodness' sake, it's knitting. I've always known.'

'You don't mind?'

Sofia shook her head.

'There was an interruption. Nobody comes at night, not this time of year anyway. Gabriella was on watch and we heard them in the street. We waited for a while and then we heard her outside with them.'

'Dear God . . . They didn't hurt her?'

Carla winced. 'I don't think so, but you know, she went with them. Was gone more than an hour.'

'You think they interfered with her?'

'No. She knew one of them. I don't think much happened, but she won't say. Her clothing wasn't torn, and she hadn't been crying. But she's so pretty, and men, they take advantage. She never says much but now she won't speak at all, just looks at the ground if I ask her what happened. You know she can be a bit dreamy, head in the clouds. I shouldn't have left her downstairs on her own.'

'It's not your fault. God damn the Germans!'

'Not Germans. Blackshirts,' Aldo growled, reminding her. 'If I get my hands on them!'

Sofia glanced at Carla. 'Do you want me to talk to her?'

Carla shook her head. 'Not yet. But, on top of everything else, I'm worried Aldo will be called up.'

'Have the papers come?'

'No,' she said miserably, glancing over at her son. '*Per Dio*, the Nazi bastards want to take our youngest now to fight their war.'

Aldo squared his shoulders. 'I'll never fight for the Germans.'

'He says he'll run off to join the *resistenza*,' his mother added with a frown. She ruffled her son's hair. 'Too hot-headed by half, my boy. Always going on about the partisans. He'll end up dead in a ditch.'

'I'll not fight for the Germans,' Aldo reiterated. 'I won't go.'

Sofia sighed deeply. She felt worried for poor Carla – as if she hadn't had enough to cope with. 'Try not to fret,' she said. 'We'll do what we can. But first, I'll find out how long Lorenzo is going to be here.'

★   ★   ★

In the dining room, Lorenzo was rising from his seat. He gave Sofia an open-hearted smile.

'I'm going to check up on some of the outlying farms,' he said. 'I had hoped we'd breakfast together but you were so long.'

'Sorry.' She wondered if he was trying to make her feel guilty but dismissed the idea, annoyed that she was questioning everything so much.

'Yields are lower than usual, not surprisingly, but I need to see for myself,' he continued, not noticing the strain she was feeling.

He knew she believed tenants should be entitled to own their land. As things stood, Lorenzo, as Conte de' Corsi, was responsible for all the farms, houses and villas on the estate. Like all the estates, they functioned under the old *mezzadria* system, a sort of sharecropping whereby he provided land, tools, machinery and maintenance in return for a half share of all the produce from the land. Once a year their olive press was used by everyone and before the war Lorenzo had paid for limited electricity and running water to be connected to all the village houses.

'Maybe it's time the system changed?' Sofia said, somewhat absently.

He gazed at her. 'I deal fairly with the farmers and workers.'

'I know but . . .'

Still gazing at her, he looked puzzled. 'What's this really about? We decided we'd make changes when the war ends. You know that. Are you all right?'

'Of course.'

'You look – I'm not sure – you look a little dishevelled.'

'Oh, for goodness' sake,' she snapped. 'What does it matter?'

'Sofia, what has got into you these days? One minute you're fine and the next you're biting my head off.'

'And you're perfect all the time, are you?' She glared at him even though he was looking at her with such softness in his grey eyes she wanted to weep. 'You're tetchy. You're hardly ever here and when you are, you're distant. If I didn't know better, I'd say you were having an affair.'

He smiled and that annoyed her more than anything.

'You hardly ever tell me what you're doing, where you're going, who you're dealing with. Nothing! What am I supposed to believe?'

'It's safer that you are kept ignorant of my activities. Anyway, haven't you been a little secretive yourself?' he said.

She felt the giveaway blush spreading up her neck and longed to be able to tell him about the Englishman and ask for his help.

'Whispering in corners with the cook. Taking phone calls late at night.'

'Once. It was only once and now I can't get through to my mother at all. I'm worried something might have happened to them both.'

'I'll check on your parents as soon as I'm back in Rome.'

'When?'

'The day after tomorrow. I'll be leaving early but I'm here today so, after I've been to the farms, we can spend the whole afternoon together and maybe tomorrow afternoon too. I'm hoping it'll make you feel better. Will it?'

No, she wanted to say. Not today. It would not make her feel better today. 'Now,' she said, changing the subject in order to get going, 'I have a few errands to run. I'll be taking the van if it's still got petrol.'

'Must you? Petrol is so scarce. Can't you take a donkey cart?'

'It's my canvas.' She paused, her stomach clenching as she considered whether to develop the lie. Was her guilt visible enough for him to see? 'I thought I'd have it framed. I don't want it to get wet.'

'Ah. You've finished it. Very well, but it does look like rain. Why not go another day?'

'I'd like to get it done. I want to give it to my mother for her birthday.'

She glanced out of the window at the gloomy clouds scudding across the sky.

'Well, be careful. When I was on my way back from Florence, anything moving was a target for the Allied planes. Take Aldo.'

'I will. We'll be all right on the little back roads.'

Once Lorenzo was out, there was no time to waste, so Sofia dressed quickly without washing and tied up her hair, then covered her head with a headscarf the way all country women did, while glancing at the silver-framed photograph of her parents on the dressing table. She prayed they were safe. Then she gathered her courage and made her way to the small side hall before marching into the little downstairs bedroom. This time the man's eyes opened, more alert than before.

'We need to move you,' she said. 'It's not safe here.'

'Thank you.' He attempted a smile, but his voice was weak.

'You *are* English?'

He spoke a few words in Italian.

'You spoke English when I first saw you.'

'Yes. I was probably too . . . well, I'm not sure.'

'When a man is barely conscious, I don't suppose a second language is on his mind.'

He gave another wan smile.

'But now? Can you tell me anything now?'

'Parachute tangled up. Got shot escaping. Somehow made it here.' His voice was hoarse, and he was finding it hard to talk.

'How long ago?' she asked gently.

He didn't reply. While she worked out what to do, he closed his eyes. What if she brought the van round to the side? It might work if Aldo helped carry him.

'My codebook?' he whispered, his voice fading even further.

'Ah yes, that's what that booklet is. I have it safe.'

He reached out and squeezed her hand.

* * *

42

When Sofia and Aldo left the front of the house, the old biddy on the corner was sitting on a chair inside her doorway in the shadow of the tower, watching. Always watching. In November. A cold November too! Maria had to be the most unpopular person in the village, poor soul. Although, at first, she had been as surprised as the rest of them when her grandson left to become a Blackshirt, now nobody knew where her sympathies truly lay. She maintained she had no idea where the boy had gone, but was she simply watching for his return or was she scrutinizing the rest of them? While everyone understood her worry, they found it hard to sympathize, and some couldn't wait for the day the boy would receive a bullet in the head.

In the old carriage yard Aldo unlocked the door. Among all the vehicles and carts, the van sat in a corner, clunky, smelly and awkward to drive. She took a deep breath and hesitated. It was so hard to know if she was doing the right thing and the van did consume precious petrol. She glanced at Aldo.

He smiled at her. 'We *are* doing the right thing.'

It delighted her that he often seemed to guess what she was thinking, but really there was no way to tell right from wrong any more. When everything was wrong, they simply did what they had to do, no questions asked. She took a breath and her resolve hardened.

Lorenzo could be overprotective, as so many men of his class were. If she was more exacting with herself, more honest, it had mostly been her own fault. She'd allowed it, relished it at first, when perhaps she should have been adamant that she was perfectly capable of handling things. Instead, without any fuss or bother, she had quietly gone about doing what she believed was right. He'd witnessed her coping, knew how much courage and inner strength she had, knew that she was indeed robust, but it had seemed easier to go on letting him feel he was her protector.

'Shall I drive?' Aldo asked, breaking into her thoughts.

'Yes, thanks. I'll sit with James. But we can't take too long. I must be back to spend the afternoon with Lorenzo.'

They climbed into the van and drove round to the side of the house.

On their journey back from the convent along the network of tracks threading the hills, the sun came out, leaving the wet landscape bright and shiny. As Sofia gazed at the panoramic rows of blue-grey hills and the patchwork of low-lying silvery cloud the beauty lifted her spirits. She felt as if the war might not touch them too much after all. How could it when a day could be as sparkling and fresh as this? And times like this were vital to preserve the precious kernel of hope that lived in her heart. These moments were her joy and inspiration. And she knew that later, if she were to lie awake worrying, she could draw on them to picture herself in a future world that was good, where the sun would shine, and they would be at peace.

Aldo stopped the van for a few minutes and they both got out to breathe the air and watch the long grasses rustling in the breeze.

'He'll be safe at the convent,' Aldo said.

'Yes.' She paused for a moment, feeling easy and relaxed with him. 'I remember when I first came to live in the countryside,' she continued as they stood side by side. 'Before you were born, of course. I'd been a city girl but, soon after I arrived, I fell in love with the whole estate and everyone on it. They welcomed me as if I were one of them.'

'My mother talks about those days,' he said.

'They were good. Really good.'

She smiled, knowing she would never forget her first winter with Lorenzo at the Castello.

'We lounged in front of roaring fires as the countryside transformed into a mystical place with mists in the valleys, purple skies above, and eventually a scattering of pure white snow.'

'Contessa, you have always been one for seeing the beauty.'

She laughed. 'Don't you see it too?'

'I do, but I'm a practical man, not so poetically inclined as you.'

Man, she thought. Hard to see him as a man.

Now, as they gazed at the pines and oaks, so dark in the clusters of woodland, the pistol preyed on her mind. Maybe Aldo could show her how to use it, but could she ever point it at another human being and pull the trigger? Could she shoot to kill? The idea seemed ridiculous.

'You know how to use a gun, don't you?' she said.

'I do,' he replied. 'For hunting.'

'Could you teach me?'

He smiled. 'Of course, but I can't see you going out to shoot wild boar.'

'No.'

There was a short silence.

She pointed at the view. 'Look how many meadows between the woods are not ploughed. With your help we women are doing what we can but it isn't enough.'

Beyond them lay the deeper woods and hills populated by the dozens of men who were in hiding. She hoped there were still some wild boar they'd be able to kill and eat.

'I think about those men at night,' she said. 'With a bitterly cold winter approaching and no warm hearths, I worry.'

'They will find a way to survive.'

She decided to tell Carla she was happy about her cooking for the men and that it was fine to use some of their supplies; it was time she did her bit to help the Allies win the war. As she stood lost in the moment the peace was brutally shattered by the deafening sound of fighter planes flying overhead in tight formation, on their way north. She clapped her hands over her ears.

'Allies, please let them be Allies,' she muttered.

Aldo nodded. 'I think they are.'

Then, when the sound of distant bombing began, she shuddered at the thought of which poor village might have been accidentally struck this time. Sometimes it felt as if the Allied pilots and gunners didn't care about the Italian people.

8.

The moment Sofia arrived home after taking the dogs for a walk the next day, she discovered there had been a phone call from Commandant Schmidt, the local German commander, while she was out, asking if Lorenzo was in residence. She held her breath for a moment. The letter she'd received informing her of their intention to requisition the village had been from this very man. When Carla had explained that Lorenzo was indeed home, the German had politely invited himself to dinner. Sofia was relieved to have already managed to spirit James away. It would be one thing Lorenzo discovering she'd been harbouring one of Germany's enemies, quite another if Schmidt found out, especially if he'd come to look the place over.

She felt grateful for a peaceful afternoon but now it was time for an evening she wasn't expecting to enjoy. She glanced out of the window at the square, while listening to the latest news, and saw the bats emptying from the arched windows of the tower and sweeping across the skyline. Then she thought of the way rumours and counter-rumours were spreading like wildfire. The Allies were close. They'd arrive any day. They heard it again and again. But now the gossip was not so good. The Allies were making slow progress across the southern parts of Italy and German resistance was stronger than expected. Battles were being fought and won but the German retreat was snail-like, allowing them time to leave terrible destruction in their wake.

She was feeling a little disheartened when Lorenzo entered their bedroom, although she was enormously relieved he was there. An evening entertaining the German on her own would not have been enjoyable.

'Radio London?' he asked as she slipped into the black satin dress she'd decided to wear. Long-sleeved, high-collared, it skimmed her hips and fell just past her knees, fitting like a second skin and emphasizing her slender shape.

'Yes. Better than the Fascist propaganda, at least. But it's not good news. Can you zip me up?'

After doing so he scratched the back of his head and she switched off the radio. They didn't speak again and there was a prolonged silence, each absorbed with their own concerns. Sofia sat at her dressing table and clipped on her diamond earrings, while he paced the length of the room.

'Well, you are pushing out the boat,' he said eventually and came to lift her hair and kiss the nape of her neck. 'You look beautiful.'

'Must create a good impression for Commandant Schmidt,' she said, but she wrinkled her nose.

He laughed. 'I'm surprised you care.'

'I was being sarcastic.'

'I know.' He smiled though his eyes looked pensive. 'You enjoyed our two afternoons together?'

'You know I did.'

He looked even more thoughtful before he spoke. 'You are the light of my life. You know that? I don't say it enough.'

She smiled at him then pinned up her hair and dabbed a little of Lanvin's Arpège on the back of her neck and on her wrists. 'You don't have to say it.'

'And you know I want things to go back to the way they were as much as you do.'

'You have to do this work for the Allies?'

He nodded. 'I think I do.'

'You couldn't just leave the ministry?'

'It might look suspicious. I'm so well placed to pass on information about food supplies, the grain stores and so on. The Allied troops will need feeding. And I hear things about the

German plans, their armaments, ability to mobilize and so on. I'm sorry I can't tell you more.'

'I wish it was just us tonight. I wish this wretched man wasn't coming.'

'What do you think he wants?'

She felt apprehensive and regretted not telling him before. 'They may billet their troops here. I had a letter a little while ago.'

He frowned, then walked over to the window to look out. After a moment he turned back to gaze at her with a perplexed expression. 'Darling, why are you only telling me now?'

'I'm sorry. I really meant to, but I hoped it would never happen. They send out dozens of these letters and often they come to nothing. I didn't want you worrying unnecessarily.'

He spread his arms wide. 'I might have been able to –'

'To what?' she interrupted. 'What, Lorenzo? There's nothing any of us can do. Anyway, let's wait and see. It may not be that at all.'

'Darling, you are jumpy.'

He was right. She was jumpy.

'Come here.'

She got up and went to him and he held her tight. 'It will be all right.'

She felt close to tears. 'Will it? Even if they take our home?'

'Trust me. We'll find a way.'

He held her at arm's length and looked into her eyes. 'Just one thing, sweetheart.' He smiled, but she could see his pupils contracting slightly.

'When I passed your studio, the door was open, and I spotted the painting of your mother still on the easel. Won't you tell me what you were really doing yesterday?'

They were interrupted by the maid calling.

Sofia breathed a sigh of relief, quickly turning towards the door. 'Later,' she said.

9

Maxine stood in the freezing hallway of the manor house in Castello de' Corsi gazing around her, having successfully found her way to the dirt road that led to this place. Now the maid, who'd opened the door, was holding out her hand for Maxine's jacket and bag.

'It's all right,' she said and clutched the bag to her chest a little awkwardly.

She'd had time to read one of the pamphlets during a stop on the way up. She'd read of partisan activities, warnings about possible future Nazi activities, and the ways people could assist the Allies. But Maxine didn't know which way the wind was blowing. She'd seen public opinion sharply divided since she'd arrived. Allied bombings were not popular when civilian casualties happened although, more than anything, most ordinary men and women wanted the Germans and the Italian Fascists gone for good.

Now, at the sound of footsteps coming from a central marble stairway, she glanced up. A small, elegant woman, all dark eyes and pale complexion with jet-black hair piled up on her head, was descending with slow, studied steps. The type of woman men adored, longed for and fought over: a Madonna. Maxine stared, feeling out of place and large by comparison. The other woman wore black and what had to be diamond earrings with a matching necklace glittering in the light from a small chandelier, her left hand resting possessively on the arm of an attractive and dignified-looking man. Both looked surprised to see her in their hallway.

She stepped forward, but the maid spoke first.

'This lady has come to see the Contessa.'

The woman reached the hall and held out her hand. She smiled but it was done without conviction. Maxine usually trusted her instincts, but this woman confused her.

'I am Sofia de' Corsi. How may I be of help?'

Maxine at once noticed Sofia's resemblance to her mother, Elsa. She had the same elegant, self-possessed way of moving and speaking too. Typical indulged aristocracy, she thought. Distant, entitled. Spoilt. Old blood, they called it, but did this woman know what her parents were really doing?

'I'm Maxine,' she said, out of earshot of the maid who had bobbed a curtsey and stepped back unobtrusively. 'I've left my motorcycle outside at the front. Will it be all right?'

Sofia's face remained impassive.

'Your parents asked me to explain things to you. It's a long story but I've been sent here by the British. Your mother also asked me to deliver something to you.'

'I see.' Sofia glanced at the maid and told her she could go then focused on the man with what Maxine considered another cool look. 'This is my husband, Lorenzo.'

The man smiled.

'Can I offer you a drink?' he asked in the courteous manner the nobility always exhibited.

'Thank you. That would be lovely.'

'Red wine?'

'Perfect.'

'Shall we go into my little salon first?' Sofia suggested. 'We can talk there. It's more private.'

Once Sofia had closed the door to her salon, Maxine unzipped her bag and drew out the box she'd been given. 'First, there's this. It's a bit odd. Your mother asked me to give it to you and remind you about the sweets.'

The other woman shook the box but gave no visible sign of understanding, though Maxine was sure the words contained a message of sorts.

'It's very good of you to bring it,' Sofia said, regarding her quizzically. 'I take it you're not from round here? I can't quite place your accent.'

'Can I speak frankly?'

Sofia gave her a guarded look and answered coolly. 'Does anyone speak frankly these days?'

To lighten the atmosphere Maxine tried a warm, engaging smile. 'My family came from Tuscany but moved to America. I was brought up bilingual.'

'I'd say there's a strong chance any Americans or English will be rounded up very soon. Anyone they consider might harm the Reich and its armed forces,' Sofia said bitterly.

And that one comment, along with Sofia's mother's sympathies, encouraged Maxine it was safe to tell her everything. 'Look, the truth is I'm working as a special operative for the Allies. I had hoped to get away with sounding Italian and not American at all.'

Sofia raised her brows. 'I see. So exactly what is it that you're here to do?'

'I have to gauge the viability of the resistance network here and then liaise between them and the British. I'm expecting to meet a British radio operator here.'

Sofia nodded. 'Ah. It's possible he may have already arrived.'

'Where is he?'

'All in good time. My mother has suggested you stay here?'

'If it's not too much bother. She thought it best, yes.'

Sofia seemed to be thinking. 'I'd better show you round the house, and then to a guest bedroom.'

'It seems very large. Three floors.'

'Not so large really. The top floor needs refurbishing so we don't use it. On this floor we have the kitchen, dining room, my studio and this salon, the main drawing room too, plus several currently unused rooms, a washroom and Lorenzo's office, of course. And the servants' quarters are attached. Do you have clothes to change into?'

'Not many. Anyway, your husband promised me a drink.'

Sofia shook her head. 'He shouldn't have. We're expecting the arrival of a German officer.'

'I'd better make myself scarce then,' Maxine said as she edged towards the doors. 'I take it my room will be upstairs?'

'Yes, all our own bedrooms and bathrooms are on the first floor.'

The Contessa's eyes still gave nothing much away as they stepped into the hall but, as they did, a loud thump on the front door was followed by excited barking coming from elsewhere.

Maxine saw it was too late to escape. Damn, or as her mother would have said, *mannaggia*. The maid had already opened the door and a man was being ushered in. He clipped his metal-heeled boots together and Sofia shot Maxine a warning frown as he bowed before them.

'Commandant Schmidt,' Sofia said, 'I am the Contessa de' Corsi and this is my good friend –'

'Massima,' Maxine interjected, remembering her cover story. 'From Rome.' And she did her best to look as if she felt at home despite an uncomfortable feeling in the pit of her stomach. 'The Contessa and I went to school together. Wonderful to meet you.'

The German smiled stiffy. Tall and thin with a slight stoop and long, elegant fingers, he wasn't young. His hair was greying and he looked terribly tired as if the world was sitting heavily on his shoulders.

Sofia smiled at him warmly. 'My apologies, my friend has only recently arrived, you understand, hasn't had time to dress for dinner yet.'

As Sofia led the way to the large drawing room, Schmidt followed with Maxine trailing behind. This room overlooked the Val d'Orcia, as did Sofia's little salon, but with an impressive array of four floor-to-ceiling windows, the panoramic view in daylight hours was even more spectacular.

'Darling,' Sofia said, 'here is the Commandant. Aren't we lucky to have him?'

Lorenzo spun round from where he was pouring drinks then finished his task before striding forward and welcoming the man.

'I see you have a piano,' Schmidt said. 'I hope you will allow me to play.'

Lorenzo smiled. 'But of course, naturally you must. Now, a little wine or would you prefer a whisky?'

The man indicated he'd like a whisky, then surveyed the room and eventually settled into the brown leather armchair near the fire, his long legs restlessly crossing and uncrossing while he sat, his hands interlaced in his lap. Maxine found his posture confusing. He looked like a career soldier ready for retirement and didn't seem as if he was enjoying being in Italy at all. She was surprised to find herself feeling a bit sorry for him – of course, among the 'enemy' there had to be men who would rather not be there at all.

'I hope you haven't been too much bothered by the bombing?' Commandant Schmidt enquired.

'Not here,' Lorenzo said. 'Although I mainly work in Rome.'

'Ah yes, compiling a report on food stores all over Italy, I understand. It will be a great help to us. Feeding the troops is always our priority. But you must have to travel a great deal?'

Maxine noticed Sofia's eyes widen a touch and behind the German's back she shot a look at her husband. Maxine couldn't read it, though there had been something guarded there.

'Indeed. I am in the process of planning my trips. I will be away for some time.'

'It's very good of you to have me here.' Schmidt smiled at Sofia. 'I hope you will allow me to visit you again, Contessa. I do miss my home comforts. I may even have to bring my second-in-command. He is young, tends to take all this very seriously, as the young usually do, whereas I . . .' He broke off and contemplated his hands.

'You, Commandant Schmidt?' Sofia prompted.

'I'm old-fashioned. And perhaps a touch more equivocal about . . . well, I suppose about life.'

Maxine wasn't sure what to make of this. What exactly was he suggesting? Did he not agree with the German Reich? Was he not a fan of Hitler?

But Sofia was smiling and answering graciously. 'You're welcome here any time. You must come again and play the piano, your man too. But what about the troops? Won't they be here?'

He gave her a little smile. 'Oh, my sincere apologies, did I not say? I sent you a second letter. Maybe you did not receive it? We shall not be needing the village at this point in time.'

Maxine could not fail to see Sofia's slight but clearly relieved intake of breath.

'Well, I hope you'll excuse me while we nip upstairs for a quick change of clothes.' She made a gesture towards Maxine. 'We won't be long.'

Maxine blinked rapidly. What on earth was she to wear?

'Come along, darling,' Sofia said, linking arms as they moved towards the door with their backs to the men. 'I've put you in the green room this time. It is your favourite, isn't it?'

Maxine took in this fabrication without expression but enjoying it all the same. This Sofia, Contessa de' Corsi, appeared to be an accomplished liar.

'Just one more thing, if you don't mind,' Schmidt added. 'We are on the lookout for a British parachutist. We believe we may have injured him. He came down not so far from here, so I was wondering if you might have overheard anything about the matter?'

'Us?' Lorenzo said, clearly annoyed at the implication. 'Obviously not. I'd have informed you immediately. You haven't heard anything, have you, Sofia?'

Sofia fingered her necklace. There was the slightest moment when Maxine noticed the corners of her mouth flicker as she fought to control a defiance that hadn't been visible before. But it was gone in an instant and her face transformed as she turned to the man, shaking her head and smiling just as graciously as she had before.

In the chill of the night, Sofia woke with a gasp, still reeling from her dream. She'd been clutching the pistol. It had felt so real she even raised her hand to look. In the dream she'd been running through the woods chased by a pack of dogs who were gaining ground. She'd called for her own dogs, but they had run away. She'd come to a halt and begun shooting but none fell, none died, and they kept on coming. She steadied her breath and tried to still her pounding heart then glanced at Lorenzo's face, ghostly blue in the moonlight. His breathing was slow and she felt confident he was deeply asleep. She slipped across to her dressing room, treading carefully round the oak floorboards she knew would creak. She moved soundlessly until she accidentally stepped on one and it made an almost human groan. A shiver ran up her spine and she listened to hear if Lorenzo's breathing had altered. When it hadn't, she found her robe, wrapped it around her body and perched on the chaise longue, drawing up her knees for comfort and warmth.

She picked up the little box Maxine had given her. Despite the cold, her palms were sweating, and she wiped them on her robe before stroking the carved surface of the box. Not surprisingly, thoughts of her mother filled her mind. As Maxine had been changing into one of Sofia's longer black skirts and a green satin blouse earlier in the evening – the skirt, nevertheless, still looking too short on her – she'd explained how Sofia's parents had been forced to leave the palazzo. Now she was sick with worry. True, they had many friends from an entire lifetime spent in Rome, and she hoped that might help.

But still she kept wondering, worrying, fretting.

It was hard to know what to think about Schmidt. He had seemed like a decent enough man. In fact, she'd rather liked him. They weren't all bastards, the Germans; take Gerhard Wolf, the German Consul in Florence. It would be hard to find a man more intent on saving the city than he. And from what she'd heard from Lorenzo, some Germans hated the Nazis almost as much as the Allies did. This time, Schmidt hadn't come to tear apart their life at the Castello, but he'd be back, and she wondered if she could trust him to be as friendly next time.

She shook the box Maxine had brought from Rome and heard something rattle. Sweets? Surely not. She slid part of the back of the box to the right and felt around for the button that opened a tiny secret compartment where her mother used to hide her violet-flavoured sweets. As she suspected, there was a folded piece of paper inside, not sweets, but what was so secret it had to be concealed?

Throughout the long dinner with Schmidt, his eyes had been on her nearly the whole time. When not on her, they'd been on Maxine. The American was vivid, natural, with huge amber eyes and gorgeous chestnut hair, the curls tumbling around her face and on to her shoulders. And when her hair caught the light it exploded into a flaming halo of red. Sofia had witnessed the bold, raw sensuousness of the woman, the curves, the full mouth, the wide engaging smile, and seen how much she had appealed to both the men in the room. Even Lorenzo had been transfixed. She would tease him about it later. But all the time this had been going on, she'd been wondering about the contents of the box.

She unfolded the paper and scanned what was clearly a hastily written note.

My Darling,

I have been approached by our friends in Florence.

The dark edges of the night closed in on Sofia and her breath caught. Friends. Which friends?

I just want you to know you can completely trust the bearer of this letter. Please work with her.

A delivery will come to you around the end of next week. Could you look after it? If you are willing, call Francesco, your vintner in Montepulciano, and ask him when he hopes to deliver the wine. Later the crates will be collected from you. Take good care of them. If you cannot help, tell Francesco you have no need of wine. Remember how we talked about ways you might be able to help? We really need this wine.

Your loving Mother

A feeling of homesickness washed through Sofia, but it was for a past long gone. Fragments, broken pieces, shards of sunny youthful days before Mussolini. And, of course, she remembered her mother insisting they all should help and that her chance would come. 'At some point, you have to choose,' she'd said, an indignant glint in her eyes. But what did this really mean? She was clearly not talking about a few crates of wine and Lorenzo wouldn't be happy if he found she was putting herself or the Castello at risk. She shivered, suspecting this was somehow tied up with James. But with Schmidt sniffing around? And *the end of next week*? Were they already in *next week*? She didn't even know how long ago her mother had given Maxine the box.

The next morning, after inspecting the sky for signs of rain and watching the crows gathering at the top of the tower, she called the dogs to her studio where they watched with adoring eyes as she added the finishing touches to the portrait of her mother. While she worked, she thought about the secret letter. She stood back, viewing her canvas, and felt pleased she had somehow captured Elsa's spirited approach to life. There was something in the eyes, determination, yes, but it was more than that. She'd struggled to achieve it and had hardly been able to identify the look she had been searching for, but 'indomitable' came close. Portraits were so much harder than landscapes.

There was a knock on the door and Aldo entered, carrying a tray of refreshments, the dogs sniffing at his heels. He smiled at her and she felt the tug of it in her heart. Whenever he came into a room she felt as if the sun had just come out.

'What's happened to the maid?' she asked.

'Giulia hasn't turned up for work today. Mother is busy so she asked me to carry this in.'

'Thank you. I hope nothing has happened to the girl.'

He shrugged. 'Hard to know.'

'Will you sit a while?'

As he pulled up a chair and gazed at the painting, she sipped at her coffee and the dogs settled at her feet while mournfully eyeing the biscuits.

'Have a couple of biscotti,' she said, handing Aldo the plate.

He took one, still contemplating the picture as he chewed, and she broke a biscuit in half for the dogs.

'Your mother?'

'You can tell?'

'Of course. It's a good likeness. Did you always want to be an artist?'

'I don't know. I lived in a home full of pictures, music and books. I guess all of that influenced me. What about you, Aldo? What do you want to do with your life?'

'I want to farm like my father did,' he said. 'But first I want to fight.'

'You're so young. Too young for that,' she said and decided to change the subject. 'What about a girlfriend? Is there anyone you have your eye on?'

He flushed a little. 'Not yet, though there's a girl I like in Buonconvento.'

'That's exciting. Tell me about her?' She passed the plate of biscotti to him again and he seemed glad of the distraction, his flush deepening. Then he lowered his eyes. 'I hardly know her and, anyway, with the war it isn't possible.'

'Surely that isn't true? People can still fall in love, can't they?'

He straightened up and looked her in the eye. 'I will be leaving, you know that, don't you, Contessa?'

When he'd been distraught after his father's death, she'd promised Carla she would always look after him, watch out for him as he grew older and ensure he stayed on the straight and narrow. In his early youth, he'd been a little wild, gone off goodness knows where, got in with a bad lot. She had taken him to Florence to broaden his horizons, Siena too, and it had been good for him to see something of the world beyond the walls of their village.

'Come on, Aldo,' she said. 'You know your mother is terrified you'll run off at any moment.'

'Contessa, I'm sorry, but I have to do the right thing.'

'And that is?'

He glanced out of the window towards the forested hills where the partisans were hiding and the fiery determination in his eyes told her exactly what he meant.

'Aldo, this isn't a game. Think of your family. They only have you. You're the man now.'

'And, as a man, I am thinking of my country.'

She could see he wouldn't change his mind and chewed her lip while wondering what to say. He really was a man now and she could sense how strongly he felt. She reached out to touch his arm and his eyes softened.

'Is there nothing I can say?'

He shook his head and she could see a confusing mixture of sadness and passion fighting within him.

'What shall I say to your mother? Won't you wait a little longer? You're so young. If I tell her I've spoken to you, she'll never forgive me for not trying harder to prevent you from going.'

He gulped back his feelings when she mentioned his mother and stared at the ground for a moment. 'Very well, I won't go yet, so there's no need for her to worry. But sooner or later I will have to.'

'Then make it later.'

He glanced up as she took his hand.

'Aldo, you know you've been like a son to me.'

'And I will always be grateful.'

'It's not your gratitude I want. It's your safety.' She squeezed his hand and her eyes filled with tears. 'Oh, my dear boy, I've known you all your life, is there nothing I can say?'

He didn't speak.

She touched his cheek. 'For me?'

His dear face reddened in anguish. 'I cannot stay, Contessa. You know I cannot. In any case, if I don't go, the Germans will only call me up to fight for them.'

Then his eyes moistened too.

'The time will come but I will be careful,' he added by way of reassurance, his eyes darker than ever.

Sofia wrapped her arms around herself. He gave her a long stare, and then, his irrepressible smile back once more, he got to his feet. 'Please don't tell my mother what I've said. It will only worry her. Let her think I'm not going, at least for now.'

'Of course,' she said, then hesitated for a moment before speaking again. 'Would you sit for me?'

He looked puzzled. 'For a picture, you mean?'

'Yes.'

'Why would you want to paint a picture of me?'

'Carla would like it.'

* * *

After Aldo had gone, Sofia read her mother's note again, feeling torn. If she only knew exactly what her mother meant by 'wine' it might help her decide. What if the delivery was weapons or explosives? She loved Lorenzo and didn't want to cause division between them, and yet, if she did what her mother asked, she might. Lorenzo would expect her to tell him, to ask his advice, and would see it as a kind of disloyalty if she didn't. She heard her mother's voice in her head. *Do it, Sofia, just do it.* And yes, with Lorenzo now back in Rome, maybe she could get away with it, without having to say anything, but he'd be home soon and how long would the delivery need to be kept at the Castello?

II.

With Lorenzo away there was an absence more worrying than the simple lack of his physical presence. The house felt emptier, as if the air had been sucked from it, making it harder to breathe. Or maybe it was the opposite? Maybe the air had become too full of something Sofia didn't understand, as if it was waiting, and not only for him to return. It felt as if all its ghosts had assembled, nudging each other and whispering, *What next? What next?*

Sofia was sitting in her little studio with its comforting smell of oils and turpentine, and French windows overlooking the garden. She busied herself for a few minutes, sketching the view and wishing life could be as straightforward as it used to be when the farmers' wives came on a Sunday afternoon to tell her their troubles and she'd do whatever she could to help. Sometimes a simple matter of providing a child with shoes, sometimes something more serious. A sick husband. A need for a loan. And she always mediated on their behalf.

But that was the past and now her most pressing concern was to take Maxine to meet James, so she put her charcoal and her sketchpad away, wiped her hands on a rag and prepared to go.

After parking the car, the two of them walked along the path that wound around the convent. The dogs had whined to come with them, but she had decided their barking might draw unwanted attention. It was a sparkling, radiant day, cloudless and not as cold as one might expect. The mimosa was still in flower and the air smelt fresh and clean, woody, green and a little bit spicy too, although Sofia was too distracted to appreciate it.

'What is it?' Maxine asked. 'Is something wrong?'

Sofia laughed. 'Is something wrong? Umm . . . now, what on earth could be wrong?'

'I meant something specific.'

Sofia sighed. 'My mother says that a delivery of some kind will be coming, and she wants me to look after it. She also says I am to trust you.'

'Well, I'm glad to hear it.'

Sofia shaded her eyes with her hand against the sun and studied Maxine's face. 'Did my mother tell you about it? What the delivery is?'

'No. But I'm hoping this British guy we're visiting is a radio engineer.'

Sofia nodded.

'Could be his radio and transmitter then?'

'Yes, could be.'

'It'll be a parachute drop, of course. There's no other way.'

'She said by the end of next week. But when did she give you the box?'

Maxine frowned. 'Over a week ago now.'

'So, it already is next week.'

'I guess it could be any day. I'm meeting a partisan leader in Montepulciano tomorrow. If your British guy confirms the drop will be soon, I'll be able to speak about it then. Arrange help.'

'He does have a name, you know. My British guy.'

Maxine smiled as Sofia knocked on a small green door at the back of the convent and the Mother Superior opened it herself.

'How is he?' Sofia asked.

The woman smiled. 'Stronger, thank goodness.'

'May I introduce my –' Sofia hesitated. 'My friend, Maxine. We call her Massima.'

The woman nodded, understanding. 'A friend of yours is a friend of ours. This way, please.'

She led them along a short corridor and opened another door

on to a pretty courtyard. Sofia looked around and saw tubs of lemon trees that in the spring would burst into flower.

'It is not overlooked here,' the nun was saying, 'and I believe the fresh air is doing him good. There he is.' She pointed to a sheltered corner where Sofia could see James relaxing with a blanket over his knees. 'He's still a little weak so try not to tire him. I'll sort out some refreshments for you.'

James turned to them as they walked across, gazing at Maxine with interest, and Sofia could again see the magnetic effect she had on men.

Maxine held out her hand as she reached him. 'Hi, I'm Maxine.'

He rose to his feet and, obviously enchanted, he smiled at her. 'You're American?'

She jokingly batted her lashes at him. 'American-Italian actually.'

'Well, either way, I'm pleased to meet you.'

'We need to get on with the business in hand,' Sofia said, just a little bit stiffly.

James immediately responded. 'Absolutely.' Then he shot Sofia a questioning look. 'Is it okay to talk?'

Sofia gave him a brief nod. 'I'm very glad to see you looking so much stronger.'

'Another few days and I'll be up and about.' He glanced at Maxine. 'I was shot when my parachute came down. Sofia brought me to the convent to recover.'

'A good Samaritan,' Maxine said with a smile. 'That's Sofia.'

They talked for a little while and then a young nun brought out a tray of coffee and small pastries. After she had left them, James confirmed the radio was expected and had been planned for approximately two weeks after his own drop.

'I have the exact location.' He pulled a piece of crumpled paper from a slightly unstitched seam in his jacket and held it out to Sofia. 'It won't be the same place I was dropped.'

66

'Thank you. I'll contact Francesco, my vintner in Montepulciano. He seems to be coordinating the "delivery" as my mother called it. Maybe you could give this piece of paper to the partisan leader you're meeting, Maxine.'

Maxine took it and then stuffed two of the pastries into her mouth. James laughed. 'Hungry?' he asked.

She swallowed and flashed him a wide smile. 'Always.'

12

The next day Maxine arrived in Montepulciano, in good time for her meeting. She'd been lucky and managed the twenty-five miles or so relatively quickly, some of it along bumpy tracks. She had even had time to visit her cousin Davide. He was the son of her mother's sister who'd married well and moved away from the farming life with Davide's father. His mother had not survived childbirth, but his father still lived with Davide and his new wife. He'd been happy to meet her, although a little cautious at first, but he'd eventually invited her to stay should she ever need to.

After she left them, Maxine set out to find the café she'd been told about, the Caffè Poliziano on the main street climbing up the hill. But on finding it, she glanced around, perplexed. This was Via Voltaia Nel Corso, as she'd been told, so therefore the right place, but she'd never seen anything quite like it. The elegant, bourgeois café, more suited to Paris or Vienna at the turn of the century, seemed an unlikely rendezvous. She hesitated on the doorstep, gazing in at the mirrored walls, the gorgeous tasselled lampshades and the smart waiters balancing silver trays as they swooped around the room. Could it be a trap? She'd left the pamphlets in the pannier on the bike, thinking it would be safer than keeping them on her person – after all, an old motorcycle was unlikely to be noticed – but now she realized that perhaps she should have brought them with her.

Go in, she told herself. *You'll only draw attention if you dither.* So she slipped inside and stood at the bar to order a hot chocolate, plus an espresso, exactly as she'd been instructed. The barman inclined his head and glanced in the direction of the main café.

'Ah yes, you have ordered the espresso for the gentleman sitting in the room on the left, nearest the window. Any cake or pastries?'

Maxine shook her head and walked into a large room with a balcony at one end. She couldn't help taking a quick peek at the incredible view over the Val di Chiana and longed to sit on one of the tiny tables out there. But she didn't linger and headed through an archway into the adjoining room where she recognized the man sitting alone at a table near the window.

As she approached, he rose to his feet. 'You know this place was established as a café in 1868?'

That had been the password Elsa had whispered in her ear and she gave him the expected reply.

'I didn't. How extraordinary.'

He held out his hand. 'Marco.'

'Yes, I remember.' It probably wasn't his real name, but she shook his hand, told him she was Maxine and worried she should have said Massima. But as he'd already heard her real name at that meeting in Rome, what could she do?

Theirs was the only occupied table in this part of the café, probably used for lunches rather than morning coffee, she thought.

'So,' he said. 'You are on time.'

His appearance had changed, his hair short, and he was well shaven, but he had the same angular looks and the same exciting caramel-coloured eyes. Plus, the same walking stick resting beside him next to his hat, a classic dark-grey felt fedora.

'I am coordinating various groups,' he said. 'It isn't easy. We have people joining us for many different reasons and they don't all get along.'

'But you will be able to help me?'

He puffed out his cheeks and shrugged. 'Depends on what you want.'

'You already know. I have to report back on what you're doing to support the Allies. And what you might be able to do.'

He frowned. 'How do I know I can trust you?'

'You saw me at Roberto and Elsa's apartment in Rome. You heard what they said. I replied correctly to your password. Oh, *and* I can show you my identification.' She reached into her bag.

He laughed. 'You think those things cannot be forged? Put it away.'

Her turn to shrug now. 'Well, it is forged, of course. But listen. I'm here on behalf of the British, as you know. And *you* understand what's happening on the ground. We can help each other.'

'Do you know the term GAP?'

'I've heard of it.'

'It's what we call a small unit of partisans – *Gruppi di Azione Patriottica*. There's one here and in many other small towns. I can introduce you.'

She glanced around at the sound of a waiter approaching their table. An elderly man who walked carefully and then laid out their drinks for them with precise movements. 'Germans outside,' he whispered to Marco and then left.

'Right,' Marco said and smiled at Maxine. 'We talk inconsequentially now. The Germans love this place.'

'Isn't it a bit risky meeting here, then?'

He laughed again. 'Right under their noses. That's the whole point. Relax, they're still outside and, anyway, they won't suspect a thing.'

But Maxine didn't feel relaxed.

He gave her hand a flirtatious stroke. 'Seriously, if you look so stiff, they'll notice. Pretend we are lovers. It's a romantic place, no?'

She glanced down and then up again and into his eyes in which she encountered the unconcealed desire men regularly regarded her with, but this time combined with a look of intense amusement. He certainly had natural charisma, but there was also a depth of melancholy in those eyes, something painful she couldn't quite put her finger on.

They were silent for a moment or two and then he was saying something conversational about the town, expanding on the detail of what there was to see, and in a flash, she'd stopped listening. Something tugged at her mind, prompting a flood of childhood memories. Her mother; always talking of Tuscany. After a moment she shook the memories away and gazed at him.

'Penny for your thoughts?' he said. 'I don't normally find women drift off in my company. Now you must take my hand properly.'

She raised her brows, pouted and, brazening it out, did as he had suggested. She wasn't sure if he was expecting her to show discomfort that they should pretend to be lovers or if he was testing her in some way.

'That's better. Now . . . how about a kiss?'

'Don't push your luck,' she replied, and laughed.

Since discovering her powers as a teenager Maxine had become a fan of dangerous liaisons and had enjoyed quite a number. Now she had the feeling this might become another. She leant forward to speak.

'What happened in Rome, after I left?'

'There was nothing incriminating. We made it look like a little soirée.'

'But the curfew?'

'Elsa told them we were guests, there to stay the night.'

'What did the Germans want?'

'They are taking over the palazzo. Everyone had an hour to pack up and get out.'

She shook her head. 'But it's awful. Where are they meant to go? Roberto and Elsa aren't young.'

'They have friends in the city.'

'Are they communists?' she asked and then frowned. 'Are you?'

'Does that scare you?'

She felt her cheeks heat up as he laughed at her.

71

'Americans are terrified of communism. But here in the countryside we're sick of never having enough. When we win the war, everything will change. But no, Elsa and Roberto are intellectuals, not communists. We all try to get along together to drive out the Nazis. It doesn't always work.'

Maxine could hear that the Germans had entered the café now, their loud, imperious voices and their terrible Italian instantly recognizable. A rush of fear mingled with the excitement from a moment ago, but she didn't glance round to look. They continued with their drinks and now Marco lifted her hand to his lips. 'I have a room.'

'Oh?'

'When I begin to rise, get to your feet too, slip on your jacket and saunter out into the street. I will pay for our drinks and follow you. Look in a shop window while you wait and then go to your motorcycle. I'll join you there.'

'A cousin of mine lives here. I was planning to go back to his house.'

'Another time.'

Maxine did as she was instructed, pausing long enough to plant a kiss on his cheek before leaving the café. The barman said something to Marco and they both burst into laughter, but Maxine couldn't be sure what about. She suspected the man had congratulated Marco on the speed of his conquest. She didn't care. This was the way she liked to live her life, always on the edge, always a hint of danger and always absolutely zero commitment.

Out in the street, Maxine crossed over to glance in a shop selling hats, scarves, overcoats and gloves. With winter coming she could do with a warm scarf, so she nipped in to choose, keeping one eye on the street. She saw Marco pull his hat brim down over his eyes as he left the café, limping slightly and leaning on his stick, then looking around to see where she'd gone. For a moment she enjoyed his expression of uncertainty but then, after quickly paying for her scarf, she went outside. He spotted her but didn't smile and she noticed he was looking in the direction of her motorcycle. Her heart banged against her ribs when she saw two Nazis were inspecting it. If she hadn't stopped to buy the scarf, they'd have caught her right beside the bike for sure.

'Walk in the opposite direction,' Marco commanded.

'The bike?'

'You still have the pamphlets?'

'In the pannier.'

'Better there than on you. Walk away now. If they don't find the pamphlets, I'll arrange for them to be distributed in local villages later. If they do, we've lost the bike.'

They began to head down the hill, Maxine on shaky legs and Marco's limp more pronounced than before. He'd raised his shoulders, slid his hands into his pockets and hunched up, seeming to shrink into himself.

They took a few more steps away before a German voice shouted out, his words unclear. She clutched Marco's hand. The German had to be ordering her to stop.

'Keep moving,' Marco hissed.

'But –?'

'Move.'

She was still shaking but did what he said, then couldn't prevent herself glancing back to see the two Nazis marching off in the direction of an officer further up the hill, who had obviously called out to them. To them. Not her.

Marco laughed as he straightened up.

Suddenly, she cottoned on. 'You knew, didn't you? You knew it wasn't about us.'

'Well, yes,' was all he said in reply.

She punched him on the arm and then began to laugh too. He'd used the hunched posture to make himself look like a useless limping man who would, therefore, be of little interest to the Nazis.

'We'll go round by the back alley, pick up the bike and then ride it a little nearer to my place. We can transfer the pamphlets to my bag. Try to look normal and we'll talk as we go. When we get to a quieter spot, tell me more about why you came here.'

Maxine considered the question as they walked.

'It's a long story,' she said as they reached a quiet street. She pictured her family and imagined how it had once been for them. Way back in November 1910 her parents and some of their extended family had disembarked at Ellis Island, New York, from the SS *Chicago*, a ship that had left from Le Havre. They'd been farmers and cattle merchants in Tuscany, but the family had grown too large for the land to support them all. Some had gone to work in Siena or Arezzo; others, like Maxine's parents, had emigrated in the hope of a better future. The country of Maxine's birth, four years later, had never felt like her true homeland and it left her with something of an identity crisis. Now, being in Tuscany frequently brought a lump to her throat. Her mother had often told the story of their long journey to America, and her continuing homesickness and glowing descriptions of home had dominated Maxine's youth. The excitement of the grape harvest, the sweet country air, the bottling of fruit and tomatoes, the wine, the fields of golden sunflowers in June, the ripe cornfields in July and August. Indeed, she sometimes believed she'd inherited her mother's occasionally melancholy disposition, and the reckless way she lived her life had been a conscious decision to counteract that.

'So?' Marco prompted. 'You drifted away again. Tell me, what else have the British asked you to do?'

'Oh,' she said, keeping it brief as she focused on him again. 'Once I've worked out where the partisans are and how numerous, I have to liaise with the Brits and then work to provide the weapons necessary to build up the partisan fighting units.'

'Really?' he scoffed. 'They send a woman to do that?'

'Apparently there haven't been many Italians willing to come back.'

He looked over her shoulder then back into her eyes but didn't give the impression that he believed her.

'So, are you coming to my place then?'

She nodded. 'You know the vintner, Francesco?'

'Of course.'

'And he is . . .?'

'A good man. You can trust him.'

'I have the location for a radio drop. Can you arrange for some men to help with that?'

'Of course. When?'

'That's the thing, we don't know for sure. Very soon, but it may mean waiting around for a couple of nights.'

That afternoon, mist was already snaking along the ground, shrouding the lower parts of the tree trunks. Without a hat or gloves, Maxine shivered in the forest's green gloom, jumping as birds burst from the trees, shrieking like devils from hell, their wings flapping. They'd hidden her motorcycle in the bushes and now Marco rarely glanced back to see if she was still following, although her footsteps and muttered curses as she struggled through dense undergrowth, her skin stinging from vicious thorns, meant he could hear her. The limp didn't seem to be bothering him now at all. When he did jerk round to check her progress, the playful expression on his face said *Are you up to this?* And Maxine would narrow her eyes and toss her chestnut curls. She didn't say she'd just seen a deer staring at her. Were there wolves too or wild dogs? She had no idea.

As she walked, her mother's voice sounded in her head, a never-ending tape of admonishment. *A nice girl waits until she has a ring on her finger. What is the matter with you? Raimondo is a good man.* Maxine didn't doubt it, but she had no desire to marry a grocer. A grocer's wife, for heaven's sake. No matter that he owned a chain of shops and was *going places*. She'd prefer to go straight to Hades, thank you very much.

After a while they approached a particularly dense clump of trees where Marco held aside the trailing vegetation to reveal a narrow path leading to what looked like a derelict stone farmhouse, standing alone in a small clearing.

'You are joking?' she said as she gazed at the roof where the holes caused by missing tiles were visible.

He shrugged.

'Your room?'

'A room is a room. I have a bed.'

She raised her brows. 'Which you no doubt share with the rats and cockroaches.'

He gazed at her with amused eyes fringed by thick dark lashes. 'I like insects . . . and animals.'

She took another look, now spotting the boarded windows and peeling paintwork, and screwed up her lips. Was she even safe here?

'We can make a fire.' He spoke nonchalantly, ignoring her expression. 'If you are cold.'

'If?'

He didn't reply, merely studied her face and gave her an enigmatic smile. She took in his bronzed skin, dark curly hair and high cheekbones. Like a gypsy. So good-looking it almost hurt and, undoubtedly, he knew it. She smiled at him. 'Well, are you going to invite me into your castle?'

Marco inclined his head, and she saw he meant it as a signal for her to follow. She swallowed her misgivings and stepped inside. He led her across an earthen floor, bypassing a room which, judging by the small table and remaining few chairs, must have once been a kitchen. Then, after throwing open a creaking dark-brown door with a theatrical flourish and making her laugh, he steered her through to the back of the house. The whole place reeked of damp, stale cigarette smoke and, rather oddly, of bitter lemons. After he'd lit a candle, she glanced around the small square room. The only window had been loosely covered with a ragged piece of cloth, but the stone floor looked clean enough. Hardly a glamorous location and yet, despite everything, she found the rustic simplicity romantic. They were not here for an intimate dinner for two. And the more rudimentary their surroundings the better. Plus, he was even more wildly striking by candlelight.

'Sit,' he ordered, taking off his hat and coat. Then he went about building a small fire, using chestnut shells for kindling and coaxing the weak flames until they blazed, while she poked at the mattress on the floor. He called it a mattress but when she examined it closely she saw it was little more than straw packed tightly inside a bag of mattress ticking. Scratchy, itchy, prickly, especially if you were naked.

'Have you got sheets?' she asked, although she already knew the answer.

'So you're the princess type?'

She laughed. 'Get a move on with that fire and I'll show you the kind of princess I am.'

'You do this often?' he said.

'Do you?'

He laughed, and she laughed with him. Then he opened a small trunk in the corner of the room. From it he withdrew a corkscrew, a bottle of red wine and two china mugs. 'They're a bit chipped but the wine still tastes good.'

He uncorked the wine, poured and handed her a mug, then sat beside her. She noticed a kind of brilliance in his eyes. Passion or the fervour of his cause? Maybe both.

Suddenly nervous, she gulped down the rich, fruity wine and held out her mug for more. Here in Tuscany she was free to be whoever she wanted to be, with no one from home to restrain her. He didn't need to know she had tweaked this version of herself and honed it until she could almost believe she'd really become the gutsy, fiercely independent individual she wanted to be. Maxine knew that if you didn't feel it, you had to fake it until it became a reality. As for the occasional stirring of a need she was unable to name, that she didn't want to name, she couldn't admit *that* even to herself.

'So, what's your story?' she said.

'No story.'

She narrowed her eyes and studied his face. 'We all have a story.'

'Not one I am willing to tell.'

'Well, just tell me one thing.'

His brow furrowed while he hesitated but then his eyes lightened. 'I can tell you that I used to be a journalist.'

'So was I.'

'Well then, I am like you.'

'I see. And are you really like me?'

'It will be interesting to find out, don't you think?'

His response made her smile, his low, soft voice enthralling her as he cast a spell. She was enjoying this.

'I worked for a while at the *Nazione*,' he added, 'the principal Tuscan daily, but it became impossible when the Germans arrived. They only wanted pieces condemning the Allies.'

They drank for a while in silence until he lifted her chin and kissed her full on the lips. Her breathing grew shallower as her body responded. She made no attempt to hide her rising desire and slipped a hand beneath his belt, pulling it loose and feeling his erection. Despite discovering that sex was a brilliant way to counteract the horrors of war, she hadn't fully appreciated how much she needed this.

Within moments he kissed her again and they fell back on the mattress, tearing at each other's clothes. Little had been said and seconds later they were lost in the act itself.

Most men didn't believe there were women who preferred this kind of coupling. No flowers and no promises of love. It was carnal, animal, visceral. Skin on skin. Flesh on flesh. And the kind of man who cared about virginity was not the kind of man

Maxine wanted. No. Far better this. No hearts to be broken. No faithfulness to be demanded, and none to be given.

Afterwards she lay beside him and watched the light changing the atmosphere in the little room. Then she stroked his now luminous skin. Pretty dancing patterns from the fire flickered on the walls, bringing them closer and making Maxine feel cosy. How must it have once been when a family lived here? She imagined a husband and wife with maybe three or four children who cared for their animals while their mother cooked tasty stews from their own produce and their father worked in the fields. She asked whose place it had been, but Marco told her there were many abandoned farms in the countryside where the inhabitants had given up the struggle to eke out a living from the land. And she understood her vision of family life here had been a fantasy. It would have been hard and lonely with viciously cold winters, especially when there had not been enough to eat.

'I need to sleep.' He had spoken rather gruffly, and now pulled a blanket over them both. 'We have work tonight.'

'Work?'

He frowned. 'The less you know . . .'

'But that's ridiculous. I need to know. It's why I've come. I told you that.'

He raised himself up on one elbow and gazed into her eyes while scratching his chin. 'You want to come? I get that. But why? Why did you volunteer for this? You are a beautiful American girl. It is not even your war.'

'It would have been if my parents had not emigrated. I have to understand what you are doing, and I need to know where the partisans are.'

'It's simple. We make trouble for the Germans. Demoralize the enemy any way we can. Hit at their German pride, you know? And the majority of the men are in the forests of Monte Amiata. Hundreds of them.'

'And here?'

'In the woods around the towns. Not so many here and a mixed bunch but we're licking them into shape.'

She gave him a look. 'And you won't let me come?'

'At this stage you'd be a liability. How did you even get this far?' he said, shaking his head. 'It really is incredible.'

'I told you, the Brits didn't have many to choose from. If you let me come, I can request more support for what you're doing.'

'We certainly need it, although we do have the farmers' support, at least. Had enough of giving up their harvest to the Germans. But as for you coming? No.'

'I'm used to danger.'

'No,' he said. 'Now let me sleep.'

'Where are you from?'

He made a groaning, exasperated sound but didn't reply.

'Well, if you won't tell me that, tell me how old you are?'

He rolled over with his back to her.

She did eventually fall into a restless sleep but at one point half woke to hear Marco moaning. When she touched his bare shoulder, she realized he was not awake and so she curled into him and slid back into sleep herself. When she fully awoke it was to the sound of gruff male voices coming from the kitchen. Marco sat bolt upright as if on alert but once he'd recognized what it was, he lit a cigarette and relaxed. She watched the glow of it in the now dark room.

'It is the men,' he said.

She clutched his arm and hissed at him. 'If you don't allow me to come, I will follow you.'

He frowned. 'Don't be a fool. You stay here or you go back to town. Maybe next time.'

She nodded. 'Very well. If that's your last word.'

13

Maxine had not been long back at the Castello when Sofia suggested Aldo should join the men for the drop. She'd wanted Aldo to feel involved without having to run away from home. Maxine had thought it a risky strategy and argued that he'd get a taste for it and then he'd be gone. Nevertheless, three nights later, and on the second night of waiting, here he was. Maxine huddled in the deep shadows of the trees with her eyes fixed on the small clearing in the valley where a fire was burning. Aldo's excitement at being included was obvious as he paced back and forth, glancing up at the sky every few minutes.

It was a clear night, thank goodness, although the excellent visibility also meant the Germans had more chance of spotting the plane and shooting it down. The pilot would still attempt the drop even if the weather was foul, in which case the equipment might well have ended up lodged in a tree. Obviously, it still might if something went wrong or the plane was shot down. They had already been waiting for three hours and the men were on edge. Even Aldo's enthusiasm was wearing thin. Nobody could tell why the plane hadn't arrived. If it didn't come before dawn approached it would be too late.

Maxine held her breath and listened to the sounds of the night: animals scratching in the undergrowth, birds' wings beating the air and the wind rustling the leaves of the trees. She smelt the smoke, the vegetation and the damp earth as she waited and watched, the darkness closing around her.

'Why is it late?' Aldo whispered.

'I don't think anyone knows.'

'I didn't expect it to be so dull.'

'Waiting is always dull. Get used to it.'

When a loud whistle pierced the air followed by the sound of an engine high above, she crossed her fingers and gazed up. Was that light she could see, an early hint of dawn maybe, or was she only imagining it in the still dark sky?

'No sight of a plane yet, but I think this is it,' she said and she could feel Aldo tense up as he stood beside her.

To guide the pilot to the target area, Marco and another partisan began flashing their torches repeatedly. Maxine narrowed her eyes to see more clearly as the plane slid into view. No interior lights had been switched on, but it circled twice and then suddenly she could make out a parachute falling. She held her breath again. If the equipment crashed to the ground it would smash into pieces – but no, the canopy opened and now two parcels were drifting downwards. The drop looked so obvious she couldn't believe the Germans wouldn't have spotted it. She saw the dark shapes of two men running to retrieve the parcels and gather up the parachute silk, then with Aldo's help they carried the parcels to the waiting motorcycles and strapped them on. Despite one being Maxine's, Marco indicated she should clamber up behind him while another partisan climbed astride the other motorcycle with Aldo on the back. Then they raced at breakneck speed through the trees and on to the narrow, tortuous lanes, finally winding up around the hill to the Castello where Sofia would be waiting.

Before they approached the huge archway into the village, the sound of a vehicle reached them from some distance behind. A German lorry or car? So soon? Had they been watching? Seen everything? In the ticking silence of the night, noises and distances were difficult to judge. Close. Far. You couldn't tell. The vehicle could be much further away than it sounded. Maxine held rigidly to Marco as he increased his speed, taking a risky shortcut through the woods, impossible for anything but a motorcycle. When they reached the village, she saw the tall gates had been left open and Sofia was pacing back and forth, not at all her usual composed self. The men pulled up and she ran to help unload the equipment.

'I think somebody might be coming,' Maxine whispered to Sofia. 'We heard a vehicle.'

Sofia seemed to consider for a moment then indicated they all should follow her to the nearest door. This she unlocked and they climbed down five steps into the shadowy basement where the wine barrels were stored.

'Here?' Marco asked, with a dubious look at Sofia. 'Not the cellars under the house?'

'There's no time for that. This is closer.' She pointed to a barrel at the back. 'It's empty. We've been using it to hide produce. Tip it up. It opens at the back. You can shove the equipment in there. We'll move it when the coast is clear.'

'Is there a lamp?'

'Use your torch. Quickly.'

Aldo steadied the barrel as the men tipped it up and then slid the equipment into the empty space. They set it down slowly and secured the back.

'Now hurry,' Sofia said, and watched as the two men wheeled the motorcycles into the darkness of the woods. Sofia and Maxine, with quite an effort, pulled the main gates shut.

'We need to make ourselves scarce before anybody notices we're out here at the crack of dawn,' said Sofia.

'Shouldn't we wait to see if a vehicle comes?'

'No, far better they find the place deserted and silent,' Sofia replied, her voice tense.

They made their way back to the house and ascended the stairs.

'Come to my room,' Sofia said.

In the bedroom a window was open and just one lamp was lit. Sofia quickly put it out and went across to look out at the square. Maxine tapped her foot restlessly, her heart still pounding with excitement. In the light from the moon she saw Sofia's shoulders relax a little. 'It's fine,' she said. 'There's no sign of anyone.'

'Can I see?'

'Take a look if you want. But I think whoever it was must have lost the trail.' She went to her bed and pulled down a corner of her eiderdown.

'You're surely not going to bed?' Maxine asked, astonished Sofia could be considering sleep.

'No.' Sofia gave a mirthless laugh. 'I'd never sleep but I need to rumple up the bedclothes and get into my nightdress. You'll have to as well.'

Maxine went to look out at the square, her hands resting on the sill, but there was still nothing to see. Disappointed by such an anticlimax after the night's adventures, she wanted more.

'Anything?' Sofia was looking at her with an amused expression.

Maxine sighed and shook her head.

Sofia sat on the edge of her bed. 'I'll knock on your door as soon as it's light. We'll go to the kitchen for coffee then.'

'And the vehicle we heard?'

'Like I said. It must have lost the trail. Now close the window and the shutters. If I hear anything, I'll deal with it. *You* stay put.'

Maxine nodded her agreement and left the room. However, whatever the Contessa might say, if anything were to happen there was no way she was going to sit in her room and miss out.

In her bedroom she undressed, put on a flimsy robe and then lay down under the chilly covers, not expecting to sleep at all.

Some hours later she awoke to see daylight slicing through the slats of the shutters. Shivering with cold, she jumped out of bed, whipped a blanket round her shoulders and then listened.

From the square, insistent German voices rang out, followed by shrill Italian ones. As doors were hammered and orders issued, people were congregating, arguing, objecting. A woman screamed and then a child began sobbing. Christ, they were here already. She opened her door and crept along the corridor to Sofia's room. She knocked gently and then entered.

Sofia was already dressed and was now brushing her hair.

'Aren't you going outside?' Maxine asked.

'Not yet.'

'Why not?'

'I will not be intimidated. They'll come for me soon enough. Let them search the village and find nothing first.'

'And then?'

'And then I shall offer them coffee.'

Maxine didn't hide her scorn. 'Always the lady?'

Sofia sighed in exasperation. 'It's what they will expect. I don't want them to think I'm worried. It would only arouse suspicion.'

'And if your husband were here?'

'Naturally he would go out, as head of the household. They'd expect it. They won't expect me.' Sofia rubbed her eyes. 'Now get dressed and come down to the kitchen for breakfast.'

'I'd still rather go outside.'

Sofia shot her a warning look. 'Do as I say. What's to be gained from going out there? They'll do whatever they're going to do anyway. Take your time.'

'Why?'

'You're filthy. In any case, it's my guess they'll be some time.'

Back in her room, Maxine washed her body as best she could at the washbasin in the corner. She didn't linger. The water was freezing and so was her room, but when she glanced in the mirror hanging on the wall she grimaced. Sofia had been right. She wiped dark streaks of mud and possibly grease from her cheeks and saw that her hair was a tangled mess. Her eyes were too bright, glittering and feverish. Too cold to wash her hair now, it would have to do. She dragged a comb through it several times with very little success. It was still a mess but maybe Sofia could lend her a ribbon.

She marched along the corridor once more and tapped on the door. Without waiting for an answer, she opened it. 'Well,' she muttered as she stared in. 'How did *you* get here?'

Sofia stared at Maxine, who was standing in her doorway with a perplexed expression on her face.

'Quickly. Come in and close the door,' she said.

Maxine came across and, with her head tilted, settled her hands on her hips. 'So? How did James get here?'

'Aldo collected him earlier. He's been sleeping in the guest room next to you.'

'And he's in your bedroom now, because . . .?'

Sofia sighed deeply.

'And undressed?' Maxine continued with a grin.

'We're trying to see if any of Lorenzo's clothes will fit. Anyway, he isn't entirely undressed.'

Maxine pulled an amused face. 'You don't have to play-act on my account. No offence, I didn't think you had it in you.'

'Oh, for goodness' sake,' Sofia snapped, because Maxine was utterly maddening. Then, seeing the funny side, she began to smile too. 'Think what you will.'

James nodded at Maxine. 'Hello, Maxine. I see you're still up for a joke.'

'Always,' she said and gave him a flirtatious look.

'And since you asked, now that the radio equipment has arrived, I'm here to operate it. They call us the Pianists, you know, us operators.'

'You know the Germans are here too? Didn't you hear them banging on the doors?' Maxine faced Sofia. 'For Christ's sake, what are you going to do with him?'

'Don't worry. I know what I'm doing.'

'They'll search the whole house.'

'Indeed.'

'How can you be so calm?'

Sofia ignored her. The truth was, she was a bag of nerves but getting a lot better at hiding them.

'James, put these on,' she said, passing him a sweater, jacket and some trousers. 'They'll have to do. Maxine, take a pile of warmer clothes from my closet and put them in your room. You have so little with you, I want to make it crystal clear to the Germans you really are staying here.'

Maxine grinned. 'Doubt they'll fit.'

'And *I* doubt the Nazis will ask you for a fashion show. Now hurry.'

'Surely you're not going to pass James off as Lorenzo?'

At this, and despite the gravity of the situation, Sofia struggled not to laugh.

'Go!'

She was not about to let Maxine into all her secrets, at least not yet, so only after she'd gone, and James was dressed, did she move her dainty dressing table aside and press a small section of the panelled wall opposite the bed. A door slowly creaked open.

'Go into this passage. It's totally sealed and concealed. After several yards, you'll find a ledge. Your code booklet is there,' she told him. 'Perch on the ledge until I knock on the panel. I may be some time. I'll knock three times, count to three, and then I'll knock three times again. Come to the door and do the same and then I'll open it.'

'Where does the passage lead?'

'I'll tell you later. And remember, as quiet as a mouse, please. Don't even cough. How's your shoulder feeling now?'

He waved her question away but, from the look on his face, it was obvious the pain still lingered.

Once he was safely hidden, she moved her dressing table back, slid her pistol into her skirt pocket – she'd taken to having it with her – and then glanced around at her high-ceilinged room, its floorboards always polished to a shine, the light softly diffused through the embroidered silk curtains she'd bought in Venice.

Five minutes later it was Anna who came to inform her that a captain was waiting in the hall.

'Thank you,' she said. 'Now, please could you knock on the guest room two doors from mine and ask Maxine to come down for breakfast?'

She made her way down the imposing main staircase. It reminded her that she still commanded status and it comforted her a little. Just being able to make an entrance was something to cling to.

'Good morning,' she said, feigning surprise. 'Whatever can I do for you at this early hour?'

He was a solidly built man, his Nazi greatcoat flapping at his ankles. He wore round horn-rimmed spectacles and had mild, myopic blue eyes which she had no doubt belied the reality of his character. She took in his smooth, unlined skin, his high forehead and thin dark-blond hair. He took a few steps towards her, each movement slow, precise, menacing, calculated to demonstrate his power over her and emphasize her own powerlessness.

'I am Captain Kaufmann. I believe you have already met Commandant Schmidt.'

With a hint of a nod, she acquiesced politely. 'But of course. He came to dinner.'

'We need to search the villa.'

'Feel free. I'd appreciate it if your men tried not to break anything. We do have some priceless antiques. You know the kind of thing. Been in my husband's family for generations. Oh, and paintings too.'

She watched him peer through the open door of her small salon and then he faced her with a tight smile. 'If I am correct, that is the golden painting of San Sebastiano by Cozzarelli. No? A rare piece.'

'Yes. My husband is very proud of it.'

'Well, you need not fear. I am not here to damage your belongings, Contessa.'

'I'm happy to hear it. So, if you don't mind me asking, what are you here for?'

'Last night there was a parachute drop.'

'Really? And what has it to do with us, Captain Kaufman?'

'It is thought whatever it was may have been brought this way. By motorcycle.'

Eyes wide, she fabricated astonishment. 'I see. And when do you think this might have happened?'

'The early hours of this morning.' He spoke concisely, his words clipped.

'Goodness,' she said, making sure she looked shocked. 'I certainly didn't hear anything, but I do sleep soundly. Maybe ask some of the villagers. Someone surely will have heard something.'

'Indeed.'

'And what do you think might have been dropped?'

His eyes narrowed with suppressed anger. 'I am not here to answer your questions.'

'Forgive me. I was just curious. But I suppose you must be worried it might have been armaments, weapons, that sort of thing.'

He didn't reply for a group of uniformed men suddenly trooped in and stamped their way upstairs. As Kaufmann barked orders at them, they immediately picked up their pace. Sofia longed to run after them, follow them to her room, prevent them from unpicking her belongings or discovering anything, but surely there was little chance they'd press the panelling in exactly the right place? Few alive knew of the hidden passage that led through the buildings all the way to the first floor of the tower at the point where it butted up against the houses. Rather like the tunnels beneath the house which snaked out to the woods, there'd been little need to go underground or use hiding places in modern times.

Kaufmann had turned from the men and was now jabbing a finger at her. 'You must unlock all the storage units,' he said. 'Woodshed, vehicle store, wine store and so on. So now, you will come with me . . .'

He headed towards the door but at that moment Maxine tore down the stairs. 'Why, hello,' she said coquettishly and smiled at him.

Kaufmann's face twitched. 'And you are?'

'Massima. But everyone calls me Massi. I'm Sofia's best friend from Rome. I'm staying here. Rome is such a bore right now, don't you think, Commandant?'

'Captain,' he muttered, and his eyebrows knitted together in suspicion. He turned away.

'*Massi*,' Sofia said pointedly. 'If you'd like to take breakfast in the dining room, I'm just going to unlock the outdoor storerooms for the Captain.'

To her credit Maxine showed no concern but simply said, 'I'm not particularly hungry, I'll help you. Breakfast can wait. Have you got the keys?'

Sofia went to the hall table and opened the top drawer. 'Here we are. Let's go.'

'What are you looking for?' Maxine addressed the German, but he ignored her.

'They're looking for weapons, I think.' Sofia spoke loudly enough for the Captain to hear.

'Oooh, how exciting. Imagine. Weapons hidden right under your nose, Sofia.'

Sofia shot her a look that she hoped said *Don't overdo it – the man is not an idiot.*

She started by taking him and two others to the vehicle store. After unlocking, she threw open one of the wide doors.

'I see you have a motorbike?'

'Yes, but it's been empty of petrol this last month. We rarely use it.' She glanced at Maxine, glad Marco had kept hold of *her* motorcycle.

The Captain put out his hand. 'The keys?'

'Hanging there on the wall.'

'Where anyone could take them?'

Sofia raised her brows. 'They'd have to get inside the shed first.'

'Who else has the shed keys?'

'Our manager has them and my husband, Lorenzo, naturally.'

'And where are they?'

'Lorenzo, I believe, is in Rome. And our manager *was* overseeing a little bit of work on our place in Florence. After the bombing, you see.'

'*Was* overseeing?'

'He was called up . . . by yourselves.'

He fixed his eyes on her. They watched each other for a few seconds, he with unblinking intensity. He was magnetic in an awful way and she stared back, caught against her will. Eventually her eyes watered and the spell was broken. But it had troubled her, and she felt sure he knew it.

He then tried the keys. The motorcycle was clearly dead.

'And when did you last open this shed?'

'We took the pony and cart to San Giovanni d'Asso recently, but that's all.'

They left the vehicle shed and she next took him to examine the wood store, hoping by the time they reached the wine store he'd have been called away. She couldn't bear to see his men shifting the neat piles of firewood into untidy heaps. Dreading what might happen later, she averted her eyes and glanced at Maxine where she stood, her hair flaming as if it were red, back-lit by the sun.

'Massima, could you keep watch?' she said. 'I need some air.'

Outside she looked up at the tower and its familiar crenellated parapets and wanted so much to hang on to her life here. Could it really be about to end? She'd always tried to be a kind person, someone happy to fit in, and ready to help wherever she could. Despite living under the yoke of Mussolini, she'd had an easy life, privileged, and able to do pretty much whatever she wanted. Of course, it hadn't been entirely painless. She'd hoped for children but after Lorenzo's accident it simply hadn't happened. She didn't know if that had been the reason; maybe he'd been injured in some inexplicable way, although the doctors hadn't come up with any answers. He'd been lucky to get out alive, unlike the rest of his family. In any case, she'd put the longing for a child away and devoted herself to her husband, the villagers, the farm-workers, her household staff and her painting. She had loved her life here and the thought of it ending sent an icy shiver up her spine.

If only they'd had time to hide the radio equipment in the tunnels the night before. She'd been living at the Castello for several months before Lorenzo told her about them and she'd been surprised when he revealed that the tunnels were accessed via a stone-built outhouse in her rose garden, of all things, and also from the basement of the house. When Italy was not a unified country and the fighting nobles were at one another's throats, their hilltop fortresses, villages and castles frequently sat atop a warren of hidden tunnels with multiple exits. Lorenzo had shown her the way through their large basement and into a maze of dark passageways, alcoves and secret rooms to the deepest cellar. From there they'd slipped into the escape tunnels.

The Captain walked out of the wood store, and she felt a cold, unnatural calm as she observed him closely; a tightly bound man, like the Commandant, wound up, coiled inside himself, but without the feeling of resignation that hung about the older man. What wouldn't she give to see every feeling, every thought, every emotion, every fear, everything this man had ever repressed or suppressed suddenly bursting forth? But it wouldn't happen today. Today, if he found the equipment, he would be jubilant.

The time had come, and as she heard Lorenzo's voice in her head – *Dignity at all times, my darling, dignity* – she took a deep breath. The feeling of calm didn't last and now, as the dread returned, she pointed towards the wine-barrel store.

As Sofia unlocked the store, she felt terribly exposed, as if every bit of her was laid bare for everyone to see. The doors opened inwards and the Captain and one of his men walked down the steps first, with Maxine following and Sofia trailing behind reluctantly.

'Is there no electric light in here?' Kaufmann asked with a grimace as he glanced back at her.

'I'll leave the door open,' she said, omitting to mention the large torch resting on a shelf concealed behind the open door.

He tapped a few of the barrels. 'Thirsty work this searching.' And then he reached for one of the tasting cups sitting on a long trestle table and laughed – a forced laugh with no enjoyment in it.

Sofia had the impression he wasn't a man who would be interested in wine. His officer stepped up, took the cup, placed it under the tap of one of the barrels and filled it. He handed the cup to Kaufmann who took a disdainful sip then slowly emptied the rest of the wine on the ground while keeping his eyes fixed on her, enjoying her discomfort as he took his time. Then he moved on to the next barrel.

'Maybe this one is better.'

Was he playing with her? Was all this for show? Or was he going to taste the wine in all the barrels *and* try the one with no wine in it? Her mouth went dry and, treading around the black hole she saw opening in front of her, she felt the rise and fall of her own breath. Too fast, too shallow. She tried to suppress all fear, and all hope. In spite of the overwhelming strain, she forced herself to look unconcerned, as if nothing of interest was happening.

Her understanding of time altered. It stretched as he moved from barrel to barrel and the relentless raid went on and on. She heard other German voices as the men strode from door to door. She heard their boots and the crows cawing above the tower. She glanced outside. From the endless white-grey sky fine rain was now falling. She shivered with apprehension and gazed at the dull greens and purples of the distant landscape on this dark, brooding day. It was bitterly cold, and she wondered if snow was far behind. Maxine, meanwhile, was smiling. She asked to taste the wine too and the Captain handed her a different cup.

'Be my guest,' he said.

Sofia was too afraid to speak but Maxine was making conversation in Italian and English and attempting a little German too. Sofia only half listened and tried not to stare at Kaufmann. Maxine did her best to engage him in the merits of different kinds of wine, but he remained monosyllabic as he arrived at the last but one barrel. He leant against it and stared at Sofia. Her palms were sticky with sweat and fear crawled up her neck as she reached the point where she barely knew how to feel. But when he remarked that her wine was merely average, her loathing knew no limits. It was a little thing, but the wine was good. Very good. Everyone knew it.

With unassailable confidence, Maxine pointed at the final barrels. 'But there are two more to go. Maybe they are more to your taste.'

Sofia didn't miss the gleam in her eyes, and the fact that she was finding this exciting. My God, she was playing a dangerous game. Sofia glanced at Kaufmann and was met with a repulsive, cold stare and that contorted smile of his. A torrent of mixed emotions surged through her and her stomach lurched in disgust. So much for calm indifference! But the anger was hardest to deal with. Sofia was not known for losing her temper. She put her hand in her pocket and felt the cool pistol nestled there.

As Kaufmann reached the final barrel, a sense of dislocation flooded her being. She was there and not there. He seemed to be waiting for her to say something and she wanted to shout out, *No!* Wanted to raise her hand, draw out the pistol and pull the trigger. Of course, she couldn't. It was an insane idea. Her mother had once said, *We don't know what we are capable of until we try.* Sofia didn't think she'd been talking about murder.

'Go ahead,' she managed instead, hoping her voice didn't shake. She gave an involuntary shudder and Maxine widened her eyes. It was a timely warning and she took a deep breath. But her mind was letting her down. As terrible scenarios took over, she felt as if she had become a shadow, transparent, hardly there. Was it possible he could see right through her?

'Or maybe you might like some breakfast now, Captain?' Maxine said, still totally unruffled.

In the breath-stopping pause, Sofia's temple throbbed. He glanced at the barrel and took a step towards it, but then, to her overwhelming relief, he accepted Maxine's invitation with the slightest of bows and stalked up the steps to the square. As Maxine passed, she squeezed Sofia's arm. On the verge of tears, Sofia felt deeply touched by the woman's support, and braced herself. Would she have even got through it without Maxine?

After the Germans had finally gone, Sofia planned to retreat to her bedroom to release James, but Maxine trailed behind her.

'Where is he?' she asked, hands on hips. 'They didn't find him so what in hell did you do with him?'

Sofia gave her a veiled smile.

'Come on,' Maxine said as if encouraging a recalcitrant child.

'You'll see,' she replied and, despite some reservations – the fewer people who knew the secrets of the Castello the better – she made her decision. She sorely needed an ally and maybe together they'd find courage, strength and a way to help each other. She took in Maxine's amused face, her amber eyes, the chestnut hair. 'Very well. Come on.'

A little later, with James safely out of the hiding place, Maxine laughed. 'Well done, you. My mother told me about these tunnels. Not here but in Poggio Santa Cecilia. My father farmed but she worked in the big house there. I still have distant cousins thereabouts.'

'The village isn't far away,' Sofia said, thinking of the beautiful high-ceilinged villa at the top of Santa Cecilia. Larger than theirs, it used to be where the grandest summer parties were held. Lorenzo and she had been drinking champagne there before the war began, when nobody believed that, even if it happened, it would go on for long.

'I intend visiting soon,' Maxine was saying. 'I so want to go.'

Sofia frowned. 'Except the Germans are using it as local headquarters. Trashing it, I heard.'

'All the more reason for going. Who knows what I might find out?'

James had been pacing the room. He knew Italian, but Sofia wanted to be completely clear about their plans, so she spoke in English. 'I'll arrange for a tray to be brought up. Then I'll work out what to do with you.'

'I can't stay here?'

'Too risky. There's an empty farmhouse halfway down the hill. It's in a copse so not easily seen unless you know it's there.'

Maxine, unabashed, smiled mischievously. 'Or I could go with James. Man and wife.'

He laughed, getting into the spirit of it. 'Now there's an offer I can't possibly refuse.'

'You may not refuse,' Sofia remarked. 'But the Germans have already seen you here, Maxine.' Then she rubbed her forehead, not knowing why she felt a bit irritated. After all, he wasn't *her* parachutist.

'Okay, okay.' Maxine spread her arms wide in an attitude of surrender. 'I know when I'm not wanted. I'll see you later.'

As Sofia and James talked, she admitted to herself how weary she felt. This level of tension was draining, but she hoped sorting out the use of the radio equipment would provide the stamina she needed to keep going. It was dangerous and, unlike Maxine, she didn't thrive on fear. As James gave her the sweetest smile, then explained what he'd been thinking, she could tell he had sensed how unsettled she was feeling.

'We either deliver the radio to one of the partisan groups immediately – I'll go with the equipment, train them to use it – or, we set it up at the top of the tower tonight. It is the perfect place. I know it's a lot to ask but the radio will work so much more efficiently at height. We'll move it afterwards.'

She gasped. The tower. She hadn't been expecting that. 'I'm not sure. We need to get our lives back on track, not derail them even further.'

He touched her hand, intending it to be a comfort, but she felt a little awkward and bowed her head. She hadn't expected friendship but, if she was honest, she liked him and didn't want him to go so soon. They all needed human contact, love, connection with friends and family, for without it they had no hope of surviving, let alone thriving.

'Very well,' she said. 'If it really means the transmission has more chance of succeeding, use the tower tonight. Just this once. There are heavy shutters and I have blackout fabric we can tack on top of them.'

'Thank you. Truth is, it's going to get a hell of a lot worse before it gets better.'

She worried he might be right. These were the days of their lives and they were steadily losing them through no fault of their own. No one knew what would be left when it was all over. If it ever was. She tried to keep positive with hopeful thoughts and visions of a rosy future, but it wasn't easy. Even before all this, they'd had the long years of Mussolini to cope with. She'd never been happy about Il Duce, as he was known, despite Lorenzo paying lip service, at first. The dictator might be good for business, he'd said, but, like everyone else, they soon realized the dreadful rumours of brutality were true. And now here they were clinging to life by their fingertips, just as surely as if they were on a sinking ship.

16

Later that day Sofia spent an hour with Aldo making preliminary sketches for her painting of him. Naturally, she had sworn him to silence. When they were finished, she found Carla and led her to the garden where they wouldn't be overheard. Carla wiped her hands on her apron and neatened her hair a little as she looked up. The sky was a dazzling iridescent blue for a change, but it was also freezing and yet, dressed only in her indoor clothes, Sofia barely noticed. She glanced around to ensure nobody could hear and then took Carla right to the back of the garden to her private area, the place where villagers would come after church on Sunday mornings to ask for help. But this was different. This time it would be Sofia asking for help.

'Now,' Sofia said. 'We've known each other for many years.'

Carla agreed, but her teeth had started to chatter and she was shivering.

Sofia felt strangely excited as she spoke, explaining that the Englishman wanted help while the partisans moved some equipment into the tower.

'Help, how?' Carla asked, looking anxious.

'Well, it will be under cover of darkness, but as Maria lives between my house and the tower, I want to ensure she doesn't suspect anything when the men cross the square right past her window. Could you sit with her, share a drop of wine? Distract her?'

Carla raised her brows in surprise. 'She'll think it mighty strange. We've barely spoken since her bastard grandson ran off with the Fascists. And anyway, why not use the hidden passage?'

It was Sofia's turn to look surprised.

Carla smiled good-naturedly and patted her hand. 'Contessa Sofia, I've lived hereabouts longer than yourself. A few of us know of it. It was my father who told me.'

'I had thought of using it, but it's blocked – I tried it out before I came to see you. I don't know how long it will take to clear but it's crucial the equipment be moved and set up to be used tonight.'

'So?' Carla frowned and narrowed her eyes. 'What is this equipment?'

Sofia was deciding what to say before she spoke. 'You mustn't breathe a word.'

Carla nodded.

'It's a transmitting radio.'

'Oh!' Carla said, seeming utterly appalled. 'If they find it –'

Sofia interrupted. 'I know – if they find it, it will be the end for me.'

'Worse. Before they kill, they torture to extract information.'

Sofia bowed her head but didn't speak.

'It is a brave thing you do,' Carla said with a slight shake of her head. 'But what if something goes wrong?'

Sofia looked up and took a long, slow breath. 'I have learnt so much from you, Carla, from all of you. Your fortitude, your courage and your determination never to give up. And now this is something I must do. The injured man, James, is a radio operator with the British army, so an ally and a friend. He is going to train Aldo to use it.'

It really was too cold to be out and Carla, frowning, vigorously rubbed her palms together during the short, uneasy silence. The wind had got up too and a few clouds had gathered again.

'Why Aldo?' she said.

'It may be the safest option for him.'

Carla gave her a knowing look. 'So, you mean he won't have to go off to live in the woods with the partisans?'

Sofia nodded. 'Unless he gets called up by the German army. And we don't really know when that will happen, or even *if* it will happen. This seems like the best solution for now.'

Carla rose to her feet but didn't look wholly convinced. 'I just hope it is, Contessa. I worry, you know.'

'Oh, Carla. I know you do. I'm just looking for the best way to keep Aldo here at home.'

Carla nodded.

'You're happy to distract Maria?'

'That will not be a problem. I can do that. But you're sure this is the right thing for my son?'

'Yes. I believe it is.'

17

Sofia pulled open a cupboard in search of a warm jersey. The tower would be bitterly cold at this time of year. She kept trying to convince herself she wasn't afraid but, all the same, she hid her gun in the small shoulder bag she wore across her body. Then she marched down to the back door, collecting Aldo from the kitchen as she went.

'You ready for this, young man?'

Aldo gave her a thoughtful look. 'I hope so.'

They found James already waiting at the door at the side of the house. Earlier, they had moved him to the farmhouse along with a few tins of sardines, a wrinkled apple and a loaf of Carla's relatively fresh bread. Now, once she'd beckoned him into the passageway, she switched on the dim light and asked if he was comfortable in his new quarters.

'Bloody cold,' he said, rubbing his hands together, and she put a finger to her lips.

'I can always put you back in the hidden passage here if you prefer.' She raised her brows, knowing full well the passage was rough and even chillier than the farmhouse, with nowhere to sit.

'I think I'll pass, Contessa.'

'Sofia will do.'

He seemed a warm and genuine man and she felt sure she'd done the right thing by joining forces with him. But you had to take care. When a person turned out to be someone entirely different from who they'd made out to be, you began to mistrust your own instincts. A couple of men had requested refuge at the Castello and because she'd had no way of telling genuine refugees from spies, she'd turned them away. When they were later discovered to have been spies and were shot by partisans, she realized she was right to have been cautious.

'You okay?' James asked, and she was surprised he'd picked up on her qualms so easily.

'What do you think?' she said a little sharply.

At that point Maxine joined them, wrapped in an oversized man's coat and with her hair tied back.

A few moments later there was a tap at the door and even though Sofia had been expecting the men, she jumped.

James gently touched her arm. 'Take a breath.'

She did so and then opened the door a crack to see two men also bundled up in thick coats, woollen hats pulled down over their foreheads.

'Marco,' one said under his breath and she recognized him from the night before.

The other one, a smaller man, muttered his name too. 'Lodo.'

'Lodovico?'

'Just Lodo.'

Sofia, James, Aldo and Maxine joined the two men outside, Sofia leading the way to the wine store, passing in front of Maria's house where, despite the late hour, a low gleam of light still shone from her window. Sofia glanced up. A cloudy night with virtually no moon would work in their favour. She hoped Carla was still with Maria, and they were both praying to San Sebastiano. Someone certainly needed to.

While the men unloaded the equipment from the wine store, she slipped over to the tower to unlock the heavy wooden door. Inside it was an ice box. Once she'd crossed the dark room, she ran her hands along the rough walls, searching with her fingertips as she fumbled for, and eventually located, a switch. Her heart thumped as she carried on up in the dim light and then eased open the door to the top room. It smelt musty, as if something had died up there.

The shutters at the windows had been left open so, inch by inch, desperate not to make a sound, she closed them and then covered them with blackout fabric tacked on to the wood.

She'd left the main door to the tower ajar and now heard footsteps on the stairs as James appeared. Aldo stood behind him in the doorway with one of the partisans – the man called Marco – both carrying the equipment. The smaller partisan followed behind with Maxine. James looked around and glanced at the narrow opening at the back.

'Old stone staircase to the roof,' she said.

He took charge of setting everything up while Sofia asked the two partisans to go back down and clear whatever was causing the blockage in the hidden passage. It led all the way behind a false wall from the first floor of the tower, through the other buildings, mainly storage facilities, to her house and her bedroom.

'Please be quick and quiet. Once we've set up the equipment and made the first transmission, we'll need to get it downstairs then hide it in the passage.'

James opened the water-tight metal container and told them it was not the suitcase type of radio.

'Wouldn't the suitcase kind have been a better idea?' Aldo asked.

'This is well padded. The suitcase wouldn't survive a parachute drop. This is a B2 radio set. Works with Morse code.'

'But harder to move around,' Aldo said, and Sofia was pleased he was engaging with this.

Maxine came up to stand beside James. 'Right then,' she said. 'What I need you to do is transmit a message to my liaison officer, Ronald. Tell him I've made contact here and that I will let him know of approximate numbers as soon as I have them. Okay?'

James nodded and then, from inside the padding within the metal container, he took out a smaller container marked 'G'.

'The transmitter and receiver are here,' he said, glancing up at Aldo.

He removed the lid from the smaller container and continued explaining everything to Aldo as he worked at setting up the equipment and the cable that functioned as an aerial. Then, after connecting the transmitter and receiver to the rechargeable power supply unit, he put on his headphones and began to tune the band selector.

He showed Aldo an envelope clipped to the inside cover of the large metal box, then removed the envelope and took out several printed pages of extremely thin paper. 'It's the operating chart.'

'How many pages are there?'

'Fourteen.'

'*Santo Cielo*, so many,' Aldo said, frowning.

Although Sofia had faith in him, Aldo looked as if he might never understand how this complex equipment worked. She'd hoped learning from James might be the perfect compromise as he'd be supporting the Allies without having to take part in even more dangerous sabotage missions.

'This last page shows the calibration charts,' James was saying.

A loud bang interrupted them. James spun round to Sofia and their eyes met.

'Maybe it's a door blowing in the wind,' she said. 'Or it could be the men removing the blockage in the passageway.'

He put a finger to his lips as they both continued to listen. She could feel her heart pounding against her ribs and struggled to stop her teeth from chattering.

'I'll go,' Maxine said.

18

Maxine slipped quickly down the stairs and out of the tower, glancing about her as she padded stealthily around the village, relieved neither to see light in any of the houses nor, so far, any sign of Germans.

The icy night-time air caught in her throat. Who knew it could be so cold in Tuscany? Her mother's nostalgia hadn't quite run to explaining about the winters. In Luisa's mind it had always been spring, with fields of red poppies, banks of wild iris, the intoxicating scent of fresh rosemary, and all of it under a seamless blue sky.

Without warning, another loud bang interrupted her thinking. Had this one come from the direction of the tower? What if the others weren't safe or something had gone terribly wrong? Maybe the Germans had found out already? She frowned. She had been listening intently and there had been no sound of any vehicle arriving.

She sniffed the lingering trace of woodsmoke in the air. An owl hooted, night birds rustled in the trees, and creatures – wild boar perhaps or maybe a fox – scratched about in the vegetable gardens. She felt she could hear the breath of the village itself – in, out, in, out – a never-ending beat. A moment later, alert to movement, she caught sight of something in one of the alleys and paused, rigid with nerves. After a few seconds she took a couple of steps back, then paused again. Nothing. Must have been her imagination. But then a twig snapped. A cat? Or crushed beneath a German boot?

She decided to glance down the alley again, her breath coming fast. This time she saw a small dark figure darting from a recessed doorway into the alley, and then vanishing around the corner at the end. For a moment she didn't dare move, uncertain whether to try to follow the person or to hurry to the tower to warn the others. Then she spotted a door swinging back and forth – at least she now knew the cause of the banging.

But she was certain she hadn't imagined the figure and, with no further hesitation, she hurried back towards the tower, considering whom of the villagers could be out this late on such a cold night. She didn't have her watch, but it had to be way after midnight now.

As she went over this in her head, the large tower door opened with a sudden creak and the small partisan called Lodo slipped out carrying some pieces of what looked like board. He melted into the night without acknowledging that he'd seen her. She heard the eerie scream of a wild cat in the distance and quickly went in through the unlocked door, located the stairs by the dim lamp and climbed cautiously. At the top she pushed the door and went in. Three heads were bent over the equipment, and only Sofia looked round. Maxine watched as James continued explaining the process to Aldo and Marco.

Sofia beckoned her over. 'What the hell was it?' she hissed.

She bristled at Sofia's imperious tone but told her about the person she'd seen running down the alley.

'Would you be able to recognize them?' Sofia asked.

Maxine shook her head.

'Pity.'

'They were small, whoever they were.'

'A woman?' Sofia asked

'Maybe. Have they finished the transmission?'

'Packing up now. We need to make this room look and smell like an artist's studio – turps, oils, that sort of thing. You can give me a hand. We'll do it later in the morning.'

'Did they clear the passageway?'

'Yes.'

As Sofia moved away, Maxine caught Marco's eye and beckoned him to follow her out.

She reached the house ahead of the others and, without anyone seeing, dragged Marco into the downstairs washroom. After that, she waited for Sofia to come in and go up to her bedroom. Once she was certain Sofia's door had closed, she tiptoed ahead of Marco and cautiously led him upstairs to her own room where she flipped on the lamp on her nightstand. Unconvinced, he shook his head, whispered it wasn't right, insisted he ought to go, but she wrapped an arm round his neck and pulled him close. Then she kissed him hard on the lips. He stopped objecting and smiled at her, his caramel-coloured eyes shining. She stroked his gleaming olive skin and ran her fingers through his dark curly hair. Like a gypsy, she thought again.

She took him by the hand and led him to her bed. There they lay fully dressed on top of the covers.

'Is this how it's going to go?' he asked.

'What?'

'We stay on top of the covers? You have noticed it's freezing?'

'I thought you could undress me. Very, very slowly.'

'Another time,' he said. 'It's too cold.'

They both began to laugh, and she put a finger to her lips, enjoying the secrecy. There was nothing quite like illicit sex.

He grinned and began to undo the buttons of her blouse very slowly, fumbling even.

'I'll show you what slowly *really* means, young lady,' he whispered when she urged him on.

He touched her with fluttering fingers, so lightly she drew in her breath. He was captivating, charming, but he was also stretching out the minutes, forcing her to wait as the pressure built inside her. If he didn't take the next step, and quickly, she was going to burst. The wicked expression on his face revealed his intent to carry on taking his time, so she narrowed her eyes and, pushing him away, removed her blouse herself. He stroked her breasts through the thin cotton of her chemise, then rubbed a thumb around her nipple. Still icily cold, she gasped and pressed against him. He slowly pulled the straps down over her shoulders and ran his tongue down the side of her neck. Her moan was designed to hurry him, but he ignored it, bending his head to kiss her shoulders still agonizingly slowly, before cupping her breasts. She arched her back and moaned again. He was strong, firm and muscular, and she pushed herself against him more insistently than before. He held the bedcovers up and eased them both under. Finally, feverish with frustration and longing, she tore off her own underwear. At first, she shivered, but then he stroked her stomach and, dizzy with wanting him, her entire body caught fire, the energy fizzing and bubbling. His hands were in her hair, his lips on her flesh. He kissed her inner thighs, still taking his time, and she finally gave herself up to the slowness of it. And, as she did, as if he had known she had surrendered, he rolled on top and thrust inside her. When it was over, legs entwined, she basked in the aftermath, sweating, her breath slowly calming. There was something different here, a sense of real connection. She was sure of it.

Before this evening she had so wanted to see Marco again, wanted to work out how she felt, but now she drew away. She was unused to this kind of hunger, had promised herself never to fall in love and had always seen marriage as entrapment. Love was the surest path to a woman's downfall.

Even her father, whom she'd once loved so much, had lost her respect when she first spotted her mother's bruises. She'd been about eight, feeling sick and not wanting to go to school. When her mother, Luisa, insisted she get dressed and go all the same, she'd clutched her mother's arm and begged to stay home. Luisa had winced then snapped at her; later, when her mother rolled up her sleeves to do the washing-up, it hadn't taken long for the penny to drop. Once Maxine had caught a glimpse of the telltale purple and yellow marks on her mother's lower arms, she worked out that it always seemed to happen when her father arrived home late smelling of drink, his nose bulbous, his cheeks red. She'd heard the shouts before, of course, without understanding her mother was being physically hurt. Once Maxine had discovered the truth, she'd cried herself to sleep on many a night.

From then on, Maxine had sworn that a monotonous life punctuated only by violence would never be her fate. Later, in her teens and developing a pronounced rebellious streak, she had attempted to talk to Luisa about the beatings, but her mother had shushed her. It had been different, she'd said, when they'd lived in Italy. Alessandro had been a good man back then. The farm had kept him fully occupied and, although running a farm was back-breaking work, their life had been rewarding. They'd been happy. Back then the drinking had only really been with meals, when everyone drank wine together, even the children. She'd sighed and said the trouble began because Alessandro had never got over leaving his homeland, even though it had been so many years ago.

'When you love someone, you love them,' she'd said rather sadly. 'No matter what.'

'Really?' Maxine had been horrified. 'No matter what? You let a man knock you about?'

With a pang of regret, she wished she'd been able to do more to help, but her mother had made more excuses, saying it was normal. It had been enough for Maxine to make up her mind. A wife bore the children, took on the brunt of the childcare, often worked outside the home too, and besides that did all the shopping, all the housework *and* looked after the elderly and the sick. Only to be bullied by a man. No. Never. Not for her. It may have been her mother's fate to be voiceless and silent in her suffering, but it never would be Maxine's.

'So why?' Marco asked, bringing her back to the present.

'Why what?'

'Why did your parents leave?'

She frowned. 'You ask me this now? Didn't I tell you?'

'Not really. I like to get things straight.'

'Checking up on my story, more like.'

'Do you blame me? We don't get many beautiful American women lending us a hand.'

'The land was no longer enough for them.'

'And that was all?'

'As far as I know. Yes.'

'And you want to see where your family came from?'

'Indeed.'

He looked puzzled. 'Couldn't you have come before the war, in peacetime?'

'Well, every time I talked to my parents about it, they persuaded me not to.'

He laughed. 'You don't strike me as someone who's easily persuaded.'

'I'm not.' She paused and scratched her ear. 'In the end, I came without their approval. Or rather, I went to London as a journalist without their approval. They just had to accept it. They don't actually know I'm here in Italy. I was instructed not to let my family know.'

'But why didn't they want you to come to Italy *before* the war?'

'I'm not sure. I was still relatively young and they didn't like Mussolini.'

'I can understand that,' said Marco with a grimace. 'We've had to put up with him since 1922.'

There was a short pause.

'Don't you want to know more about me?' he asked.

Surprised, she half sat up and gazed down at him. He reached up to stroke her hair.

'I do,' she said. 'I didn't want to ask . . . I thought . . .'

'You're right. We train ourselves not to reveal who we really are.'

'Maybe tell me why you joined the partisans?'

He rubbed his eyes and she lay back down to snuggle up close with a palm on his chest so that she could feel his heart.

'Before the war my older brother was taken by the Fascists. We never saw him again.'

'I'm so sorry.'

'It happened, and not only to us. But I swore when the time was right, I would fight them. My brother never supported Mussolini, few of us really did, but he'd been too outspoken, and then one night they came. We don't know what they did to him, but we can guess. I still have a sister, but the loss of my brother broke my mother.'

'Oh, Marco.'

He gazed into her eyes and they were silent for a long time. Moved by his passion, both for the cause and as a man, she truly admired him.

He was the one who broke the silence. 'Do you have brothers or sisters?'

'One brother, a year older than me.'

'He's good to you?'

'Good enough.'

He sighed. 'We can't make a habit of this, you know,' he said.

The pleasure evaporated and she experienced a well of sadness opening. She didn't want to hear this and felt torn. 'Why not?' she asked in a low voice.

'Because it isn't safe. We have to use our discretion, maintain our separate identities.'

'And what about feelings?' she asked.

'They become a weakness. The enemy is always on the lookout for weak links in the chain.'

'Well,' she said, and tried for a more light-hearted response than she really felt. 'We'd better make the most of it now.'

He kissed her on the lips then shook his head. 'It's time to sleep.'

She switched off the light but as his breathing began to

deepen, her thoughts churned. Why did she have to find someone she liked so much at such an impossible time?

'Are you still awake?' she said.

'Mmmm?'

'I want to come on your next mission, whatever it is.'

'Very well.'

'Very well?' she said, surprised.

He laughed. 'Anything for a night's sleep!'

19

Sofia felt reluctant to wake and surfaced slowly, rubbing her cold arms. And when she opened the curtains, she drew back at the sight of a vicious wind blowing the trees about. But at least it was moving the clouds away, and patches of brilliant blue were beginning to emerge. Hoping fresh air would lighten her mood, she dressed quickly and went downstairs where she reached for Lorenzo's old coat, which usually hung on a hook by the back door. He was so tall it trailed along the ground when she wore it, but she liked the spicy smell of his aftershave and his cigars and often slipped it on for comfort as well as warmth. Now, as she found the coat missing, she remembered that Maxine had been wearing it in the tower.

Outside, she glanced up at the tower. Maybe she should have left the shutters open, as they had been before their transmission. It was possible someone might spot they were now closed, so she headed back inside and fished out the key from its new hiding place.

At the top of the tower everything remained exactly as they'd left it. In the downstairs room, James had pulled a linen cupboard across the doorway to the secret passage and today she would load it with paints, brushes, turpentine and rags, plus some of her books on art. And she'd ask Aldo to carry her two easels, with the latest work in progress, right to the top. Thinking of her canvas reminded her that Lorenzo had not questioned her about it again. She hated that he knew she hadn't taken the painting to be framed and that she'd lied to him. The only thing she could do was to own up to the truth, tell him about James, and she would, next time he was home. Lorenzo didn't often push for answers about anything; he usually dropped some-thing into the conversation, leaving it there until she was ready. She didn't enjoy lying. She had told so many small lies, although most were lies of omission. But it was so easy to delude oneself, manipulate the story, believe the lie, save face. Especially now. It wasn't even about pulling the wool over somebody else's eyes when one's own were so ready to be fooled. She com-forted herself that at least her domestic lies had not been outright falsehoods.

She removed the cloth from the windows, rolling it up before opening the shutters. Then she headed back downstairs.

In the few minutes she'd been in the tower the sky had changed. Now a shimmering blue as far as the eye could see, it made her feel a little happier as she made for the cobbled path-ways around the edges of the village. She skirted the vegetable patches and the empty chicken coops and then, striding past sev-eral winding terraces of two-storey houses, some with tiny loggias, she breathed more deeply, the exercise driving back the anxieties of the night.

As she arrived at her favourite spot, she looked over the wall and across to the sensuous contours of the Val d'Orcia, with dusky blue Monte Amiata in the distance and all the valleys spectacularly wreathed in white mist. She felt as if the scene had been laid out for her alone, the view soothing her as it always did, no matter the season. Once she felt brighter, she made her way back, passing by one or two village women, headscarves tied firmly at the back of their necks, as they diligently scrubbed their front doorsteps. It warmed her heart and, struck by the way, despite war, deprivation and loss, the women still main-tained their standards, she smiled at them. Then she stopped to exchange a word with Sara and her next-door neighbour, young Federica, whose unfortunate little son had a cleft lip and watched in silence, sucking his thumb.

When she passed the small churchyard at the side of the

tower, she looked up to watch an eagle wheeling across the sky as it flew north, where it would be even colder, and then, looking down again, she spotted a small figure hunched up in an alcove.

'Gabriella,' she said, surprised. 'Is it you?'

The girl bent her head, trembling as she shifted even closer to hug the wall.

'Gabriella. What on earth are you doing?'

Sofia walked closer and held out a hand to the girl, which she ignored. Twigs and leaves had become caught up in her tangled hair and her skin was so blue it scared Sofia. Surely she hadn't been out all night?

'Come on. We need to get you into the warm. Where's your little dog, Beni?'

Sofia had spoken gently but Gabriella still wouldn't move. She wondered if she ought to fetch Carla, but if she left the girl alone, there was a possibility she might wander off again. She decided to take a sterner approach.

'Gabriella. This will not do. I insist you come inside before you catch your death.'

Now, hearing the command in her mistress's voice, the girl glanced up, and then she struggled shakily to her feet.

'Have you been out all night?'

Gabriella nodded and Sofia realized it must have been she who Maxine had seen darting down the alley. At that moment, her sister, Anna, appeared around the corner with little Alberto in tow. She paused as she took in the scene.

'What –' she began with an angry look.

Sofia held up a hand. 'Gabriella is going inside to get warm, aren't you, dear?'

Gabriella barely moved but her eyes flickered.

'Per Dio,' Anna began again, 'why will she never open her mouth and speak?'

Sofia silenced her with a look and helped Gabriella to start walking towards the house.

But Anna hadn't finished and, eyes ablaze, the words burst from her. 'My mother has spoilt the girl. Now look at her. Has she been out all night? And doing what, may I ask?'

'Anna, you're right,' Sofia said. 'There are questions to be answered, but first she needs to warm up and have something to eat.'

'Of course, Contessa. I'm sorry, I didn't mean to speak out of turn.'

'Forget it. You're worried, I know.'

Anna's little boy began to tug at her skirt and whine. 'I'm just taking Alberto to the house of Rosalia,' she said. 'I have . . . something . . .'

'It's fine. I understand.'

Anna studied Sofia's face for a moment as if wondering how much the mistress knew about her courier activities. Sofia gave her a little nod and Anna took her leave.

When Sofia and Gabriella reached the kitchen, Sofia pushed open the door to find Carla in something of a flap.

'Gabriella,' she cried, her voice trembling. 'I have been looking for you everywhere, child. Where have you been?'

As Gabriella remained mute, Sofia decided to intervene. 'I found her in the churchyard. I'm afraid she has been out all night.'

Hands on hips, Carla frowned, angrier now. 'Why? What the devil?'

'I can keep her with me,' Sofia said. 'Try to get her to tell me what she's been up to.'

Carla straightened her shoulders before she spoke. 'No, Contessa. Thank you for offering, but I am happy to deal with my daughter myself. I'll soon get to the bottom of this.'

Carla followed Gabriella into her bedroom and Sofia heard Carla's raised voice for a few minutes. Then there was only silence.

When Carla came back, she stood by the stove and shook her

head. 'She's not saying anything. Not yet. I think she needs to sleep. I've wrapped her in a blanket and I'll take her a hot drink in a little while, see if that helps.'

Sofia nodded. 'Give her some time.'

'Yes. You're right.'

'So, what happened with Maria last night?'

'I offered her wine and a fine cheese we'd been hiding from the Germans. Told her it was time we made our peace.'

'And she accepted that?'

'Yes, and in the end it went well. She didn't notice a thing.'

Carla took out a scrubbing brush, filled a bowl with soapy water and began to tackle the kitchen table.

When Aldo came in from the garden, looking hungry, Sofia winked at him to remind him not to say anything about the sketches or the painting in front of Carla and he gave her a wide-eyed, conspiratorial look.

Carla finished scrubbing the table, then busied herself with stoking the stove. After that she fetched the broom from the cupboard, but as she was about to sweep, Aldo took hold of it and he swept the floor instead. Then he laid out everything they'd need for breakfast while his mother brewed the coffee, taking the first cup she poured through to Gabriella.

Sofia smiled at Aldo as he seated himself. Few men would stoop to do women's work, but he had always helped his mother.

'I like having breakfast with you, young man,' she said as she settled opposite Aldo. 'How are you after last night?'

He gave her a self-conscious half-smile. 'I don't know if I'll ever understand the radio.'

She patted his hand. 'You will.'

When Carla came back into the kitchen, Sofia asked how Gabriella was.

'Sleepy,' Carla replied and then shrugged. 'We'll have to see.'

Then she unwrapped a small loaf baked the afternoon before, a few home-grown tomatoes, a bottle of their own olive oil and some salt. She sliced the tomatoes thinly and unwrapped the tiny pastries she'd made along with the bread.

'Any dried peaches?' Sofia asked, knowing they were Aldo's favourites.

Carla, a great believer in the comfort of food, nodded and went to the pantry where she kept the jar hidden.

'Can you come to sit for me for a while?' Sofia whispered while Carla's back was turned. 'I should finish the preliminary sketches today.'

20

It was almost dark and, in the relative safety of an abandoned farmhouse, Marco was gazing at Maxine intently. 'You may report on our numbers, our lack of weapons and our locations but no names. You understand?' He gripped her by the shoulders and as he did so his fingers dug in, hurting her. 'You understand?'

She bobbed her head as she searched for her underwear. Where the hell was her bra?

'And you cannot speak to anyone here of what you see tonight. If we face any problems, you'll be on your own. You hide or you run.'

She found her bra and caught the blouse he threw at her, and then they both dressed quickly. As she gazed at Marco, he hung a pair of field binoculars round his neck.

'What?' he said.

'Where on earth did you get hold of those?'

He laughed and came across to kiss her on the lips. 'I can get hold of anything.'

They slipped through to the kitchen, where a group of hard-eyed men were gathered. A thin, shifty-looking older man leered at her and made a vulgar comment at her expense. The men laughed and then ignored her. She spotted Lodo, from the other night, but then was surprised to see Aldo too, his wild eyes so terribly young and full of fear and yet he was smiling bravely.

She grabbed hold of his elbow and whispered. 'I thought you were just going to learn how to operate the radio?'

He shook his head. 'That's what I told my mother and the Contessa, but it's not enough. I want to see action.'

'And Marco agreed to this?'

'I gave him no option. I followed and here I am.'

Maxine glanced around her. They all wore dark clothing, and everyone had covered their shoes with thick socks.

'You too.' Marco handed her a pair of socks. 'They help keep us silent. The village women knit them for us.'

'Ready, Aldo?' the thin man asked the boy.

Marco butted in. 'No real names. Call him The Kid.'

Aldo grinned.

Maxine sensed the men were overly excited. The fear of facing danger and being caught mixed with the thrill of possible success was a lethal combination. As the group set off, one of them called out to Aldo.

'Kid, you walk with me.'

Maxine ducked her head under a low-hanging branch and, absorbing the energy of their excitement, she followed.

Nobody spoke until about forty-five minutes later when the group neared a railway track. Maxine concluded they were about to undertake some form of railroad sabotage. Three of the men carried rucksacks which, she guessed, must all be packed with explosives.

'If you hear a cough,' Marco whispered to her before moving away, 'it's a signal meaning a guard is approaching. We are hoping to blow up a Nazi supply train with freight carriages full of food. But you stay back here.'

From her vantage point and in the faint light from her dying torch, she watched as the three men pulled out odd containers shaped like long salami sausages. Then she held her breath as they crept down to the track running along the valley to San Giovanni d'Asso. On the small bridge over the road they began to lay the explosives under the flange of the rail so that when the train wheels ran over them, they'd go off on contact. The object was not only to derail the entire train but also to destroy the tracks. Every now and then their hands dislodged a few stones that clattered as they rolled away, making a terrible din in the thick silence of the night. Each time it happened they froze in fear of being discovered. In the darkness Maxine spotted the glint of Marco's field glasses. How much could he see? The two men working as lookouts stood on slightly higher ground surveying the scene, ready to cough or whistle if they spotted anyone moving. The atmosphere was strained and the longer it went on the more rigid she became. The night was startlingly cold, and she shivered incessantly.

Without warning a brilliant flash lit up the dark as if daylight had come early. A Nazi patrol using flares! Ferocious shouting in German rang out and the partisans began to run. Gunshots followed and Maxine saw Aldo fall to the ground. She covered her mouth to stop the scream, but then he got to his feet and began to run again. Relieved, she watched for a couple of seconds and then, just as she began to turn away, was horrified to see one of the Germans grab Aldo and throw him to the ground. Once more, the boy staggered to his feet. She swivelled round to search for Marco, but there was nothing she could do.

The other men were running, melting back into the woods and separating. And then her own survival instinct kicked in and she was forced to do the same. She raced back into the woods, tripping over her feet, while branches clawed and scratched at her face, sticks and twigs cracking beneath her feet. Water dripped from the branches above. Animals rustled, scurried, snuffled among the trees. Wild boar? Did they attack? She couldn't see but carried on running until she caught her foot in a tangle of tree roots and fell flat on her face, the impact winding her. The stink of earth and rotting vegetation filled her nostrils and when a vile taste reached her mouth she vomited. Wet through, she forced herself up and stumbled on, barely aware of where she was heading, her breath coming fast from the effort of running uphill. The wind whistled in the trees and in the pitch-black everything seemed to be moving. She slammed straight into a large oak tree and fought to regain her breath but then cramp painfully contracted her calf muscle and she could not run. Dogs began barking. German dogs? Coming closer or heading further away? She dragged herself off, going more steeply uphill now, limping in pain and in the grip of a kind of fear she'd never experienced before.

The woods were dangerous, terrifying. And she was being hunted. Were they circling ahead of her, getting ready to trap her? At the sound of footsteps crashing through the undergrowth she squatted down to conceal herself. She heard the boots of a German soldier as he stumbled through the bracken, poking at it with his rifle. How far? Two feet away, three? She held her breath. The German swore as another bellowed orders. Then the man retraced his steps, passing right beside her again, only inches away.

After a few moments more she let out her breath.

Sounds were travelling strangely now. Altered. Distorted. And voices were roaring, coming out of nowhere. *Halt. Halt.* The yelling echoed inside her head. *Halt. Halt.* Where were they? Her mouth dried. She couldn't swallow. She couldn't see. One moment she was hot, the next freezing cold. And then the burst of another shot paralysed her. Heart thumping, she imagined the bullet tearing into her flesh so convincingly that for a moment she believed it had really happened. A further shot rang out and then another. Had they caught someone? Marco? Had they caught Marco? But how had the Germans even known the partisans would be there? In that moment as she stood still, it became blindingly clear someone must have given them away.

After an age the shots ceased and the voices faded. In utter relief, she sniffed the air. Woodsmoke? She followed the trail ahead of her until she reached a small farmhouse standing on its own with a barn and shed alongside it. Dishevelled and bleeding from cuts and scratches, she headed for the barn. She felt hopeful that Marco had managed to get away but what about Aldo? Oh God! Had he managed to escape too?

21

The following day Sofia heard a rap on her exterior door, the one that opened straight out into what used to be her rose garden. Then came a whispered voice. She unlocked it and Carla's daughter, Anna, practically fell into the room, looking red-faced and agitated. She glanced towards the door leading to the main part of the house. 'My mother does not know I'm here.'

As Sofia locked the door, Anna exhaled slowly, deliberately, as if trying to hold herself together.

'Won't you sit?'

Anna remained standing, her face drawn, her eyes screwed up in anguish.

'So, tell me,' demanded Sofia.

'It's Aldo.' Anna gulped back a sob.

A feeling of dread began to spread through Sofia's chest as she waited for Anna to continue.

'They have him.'

'Who, Anna? Who has him?'

Anna hung her head and, when she looked up, her dark-brown eyes were spilling over with tears.

Sofia's heart lurched. 'Oh, Anna, come and sit with me.'

She stumbled over and Sofia held out her arms for her. They both perched on the little chintz sofa while Anna wept.

'Tell me everything. Start at the beginning.'

In a rush, Anna recounted a rumour. 'They're saying Aldo may have been shot during partisan activity.'

'Aldo was involved? They know this?'

'A man came at dawn. He didn't know for sure if it was Aldo, or even if he's alive or dead. But they think he was taken to the police station in Buonconvento.'

'Shot by Germans?'

Anna nodded, rubbing her forehead in distress. 'He said someone must have betrayed the men because the Germans were waiting for them. I don't know what to do. Aldo didn't come home last night and I dare not tell my mother.'

'But why was he taken to Buonconvento?'

'The rumour is one of the partisans came from there. Would you come with me? Help me find out what happened?'

'You don't have to ask,' Sofia said, thinking it over for a moment. 'We'll take our shopping baskets and let's go by the dirt road in a pony and cart to allay suspicion. But we must be vigilant and look as if we're simply there to shop.'

Anna gazed at her. 'If a German was killed, they will execute five men from each village the partisans came from.'

'The only one they captured is Aldo?'

'I don't know,' Anna answered miserably.

'Right,' Sofia said, forcing herself to regain her composure. 'Wait for me outside the main gate. Don't let Carla see you. I'll need half an hour to get dressed and to fetch the pony and cart. Where is your little boy?'

'My neighbour has him.'

'Good. Keep your spirits up. We don't even know for sure it's Aldo they captured.'

Anna took a long, shuddering breath and nodded.

They barely spoke on the tortuous journey there, and made slow progress, the track curling round the hills and rocky outcrops and down through several valleys. At Buonconvento, they entered the walled village through an enormous wooden door at the northern gate towards Siena, the Porta Senese. The village was located where the rivers Arbia and Ombrone converged and until recent times had been a welcome stopping place for travellers. The name meant 'happy place', though Sofia couldn't think of a more inappropriate description that day. She felt sick with anxiety and could see Anna was finding it hard to control her nerves.

'Come on,' Sofia said. 'We don't know anything yet.'

They found Via Soccini, the main street, completely empty. Not knowing why it was, they decided to leave the pony tied up and walk through the tangle of alleys and backstreets spreading out behind it. Sofia usually drove to Buonconvento on the main road and her favourite place was the little square at the end of Via Oscura. She'd always loved this town with its medieval streets and tall, ornate red-brick palazzos. Even the narrow backstreets were picturesque. Yet here, too, they passed not a single soul. No one hanging out washing, no one sweeping their front step. And all they heard were the sounds of their own footsteps on the cobbles. It felt like a ghost town. Eventually they came across a woman standing in a doorway staring at the ground.

'Excuse me,' Sofia began, but the woman just pointed to the other end of the town.

Sofia's anxiety deepened. Something was terribly wrong. Buonconvento was usually a bustling place, even since the war had begun. Now only a jarring emptiness met them at every corner, that and a strange whispering that seemed to be carried on the air.

In the end they headed back to the main street and headed for the Porta Romana on the south side.

And then they saw them.

The two bodies, their flesh covered in red welts, their fingers black, their faces purple with bruises. A lumpen feeling in Sofia's throat stole her breath.

Anna clutched her arm and they joined a small, silent crowd staring up at the men hanging from the main gate. You could neither enter nor leave without seeing them and straight away Sofia knew one of them was the slender boy she had always loved. The other was the partisan, Lodo. She clamped a hand over her mouth to suppress the screaming sound in her head. The air around her split, her eyes blurred, and the houses and people shifted so all she could see was Aldo. Some of the crowd shuffled back, aghast, while others crept forward, mesmerized by the bitter smell of death, the sickly-sweet metallic taste of blood on their tongues, the stink of faeces in their nostrils, the ghastly silence of the street broken only by a baby's cry and the whispering that did not stop.

Unable to bear the sight, Sofia closed her eyes for a second and, when she opened them again, knew she was forever changed; she had instantly become a completely different person in a completely different world. This act of utter provocation incited such a feeling of rage and revulsion that it flooded her whole body. She tasted blood and salt in her mouth and the kind of burning anger she'd never experienced before. She longed to rush up to them and cut their bodies down, wash their poor battered skin, bring them back, and yet she knew she could not. Despite exploding inside, she could not even show she knew who the men were. Anna was rigid, and Sofia was holding on to her as if they each might crumple and fall without the other. They managed to remain standing, frozen in disbelief, but Sofia's mind filled with images of the mischievous little boy Aldo had once been. She saw him playing on his cart or up to monkey business somewhere in the village – his curly hair falling over one gleeful eye – but forgiven because of his irresistibly open smile. To see his body hanging there, head lolling to one side, his bones broken, his life destroyed, hurt her in a way she could never have imagined. At a spasm of pain, an actual slicing physical pain, she struggled not to cave in. She must stifle any expression of grief until they got away from this terrible place. She glanced up to the left and, in one of the windows overlooking the scene, she saw the stony face of a German officer, the cold indifference of his raised eyebrows igniting an even greater storm inside her. Kaufmann. He stared straight at her and she felt such hatred that she was gripped by certainty. She could kill. She wanted to kill. And she came so close to violence in her mind that she frightened herself.

She tried to tug Anna away. 'Come on. We have to go.'

'I can't leave him. Not yet.'

Of course, Sofia understood, so they stayed, although it was far too risky.

There was a commotion behind them from a larger crowd forming back there. The next thing Sofia saw was Carla pushing her way to the front, the life draining from her face.

'Who told her?' Sofia whispered, but Anna had stiffened.

Sofia waited for the scream to come but there was just the sound of muttering behind them. Time stopped as she watched in an agony of suspense, but Carla seemed to be in a trance, of the world but no longer in it. If someone broke the trance, what then? Would she break down, start screaming for her poor dead boy? Do exactly what the Germans wanted them to do?

Then she spotted Maxine, edging her way towards Carla, taking Carla's arm and appearing to say something. Carla blinked rapidly but Sofia got the feeling she was not seeing anything now. The shock had crushed her, and Maxine was able to lead her by the arm away from the terrible sight of her only son.

Fired with a sudden and ferocious determination, Sofia pulled Anna away and they stumbled after Maxine. And in that moment Sofia vowed that for as long as it might take, she would do everything in her power to rid her country of these vile interlopers. Aldo's death would not go unavenged. The lovable boy she had known since birth would not have died in vain. And when she remembered the pistol her husband had given her, she itched to pull the trigger.

22.

December 1943

Aldo's absence filled every room. The waves of grief were sudden and overwhelming and day after day the shock repeated anew as if for the first time. His cheeky smile haunted Sofia and, no matter where she went, he was there; she couldn't convince herself she'd never see him again. Over and over she saw him hanging, and the terrible image broke her. Nothing relieved the ache in her chest, so God only knew how it must be for Carla. She wished with all her heart Lorenzo would come home, for his presence would be such a comfort. She tried to picture him there, standing by the door, newly arrived and holding out his arms to her.

When she had first met Lorenzo, his confidence in his own identity and his ease with himself made it easy to relax around him. Commandant Schmidt, the German officer who had invited himself to dinner the night Maxine had arrived, was the exact opposite, a man who didn't appear comfortable at all. Nervy, rangy and too thin, he entered the salon now, taking long strides forward, then smiling. She had the same impression she'd had before that here was a man who'd rather have been putting his feet up in front of a fire at home with his wife.

As she had to maintain his trust in her, she smiled back and held out her hand to be civil. He kissed it and she smelt his peppery cologne, and it was only then it struck her that he wasn't alone, and that Kaufmann was standing right behind him. And he was a very different kettle of fish. Schmidt noticed her glance over his shoulder and bent briefly to acknowledge the other man.

'Captain Kaufmann,' he said.

'Yes, we've met,' Sofia said, turning to Kaufmann and taking in the man's smooth, unlined skin, his glassy pale-blue eyes behind the horn-rimmed spectacles, his high forehead and thin dark-blond hair. A perfect example of Aryan manhood, she thought.

Kaufmann gave her a tight little bow and then focused his attention on the room.

'Welcome,' she said, probably a touch too stiffly, but not a flicker of response came from him. Instead, while Schmidt settled himself in an armchair, crossing and uncrossing his legs as he had before, Kaufmann walked slowly round the small room, sensuously stroking objects then bending to examine them closely, picking one up then exchanging it with another. What he expected to find she had no idea.

Although she was trying to pay attention to Schmidt, from the corner of her eye she was observing the other man. He was now standing, feet wide apart, hands clasped behind his back, in front of her favourite painting as if mesmerized by it.

'This *is* a Cozzarelli. I remember seeing it here before.' He turned back to look at her. 'Of the Sienese school, influenced by Byzantine art and less well known than the Florentine.'

'Yes.'

He gave her a long, cold stare. 'We are not lacking in the finer sensibilities, whatever you may think. I myself am something of a collector of Italian art. I believe there may have been more than one of San Sebastiano.'

'My husband would know. This one has been in the family for many generations. The villagers see San Sebastiano as a protector.'

She felt a shiver of revulsion as she recalled the way Kaufmann had been staring down at her in Buonconvento. His being here at this time couldn't be a coincidence.

And now Schmidt was speaking again, looking at her solicitously and speaking kindly. 'You seem distracted, Contessa. Are you quite well?'

She rubbed her temple and told herself to keep as close to the truth as possible. 'My sincere apologies, Commandant Schmidt. I don't mean to be. It's just . . . well, I have a rather bad headache, you see.'

Heartache, not headache, she thought, as the terrible image of Aldo returned with that sickening stench of blood, faeces and fear.

'Well, we won't take up too much of your time. I'm only here to ask if you know of any men who might be missing from your village?'

She hesitated for a fraction too long and hoped he hadn't noticed. 'Oh, I see. I haven't heard of any, though naturally we also have the outlying farms and I wouldn't necessarily know, at least not straight away.'

Schmidt nodded but Kaufmann walked over, frowning, and then, with a slight tilt to his head, said, 'Really?'

Schmidt glanced at the man. 'I'm sure we can trust the Contessa.'

Kaufmann arched his brows as he studied her face. 'As I understand it, you have your finger very much on the pulse, especially while your husband is absent.'

'Well, I do my best.'

'I imagine it must be difficult,' the Commandant interjected, and Kaufmann returned to the objects he had previously been examining.

She took a deep breath. 'I'm used to it. Now, may I offer you both a coffee?'

The Commandant shook his head, but she could tell he'd like nothing more than a cup of coffee and a brief respite from the war. 'Much as that would be delightful, I'm afraid we are somewhat short of time.'

Kaufmann looked up while stroking a porcelain shepherdess. 'You like English *objets d'art*?' he asked.

She gave him a small polite smile. 'I enjoy collecting all sorts

133

of ornaments. We have many more in our main drawing room if you'd like to see.'

'You speak English?' he said, ignoring her offer.

'I do.'

He shot her a suspicious look. 'And how is that?'

'I spent a year in London. My parents considered it an essential part of my education.'

He glanced down, picked a hair from his sleeve very deliberately, then gazed at her for a moment before speaking. She waited, feeling sick, fearing something unpleasant was coming.

'Tell me, Contessa,' he finally said, narrowing his eyes. 'One final question. Have you been in Buonconvento lately?'

23

When Sofia went to check on Carla, she found her sitting at the kitchen table while Anna bustled around making coffee and slicing a fresh loaf. The room smelt of baking, herbs and vegetable soup, and Sofia's stomach clenched in a vice-like grip. She had not been able to face much in the way of food since seeing Aldo.

As Sofia watched Carla, she pictured Aldo's final moments. Had they tortured him before they murdered him? Of course. Had he been scared? Known he was going to die? That too. Above all, they would have demanded names. She couldn't be sure and prayed he had not given in, but he'd been only seventeen. Too young to die for a cause.

Sofia thought back to Carla's husband, Enrico's, last hours, the gasping for breath, the agony he must have experienced as the cancer took him. She knew Carla had believed it to be the worst thing that could ever happen. How wrong she'd been. Because now to see Aldo treated as if he were no more than a worthless carcass, it was worse than brutal. It was savage. She pictured his dear face, the light and animation in his smiling eyes, and she did not know how Carla would ever endure this.

Maxine was now sitting at the table as well and pushing a plate with bread and sliced tomatoes towards Carla. Sofia could smell the aroma of garlic and olive oil. Suddenly Carla swept the plate to the ground where it shattered on the hard flagstones. Nobody reacted. It was as if a mantle of unnatural calm had been agreed, as if that might somehow lessen the pain.

Sofia remained silent, while Anna, clutching a dustpan and brush, and red-eyed from weeping, knelt on the floor to clear up the mess.

'Captain Kaufmann has been,' Sofia said, rubbing her own eyes. 'He may come back.'

Anna straightened up. 'That's not good.'

Maxine got up and walked over to Sofia. 'Does he know anything?'

'Hard to tell. I think they suspect something.'

'They?'

'He had Commandant Schmidt with him. But I think Kaufmann may have seen me at Buonconvento.'

Anna gasped. 'He recognized us? It's my fault, I knew I shouldn't have asked you to stay. Once we'd seen what had happened, we should have left.'

'How could we not stay?' Sofia spoke gently. 'There's no point assigning blame. Anyway, he recognized *me*. Not you.'

'They *will* be back,' Maxine added.

Sofia recalled how Kaufmann had looked at her. 'I feel he can see right through me – and the way he smiles, a twisted kind of way, contorted, a smile that doesn't reach his eyes.'

And she remembered that when he had bowed and spun on his heels to leave, she had become conscious that all the time he'd been here, she'd been aware of a deeply unsettling underlying cruelty.

'The Commandant was different,' she said. 'Better somehow.' She realized her hands were shaking. 'But they know more than they're saying. I'm worried somebody must have told them Aldo came from here.'

'Most of the locals would die rather than give anything away,' Anna said.

Sofia sighed then came over and gently placed a hand on Carla's shoulder. There was nothing anyone could do. They were waiting for Carla to voice her sorrow, but it seemed she'd fallen mute.

'Contessa,' Anna said, 'there's something else. Gabriella is saying she's in love, but won't say who with. She has this peculiar secret smile fixed to her face. It worries me.'

'Would you like me to talk to her?' Sofia offered.

'I don't know,' Anna said. 'Maybe Mother will when she's feeling a bit stronger.'

'Very well.'

As Sofia and Maxine left the room, Sofia's thoughts drifted back to when Carla and Enrico had still been living at the farm and Carla's children had been young. Carla's job had included feeding the courtyard animals: usually turkeys, ducks, guinea fowl and chickens. She prepared all the meat for the entire year, butchering the carcasses and making the sausages for the family. She'd helped thresh the wheat and harvest the grapes, olives and tobacco, and she prepared meals for the farmers. It had been a busy world, but laughter and fun with the children meant it had been a happy one too. Poor Carla. How she must miss those days.

24.

From the kitchen Maxine and Sofia walked out to the vegetable garden where they wandered the paths between the sparse brassicas. It was chilly and Maxine shivered. Sofia seemed preoccupied, although it was hardly surprising considering what had happened.

'I was there, you know,' Maxine said. 'I didn't know if you'd heard that.'

'There?'

'The night they caught Aldo.'

She could see Sofia scrutinizing her, eyes narrowed. 'Good heavens. How awful.'

'It was, and terrifying too.' Maxine took a long breath and then spoke very gently. 'Look, Sofia, I truly understand how dreadfully hard this is for you, but we can't let ourselves give up. We have to go on. And we have to do it for Aldo's sake and for all the others who died trying to fight back.'

Sofia nodded slowly. 'I know. It's just I'm not sure how to put it behind me. I'd known Aldo all his life and I loved him. I was making a painting of him as a gift for Carla. Do you think it's still the right thing to do?'

'I think, in time, she would grow to love it.'

Sofia heaved a sigh.

Maxine took her hand. 'What happened to Aldo is terrible, I know. Nothing can make that better.'

There were a few moments of silence.

'But there's more work to do and I have to get in touch with my contact again, let him know what I've found out about the partisans here.'

'And that is?'

'That there are many men willing to fight but they are hungry, and their armaments are few. Marco is gradually organizing them into convincing units, but we have to get hold of weapons, ammunition and food.'

'How?'

'Well, as far as weapons are concerned, we have a contact who works in the outer office of the German Consul in Florence. Apparently, he has information.'

'And food?'

'I'm meeting Marco to talk about that.'

The wind got up, rustling the leaves of the trees and blowing the grass about. Sofia pulled a hesitant face and brushed the hair from her eyes. 'So, tonight? You want to transmit tonight?'

'As soon as possible.'

'Not from the tower. They'll be watching us.'

'No. We'll take the equipment away.'

'You won't need me.'

Maxine shook her head. 'James and I will remove the equipment under cover of darkness and transport it to the attic of the new farm he has been staying in. It's further away but relatively high up, and we have to keep moving the radio anyway or their triangulation will catch us out. We'll transmit everything I now know and hope to receive further instructions.'

They were silent for a few minutes.

'What was that Anna said about Gabriella?' Maxine asked.

Sofia pulled a face. 'She thinks she's in love. She's not stupid but school was tricky for her.'

'How do you mean?'

'She's a bit stubborn.'

'You mean simple-minded?'

'No, not exactly. But the stubbornness and refusal to learn are hard to handle. I don't like to pigeonhole her. She is who she is. Dreamy, inattentive, a bit vague. I tried to teach her to read but it was hopeless. She used to say the letters didn't keep still on the page. We gave up in the end, but she's good at other things, knows her plants and flowers and is wonderful with animals. Her little three-legged dog adores her.'

'Ah, so it's young love.'

'Indeed . . . Shall we go in? It's freezing.'

The next day Maxine and Marco were shivering in a small clearing in the dense woods close to San Giovanni d'Asso, with an unusually fat partisan called Fazio and a couple of others. The men were kicking the ground to keep warm as they discussed the best way to get food to the partisans. Marco had previously suggested that each of them try to get hold of a chicken, some sausage or a bag of potatoes. Anything was better than nothing, after all, but they hadn't come up with much, except for Fazio who had a goose under his arm.

'Where the hell did you get that?' Marco asked, taking off his hat and scratching the back of his head.

Fazio narrowed his eyes. 'What's it to you?'

'We can't steal from those who have so little, you know that. One of the widows in San Giovanni used to keep geese.'

Fazio's face twitched. 'She gave it to me.'

Maxine sighed. 'Can we just get on with it? Surely we need to be relieving the Germans of their food supplies?'

'Easier said than done,' Fazio muttered and then spat on the ground.

'We know there is a German food camp not far from here,' Maxine said. 'Can't you target that?'

Marco nodded. 'Exactly what I'm thinking. And there's a farm not far from it. It belongs to Farmer Galdino. He's old now, but I think he will help us. If he does, we'll keep a lookout at the food camp tonight and then sleep in his barn. Fazio, you know where it is?'

Fazio nodded.

'Get the rest of the men to meet us there tomorrow night at ten. You, Maxine, need to press the British to drop more food parcels. That way we all play a part.'

As the men slipped away Marco took hold of Maxine's hand. 'Come to the farm with me.'

'Okay.' She squeezed his hand then let it go. 'Listen, Marco, my British liaison, Ronald, has ordered accelerated action. More disruption, nothing less than an armed uprising. Can you let the men know this? I realize it's a challenge with the partisans still disorganized.'

'A challenge? It's hell. That's what it is. We're doing all we can. But it's hard. Our men are facing danger, oppression, hunger and cold, with no end in sight.'

'I know.'

'When were you in radio contact with Ronald?'

'Last night. He also wants increased intelligence about enemy movements.'

'We can try to do that *and* speed up the sabotage, I suppose, but it's putting a strain on the men. The longer it goes on the harder it gets, physically and mentally.'

'And yet we have no choice. You have to keep the pressure up, encourage the patrols to harass the Germans wherever they can.'

'And then we have to be on the lookout for the spies who act as partisans by day and informants to the Nazis by night.'

'I have faith in you.'

As they walked on together, they eventually reached what must have once been a beautiful old farmhouse. Maxine could see how neglected it had become.

'Who lives here now?' she asked.

'The old, the young.'

He walked up to the door and knocked.

A thin woman with white hair and wearing a worn blue apron opened the door and led them into a smoky room where, without a word, she offered them both chairs. It was clear to Maxine that Marco was already known to her.

The fire was small and the room was cold. Maxine and Marco sat down and looked around. An old man with a bent back and a bad cough was leaning against the wall near the chimney and a much younger woman was sitting on the other side of the fire cradling a crying baby in her arms.

The old man, who Maxine reckoned had to be Farmer Galdino, looked at the young woman and sighed. 'Can't you keep the child quiet?' he muttered.

'He's hungry. You know that.'

Marco explained the plan to them and as he did the young woman began to cry. He rose to his feet and went to kneel at her side.

'They hanged him,' she whispered. 'They hanged my Lodo.'

'I know.'

She wiped her eyes with her skirt. 'So yes, you can use the barn.'

'And if you get hold of food, bring some to us,' the old woman said. 'That's all we ask.'

The old man nodded but didn't speak.

25

It was December the eighth, the feast day of the Immaculate Conception, and the villagers considered this national holiday the official start of the winter season. For the religious among them, and that was most, it was one of the most sacred celebrations in the spiritual calendar. For everyone else it symbolized the beginning of the lead-up to Christmas. It used to be a weekend when candles were lit and homes decorated with branches hauled in from the woods and flowers they'd dried at the end of summer. Nativity scenes would be prepared and in some towns and villages Christmas markets popped up too, but not this year. As dawn was breaking Sofia gazed out at a sky which looked as hard and grey as flint and heard the church bells ringing. That was something, at least, but how was it the Nazis could inflict their characteristics even on their beautiful Tuscan sky? She lay back on her bed and listened.

A little later she was called to the main drawing room. With a heavy heart she saw Schmidt standing with his back to her, arms folded behind him, staring out of the window towards the tower. How tall he was, thin, stooped and tired-looking. She almost pitied him. He heard her footsteps and immediately spun round. She noticed the sombre look on his face but forced herself to smile.

'Commandant, how nice to see you again so soon. But how we could do with some sunshine, don't you agree? Will you sit? I can order coffee and some newly baked pastries.' Just in time she stopped the words from running away with her.

'That is kind but today I have no hunger, Contessa.'

'Ah . . . Well, will you sit? The red velvet is the most comfortable or the wing-back chair.'

He walked towards the velvet chair but stopped and stood beside her, so close she could detect the onions on his breath.

'How may I help you today?' she asked.

He smiled. 'That, my dear lady, will be up to Captain Kaufmann.'

Her heart sank. 'He's here?'

'He will be.'

She wondered what he knew or, more to the point, what he thought *she* knew.

'Your husband is still away?'

'He is, but I expect him back soon.'

He nodded. 'That's good. I don't like to think of you alone here.'

She remained mute and discovered she was clenching her hands.

'You are a little nervous today?'

She wanted to scream. *Of course I'm nervous. Undeniably, I'm nervous. What do you expect?*

'There is nothing to be nervous about, Contessa. At least, I hope not.'

'Tell me, Commandant, were you a doctor?'

He looked taken aback.

'I mean before. Were you a doctor?'

'Whatever makes you think that?'

'Your questions. You seem a compassionate man,' she said and then quickly changed the subject. 'Would you like to play? The piano, I mean.'

'How kind,' he said, 'but here is Captain Kaufmann now. I will take a turn about the grounds instead. See if that sun has had a chance to come out.' Then he smiled at her and left the room.

'Contessa,' Kaufmann said as he entered. 'You are well?'

She nodded and tried for a confident smile but knew when it came it was tremulous.

'Well,' he said. 'I have a few questions.'

She forced another smile. 'First, Captain Kaufmann, I am going to call for some pastries.'

'You haven't eaten breakfast yet?'

'No. I came straight here.'

He must have imagined she would ring a bell. Instead, she left him to it and once out of there leant against the hall door, taking shallow, shuddering breaths and fighting to calm herself. She pinched the skin at the bridge of her nose to try to release the tension. All she wanted was to flee, but instead she headed for the kitchen where she found Anna attempting to comfort a weeping Gabriella.

'Has he gone, madam?' Anna asked.

'No. I came to request pastries. If I don't eat soon, I think I'll collapse, although my stomach is churning so badly, I don't know if I can even eat.'

'I will ask the maid to bring them.'

'Have you found anything out?' Sofia indicated Gabriella, whose face was buried in Anna's skirts while her little dog, Beni, whined his distress.

Anna shrugged.

'Well, I'd better go back.'

'Why is he here?'

'So far, no idea. He's very cagey.'

She took her leave then, and before re-entering the main drawing room she drew back her shoulders. He turned to watch as she came in, his insufferable pale-blue eyes boring right through her.

'Did I tell you how much you remind me of my aunt?'

'I'm afraid I don't remember.'

He smiled coldly. 'Ah, well. I'm sure I did. Do you dance, Contessa?'

She frowned. 'Before the war.'

'My aunt dances. She is a very attractive woman, like yourself.'

He walked across to her and touched her cheek. She swallowed, struggling not to flinch at his touch and the sickly, syrupy smell that clung to his breath. His next words confirmed her worst suspicions.

'Ah, Contessa. I so wish you had told me the truth when I was last here.'

Stricken, she couldn't speak, and felt as if he'd stabbed a knife right into her heart. It was a sharp pain so real she feared he was about to slice her open and all her secrets would spill out. Against her will they'd fall, spreading across the floor for all the world to see. She was very afraid.

'Do not be frightened,' he said, clearly understanding. 'But, you see, we do not relish being lied to.'

'Lied to?' She pressed her lips together and felt the walls of the Castello – the walls that had kept them safe for generations – closing in on her.

'Am I making you feel uncomfortable?'

'Not at all,' she said, but the ground she stood on was caving in. Cracks were opening around her. Cracks through which she would fall at any moment. Cracks which would mean the end. *Lorenzo. Lorenzo. I need you.*

'We have discovered the first name of one of the men we caught,' he said, almost nonchalantly.

She steeled herself. 'And how is that to do with me?'

'Does the name Aldo mean anything to you?'

She had to think very quickly. If he already knew, a denial would only make things worse, and she suspected he *did* know, here to catch her out in another lie. She made a snap decision.

'Contessa?'

'Sorry. Yes. We do have an Aldo here.'

'I think you'll find you *had* an Aldo here,' he said with a smile that bordered on a sneer. 'Why didn't you tell us when I asked you if anyone was missing?'

'Is he missing?'

'Not any more.' Now he sniffed disdainfully, and the knife twisted inside her. Assaulted by the memory, she thought of his men snuffing out Aldo's young life and felt the anger rising. A single word rang in her head over and over.

Murderer.

Murderer.

Murderer.

'We were given information. It allowed us to trace him to you. Or should I say to your cook.'

She shook her head.

'Scum, dear lady. Why are you trying to protect the likes of him?'

Too late to stop herself, she snapped back. 'Well, if I was, it would have been too late, wouldn't it?'

He laughed as if he meant it. 'Such spirit! I do like to see a bit of temperament in a woman. Makes it more fun.'

She eyed him angrily and hoped she hadn't given too much away.

'Now, about the unfortunate young man. One of us will need to speak to his mother.'

'That won't be a problem.'

'But you still have not told me why you didn't recognize him.'

'If you are talking about the two men you hanged at Buonconvento, they had both been so brutalized, I'm sure nobody could have known who they were.'

He looked offended. 'You think I am a brutal man?'

'I didn't say that. But it was a horrific sight. I glanced up and then immediately looked away.'

'Certainly, it wasn't pretty. But, you see, I was keeping watch and I'm sure I saw you staring.'

'I don't remember.'

'We do like to flush out the relatives if we can.'

'If it really *was* our Aldo, he was only a boy.'

He gave her an incredulous look. 'A boy who would have had no qualms in killing one of *us*. You'd be surprised how young some of them are.' He paused. 'Now, I imagine you are wondering what we are going to do?'

Her throat tightened.

'Well, I will allow that for a female member of the nobility, a woman of your sensibility, to see two men hanging might have been such a shock that you did not recognize the partisan, Aldo.'

'For God's sake, Aldo couldn't have been a partisan.'

'And you know that how?'

She couldn't find the words and tried her best to swallow.

'Contessa?'

'I swear I didn't know it was him. If I was staring, I certainly don't recall it. All I remember was the awful shock of seeing two men strung up. The sight . . .' She paused, covering her mouth with her hand for a moment. 'The smell . . . I had no idea one might have been Aldo.'

'Well, let's hope you are telling me the truth.' He paused. 'In any case, I'm sure you will be able to find a way to reward us for our lenience.'

'Oh?'

'By allowing Commandant Schmidt to use your piano, I mean.'

'And you?' she asked.

'Me? I like the look of your paintings, Contessa.'

'I see.'

'I will be coming back to interview your cook. We are always on the lookout for partisan sympathizers.'

With that, he snapped his heels together and swiftly left the room. As soon as she heard Giulia, their maid, showing him out, followed by the sound of his vehicle leaving, she rushed to the downstairs lavatory and vomited until there was nothing left. Of course, he had not believed her story, so why was he playing this game with her?

26.

January 1944

The church bells woke Sofia that icy January morning. She left Lorenzo sleeping and looked out from her bedroom window, catching her breath when she saw the magically transformed landscape. She loved the first snowfall of the season: the sky the colour of lavender, the air shimmering in the weak sunlight and every rooftop blanketed in a dusting of white. But as she gazed at the dark trees standing out in silhouette against the brightness of the newly carpeted fields, she feared for the partisans in the woods. They tried to watch over them, the women continuing to knit sweaters and thick scarves to guard against the cold, but it would never be enough, and the men needed to build telltale fires if they were to survive.

And it wasn't only the partisans who needed their help. Marco's men had managed a raid on a German food camp and that was keeping them going. But towards the end of December dozens of homeless men, women and children had trailed along the roads and through the woods nearby in their attempt to reach the Allies in the south. Sofia had arranged for food to be given to some of them but there just wasn't enough for all. Some were escaped British prisoners, who had either stormed their way out or been released by Italian soldiers, but with so many Germans in the area, their predicament was perilous, especially in the freezing conditions. Several of their older farmers offered temporary shelter but no one knew how or if they'd be able to pass through German lines. And then, on Christmas Day, radio news had reported the bombing of Pisa.

Kaufmann had returned to interview Carla, but, after intimidating her and threatening her, concluded there was nothing more to be gained, at least for now. Sofia had been terrified they'd take five men from the Castello to be slaughtered in an act of revenge for the raid, but they seemed to have been satisfied with hanging Aldo and Lodo. Sofia's relief was profound as any men left were either old or frail. Just before Kaufmann was leaving the Castello after speaking to Carla, he had demanded to see the painting of San Sebastiano again. He had stared silently for some minutes, rubbing his hands together, then he'd stiffened, drawn back his shoulders and left. Something about the proprietorial look in his eyes had been deeply unsettling and Sofia had considered hiding the picture and pretending it had been sold but, in the end, she'd opted not to.

It was bitterly cold as she came downstairs. Maxine and Marco were standing in the small hallway leading to the back door, heads together and whispering furtively. Sofia felt a flash of annoyance, partly because she was still in her robe with only a woollen shawl wrapped round her shoulders, and partly because she had not given permission for Marco to stay the night. But, by the look of things, he had. She watched them for a moment until, obviously sensing her presence, they both turned to face her.

'Oh,' Maxine said, rubbing her eyes.

'Oh, indeed,' Sofia replied.

'Marco is just leaving.'

Sofia felt her jaw stiffening. 'He stayed the night?'

Maxine shrugged.

'Look, Maxine, you really can't invite just anybody to stay here.'

'He isn't *just* anybody.'

'For God's sake, he's a partisan in *my* house. Do you not understand?'

'The equipment was in *your* tunnels,' she retorted. Maxine, fierce, was a force to be reckoned with, but Sofia was not intimidated.

'My husband is *here*,' she hissed, 'not in the damn tunnels. This cannot happen again.'

'Surely he wouldn't mind?'

'What do you mean?'

Maxine frowned. 'Well, he clearly isn't on the side of the bloody Nazis, is he?'

'Whatever he is doing, it is not a suitable subject for conversation.'

'Ah . . . well.' Maxine's mouth twisted to one side and she patted Marco's arm affectionately. 'Anyway, we have news.'

'Good news?'

'I think so. The network of *staffettas* delivered a message requesting I make urgent radio contact with Ronald. We tried repeatedly, James and I, but the connection kept failing. The mountain topography creates problems, you see. But, thanks to the message precedence system, we finally made good contact yesterday. We now know the Germans have drawn up plans for the defence of Italian cities, including a huge arsenal to be stored in the centre of Florence.'

'Where?'

'That we don't know. We *do* know the weapons will be arriving by train in crates from the Beretta factory in Lombardy. Sub-machine guns, rifles, pistols. They manufactured them all for the Italian military until the Germans appropriated the factory for themselves following the armistice.'

'Lorenzo used to know the chairman of Beretta,' Sofia said.

'Well, he's probably long gone. Anyway, there's more. I've been tasked with befriending an SS officer called Bruckner,' Maxine said. 'Gustav Bruckner. Normally he's based in Florence, but he works with Kesselring, the Commander-in-chief, and we believe he'll be the one to decide where the armaments will be stored.'

Marco nodded. 'We know he's going to be in Montepulciano for meetings with officers from Rome.'

'I'm planning to go there and meet up with this Bruckner,' Maxine said.

'And I'm in contact with some of the Florentine partisans who I'm certain will do what they can to help us locate the arsenal,' Marco added.

'So, your objective will be to relieve the Germans of their new arsenal in the city?' Sofia asked.

'Right.'

'I have a cousin with whom I can stay in Montepulciano,' Maxine put in. 'Marco knows where the Germans drink, the bars they go to, where they eat. I hope to get to know Bruckner, find out what I can and then meet up with the partisan unit in Florence.'

'They will want to know why you're in Montepulciano, who you are – and if they find out you're . . .' Sofia shrugged, but her meaning was clear. 'And you'll need clothes. The right kind of clothes.'

Maxine nodded. 'That's true.'

As Sofia considered this, she remembered they still had a wardrobe full of Lorenzo's sister's clothes. After the car accident in which Lorenzo's father, his mother and his sister had perished in Switzerland just a few months after their wedding, Sofia hadn't had the heart to get rid of them, and his sister had been a similar size to Maxine.

Marco gave Sofia an enquiring look. 'You have friends in Florence?'

'Yes, many, we have a small palazzo there. But you know about the arrests by the SS – the questions, the torture?'

He nodded, no doubt also thinking about the place the people had dubbed the Villa Triste in Via Bolognese, the headquarters of the SS.

'It's hardly safe,' Sofia added.

'They're more preoccupied with rounding up the remaining Jews there than digging out the partisans at the moment.'

Maxine reached out a hand to Sofia. 'I'll need somewhere to stay when I'm in Florence. It would be a helpful cover if you could be there too. Gives me a reason to be there, as your friend.'

'And, Contessa, you must have contacts?' Marco added.

'Yes. I know the German Consul, Gerhard Wolf. And I know one of the more sympathetic German residents, if he's still there. A young man called Reinhard. He used to be a lawyer before the war and could be useful.'

Maxine brightened. 'We have a man who works as a clerk in the outer office of the German Consul. So that's perfect. You can try to get an appointment with Wolf and I'll come to Florence as soon as I can.'

'Very well. I'll open up the palazzo, but don't expect too much.'

Marco was looking at Sofia encouragingly. 'Don't forget, the resistance is growing. The enforced use of thousands of our men as labourers has gone against the Germans. They'll make mistakes.'

The next morning, Sofia woke with Lorenzo curled up against her, comforted by the soapy sandalwood smell of him, her underlying anxiety outweighed by the very real joy of being so close. They'd always slept this way, with him curled up behind her or sometimes the other way round. She had been missing his warmth, and she felt safer now, although she'd been able to tell something was troubling him. She'd asked him about it the night before, but he'd just shaken his head and said his job was becoming more difficult; he couldn't rid himself of the feeling that he was being kept under observation.

Of course, that had worried her.

She recalled the first time Lorenzo had turned those gentle grey eyes in her direction and how she'd felt as if he'd been able to see right inside her. It had taken her by surprise and left her tongue-tied. When a man sees past your defences for the first time it's terribly thrilling and new, but it leaves you exposed too. Lorenzo had never taken advantage of her vulnerability. But now he seemed to be erecting shields, as if he had become the vulnerable one.

There'd been a heavier fall of snow during the night and, when they rose, she found they were completely cut off. No telephone, no electricity and therefore no radio. There'd be no post until the snow cleared, and Sofia felt very relieved Lorenzo was home. After breakfast, despite the biting cold, they wrapped up in woollen coats, scarves, hats and gloves, and set off for a walk in the snow with the dogs at their heels.

Outside, the whole world had been silenced and, although cold, it was also very beautiful, the heavy white sky so low you felt you might reach out and touch it. In thick sheepskin boots they picked their way along one of the tracks leading to the road to San Giovanni d'Asso. Sofia loved to breathe the chill air and watch her breath escaping in a cloud then mingling with Lorenzo's.

'Why this way?' she asked as he took her arm.

'The road is safer.'

'From bombs?'

'From snowdrifts, silly.'

They both laughed and she felt a little lighter than before.

'I wanted to tell you about Rome,' Lorenzo said, changing the subject. 'I've never seen anything like it. People are hiding all over the city in fear for their lives. There's constant machine-gun fire and the *boom* of hand grenades hounds us literally night and day. And all this in maybe one of the worst winters.'

Sofia's heart plummeted in worry for her parents. 'Not maybe. It's the coldest winter I've ever known.'

'There's strong resistance though and sporadic sniping at Germans and Fascists too. Unfortunately, there are too many opposing partisan groups and they don't always work together.'

She hardly dared ask and, when she spoke, her voice was a whisper. 'My parents?'

'They're safe enough for now. But every time a grenade

explodes, everybody in the vicinity is arrested. The worst thing is that faith in the Allies is weakening and food has become terribly scarce.'

'What is happening with the Allies?'

'The British army are almost at a standstill. We hear they've only advanced twenty miles in two months.'

'I hadn't realized it was that bad.'

'The conditions are hellish. It's wet, freezing and muddy. They're moving forward inch by inch over the mountains, with no tree cover, fired on by the Germans from the top. Mortar bombs, grenades, machine guns, the lot. They need to get to Rome, but God only knows how long it will take with the mountains as impregnable as fortresses.'

'I feel for them,' she said and reached for Lorenzo's hand. 'What do you think I should do about my parents?'

'When I go back, I'll try to persuade them to come here, but write to your mother too. I'll do my best to deliver it.'

'Maybe I should go to her. Do you have a new address? I don't think my last letter could have reached her.'

'I know. It's because they keep having to move on.'

'Oh, Lorenzo,' she said, and a sob caught in her throat. Then scalding tears began dripping on to her freezing cheeks as she imagined her poor parents being forced to lead such a marginalized life.

He wrapped his arms round her and they stood for a few minutes, as still and silent as the land around them, both with their own thoughts.

Then he pulled back before wiping her tears away. 'Come on, my darling. Let's walk and afterwards we'll spend the rest of the day beside the fire. If Giulia hasn't lit it, I will. How does that sound?'

'It sounds wonderful, but I'm afraid Giulia has gone back to live with her ailing grandmother in Pisa. You remember she lived there for a while before she returned here.'

'When did that happen?'

'Yesterday. She'd been unreliable for a while and then she upped and went, just leaving a message with Carla.'

'Ah. Can you manage without her?'

'Absolutely.'

'You won't miss her?'

'She wasn't here for long, so no.'

'It's the little things we miss most of all,' he said. 'Isn't it?'

She nodded, remembering all the familiar rituals that bound them together and formed the foundations of their lives; the little things they took for granted until they were gone. She longed for the ordinariness of their old routines, the way day followed day in peace and certainty.

'What are you thinking?' he asked. 'Something bothering you?'

She knew she had to raise the subject of Florence.

'I was thinking of maybe spending a little time in Florence, that's all. If you don't mind.'

'Really? The place will need airing and Florence isn't safe. And what about the damage to the palazzo?'

'It's been dealt with. There wasn't much.' She ignored his disapproving expression. 'I can take Anna with me and we have so many friends there.'

He tilted his head to one side and gazed at her, his eyes full of love and concern. 'I wish you wouldn't. Why the sudden change?'

'Oh . . . I don't know.' Her voice faltered, she took a steadying breath and then she told him everything. Told him about her mother's letter, about James and the radio, about her involvement with the partisans and about Maxine's task to find out where the Nazi weapons were to be stored in Florence.

He stood absolutely still, staring at the ground. When finally he looked up and held out a hand to her, his eyes were dark with anxiety. 'Oh God, Sofia. Damn it! All this is terribly dangerous. At this stage of the war, even knowing Maxine could put you in jeopardy. Anything could happen. I want you to keep out of it. You *must* keep out of it.'

She shook her head. 'That's impossible. Aldo's death changed everything for me.'

Lorenzo gazed at her, so troubled she almost changed her mind. Almost, but not quite.

'I understand that,' he said. 'But, nevertheless, I can't let you go.'

'And I can't just stand by. I won't have to do much. Truly. Maxine will be there and Anna too. They'll be doing the work. But if I'm there it gives them a plausible reason to be staying in our palazzo and I want to meet up with Gerhard Wolf too.'

'Dear God. This is crazy! Must you? When he came to our house, it was well before the armistice. Remember, we were on the same side as the Germans then.'

'He may know something.'

Lorenzo sighed. 'He won't be able to say, even if he does.'

'Maybe not.' She took a breath. 'Look, Lorenzo, I *am* going to go. But I'd much rather go *with* your blessing than without it.'

A nerve in his jaw was pulsing furiously and she could see how dreadfully upset he was. 'If anything happens to you –'

'It won't,' she interrupted. 'I promise.'

He took a long, slow breath and nodded.

'Do you know if Reinhard is still in Florence?' she asked. 'The lawyer. You remember him? I found him rather sympathetic before the war.'

'He was arrested.'

'You're sure?'

'Spying for the Allies.'

'And you? Is that what you're doing too?'

'I'm doing what I can, as you already know. When I can, I pass on detailed information to the Allies.'

'About the whereabouts of foodstuffs?'

'Correct.'

She smiled, knowing there was more, but also knowing he'd

be unlikely to give her details. 'And what you said about feeling you're being watched. You will be careful?'

'Of course.'

'Do you think you might be able to arrange for my parents to come here to the Castello?'

'I'll try.'

There was a pause before he spoke again.

'Well,' he said, 'if you're really determined to go, I can't stop you. At least you won't be quite as cold in Florence as you are here.'

She gave him a small, grateful smile.

'Look,' he said, 'it's snowing again.'

She watched the white crystals dancing in the air.

'You are my light,' he said and stroked some snow from her hair with an icy gloved hand.

'You always say that.'

'Because it's true.' He gazed into her eyes. 'Promise me you will stay safe.'

And, although he was smiling, she could tell he would not stop worrying about her visit to Florence.

'I'll be safe,' she said. 'Now come on.'

Their boots sank into the snow as they crunched their way back, holding hands for balance, and for more than that: for love, for hope, for a future. A burst of sunlight shot through a gap in the snowy clouds, firing up the distant hills in shades of red and gold. Sofia glanced back at their deep footprints, planting them in her memory and knowing this moment with Lorenzo was one she had to preserve.

27

Maxine sat in her cousin Davide's drawing room in his house in the medieval hilltop town of Montepulciano. With the shutters closed, and heavy velvet curtains drawn across the two windows facing the garden, the room felt claustrophobic. She breathed in the sour air in the little-used room and, despite the cold, longed to throw open a window. No welcome fire burned in the grate and only two candles lit the room. It was now the twenty-second of January.

When she'd first met up with her cousin, Davide, back in the late autumn, he'd been a little reticent at first, as he'd never met her before, but had eventually agreed she could stay with him and his family if she ever needed. There had been some tense days in the town since the execution, a week before, of six local peasants who'd helped conceal and feed escaped prisoners. Maxine had met two of the dead the day before it had happened and had been shaken by the news. The men had been ordinary working people, too old to be called up, and with extended families who relied on them.

Marco had taken her to talk with some of the local partisans but with even more Fascist militiamen arriving in town intent on helping the Gestapo weed out those who continued to undermine the work of the German Reich, many were now in hiding.

Maxine and Lara, her cousin's wife, were waiting for Davide to come into the drawing room. They listened as he made his way down the creaking stairs and then entered the room. He winked at them both before setting up the secret radio he usually kept hidden in the attic. It was the most thrilling moment of the day and Maxine's heart pounded in expectation as they all drew close, huddling round to hear, hungry for the day's news. As Davide fiddled with the knobs, the set whistled and, at first, the sound was disappointingly intermittent. A crackle. A hiss. A word. Even when they began to hear speech, the words were impossibly scrambled. Maxine held her breath. Would anything come through tonight? Lately the lack of good news had been agonizing: people were losing heart, resentment was growing and some believed the Germans really were going to win the war. And with what seemed like indiscriminate bombing by the Allies, some even thought it might be better if they did. Unsurprisingly, the Allies were aiming for railway lines, stations, assembly storage areas, holding areas and so on, but when village after village took a direct hit, people became angry. The crackles continued but then came the Allied radio broadcasters, who at nine o'clock sometimes sent encrypted messages for the resistance. Occasionally 'personal messages' were hidden in its broadcasts of news and entertainment to occupied Europe. Often, there were coded messages intended for secret agents. She worried the station wouldn't come through clearly but, at last, it did, thin and high-pitched, but enough for them to hear.

To begin with, silenced by disbelief, they exchanged cautious glances. There had not been an encrypted message, just this incredible news. Could it be true? Could they really be so close? The newsreader repeated the message: the Allies had landed at Nettuno, just over sixty-five kilometres south of Rome. Not only that, there had also been massive Allied bombing of German cities; anxiety was now spreading among the German population, some of whom feared they might lose the war after all.

Davide gave a joyful shout, clapped Maxine on the back and kissed his wife on both cheeks. 'This calls for only the very best.' He punched the air in jubilation, and then left the room.

Maxine smiled at Lara. 'Wonderful, isn't it? Let's hope they liberate Rome soon, eh?'

Although not a partisan, Davide fully supported those taking a more active role than he. A lawyer by profession, he might have been expected to support the Fascists. Instead, quietly and very much behind the scenes, he worked at assisting people who'd been wrongly arrested and arranged safe houses for those under threat. It had taken time for Maxine to find this out but, in the end, he'd trusted her enough to reveal what he'd been doing.

He came back into the small drawing room holding aloft a bottle of his best red wine.

Chuckling, pleased with himself, he uncorked it and poured three glassfuls. 'I've kept this hidden. Saving it for an occasion like this.'

A few days later, Maxine met up with Marco at the Caffè Poliziano on the Via Voltaia Nel Corso, the place where they had met before. It was early and still quiet, so they chose a table overlooking the stupendous view. As they both gazed out of the window, she glanced sideways at Marco's profile. He turned his head to face her and she was suddenly rocked by the intensity of his eyes. For one dizzying moment her heart somersaulted and, confused by these blossoming emotions, she didn't catch what he'd said.

'Aren't you listening?'

'Sorry.' She didn't want to tell him why, so muttered something about the view. Why did being with Marco always make her feel like a fraud? Something about him penetrated the walls she'd so painstakingly built up over the years and if, as she suspected, he could see who she really was, it unnerved her.

He gave her a withering look, his face grim. '*Santo Cielo*, never mind the view. Don't you realize a state of emergency has been declared in Rome?'

'Yes, I heard.'

'There's no food, the roads out are blocked and the water system has packed up.'

'How are they meant to survive?'

'Everyone is banking on the Allies arriving quickly.'

Maxine heaved a sigh. 'What if they don't?' She gazed at him, but he didn't speak. After all, what could he say? It was truly awful.

He shook his head. 'The Germans won't give up without a fight,' he said. 'Long columns are already winding their way to Rome from Siena.'

'You've seen them?'

'Yes. Not a pretty sight. The men have been counting them. Lying in ditches and under cover of bushes. The Allies will need that information.'

They both turned to look out of the window. How incongruous to be staring out at a landscape shining so prettily in the winter sun, with a sky so blue it didn't seem real, when such devastation was happening not so very far from them.

'So . . .?' he said with a quizzical look and drew closer to her.

She glanced behind her to check who was in the room. 'I'm afraid we're no nearer to knowing where the German arsenal in Florence is. I've tracked down Bruckner though. He is definitely here and he drinks in the Piazza Grande.'

'No shortage of excellent wine in the palazzo there,' Marco said.

Maxine knew Montepulciano was renowned for its Vino Nobile so, naturally, the Germans had raided the wine cellars of the fourteenth-century palazzo they'd commandeered just off the Piazza Grande at the top of town.

'You'll need to be quick,' Marco added. 'I don't think he'll be here much longer.'

'I'm planning to do it tonight. You have the name of the bartender who'll get me in?'

'Yes, Ricardo, he's the one who lets the girls in. I'll introduce you.'

She pulled a wry face. 'I'm going to say I'm here because my mother sent me away from Rome before the roads became blocked. I can tell him I've been staying with a friend in the countryside but that I'm at my cousin's now and looking for work. They swallow anything that comes from a pretty face.'

'Unless they think you're a prostitute.'

Maxine gave Marco a *so what* look then gazed at him. 'What about you? Do you have anything for me?'

'Yes. When you reach Florence, you need to contact the partisan leader, Ballerini. He'll be able to give you the lowdown on what's happening in and around Florence, and you can pass it on to the Allies via Radio Cora.'

'What does Radio Cora stand for?'

'The Radio Commission. A clandestine radio they use for contact between the Allies and the resistance. The password to make the connection to Radio London is "The Arno flows in Florence". It's a pretty rudimentary radio system that needs to be frequently moved, much like the one James operates.'

'Okay. So, once I'm in Florence, I'll get moving with this Ballerini. See what we can do together.'

'Yes. I'll be needed here and at Monte Amiata so he's your best bet. And go to 12 Piazza d'Azeglio to meet up with the clerk who works in the German Consul's office.'

'Gerhard Wolf's office?'

'Yes.'

She nodded and then, with her head tilted to one side, gave him a teasing smile. 'Let's go. Where's your hat?'

He shrugged. 'I lost it.'

'I know what you said before about keeping our distance, but . . .'

He knitted his brows together in mock outrage. 'I cannot imagine what you might be suggesting.'

'My cousin is at work and his wife is out today so . . .'

'You'd like to invite me round for coffee?'

She grinned with pleasure. 'Exactly.'

* * *

Maxine loved the town's elegant Renaissance palaces, its age-old churches and all the little squares and secret corners. The views lifted her spirits when she tired of the war and she'd stand gazing out across either the wonderful Val d'Orcia or the Val di Chiana valleys surrounding it. And it was with lifted spirits that she walked ahead of Marco to Davide's house. She hadn't expected him to agree to come but now that he had she was determined to make the most of their time together.

After making love in her little bedroom on the third floor they lay in bed and talked. He told her of his hopes for the future, and how much he wanted a family of his own one day, that somehow it would make up for the loss of his brother. He told her he had a sister and a nephew, and he wanted to make things better for them.

She was surprised and said so.

He smiled. 'I don't often allow myself the luxury of imagining good things.'

'Maybe thinking about better times makes all this more bearable.'

He shook his head. 'I know what you mean, but I think it makes it more painful. I've found that it's only by toughening up that I can do what I do.'

She sat up, plumped the pillow behind her, then gazed down at his closed eyes, reaching out to gently stroke the contours of his brow.

'It's hard, isn't it?' she said.

His eyes flew open and their eyes locked. 'What?'

'Love. Or, rather, living without love.'

He sniffed. 'Is that what you think I'm doing?'

She shrugged. 'Maybe you have to.'

They were silent for a few moments.

'Don't you think love can balance out the horror of war, just a little?' she asked.

'You tell me. Can it?'

'I want to believe so.'

He looked away from her. 'Is it truly possible to love when the world has grown so dark?'

She sighed. 'What's left without it?'

'War. There is only war.'

Something about the gravity of his voice silenced her.

'Feelings weaken you, affect your decisions, put you in danger, others too. That's why we have to completely cut ourselves off from our families and assume a different identity.'

'So, you're not really Marco?'

'Correct.'

'But, "not" Marco, you *do* have feelings.'

Their eyes met again, and he narrowed his gaze.

'Yes. You do,' she said resolutely, not wanting to give up on this. 'You feel guilty because your brother was taken, and you weren't. That's why you're doing what you do, isn't it?'

He stiffened.

'You feel fear too and anger. I know you do.'

'And you don't?'

'Of course I do. I'm not saying I don't. I feel panic, uncertainty, doubt, all sorts of things. But you can't feel all those things and not feel love.'

'That's crazy. Why not?'

'Because if you close off love, you close off everything else as well.'

'And you know this how?'

'My father. Something happened. In the past. I don't know what. They've never talked about it in front of me, but I've overheard my mother whispering with her friends. Whatever it was, my father closed off, shut down his feelings, his heart. Sometimes I think the only emotion left to him is rage.'

'And you think we can't survive on anger alone? That's what you're saying?'

'We can survive but it isn't really living, is it?'

He stared at her. 'You think anger is the worst thing?'

'I don't know. What is?'

'Since the war, or ever?'

'Either.'

He seemed to consider it. 'Apathy. That's the worst.'

She nodded. 'Yes. I think you're right. Especially now.'

'Well, nobody could ever accuse you of being apathetic.' He paused for a moment before he spoke again, and she saw him swallow a lump in his throat.

'I still see him everywhere,' he said.

'Your brother?'

He nodded. 'I see him walking down the street, sitting in a café, bringing in the harvest. I see him with my parents, my sister. I see the father he would have one day become, the children he might have had.'

'You've already said you're doing this for him. Isn't that love?'

'Or revenge. Have you thought of that?'

She gazed at him. 'It's not revenge I see in your eyes, Marco.'

'What do you see?'

She raised her brows, took hold of his hand and drew it to her lips. He had the grace to smile. *Oh, this man, this man,* she thought, *how I do love you.*

That night Maxine lounged on a velvet chaise longue in the palazzo commandeered by the Nazis, occasionally tipping the wine she was supposedly drinking into a potted plant behind her. Although she enjoyed nothing more than an excellent *vino rosso*, she needed to keep her wits about her. While they already had their contact in the office of the German Consul in Florence, Maxine still needed to meet Bruckner, the man she believed would be making a decision about the site for the storage of the new arsenal.

She was listening to an extremely tedious Captain Vogler, Baltasar Vogler, who was claiming that his Christian name meant he was protected by God – 'As all we Germans are.' He laughed and then went on to complain about the evil workforce strikes in the north of Italy.

'But do not worry,' he was saying, 'we have sorted them, all right.'

Maxine smiled with what she hoped was an admiring look but secretly wished she could snip off the lock of light-brown hair that fell into his piggy-looking eyes. Unusually small and stocky – most of the officers were at least tall – he smelt unattractively meaty. As if he'd gone a little bit 'off'. She smiled again at the image of him slowly rotting from the inside out, and sure enough he took the smile to mean she was hanging on his every word.

'You wish to know how?' he asked, and then carried on without waiting for her to answer, boasting that they'd simply shot one tenth of the workforce. 'They get back to work pretty damn quickly, I can inform you.' He laughed as if he'd told a hilariously funny joke.

Maxine, feeling sickened, managed to maintain her smile, while keeping one eye on the door and remaining aware of the other two men in the room, who appeared to be engrossed in conversation. Vogler loved the sound of his own voice and Maxine had little to do but appear to be listening. When he placed a sweaty palm on her knee, she could feel the sticky heat of it through her silk dress. Peacock blue and one of Sofia's dead sister-in-law's, it was admittedly out of date, but the colour enhanced the red in her hair and set off her red lipstick too.

The door suddenly swung open. A man walked in, still not especially tall but muscular, with cropped, very blond hair, dressed in the uniform of an SS officer with four silver pips centred on a collar patch. Was this Bruckner? She held her breath as a spike of fear travelled up her spine, then she gave him a tentative smile. The SS had originally been an elite squad formed to defend Hitler but were now the dominant organization in charge of security, surveillance and terror both in Germany and German-occupied Europe. She would need to tread very carefully.

'Ah, Major Bruckner, what can I get you?' Vogler said, jumping to his feet.

'We have beer?'

'No. Only the red wine.' The stocky officer laughed but Bruckner just shrugged.

As Vogler went off to open another bottle, Bruckner gazed down at Maxine. She lowered her lashes before looking up again and gazing into the greenest eyes she'd ever seen. What a pity he was a Nazi. She contemplated what it might mean to sleep with such a man, whether the end could ever justify the means, whatever the cost. If she could forget who he was for a moment, this might not be so bad. *If* she could forget. She thought of what Marco had said about feelings weakening you, putting you in danger, and she longed to be back with him rather than doing this.

'I'm Massima,' she said, forcing herself to focus.

His eyes danced. 'Pretty dress.'

After Vogler had brought in two uncorked bottles of red, Bruckner waved him away and the other man left the room, followed by the two who'd been hovering by the fireplace.

Bruckner studied Maxine's face. 'So, you are from here?'

Maxine held up under his scrutiny as she shook her head. Then told him how surprised she was at hearing such excellent Italian.

'Ah, we used to come here when I was a child. My mother loved Italy, especially the lakes. Lugano was her favourite, but she loved Tuscany too. We all did.'

'Loved?'

He gazed down at her. 'Sadly, she is no longer with us. Our apartment building was bombed. Only my father and I survived because we were not at home. My brother and younger sister also died.'

'I am so sorry,' she said, and realized she meant it. There was a terrible loss of innocent souls on both sides, after all.

'You have an unusual accent, I think.'

Wrong-footed, she had to think quickly. Her mother's voice warned her to be careful, and the very British voice of Ronald, her liaison officer, joined in. 'Stick to the truth, or as near to the truth as you can.' That had been his mantra.

'I spent some years in New York with relatives when I was younger,' she said. 'But I'm from Rome. I'm staying with my cousin here in Montepulciano.'

There was a short silence.

'Won't you sit, Herr Bruckner?'

'Call me Gustav. I'm off duty tonight.'

He sat close to her and she breathed in his lemony scent. 'You smell nice.'

'You too. What is it?'

Maxine had considered very carefully before coming to Italy and the scent she had chosen was possibly the sexiest one ever created, bursting with the earthiness of patchouli and blended with carnation and vanilla.

'Dana's Tabu,' she told him.

'Sensual,' he said in a soft voice. 'Animal . . . I think you must be a dangerous woman.'

The look she directed at him told him she was.

They spent an hour talking and she found she rather liked him. There was something different about him and she sensed he was a bit of a fish out of water, although he must also be ruthless to have risen to the level of Sturmbannführer, or Major, so young. He told her he'd been training to be a doctor until war broke out, when he had signed up for duty in the Wehrmacht instead. He'd wanted to fight for the Fatherland and defend the country he loved, and had been an assault unit leader. His uncle was a Vice Commander-in-chief of the armed forces, who had given him a leg-up.

'It was an outrage when Italy changed sides,' he said, and she noted the scathing tone of his voice.

'Not all of us changed,' she said. 'You should have seen Mussolini on his white horse proclaiming his goal to unify Italy.'

'A proud man. Like our Führer. But he never was strong enough. You cannot be weak, or tolerate weakness, if you want to change the world.'

With secret pleasure she remembered the ways in which the equally determined partisans were aiming to change the world by crippling the Nazi war machine.

There was a lull in their conversation and he got up to stoke the fire. Maxine decided it was time to steer the evening in the direction she wanted it to go. When he came back, this time sitting even closer to her, she placed a hand on his wrist.

'Are you here for long?' she asked, her voice deliberately husky.

He shook his head. 'I'm here for a couple of days then back to Florence.'

She smiled and stroked his wrist. 'More wine?'

He nodded.

He had been steadily drinking and his eyes were beginning to get the hazy look of a man who wants only one thing. In order to keep him keen, Maxine rose to her feet.

'Will you be here tomorrow night?' she asked.

He leant back, his arm resting along one side of the sofa, legs spread wide. 'Will you?'

She smiled provocatively. 'Of course. Where else would I want to be?'

'Then I will be here too.'

'Then you'll be off to Florence.'

He gave her an unfathomable look. 'Plenty of time before that.'

'I'd like to go to Florence. It's so dull here.'

'What would you do there?'

'Maybe find a job. I have a friend who lives near the river. So, perhaps I'll go by train and stay with her.'

'You have all your documents?'

She raised her brows. 'Of course.' Her fake documents, provided by the nuns she had been taken to south of Rome, had served her well so far.

Then she blew him a kiss and made her escape. If she could just persuade him to give her a lift to Florence . . .

28

Lorenzo was back in Rome again and Sofia was preparing for her trip to Florence. The night before her departure, she was surprised to find James at the back door. He was rubbing his hands and blowing on them at the same time. 'I hope you don't mind,' he said, his lips blue with cold. 'I know it's late, but it's damp and freezing at the farm and I daren't light a fire.'

She considered for a moment, glad the dogs were asleep in the kitchen for their barking would be loud enough to wake the dead. 'It's probably best if you come up to my room. I can light a fire. If anything happens, you'll be able to quickly slip into the passage from there.'

'Thank you.'

'It's important you don't get ill again. Are you hungry?'

He made it clear that he was by tapping his stomach.

'We may have some leftover rabbit pie. I'll look. You remember the way up?'

He nodded. 'Is Maxine here?'

'No. She's still in Montepulciano. Go on up now. Nobody will see.'

As he headed towards the stairs, Sofia went to the kitchen where she found Carla still wiping down the table.

'Oh,' she said, surprised. 'You're still up.'

'I'm happy to get you something.'

'Ah . . . Yes. Do we have any rabbit pie left?'

Carla went to the larder and returned with a slice of pie on a plate, which she placed on the table. 'I'll get you a fork.'

She studied Sofia's face with a concerned look. 'Are you all right, Contessa?'

'Yes. Why wouldn't I be?'

Carla narrowed her eyes inquiringly. 'You are a little pale and you never eat late at night.'

'Nothing gets past you, does it, Carla? But, honestly, I'm fine. The pie is for James. He's cold and he's hungry.'

She picked up the plate and fork Carla handed her. 'I'll take it to my room.'

Back upstairs, a built fire used to always be at the ready. Giulia would prepare it every day, but now Sofia took care of it herself and, following Giulia's example, she kept her supplies well stocked. She could employ another maid, of course, but with things as they were, she preferred not to have anyone new working in the household. She handed James the pie, then busied herself by crumpling the paper, adding the kindling and a few bone-dry smaller pieces of wood, all the while conscious of him watching her every move. It was an odd, rather awkward situation and she felt it keenly. When she struck the match, the fire blazed up quickly and she drew up both the bedroom chairs before it.

She wasn't looking at him, but she could sense he was still gazing at her. When she did glance up, she couldn't quite read his expression – there was something a bit soulful about his eyes and she wondered if he was feeling homesick. She felt as if she were absorbing the sadness from the depths of those very blue eyes and found herself wanting to comfort him.

He finished the pie and flashed her a smile. 'Thank you. You're very generous.'

'Not at all.'

'I've been looking for locations,' he said.

'Locations?' She realized she must sound stupid.

'New sites where we might be able to set up the radio, not just the farm I'm staying in.'

'And did you find any?'

'Yes, one or two. An abandoned church tower, a high-ceilinged barn at the top of a hill.' He gave her a warm, familiar look and suddenly she felt prickly and exposed.

'So . . . how are you?' he asked.

She stiffened, aware that she wasn't usually as self-conscious as this. 'I'm fine.'

The conversation had already become stilted, a result of her growing unease at being alone in her bedroom so late at night with an attractive man who was not her husband.

'Sorry,' he said, clearly sensing her discomfort. 'I'd better go.'

She didn't reply at first. Should she send him away or simply brush his suggestion aside? She hadn't the heart to send him straight back to a freezing house a considerable walk away so, trying to keep her tone neutral, she offered him some extra blankets.

'Thank you.' He began to rise.

After a moment's hesitation and wanting to rescue the situation, she added, 'Look, really . . . you don't have to go yet. Please warm yourself up properly first.'

He sat back down. 'You're very kind.'

There was a pause that soon turned into a long silence.

'Can you tell me anything about your life?' she eventually asked. 'Back home, I mean.'

He rubbed his chin and looked resigned. 'I'm afraid we're not allowed to share personal information.'

'Of course not. Stupid question.'

'Not stupid. Normal. Well . . . if things were normal, I mean.'

They fell silent again and then, suddenly, both spoke at the same time. 'Go on,' she said. 'You first.'

He smiled and she felt so disarmed by the light in his eyes that all manner of complicated responses rose up inside her.

'Oh, to hell with it,' he said. 'It's hardly going to lose us the war, is it? I'm from Gloucestershire. A place called Stroud. Well, one of the villages nearby, in fact.'

'Won't you tell me what it's like? I've only ever been to London.'

'It's very different from London. Lovely Cotswold stone cottages dotted around the hills, and some very grand houses too,' he said, warming to the topic.

'It sounds delightful. You must miss it.'

'I do. My parents live in Minchinhampton, near the common. It's where I used to walk our Labrador.'

'What's his name?'

'Dead now, I'm afraid, but I called him Pluto.'

She laughed. 'Funny name for a dog.'

They talked comfortably for an hour. He told her about England – his fiancée, Margaret, his home, his favourite food. Apparently, everyone in England talked about food, or dreamt about it, just like they did. He told her about bangers and mash, and cottage pie, roast dinners and apple crumble. She told him the food in London hadn't been great.

'Godawful,' he said, pulling a face, and they both laughed.

As they sat together by the fire, she felt cocooned in a precious oasis of peace.

'What about you?' he asked. 'Where did you grow up?'

'Rome. The walls of our apartment were lined with books and paintings.' She smiled at the memory. 'My father despaired because Mother was forever hunting for rare books or pictures and carting them home. They were thoughtful people and good parents. As a treat, I was sometimes allowed to stay up for their monthly musical evenings.'

'Sounds wonderful.'

As she thought about the past, a wave of sadness went through her. 'Yes, it was. For a while. My parents' friends were artists and writers, musicians, poets, actors. Not the kind to carry the Fascist card. But gradually they became fewer in number.'

'What happened?'

'Mussolini happened. Some disappeared and were never heard of again. Others went abroad. America mainly. It broke my mother's heart.'

'I imagine your husband's background was somewhat different.'

'The nobility tended to support Mussolini.'

'Your husband too?'

She gave him a noncommittal shrug and sank into thoughts about Lorenzo. Although she'd been fully aware of his grave misgivings on the subject of Mussolini, he hadn't been actively outspoken against the man. Few had, and when they did, they lived to regret it if they lived at all. But in any case, generally speaking, Lorenzo had never been as forthright as she. His personality was different and, as he'd been brought up to be less open, maybe it was natural for him to be a little more reticent.

'He doesn't support Mussolini, and he's a good man, a really good man,' she said. 'But he holds a lot in reserve.'

'And you're all right with that?'

'Aren't most men uncommunicative, at least some of the time?'

He bent forward and gazed at her with a quizzical look, but she didn't quite trust herself to add anything more, even if she had wanted to, and she wasn't sure that she did. She felt he wanted to say something, something that was right on the tip of his tongue, but then he sat back and shook his head, turning his eyes away.

They sat in silence for a few minutes and she became aware that her earlier discomfort had completely vanished; the companionship she felt being with him and the directness of the conversation had been comforting. There was a straightforwardness about him that she liked and it was clear a delicate bond had begun to spring up between them.

It was as if they'd agreed to talk about everything but the war, until suddenly she couldn't help herself. 'Will the Allies win?' she said and heard the tremble in her own voice.

He took a deep breath and exhaled slowly. 'I bloody well hope so.'

'But it's more complicated than winning or losing, isn't it?

The whole thing is insanity. It shouldn't even be happening, should it?'

He groaned at the truth of this. 'None of us want it.'

'My mother says that amid darkness there is always light.'

'And you believe her?'

'I want to . . . but I know the reverse is also true.'

As the hour grew later, she was beginning to feel sleepy and couldn't help yawning.

'I'm so sorry,' he said, instantly rising to his feet. 'I'm keeping you up and you need your sleep.'

She got up too and, feeling lonely and longing for further human contact, she only just stopped herself from suggesting he stay longer.

He gazed at her as if he could read her mind. 'Thank you,' he said, taking her hand and putting it to his lips. She leant into him, felt his heart thump, and realized how warm he now was. A few moments passed, then she pulled away, suddenly wishing she hadn't allowed this intimacy.

'I'm so sorry,' he said, looking crestfallen.

'It's fine,' she replied. 'But you'd better go now. I'll come down and lock the door after you.'

29.

Florence

Lorenzo had been right. When Sofia and Anna arrived in German-occupied central Florence, it wasn't quite as cold as the Castello, but still the damp crept into their bones. Sofia recalled her very first visit to Lorenzo's family palazzo, how stunned she had been by its beauty, with its arched windows right across the front and the huge main doorway. Their last visit here had been back in September, and they'd been lucky. There'd been no air-raid sirens when the Allied bombers targeted the city, and they'd been relaxing in the salon unaware of what was about to happen. When the awful whistling began, Sofia ran to Lorenzo and they held each other, listening as each shrill shriek was followed by a rumbling sound, ending in an explosion that made you feel you were going crazy. As the nightmare went on and the Allied bombs fell hard and fast, they waited, hardly breathing, not knowing if they would live. She prayed and prayed, and she meant it. And she tried very hard not to think about what might happen if they were unlucky. Miraculously they were left unscathed, with just a few of their palazzo windows shattered, but they found out several buildings had been destroyed and at least two hundred civilians killed. It was hard to stomach. The British and American forces had been their enemies but, overnight, became their friends. Now they were blowing up bridges and railway tracks to make life difficult for the Germans, but it was hurting the ordinary citizens too.

This was the first time she had returned since then and the whole house echoed with Lorenzo's absence. Nothing improper had really taken place, but perhaps spending time alone with

James the night before had made her more aware of how much she needed her husband to be near her. Was that wrong? She could cope. She could cope perfectly well, but she longed for him to be there, in the dark, shuttered rooms and in her bed. She whipped off the muslin dust sheets covering the furniture in every room and that helped a bit. The four-storey palazzo was far too big for them and there had been an exciting plan to refurbish it into four apartments but when the war came along the project had ground to a halt.

When they were first married, she'd had to build her confidence in the role of Contessa and, especially here, it had felt like a performance until, gradually, she'd fallen into step with the way of things. Before her death, Lorenzo's mother had gone out of her way to be kind. Sofia had been visiting her parents in Rome when the terrible accident had struck Lorenzo and his family. As the only one to escape the car with his life, his guilt and sorrow had been devastating to see. She'd done everything she could to help him, until eventually the light had begun slowly to return to his eyes.

Now, while the ever-practical Anna concocted something to eat, Sofia lit a fire in the drawing room and thought again of James. Loneliness and living in fear could lead you to a place you never would have imagined in peacetime. After the fire had caught and the room had filled with smoke, she longed to clear her head so decided to take a walk. She slipped into a long black coat with a thick fur collar and matching hat. Unsure how safe it was, she considered taking her gun but decided against it. Not a good idea if she were to be stopped and searched.

It must have been raining heavily earlier because she had to pick her way over puddles in the cobbled streets and avoid water dripping from the deep eaves of the buildings. She passed very few locals but there were Germans, their lorries and their military vehicles in evidence everywhere. She headed along the Lungarno for the Ponte Vecchio, where it straddled the river Arno on low arches.

When the Medici family transferred from their original palazzo to the Palazzo Pitti, they built a connecting passageway from the Uffizi to the Palazzo Pitti on the other side of the river so they could cross while remaining hidden from the ordinary people. She could see the row of small windows along the walls of the Corridoio Vasariano which ran above the jewellery shops on the bridge. When Lorenzo and she met all those years ago, this had been their favourite romantic spot. By day the sky had always seemed to be a clear azure blue while the sun lit the buildings so brightly, they shone as if made of palest gold. The memories tugged at her heart, especially from those early evenings, the magical hour when they sauntered arm in arm along the riverbank beneath a velvety violet sky. The hour when the surrounding hills softened to dusky blue, the golden reflections of ancient houses shimmered in the water and the scent of orange blossom hung in the air. She felt a stab of panic when it struck her that the German retreat from, or defence of, this beautiful city might mean the destruction of this ancient bridge. She knew she had to do her best to find out if any of her friends had heard rumours about where German weapons were being stockpiled. The partisans badly needed them if they were to assist the Allies in liberating Florence.

As dusk approached, a diaphanous white mist rose up above the river. She reluctantly moved away and soon, hearing gunshots, began scurrying along, pulling her fur collar around her face as the bitterly cold wind drove her home. When she reached the palazzo, she glanced up at the two wrought-iron lanterns above the door fixed into the rusticated stone wall. No bulbs inside them now. Then, as she pushed open the great wooden front door and entered the fifteenth-century inner courtyard, the aroma of frying onions and garlic greeted her. Life must go on and, thank God, it did. She ignored the wide stone stairs leading up to her quarters and instead made her way to the tiled kitchen where Anna greeted her with a warm smile.

'Are you happy to eat in here, Contessa?'

Sofia agreed and straight away sat at the table where Anna had already poured two glasses of wine.

Two days later, when Sofia opened her eyes in the morning, she saw bright light bouncing off the wall opposite her bed. This was the day. She'd had to phone the consulate office twice before she'd been able to speak to Gerhard Wolf, the German diplomat currently serving as Consul. But she'd successfully made the appointment for today and was now feeling pleased with herself. Her heart lifted even further when, glancing out of the window, she saw the clouds had dispersed and she was greeted by a shimmering day. She was glad of the good weather for her meeting.

As lovers of fine art, Wolf and Lorenzo had met before the war at an exhibition in the National Gallery in London during June 1935, and then again in Berlin a month later. There they had become friends and corresponded until war had broken out. Then, when Wolf was posted to Florence, Lorenzo had invited him to their house. So, as Lorenzo's wife, it hadn't been difficult for Sofia to arrange this meeting. She knew Wolf had been born in Dresden, and that he'd studied philosophy, art history and literature. As a cultured man he had resisted joining the Nazi party at first and only did so when it became evident that his diplomatic work could not continue otherwise. Among Sofia's friends it was whispered he had helped Jews escape and was now doing his best to prevent significant artworks from being appropriated and shipped back to Berlin.

As Sofia remembered the one occasion she had met Wolf, she looked down at their small garden now bright and shiny in the sunshine. She'd met him here in this house, one early summer, and they'd all enjoyed cocktails in the garden. Few of the houses had gardens, especially so close to the river, so theirs was precious despite being overlooked by the backs of other townhouses.

She decided that after seeing Wolf she would call on friends, let them know she was there and find out how they were doing. Unsurprisingly, many had already fled or been forced out, their houses requisitioned along with the best hotels. Lorenzo had told her the Germans were using the synagogue on Via Farini as a warehouse and stables, so maybe there was a chance the armaments might be stored there too. She would do her best to find out what she could.

30

Sofia was due to meet with Wolf in a café not far from the consulate. On the phone he'd told her the consulate itself was an inferior sort of a place, not at all what one would normally expect, and he preferred they meet in a café instead. She'd thought it a bit clandestine but had arrived early and chosen a table in a quiet corner at the back.

When he walked in, she instantly recognized the solidly built man with a kind face. She rose from her seat and they shook hands.

'Thank you for meeting me,' she said.

'It is my pleasure. I remember you well. How is your husband?'

'He's in Rome at present.' She fudged her reply as she didn't actually know where, or how, Lorenzo currently was.

'Still at the ministry?'

She nodded.

'So.' He clasped his hands together, fingers pointing upwards. 'What can I do for you?'

'Well, I'm not really sure. I expect you know how concerned we are to avoid damage here in Florence.'

'Well, yes, of course, but obviously . . .' He paused and smiled sympathetically. 'I have no influence over the Allied bombing.'

She smiled back. 'True. I hope you don't mind me mentioning it but people are saying you have been instrumental in preserving or should I say *protecting* artworks from being removed from Italy.'

He glanced around the room to check if anyone was in earshot. 'My dear lady, you must understand I cannot comment. I am a German citizen and, as such, of course I support my country in winning this war.'

'I understand.'

She thought for a moment before trying a different tack. 'We've heard that when the German army retreats, they tend to leave destruction behind them. Is that correct?'

He gazed at the table for a few moments, then looked up at her, sadness in his kind eyes. 'It is to be deeply regretted . . . Look, Contessa, I am only talking with you now because of my previous friendship with Lorenzo.'

She nodded.

'Florence, as you know, was a city of wealthy bankers and merchants in the thirteenth and fourteenth centuries. They spent their great wealth on extraordinary architecture and filled their palaces with fine art and wonderful frescoes. How can any thinking man bear to see it destroyed?'

She shook her head.

'I tell you that because I am trying to retain my humanity at an extremely testing time. I do my best to alleviate suffering if it is in my power, and I aim to preserve whatever I can of the majesty of Florence. I do not wish the world to lose what you have here.'

'Of course. And I imagine you are not party to Kesselring's intentions?'

He shrugged and looked up at the ceiling. She waited, anxiously watching the internal struggle reflected in Wolf's face, his jaw pulsing and signs of tension showing in his brow. She could tell he would have liked to say more and felt sorry for putting him in a quandary.

Eventually he sighed and looked at her again. 'Although Kesselring is a genial man, my powers, as far as our Commander-in-chief is concerned, are extremely limited. And now I'm afraid you must excuse me.'

He rose to his feet and shook her hand before leaving.

31

They set off from Montepulciano at five in the morning to avoid the Allied bombing. Maxine sat with Major Gustav Bruckner in the back of the chauffeur-driven car. On their third meeting, he'd offered to give her a lift to Florence and, of course, she'd swiftly accepted. She gazed out at the barren landscape and longed for the fresh lemony light of a spring morning.

Captain Vogler was sitting morosely in the front passenger seat and not adding a word to the already limited conversation. Bruckner patted Maxine's knee but, although obviously attracted to her, he had been in no rush to do more. They'd mainly spent their time engrossed in lively talk, which is why she found this silence unsettling. If anything was wrong, she could hardly make a dash from a car occupied by three Germans.

She considered the things Bruckner had revealed about himself. Unmarried, he did not have a fiancée or steady girlfriend back home. Although he intended to finish his medical training once they won the war, he had no interest in settling down. He wanted to travel. In Germany he'd ridden a motorcycle, which he preferred to driving an automobile. He enjoyed reading and the theatre, but most of all he loved opera. In short, he was a cultured man. If he hadn't been the enemy, she could have really liked him. In fact, she did like him and had to remind herself he was also a ruthless SS officer.

But everybody had different, maybe even conflicting aspects to their character. She certainly had. When her mother, Luisa, had persisted in urging her to marry the grocer, she'd defiantly retorted, 'No. I want to be myself.' When asked to explain exactly what that self was, she'd floundered. What she really wanted, what she longed for, was an open life, one in which she could *find out* about herself and thrive, not simply survive as her mother had done. And she was certainly finding out now. She'd discovered something of her courage and her fearlessness but had concluded courage was only valid in the face of fear. If it came easily, it wasn't courage at all. Courage was a choice.

'Join me for lunch,' the Major said suddenly. 'I know somewhere quiet and modest where we won't be disturbed. Will you be able to make your way to your friend's place afterwards?'

Maxine smiled. 'Of course, and how lovely. I hadn't expected to be fed as well as given a lift.'

'Or, if you prefer, I can instruct my driver to drop you at your friend's place as soon as we arrive.'

'It's fine. I'm hungry.'

He gave her a warm smile.

As they drew up at the grand six-storey Excelsior hotel situated on the north bank of the Arno and facing Piazza Ognissanti, it was busier than Maxine had expected. German trucks were parked right around the piazza and cars were constantly pulling up. He asked her to wait outside for a moment and then he went in. Obviously the building had been requisitioned but even so, when she glanced through the window to watch Bruckner, she was taken aback by the grand marble-pillared entrance hall teeming with German and Fascist officers and not a single woman in sight.

After lunch she went to find 12 Piazza d'Azeglio, the address Marco had given her where she would meet Gerhard Wolf's clerk and find out more about the partisan leader Ballerini. The square, it turned out, was a beautiful formal garden that looked as if it had been inspired by the squares she'd briefly enjoyed when she'd been in London. There were trees, hackberry and sycamore, several pathways and flower beds, and the buildings surrounding the square were not medieval but looked as if they had been built in the eighteenth and nineteenth centuries.

A middle-aged woman with a hook nose and dyed black hair opened up at her knock, and after Maxine delivered the password, she was shown into a back room, where she met with a neat, bespectacled young man who was pacing back and forth, looking nervous and worried. He held out his hand.

'Antonio.'

'Was that your mother?' she asked.

He shook his head. 'I don't live here.'

'Partisans?'

He nodded.

At that moment another man entered the room. He looked down at heel and hungry, and Maxine could tell by the tight expression on his thin face that he was one of the Florentine partisans. He said his name was Stefano.

She clarified who she was, and then Antonio explained that he was a clerk in the office of the German Consul and that he had information. Two Nazi officers were due to meet with Wolf in a few days' time. He'd heard one of them would be Kesselring, and he was planning to listen in to what was being said. Looking at Antonio, Maxine doubted the man would have the skill to do so undetected, but as he was all they had she had to pin her hopes on him.

'Kesselring,' she remarked with a whistle. Kesselring, the man who was in direct command of all German forces in Italy. 'What is the meeting for?'

Stefano spoke up this time. 'Antonio has already picked up that it may be to do with the arrangement for the storage of armaments. That's why the partisan Marco sent you to us. Wolf is worried that some weapons have already been stored in a major palazzo, though we don't yet know which one.'

Maxine frowned. 'But he's a German – he thinks that's a problem because –?'

'Because if it's hit by Allied bombs the entire street might go up in smoke and all the palazzos with it. Wolf is determined to preserve as much of Renaissance and medieval Florence as he can.

'We now know the consignment from the Beretta factory will be arriving any day. We are keeping a watch on the station here and those just outside Florence too. But since some Beretta sub-machine guns were appropriated from the factory by partisans last October, the Germans have doubled their security on the trains.'

'The consulate is very small,' Antonio said. 'Only four rooms between the German Evangelical mission and the Lutheran pastorate. It's not too difficult to overhear if you know how.'

Maxine nodded and Antonio continued.

'Wolf removed Hitler's portrait, you know, from where it was hanging behind his desk. He took it down and replaced it with a lithograph of Goethe instead. Head and shoulders, turned three-quarter length to the left and wearing a fur collar.'

'Kesselring won't like that,' Maxine said, and they all smiled.

'Wolf is a good man,' Antonio said. 'He had his work cut out to persuade the Nazis to post him as consul here. He came three years ago with his wife and daughter. I'll get a message to you saying when and where to meet me when – or if – I have more information.'

'You know about Radio Cora?' Stefano said, looking directly at her. 'That's how you'll be able to let the Allies know where the armaments are, and you'll be able to disclose whether we get them or not. They might find a way to help us.'

'I need to let my liaison officer know about the situation here too.'

'How do you mean?'

'Where the partisans are, how many there are and so on, not just whether they have weapons. I was told to find Ballerini.'

Stefano sighed. 'Ballerini was killed recently. A brave man. Our anarchist leader.'

'I'm sorry to hear it,' she said, but – *damn!* – she hadn't expected that.

'And in December Manetti and Ristori, the leaders of the

other group, were shot. They used to hole up in Monte Morello. It's the highest mountain in the Florence plain and takes about four hours to get to on foot. Maybe half an hour in a vehicle.'

'So who is leader now?'

He pulled a face. 'It's early days. Ballerini's group have joined with another group called the Garibaldi Black Wolves. They are in the Calvana Mountains now.'

'Where is that?'

'About forty kilometres away. There are hidden trails through the forests, hills and small rural villages and that's where they are.'

'And what about in Florence itself?'

'People come and go. You want Luca, he'll tell you.'

'And Luca is –'

She was interrupted at that moment by the middle-aged woman coming back in. 'Quick. Four of them. In the street heading this way.'

Antonio paled but seemed to know what to do. He and Stefano indicated Maxine should follow them to the back of the house and then out through an alley which opened into the street a few yards up from where the four German soldiers were now standing. Maxine went first and tried to look nonchalant as she sauntered up the street and away from them. At first, she thought she'd got away with it but then, unsettled by a weird mixture of caution in her bones and nervousness in her blood, she worried she had not. With a sharp intake of breath, she quickly turned to her right, hoping to double back on herself and walk in what she thought was the right direction for the river and away from the men.

She needed to make her way to the Ponte Vecchio and hoped to easily follow Sofia's directions to the house. But then her stomach tightened, even before she saw the four soldiers swaggering down the street and coming her way. They had simply gone the other way around and were now heading her off. One look at their arrogant stride and the rifles slung over their shoulders was all it took to realize she was about to become their prey. The tallest of them stared at her, unblinking, his icy-blue eyes expressionless.

'Papers,' he ordered and held out a gloved hand while one of the others lit a cigarette.

She clenched her jaw as she pulled out her false papers and handed them over. Would they pass muster this time? The minutes passed slowly, and her mouth became dry. She began to count in her head. It helped distract her from the fear. At any moment the man might suspect the papers were phoney and, if that happened, she'd need her wits about her.

The man continued to make a meal of it, sharing a joke in German with the other three, who clapped him on the back and guffawed. They gave her sideways looks, enjoying her discomfort, and the tall one raised his brows as he scrutinized her.

'What were you doing in Piazza d'Azeglio?' he asked. 'We have been keeping a watch there.'

'I was asking for directions.'

He tilted his head to one side. 'Where to?'

'My friend's house.'

'And where is that?'

'The Lungarno, further along from the Ponte Vecchio.'

He whistled. 'Fine friends you must have.'

They spoke in German for a few minutes, almost none of which she understood, and only after they had taunted her a little longer did they hand the papers back.

'You'll have to run if you want to make it.' He glanced at his wristwatch and tapped it. 'Curfew.'

'I'm not sure I fancy her chances,' one of the others said.

She ignored this, let out a long, slow breath and walked briskly on, aware they were still watching her.

The curfew had not yet begun, but the German and Fascist patrols were everywhere and she could now hear that the four soldiers were still following her. She darted down an alley hoping it might be a short cut in the right direction but, spying the men ahead of her now, backed out smartly, heart racing. How had they managed to do that? But there were so many interconnecting roads and alleys, anything was possible. *Get a grip*, she ordered herself. *Get a grip*. After that she had to retrace her steps, except now all the streets and alleys were looking alike. Bewildered, she swivelled round trying to decide which way to go and, at a complete loss, scratched the back of her neck as she deliberated. She glanced at her watch. Only five minutes until the curfew began.

With her back tight against cold stone walls, she slipped from one cobbled alley to another, glancing in at dimly lit, smoky bars where ruddy-faced German soldiers were drinking and clapping while pounding out the rhythm on the tables. She jumped when a dog began barking behind her. A patrol dog?

A woman shouted somewhere and jackboots pounded on the street. But where? She brushed up against a windowsill, trying to conceal herself, and accidentally set a pot of herbs clattering to the ground, their scent filling the air. She froze as a German voice shouted *Halt*, followed by another more insistent *Halt!* Surely not those four men again? She mouthed an obscenity and then, chancing her luck, ran fast as she headed for the river and whichever bridge she happened across. If the worst came to the worst, there would be hiding places beneath the bridges or even on the boats.

She knew her luck was in when she reached the Ponte Vecchio, but she could also see it was heavily guarded. She spotted the Uffizi extending out towards the river, flanked by arches and fancy columns. Instead of following the river she'd have to use the backstreets and locate the correct rear entrance, but still she made several wrong turns in this maze of a medieval city. Eventually, with relief flooding her body, she found the narrow alley where, at the end, she saw the tall iron gates Sofia had described.

She glanced up. In the gathering gloom, she fumbled about in a row of flowerpots resting against the wall and eventually winkled out the key. Sofia must have oiled the lock and the hinges because the key turned easily and she was able to slowly ease the gate open.

She reached the back of the enormous house, knocked and waited. Nobody answered. Something was rustling in the undergrowth and now she could see the moon through a break in the cloud. She was about to throw a stone at one of the windows when a shutter was opened above her and, with a huge rush of relief, she saw Sofia peering out.

A few moments later Sofia had opened the door, grabbed Maxine's arm and pulled her inside a gloomy vestibule.

Maxine exhaled noisily. 'Phew. I was beginning to think you'd never come.'

'Let's go through to the kitchen.'

Once inside the kitchen Maxine could see the lights had been kept low and the shutters were firmly bolted. Anna sat at the table, staring up at her with unfathomable eyes.

'So,' Anna said. 'You took your time.'

'I only got here today, but you'll want to hear what I have to say.'

'I can offer you an *aperitivo*,' Sofia said, fetching a bottle and a plate of tomato and garlic bruschetta.

Maxine remembered her mother fondly describing the tradition of being served an *aperitivo*. Not just a pre-dinner drink, as Maxine had imagined, but offered with tasty morsels. Maxine herself had been hungrily looking forward to trying bruschetta with a variety of toppings: slices of mortadella or prosciutto, maybe mozzarella, or tomato and basil. And yet she had only seen it on the tables frequented by Germans in the Caffè Paszkowski: or in other bright, shiny places.

She pulled out a chair and sat opposite Anna. Sofia, looking far too pale, was now standing with her back to the range. The kitchen wasn't warm.

Maxine went on to tell them about meeting Bruckner and how he'd given her a lift, and then she told them about her meeting with Antonio, Gerhard Wolf's clerk, and the partisan, Stefano.

Sofia nodded. 'I met with Gerhard Wolf myself. He didn't give much away. I got the feeling he would have liked to say more but could not.'

32

Sofia woke with her mouth watering, feeling disappointed the creamy fig and ricotta tart she could taste had been only a dream. She and her mother used to prepare it together. Her job had been to grind the almonds and make the pastry by adding the almonds to the flour, then together they'd create the filling by combining drained ricotta with eggs, honey, lemon zest and vanilla. Once they'd taken it out of the oven, they decorated it with quarters of sliced figs. Delicious.

She was sure these dreams of the past were her way of escaping the present and groaned at the icy cold as she swung her legs to the side and then slid out of bed. She dressed without washing, then braved the empty, echoing halls and corridors where the shutters were rattling in the wind. When she reached the kitchen, Anna was already stoking the range and the boiler. At least they had a supply of unused fuel here, although how long it would last or how long they'd need it to last was unknown. The uncertainty of everything left her feeling ill at ease, but for Anna's sake she rallied and gave her a smile.

'Did you sleep well, Anna?'

Anna pulled an exhausted face. 'Well, you know . . .'

'Yes.'

They drifted into silence as Anna brewed the coffee.

'Goodness,' Sofia said, suddenly realizing the coffee was real.

Delighted with herself, Anna pointed at a cupboard. 'I found it at the back of that cupboard, already ground and rock hard. Had to pound the life out of it.'

She poured them both a cup.

And even though Sofia could tell it had lost some of its

flavour, the taste still brought tears to her eyes. Memories. Always the memories of better times.

'I was dreaming of food again,' she said.

Anna's mouth turned down at the corners. 'It's because we're always hungry. I don't dream at all.'

'We all dream. It's the way we make sense of things. You just don't remember.'

Anna tilted her head to one side, thinking. 'I dream of my husband sometimes, or I used to.'

Sofia shot her a sympathetic look. 'It's been hard on you.'

'On so many,' Anna added.

They both stayed silent for a moment, contemplating.

'Maxine not up?' Sofia said eventually.

Anna shook her head.

But just a few minutes later Sofia heard Maxine as she came to the doorway and turned to look at her. Wrapped in a blanket, her curly chestnut hair tangled about her shoulders, she still looked beautiful.

'Darn this freezing mausoleum,' she said as she stalked in, sat at the table and reached out to pour herself some coffee. 'The real stuff, eh? What's to eat?'

Anna was slicing the last of two loaves they'd brought with them. Stale now, so she toasted the slices in the pan before bringing over salt and olive oil.

'What I wouldn't give for a cheesy bagel.' Maxine inhaled and then shrugged at the thought before stuffing bread into her mouth.

Sofia laughed. 'I've been dreaming of food too.'

'Chocolate brownies?'

'No. Fig and ricotta tart.'

'Oh, my goodness, my mother used to make that.'

'Tell us what you know about her village.'

A dreamy look softened Maxine's gaze. 'It's called Poggio Santa Cecilia, as you already know, and it's perched high up on a hill. Siena isn't far by car. The farmhouses are clustered outside the village – my parents had one with a rooftop pigeon loft. My mother loved it. There are olive groves, vineyards, agricultural lands, woodlands, plus two lakes on the estate where she told me she used to swim. I'm not sure it was allowed but she did it anyway.'

'It's a beautiful place,' Anna said. 'I went there once.'

Sofia watched as Maxine's eyes grew softer still. 'My mother says it's the most peaceful place in the world.'

Sofia nodded. 'She must have hated leaving.'

'She did.'

Maxine's face changed and Sofia felt she was pining for something she'd never had.

'And there are orchards, Mother said. Plums and apples too. The village is enclosed by the crumbling walls of an old castle.'

'I've sat on those walls,' Sofia said, 'and I know most of the buildings go back to the fifteenth century.'

'Estate workers live there as well as the aristocratic family who own the whole shebang.' Maxine's lip curled as she scoffed, then she reddened as she glanced at Sofia. 'No offence.'

'None taken,' Sofia said. 'By birth, I'm a commoner.' Then she reminded Maxine of her plan to visit the village.

'I still want to. Things keep getting in the way. And I hate to think of Germans living there. My mother would die if she knew. I wish my parents hadn't had to leave Tuscany.'

'I went to Santa Cecilia a number of times before the war,' said Sofia, 'parties, recitals, that sort of thing. The main villa has these lovely panelled ceilings and frescoes on the walls. There are huge fireplaces and a wide stone staircase up to the first floor where a salon leads to a glass-walled solarium overlooking the terraced gardens. Our place at the Castello is tiny by comparison. But Santa Cecilia is not what it used to be. The family who own it moved out. Only the grandmother has stayed on, a lovely old lady, but I heard she's now in a village house since the Germans requisitioned the manor.'

'It's a damn cheek, isn't it? Maybe I'll go when all this is over.'

'Mmm.'

'Would you consider coming with me?' Maxine added as an afterthought. 'If you know someone at the village, it could give us an excuse for visiting. We could go on my motorcycle.'

Sofia laughed but was aware of the vulnerability in Maxine's eyes. She didn't give a lot away but there was more to Maxine than you first realized. She'd seen it in the way she gazed at Marco too, and visiting her parents' village clearly mattered.

'Riding pillion on a motorcycle would certainly be a change,' Sofia said. 'Lorenzo rides but I never have. I'm sure I'd end up in a hedge.'

'You'll love it,' Maxine replied and smiled warmly.

Sofia was aware they were talking about the things that were guaranteed to make them feel happier. Sometimes they just had to.

'I heard firing in the night,' Maxine said suddenly. 'Did you?'

'Every night. Doesn't matter how often you hear it, it's always awful.'

Maxine turned to Anna. 'Could you contact some of the local *staffettas*? One of them should know where I can find a partisan called Luca.'

'Who is he?'

'I think he may be the new leader around here.'

33

February 1944

Although most of Maxine's hopes for information were now pinned on Wolf's clerk, Antonio, she knew she might still gain an advantage by knowing Bruckner. So, once the morning mist had cleared, she spent a few hours keeping an eye out for him, modestly dressed in an old brown coat, her scarf wrapped round the lower part of her face and a woollen hat pulled low, plus a pair of wire-rimmed spectacles. The last thing she wanted was to attract attention.

The shops were almost empty and Maxine saw why when she spotted German lorries picking up merchandise from every single one. She trusted the shopkeepers had been canny enough to hide some of their goods. She sauntered up the Viale Michelangelo and was impressed by the Piazza Signoria with its famous tower and loggia. While doing all this, she spied out the bars Marco had listed and kept her eyes peeled for Bruckner, ensuring he didn't spot her until she was ready.

While she paced, she contemplated the British officer with whom she liaised. Ronald was quite a posh chap, but she knew nothing else about him. He had been helpful and kind but always distant. Perhaps it was the British stiff upper lip. She didn't know. In any case, the more the Allies knew about the area, and whom they could or could not trust, the easier it would be when they pushed northwards and drove the Germans back, especially if the partisans were well armed. Later in the day she intended to make contact with Luca.

She spotted Bruckner eating early with another officer, so she skulked in the shadows and waited, ready to cast off her coat, scarf and hat to reveal a red silk dress when she intercepted him.

A few moments later she almost missed him when, with long, purposeful strides, he vacated the restaurant with the other man, whom Maxine now recognized as Baltasar Vogler. She followed them and, with no time to cast off her outer clothing, she watched from the other side of the square as the two men made their way towards the Excelsior hotel. Vogler went in first and then, a second or two later, Bruckner entered. At the exact same moment two men in dark clothing came racing past and sent her flying. In the seconds during which she restored her balance a tremendous noise rocked the piazza. Despite standing on the opposite side of the square, the full force of the blast slammed into her. Blinded by the dust, her eyes were stinging and, aware of shrapnel striking masonry and glass, she sank down and covered her head with her arms. When the noise subsided a little, she wiped her eyes with her sleeve, but it was impossible to see anything through the clouds of dust and smoke ballooning in front of her. Men shouted and women screamed but she couldn't tell from where. She scrambled to her feet, wanting to get away quickly, but was hampered by the rubble, brick, mortar and glass strewn all over the ground, and stumbled. Now little fires dotted the piazza too and gradually, despite the smoke, she was able to see flames surging from the windows of the hotel. Had the bomb been planted there? Or had it been thrown in? She remembered the two men she'd seen running away and then gave a fleeting thought to Gustav Bruckner. If her one good German connection had been killed, it was even more urgent she find Luca quickly. Luca and Antonio were all she had.

34

A few moments earlier Sofia had just settled into the cosy salon overlooking the river when she was startled by a loud blast. She put down her book, rose to her feet and rushed to the hall window from where she saw a pall of smoke rising over an area of the city.

When, fifteen minutes later, Maxine burst in, her face raw with cold, Sofia stared in astonishment. Like a living phantom, Maxine was coated in fine grey dust: on her face, in her hair, all over her clothes. And, to top it all, she was shivering uncontrollably. As she attempted to speak, her red-rimmed eyes scanned the room, glittering as if in shock. Sofia offered to make her a hot drink, but she could hardly catch her breath and, still unable to say anything, doubled up as if in physical pain.

As soon as Maxine straightened up, Sofia wrapped her arms round her shoulders, pulling her close. As Maxine gradually settled and her breathing calmed, Sofia drew back and studied her face. 'I heard the blast. What happened?'

Maxine squeezed her eyes shut for a second and, when she opened them, Sofia noticed how hollow they looked.

'Can you tell me?'

'A bomb . . .' Her voice came out rasping and unclear.

'Where? I didn't hear any planes.'

She took a long, deep breath and exhaled slowly.

'It's all right. Take your time.'

'Not the Allies. Near the Excelsior hotel. I was watching Bruckner walking in through the main doors and the next second – *boom* . . .'

'Is he dead?'

'I don't know. Probably. I had to run. I don't know why I'm so shaken really. I'm not usually so pathetic.'

'Don't be silly. You're the least pathetic person I know. It was unexpected. That's all. You've had a shock.'

'I thought I was shockproof,' she said with a wry smile.

Sofia shook her head. 'None of us are.'

'They'll extend the curfew,' Anna muttered as she entered the room, still wearing her coat and looking weary. '*Per Dio*, these hotheads make it impossible for the rest of us.'

Maxine spun round to look at her. 'Did you see it?'

Anna threw herself into a chair, then glanced at Sofia as if for consent to sit down.

Sofia smiled at her. 'Come on. I think we're past these old differences, aren't we? It's fine. Make yourself comfortable.'

'*Madonna*,' Anna said, looking across at Maxine who was now standing with her back to one of the two shuttered windows. 'Look at the state of you! No, I didn't see it, but I heard it.'

'Thank God you're both safe,' Sofia said, 'although you need to get cleaned up, Maxine. Did anyone see you near the hotel?'

Maxine shook her head. 'No one would have noticed me. I was wearing that old overcoat with a hat and scarf.'

Anna indicated that no one had seen her either. 'I came back the long way round, but there were quite a few people out on the streets. They can't arrest all of us.'

'Can't they?' Maxine said bitterly.

Anna looked at the other two gloomily. 'There'll be reprisals.'

The very real possibility of that made Sofia feel physically sick.

Maxine looked glum. 'I'll have to find out if Bruckner is dead.'

Early the next morning Sofia was pacing the garden, restless and edgy, waiting to hear news of what was going on in the city following the bomb blast. They had no radio so Anna had gone out to see what she could learn.

When she heard the back gate open and saw Anna entering

the garden, it was obvious from her drawn, anxious face the news wasn't good. When she spoke, she was breathless, almost panting, and the words came out in a rapid stream.

'I came back as quickly as I could. Throughout the night the Germans have been rounding up anyone known to be even remotely sympathetic to the partisans. Plus anyone who doesn't actively support the German Reich.'

'So now only the Fascists are safe.'

'Exactly.'

'What have we come to . . .' Sofia didn't finish her sentence. 'Did you meet anyone?'

'Since the bomb blast many of the men have gone, in prison or headed for the hills. There is a woman, though – Irma, she's called.'

'A *staffetta* like you?'

'Yes. She says she'll meet with Maxine at three today in Via Faenza. Introduce her to Luca, their unit leader.'

'And the bomb?'

'They're saying a bomb was thrown into the hotel,' she said. 'I wish we could go home now. It's terrible out there. People are starving, fighting over scraps of food thrown away by the restaurants. Getting themselves shot for trying to smuggle out food for their families.'

Home. Sofia felt low as she thought of the Castello and longed to be there too.

'I need to tell Maxine about Irma,' Anna added.

They remained silent for a few minutes.

'Tell me something good,' Sofia said eventually. 'Tell me something to make up for all this.'

Anna stared back with a hopeless expression.

'Anything? Something?'

Anna rubbed her neck as she considered it. 'My little boy, Alberto. He's good.'

'I agree,' Sofia said. 'He's a sweetie.' And then her mind went wandering over the sunlit days of the past, Lorenzo kissing her forehead for the first time and in full view of her parents. Her father's raised eyebrows, her mother's gentle smile. And then, once they were engaged, off they went exploring the walled hill-top villages and towns of Tuscany.

'It's why we're doing all this, isn't it?' Anna was saying, and Sofia came back to the present with a jolt. 'To get our country back and for all our children to grow up in peace.'

'It will happen,' Sofia said. 'The Allies *will* win. We have to keep believing.'

35

It was barely light when Anna answered the door to a thin-faced Italian woman who glanced furtively to either side and then behind her.

'Yes?' Anna said.

The woman spoke rapidly and in a low, urgent voice. 'Tell Massima, Antonio will be waiting for her at 12 Piazza d'Azeglio. Ten o'clock sharp. Do not be late.'

Anna started to thank her, but the woman scurried away before she'd finished her sentence. She went upstairs, woke Maxine, passed on the message, and then went down to prepare breakfast with Maxine trailing behind in her robe.

'Was that all she said? Did she tell you her name?'

Anna shook her head.

'Do you think she might be working for the Germans? One of them told me they'd been watching the square.'

'I believed her,' Anna said. 'What more can I say?'

'What did she look like?'

'Middle-aged. Very black hair and a prominent nose.'

'A hook nose, would you say?'

Anna nodded. 'At least you'll have plenty of time before you meet Irma in Via Faenza at three.'

Maxine was eager to hear Antonio's news but first she was curious to see the aftermath of the bomb attack at the hotel. She had tied up her hair, hidden now beneath the kind of plain headscarf so many of the women wore. She had put on a drab grey coat and had applied none of her trademark red lipstick.

When she reached the Excelsior, she saw several workmen

were already repairing the damage. She loitered for a moment to give the impression that she was just a nosy Italian housewife, then she approached a bullish-looking Italian man who was strutting about giving orders to the other workmen. She sidled up then paused beside him, hands on hips.

'Well!' she exclaimed, puffing out her cheeks. 'My husband, Tomasso, said it was a right old mess. He wasn't wrong, was he? How long will it take to put right?'

The man shrugged. 'Too long.'

'Anyone killed?' she asked.

'What's it to you?'

'I don't live far. I heard the blast. Everyone in the street heard. Tomasso said someone must have been killed. I thought it might have been gas, but Tomasso bet me it was a bomb.'

'And now you've come to gawk?'

She frowned, arms folded in front of her, as if taking umbrage. 'No-o-o. I'm on my way to see a friend. I was just passing.'

'Just passing, eh? Well, for your information, an influential SS officer was indeed killed here, name of Bruckner. That's what we heard, anyway. They don't tell us much, to be honest.'

He turned away to shout at one of his workmen and Maxine took the chance to slip away. If Bruckner would no longer be the one deciding where the arsenal was destined to be housed, who would? His death left her feeling a bit blue, with a sudden longing to taste, feel and touch the old familiar things of home. She loved the bustle of New York, the delicious cheesecake, the trams, the steam rising from the subway. Most of all she missed sitting out on the front step watching the world go by in the clammy heat of summer. And, of course, there were no Nazis and no war. But New York seemed so distant and, for all that Maxine missed it, it might just as well have been at the ends of the earth.

Had she been insane to come to Italy, lured by what she'd stupidly imagined was excitement? Could she really have been so shallow? Not surprisingly, it had never been that simple, and now, beginning to understand herself a little better, she was becoming aware of how hurt she had been all those years ago. She had adored her father, and his violence towards her mother was the pain she never spoke of. In fact, she had done everything she could to suppress it. But it had certainly shaped her decision to never let anything like it happen to her. Instead, she'd striven to be fearless and courageous, and yet there were still times when she did not feel either of those things. Perhaps that was normal.

And what with Bruckner's death and now her clandestine meeting with Antonio ahead, she began to imagine that every passing stranger might pose a threat. She shook herself out of it by forcing herself to look at people, really look at them, and as she did their dull eyes revealed only their instinctive fight to remain invisible. These people were not a threat, they never could be – they were hungry and without hope, and she pitied them.

At five past ten she arrived in Piazza d'Azeglio where she walked up and down, then along the pathways of the garden and round the perimeter of the square. After a few moments, she slipped into a side alley to keep a lookout but could see no obvious signs of German surveillance, at least not from the street. Of course, she had no idea whether they might be watching from one of the high windows opposite. Eventually she knocked at the same house as before and the same woman opened up.

'You're late,' she said.

'Sorry. It was further than I remembered. Is Antonio here?'

The woman nodded and took her through the house and into a garden. She then pushed open the back door of a house adjoining the garden. They entered and she pointed at a door on the left. 'He's in there. When you leave, don't come back to Piazza d'Azeglio. Go out through the front door of this house and leave by Via della Colonna.'

Maxine opened the door on the left and found Antonio standing there, staring out of the window.

'I have to be quick,' he said, his voice tense. 'Three partisans were discovered hiding in one of the houses in the piazza at dawn today. They were all shot.'

'By Germans?'

'No. The Italian Fascists. But we expect the Germans will search all the houses in the square now. They were annoyed the partisans were not taken to the Villa Triste to be questioned before being shot.'

'So, what is it you have to tell me?'

'Kesselring came to meet with Wolf. He had another man with him whose name was Vogel or Volker, something like that.'

'Vogler?'

'Yes. That was it. I didn't hear everything, but Wolf became very angry. It was unlike him to raise his voice, but it did help me. He, and I think it must have been Kesselring, were arguing about the storage of armaments in Renaissance palazzos. Kesselring insisted they had to be in the heart of the city, where they'd be impossible to raid, whereas Wolf wanted them in the outskirts.'

'So?'

'So, they reached a compromise,' and here he gave her the first smile she'd seen. 'The old Carabinieri barracks, near the train station! That's what swung it. The crates will come in by train in forty-eight hours' time and then trucks will take them just a short easy distance to the barracks.'

'And the Carabinieri themselves?'

'You may know that as a military police force under Mussolini, they were entrusted with suppressing opposition, except that once the armistice was signed, the Nazis disbanded most units.'

'Ah.'

'Some of the southern Carabinieri joined the resistance, while in the north they remained predominantly Fascist. The Germans disarmed most but for the few they still use for security and guard duty. Luca used to be part of the Carabinieri, and he knows the barracks inside out.'

'I'm meeting up with him today, I hope. Do we know the extent of the goods coming in?'

'No. And neither do we know who will be guarding the barracks. Tell Luca everything I've told you.'

As it approached three in the afternoon, Maxine headed over to Via Faenza in the pouring rain. It was a narrow street in the station area, where she was to meet up with Irma, the *staffetta* with whom Anna had already made contact. Once there, she whispered the password Marco had given her and Irma silently scrutinized her. She was small with a steely, determined look in her greenish-grey eyes. After a few moments she beckoned Maxine to follow her up the stairs.

At the top Maxine looked around at the bare room, wondering why two wooden chairs were sitting in the middle. She held out her arms, dripping water on to the floorboards. 'I'm soaked.'

'I can see that.'

'Is this your house?'

The woman pursed her lips and gave Maxine a long, cold stare. 'Why would you ask that?'

'Sorry. I didn't mean –'

'Who are you?' Irma asked, sounding hostile, and Maxine wouldn't have been surprised if there was no one she trusted.

'I'm Massima.'

'Not your real name?'

'No.'

Irma nodded. 'Good. So . . . tell me why you are here.'

'I'm here to see Luca.'

'Look, people come and go. This is a safe house. I don't know who owns it. Houses are abandoned all over the city. As for Luca, he comes and goes too. We are GAP . . . you know it?'

'Of course. *Gruppi di Azione Patriottica.*'

'Well, since the bomb, the hotel bomb that is, many of the

men have scattered.' Her brow furrowed and Maxine could see the distress in this brittle woman's eyes.

'I'm sorry.'

'Or they have been arrested. We move around. People go missing. Dead or alive, nobody knows. You wait, you hope. *Merda*, you don't know if your husband or brother has been tortured, shot or taken to their labour camps.'

Maxine lowered her eyes in sympathy. 'The men in hiding, they'll be back?'

'Of course.'

'Did you lose somebody?' Maxine asked hesitantly.

Irma laughed bitterly. 'Lose? Oh yes. My husband was lost all right. Blinded and thrown out into the street like a dog. Crawled home by touch alone.'

'He's still alive?'

'No. He asked for his gun and then shot himself right in front of me.'

Maxine gazed at the floor. 'I'm so sorry.'

Irma looked up at the ceiling and then at Maxine, narrowing her eyes. 'Have you ever killed anyone?'

Maxine shook her head.

'They say it's hard for women. Because we are the ones who look after the babies, they think we cannot kill so easily. What do you think?'

'I think a woman is capable of anything a man can do and more.'

At that point the door opened and a small wiry man with very dark eyebrows and alarming black eyes stalked in. He and Irma exchanged glances then he sat on one of the chairs, staring at Maxine. 'So?'

Maxine began to speak. 'I was expecting to meet with Ballerini but I've only recently found out he's dead and that you are now the person to see.'

'Continue,' he said, his face grim.

She went on to explain that she was working with the British and that her task had been to identify the extent of the resistance in the area, particularly how much they would be able to help in the liberation of Florence.

'And that's it?'

'No. I have been instructed to identify where, when and how we can work together to relieve the Nazis of their store of armaments.'

Then she went on to tell him everything Antonio had said.

He whistled and finally his eyes lit up. 'So, we have work to do.'

'Can *you* arm enough men for a raid?'

'Most of the men are in the hills and mountains now, but we can get enough back in through the sewer system.'

'Jesus, really?'

He shrugged and sniffed. 'The other problem will be vehicles. We'll have to take the stuff out of the city. I can get my hands on one, or possibly two, Fiat 262 trucks and the petrol we'll need, and I can probably arm a unit of about eight men.'

'Will it be enough?'

He shrugged. 'How many of you are there?'

'Three.'

'Good men?'

'Women.'

He raised his brows. 'We'll increase our watch at the station and at the Carabinieri barracks and wait for a couple of days after the goods have arrived. Then we'll strike. A *staffetta* will let you know when we need you. I will keep the plan simple and use you three women as lookouts.'

Maxine entered Sofia's house by the back gates and found the door to the house unlocked. Upstairs, she discovered Sofia and Anna twiddling the knobs of a radio.

'Are you insane?' she chided. 'The back door wasn't locked. Anyone could have come in and found you like this.'

Sofia jumped up as if she'd been scalded. 'Sorry. My fault.'

Maxine pulled a face. 'I thought you didn't have a radio here.'

'Me too, but I got fed up waiting with nothing to do, so went up into one of the attics with Anna and found it.'

'Clever you.'

'I want to see if we can receive the Allied radio broadcasts at nine. I'm hoping they might send a coded message for the resistance that you may understand.'

'We also found piles of old clothes,' Anna added. 'Coats, jackets, all sorts of things. Some might prove useful. Anyway, what's your news? Did you find out about Bruckner?'

'He's dead. But I have made progress. Antonio knows where the armaments are going to be stored and the leader of the partisan unit wants our help as lookouts during the raid. Are you both willing?'

Maxine watched as Sofia went over to the window and pressed her cheek against the glass. She stood for a few moments shivering and Maxine could see the anxiety in her eyes. Then she left the window and came back to them.

'I will need to think about it,' Sofia said. 'Now, though, we need to warm up. Anna, please will you build a good strong fire?'

'Brilliant idea,' Maxine said. She groaned and took off her coat. 'With all this filthy rain, I'm soaked through.'

'The problem is,' Sofia said, rubbing her eyes, 'we've forgotten how to be happy.'

Anna gave her a grim smile. 'Hardly surprising.'

But Maxine had livened up and fixed her eyes on Sofia. 'Do we have wine?'

'We do.'

'Hurrah to vino!' she said. 'I propose we forget about everything for one evening. Absolutely everything. I feel like getting roaring drunk.'

36

The evening had passed in a blur of restrained laughter and nostalgic reminiscence and gradually the feeling of anxiety had given way. In the morning Sofia watched the red sun rising above the hills and then Lorenzo phoned to check that she was keeping safe. She'd been longing to hear his voice but obviously couldn't talk about their plans or about anything of significance on the telephone. She kept her voice light enough to convince him not to worry too much. He, in turn, told her he was fine but not to be concerned if she couldn't make contact for a while as the phone lines were frequently down in Rome. She didn't ask what he was doing. Knew he couldn't, or wouldn't, say. When she asked about her parents, he told her they were safe and choosing to stay in Rome. After she put the phone down, she hugged herself and took several deep breaths, whispering, 'I love you. I love you. I love you.' Lorenzo would be all right. He was careful.

Now she needed time to think so she took an early-morning walk through a glittering and silvery Florence. The sky was blue and the sunshine was spilling into all the city's nooks and crannies. If you hadn't known any better, you'd have thought it was a normal day, and not the day after a suggestion you might have to play a part in an extremely dangerous raid. She thought back to Aldo's death and remembered how much she'd wanted to kill Kaufmann as he'd stared down at her so coldly. But could she really have done it? And if she were to do it, would he be another casualty of war or, if she was honest, would his death really be the result of vengeance? The taking of a single life, even amid the death and devastation they saw daily, was so appalling she couldn't begin to comprehend it. Once, she would have sworn she could tell right from wrong – now the boundaries between good and evil had become so blurred.

Despite the sunshine, the city smelt damp. In the huge Piazza della Repubblica, the nineteenth-century square built on the site of the Roman forum and subsequently its old, long-since-demolished ghetto, she had the distinct feeling she was being watched, but put it down to her imagination getting the upper hand. She recalled the times Lorenzo and she had wandered there, eaten *tagliatelle al tartufo* at one of the restaurants or delicious pastries in their favourite café, the Caffè Giubbe Rosse, named after the red jackets worn by the waiters. In wet weather they'd retreat inside its smoky wood-panelled rooms and stay for hours, putting the world to rights as they sipped their coffee. And when it was fine, they'd relax outside at a pretty table with a red-and-white tablecloth in the shade of a large awning and laugh and talk and watch the people passing by.

They could never have imagined what she could see today. No market, and the only vehicles German lorries and military cars.

She decided to walk to the Ponte Vecchio, cross the river there and make her way to San Niccolò and the Giardino Bardini with its grottoes, orangery, marble statues and fountains. It wasn't open to the public, but Lorenzo knew the owner and they used to have permission to take the steps climbing up to the seventeenth-century Villa Bardini from where you could gaze down at the city. They used to come in April and May, when the azaleas, peonies and wisteria would be in bloom. Today, hoping it would be quiet, she just wanted the exercise of climbing the hill and a restorative half-hour in the garden.

When she arrived at the top, extremely out of breath from the steep climb, she sat on one of the steps, closed her eyes and lifted her face to the sun, comforted by the peace and safety of nature.

Absorbed in herself, she was only vaguely aware of some-one speaking. When the voice was followed by a cough and the mention of her name, she was jolted out of her reverie. She recognized the voice. The wind whipped around her and she suddenly felt so alone she wanted to weep. She looked up, shading her eyes from the sun, trying to disguise her anxiety at seeing him.

'I thought it was you,' he said stiffly. 'You are very far from the Castello.'

'Good morning, Captain Kaufmann.'

He glanced around at the garden before meeting her eyes. '*Major* Kaufmann now. It is pleasing here, no? On such a lovely day.'

She was taken aback at these superficial pleasantries, unsure how to respond, and she wondered if he had been following her.

He smiled that same smile, the twisted one that never reached his eyes. 'We are using the villa here,' he said, pointing vaguely to the area beyond the top of the steps. 'May I join you?'

Without waiting for a reply, he sat next to her. She wanted to tell him, *No, I do not want you to ruin my peace, not now, not ever*, but she couldn't.

'Are you going back to Siena or Buonconvento? To rejoin the Commandant, I mean?'

'Most probably . . .' He shrugged but made no further comment about Schmidt. 'I find I like Florence.'

'Surely you're not here to sightsee?'

His mirthless laugh unsettled her.

'We are making plans, holding meetings . . . deciding on the future of Italy.' He laughed again, his voice icy with contempt as he continued. 'And the rest of Europe, of course.'

She drew in her breath but did not retaliate.

'Now that I have you,' he said, looking over her shoulder and then back to stare right into her eyes with unmistakable disdain, 'I trust you'll permit me to call on you at your palazzo.'

She blinked rapidly under his scrutiny, knowing full well he didn't need her permission. 'You know where it is?'

He inclined his head. 'There is very little we do not know, if you understand me.'

She ignored this last comment. 'When would you like to come?'

'I'll drop by when I have the chance. I hear your husband keeps an especially fine cellar.' He paused before changing the subject. 'Does he own any other Cozzarelli paintings? I think I may have mentioned I'm a collector. I like to surround myself with only the very best.'

'My husband doesn't have others, at least not any I'm aware of.'

'He painted on wooden panels, you know, Cozzarelli.' Kaufmann rose to his feet. 'Quite wonderful. And he painted the altar piece at Montepulciano . . . Have you seen it?'

'Certainly.'

He flicked off the few leaves that had adhered to his uniform. 'Well, it has been most enjoyable, but now I must take my leave.'

After he'd gone, she sat a little longer, feeling the light draining from her day. The last thing any of them needed was the Major sniffing around at the palazzo.

When Sofia arrived back, the aroma of real coffee greeted her. Again? As she made for the stairs to the kitchen she wondered how much Anna had discovered squirrelled away at the back of the cupboard. In the kitchen she found Maxine and Anna deeply engrossed in discussing the proposed raid on the Carabinieri barracks.

'Before you go any further –' Sofia said, and told them about seeing the Major and his intention to visit her.

'Oh hell!' Maxine exclaimed and ran her fingers through her curls. 'Let's hope this is all done and dusted before then.'

37

Sofia could neither eat nor sleep and, now that the night of the raid had arrived, she longed for it to be over so much she could barely breathe. Maxine had been briefed the day before and now Luca's men were in place, hidden in buildings around the barracks on Via Fume and in the Valfonda gardens. Very few men were staying in the Carabinieri barracks these days as most had already absconded or been disarmed. The few who remained had been coerced into guarding the usual foodstuffs stored there and, as far as any of them knew, that was all there was. But now a new consignment had arrived and not of flour or beans. Two armed Carabinieri patrolled the perimeter, remaining outside for approximately an hour each time, one at the front, the other at the back of the long complex, then one at a time they went inside for fifteen minutes, so there would always be one of them outside. While these two were outside together, the plan was that Luca's partisans would get inside during the brief blind spot at the side of the building between the two patrolling men at the front and back. Once inside they would knock out the interior guards, bind them, blindfold them and gag them. They couldn't shoot the two men on the outside, nor could they remove them, because any passing German patrol might hear the noise or spot their absence. Plus, they had all been warned not to shoot unless Allied bombing was loud enough to disguise the sound. A few days earlier, Luca had captured the brother of one of the Carabinieri whose job it was to guard the inside and was trading the brother's life in exchange for the side door to be left locked, but unbolted. The lock wouldn't be hard to break. Afterwards, the Carabinieri guard and his brother would be given safe passage to the mountains.

At one in the morning, Sofia, Maxine and Anna left the palazzo and individually made their way to the Santa Maria Novella neighbourhood near the station. Sofia was carrying her pistol while Anna and Maxine both had knives. With an old scarf from the attic wrapped round to mask her face and her hat pulled low, Sofia waited at one end of a grim alley. It split off from a narrow street close to the train station and smelt of rotting vegetables and animal excrement. Anna, dressed like a man, waited at the other end. The waiting went on forever. Time stopped and, in the stillness of that horrible alley, Sofia listened to the sounds of the city and the hills all around them, just a low rumble at this time, but distinguishable all the same. She pictured everyone in the dark buildings, sleeping or trying to. And there was a part of her longing to call a halt to this. But then, after a few moments, Maxine and Irma arrived, dressed as prostitutes might, and it was already unstoppable.

Maxine and Anna walked together, sauntering casually, keeping to the darkest places. There were no street lights and no moon, but their job was to watch for anything unusual. Sofia remained in the alley as much out of sight as possible, but with a good view of the side door of the barracks. Luca was watching for the exact moment that the men could not be seen by either guard. Then he signalled, and he and five partisans dressed in dark clothing crept rapidly along Sofia's alley to the side entrance. They didn't have any trouble breaking the lock and, once they were in, Irma slipped in too. She was to wait just inside the door. If anything alarming was spotted, Maxine, Anna or Sofia would enter the building by the side door and warn Irma. She would then alert the men.

As a vehicle slid down the street at the end of Sofia's alley, she saw the dark figure of the driver accompanied by another man. She glanced around the corner after the car had passed to her right. She recognized the car; not an ordinary patrol car but the same type Lorenzo drove. Lorenzo's was an older model, but this was one of the new Lancia Artenas, built at the request of the Italian army to chauffeur officers around. She watched as it pulled up and a man carrying a briefcase climbed out. She held her breath, unsure what to do, attempting to mentally rehearse the instructions she'd been given. While the man went into a house, she waited. A few moments later he came out without the briefcase, signalled to the driver to open the car window and leant in to speak. Then he got into the back and the car slowly moved off. She breathed a sigh of relief and, at the same moment, heard the first bomb fall in the direction of Fiesole.

The time was passing incredibly slowly, and Sofia had no idea how things were going inside the barracks. Apart from that one passing Lancia, she had seen nothing. Eventually she could just make out a Fiat truck heading her way from the direction of Via Bernardo Cennini. It pulled up right outside the side entrance, three men got out and successfully jumped the guards, first one then the other, daring to shoot as the noise was now masked by close Allied bombing. They dragged the bodies inside then began bringing out crates and loading them into the truck. Just as they finished, Irma came out and climbed into the truck with another man and the driver. Luca and the rest of the men slipped away.

It was just as well that Luca had only managed to get hold of one truck because soon after it pulled away, the Lancia reappeared and skidded to a halt. Had there been another truck being loaded up they'd have been caught. The Lancia stopped at the precise moment Maxine was coming round the side of the building and a German officer in uniform was already getting out of the car. He drew his revolver and beckoned her to approach him. Sofia's pulse was going so fast she thought she was going to vomit as she saw it was too late for Maxine to run. The driver remained in the car with the window wound down. The officer had his back to the car and didn't see Luca appear from a side alley and put a gun to the driver's head. From the corner of her eye Sofia saw Anna creep towards Maxine and the German officer, then draw back into the shadow of a recessed doorway close by. To keep an eye on Maxine, Sofia thought.

'Did you hear a vehicle?' Sofia heard the officer ask Maxine.

'Yes, yours.'

'Not my car, idiot. Sounded like a truck.'

She shook her head.

'Hold on, don't I know you?'

She nodded and held out a cigarette case.

'Massima, right?' he said. 'What are you doing out so late?'

Then everything happened so fast Sofia could hardly believe it. The man declined her offered cigarette and put his revolver back in its holster while he dug in his pocket to take out one of his own cigarettes. Probably the Turkish type that some of them smoked, Sofia thought. He put it in his mouth and bent his head as she offered him a light.

'Must be out of fuel,' Maxine said, giggling flirtatiously as she looked up. 'Sorry. Anyway, I have matches.'

Maxine took a box of matches from her bag, struck one and, when he bent his head again, lit his cigarette.

At that moment Sofia spotted the driver of the car lunge forward, slamming the car horn as he did, the sound blasting out just before Luca shot him dead. The officer reacted swiftly, looking up and round, then back again, his eyes wide. And in the sudden realization that Maxine was somehow involved in this, he grabbed her arm.

'What the hell?' He spat out the words.

With his other hand he withdrew his revolver and held it point-blank at her chest. 'You will pay for this,' he growled.

Then he half twisted them both to glance back at the car, while still maintaining his grip on her arm and the gun to her chest. With his eyes fixed on the slumped body of his driver, he failed to spot Anna, who had silently leapt out at lightning speed and was now right behind him.

She withdrew her knife from her pocket, grabbed his hair, pulled his head back and then slit his throat from side to side with enough strength to sever a major artery and his windpipe. In that split second of shock, Maxine managed to knock his revolver to the ground. As the blood gushed out, Maxine shied away from the man. The blood pumped and pumped in a wide arc on to the wall and on to the cobblestones. He made a terrible gurgling sound and, finally, slumped to the ground, senseless.

In her rising panic, Sofia hesitated, almost paralysed, and tried to will herself to be calm. It didn't work but she recovered enough to take off her coat and run to Maxine, who was now soaked in blood. There was very little light, but they could see enough to stare at each other, wide-eyed in terror, and then at the dark stain of blood pooling in a dip in the street.

'Thank you, Anna,' Maxine whispered, then squatted beside the man. 'I do know him,' she whispered. 'Vogler. That's who he is.'

'Is he dead yet?' Anna asked.

'Almost. He's bleeding out. Jesus, the smell!'

Sofia watched the gruesome sight of the blood still seeping from the ragged fleshy cut in his neck, then she threw the coat at Maxine. 'Quick. Put this on. It will cover the blood on your clothes.'

'Hurry. We need to get out of here, and fast,' Anna hissed. 'I'll go with Sofia. Maxine, you go the longer way round.'

As they left, Sofia was trembling uncontrollably from the shock, but Anna was unnaturally calm. When they reached the Ponte Vecchio, Sofia's voice quivered as she whispered, 'Have you done that before?'

'Only to a pig.' Anna gave a bitter laugh. 'It wasn't very different.'

'You need to wipe your shoes. They're covered in blood.'

'There's blood all over me. Lucky it's dark.'

Sofia's breath caught in her throat and her mouth tasted sour; even though she hadn't had to pull the trigger or use a knife, she had witnessed the killing of a man. A German man, but still a man, and she had no idea how to process it.

'Don't think,' Anna said as if she could tell what Sofia was feeling. 'Don't go over it in your head. We need to get back without being caught, burn the clothes and get clean. That's it. Plenty of time to think tomorrow. Tonight, we sleep.'

As Sofia's terror gave way to common sense and self-preservation, she didn't say that she couldn't imagine ever being able to sleep again.

38.

After the murder of Vogler and his driver, and the raid on the barracks, there were roadblocks and multiple checkpoints everywhere. Cornered like animals, the three women had to wait it out. The rumour was that a mountain of machine guns, mortars, pistols and ammunition had been stolen and the Germans were furious. Nobody could leave the city and armed police patrolled the streets and stations day and night. It was twenty-four hours since Anna had killed Vogler, and although Sofia was sure she had most likely saved Maxine's life by doing so, she felt sick about the whole thing. She walked the corridors and wandered the empty rooms, trying to find a place in this huge house where she could feel safe. Even as she escaped to her bedroom and slammed the door, fear snapped at her heels and she failed to shut it out.

She longed to leave Florence, the city she had once loved above all others, and she lay wide awake in the dark hour before dawn, shaking with misery. What they had done was incomprehensible. Could it have really happened? Or was she caught in an endless nightmare from which she could not awaken? Things were moving too fast. *Hold on*, she wanted to say. Couldn't they simply go back and think? When she did get up, the ache in her bones deepened by the hour. Haunted by the killing, she prowled the silent house and longed for Lorenzo to keep her rooted in the life they used to have. But even he could not make this right and she felt unnerving changes moving within her.

Was it ever acceptable to kill, she found herself wondering again. She heard people say that after you'd killed once the second time would be easier, but she had to hope she would never witness such a thing again. Anna didn't have any such qualms. To her he was a German and it was because of the Germans she had lost a beloved husband and a brother too. To her, there was no point brooding. No, they had to get on with living as normally as possible, especially if Major Kaufmann came calling as he had suggested he might. How would Sofia manage to conceal her guilt if she couldn't make a show of appearing to be her normal self? She slipped out to the garden, hoping for solace, but it was no longer the birds she heard, it was the sound of boots thumping on cobbles and Germans shouting, bullying, ordering, laughing. In her mind's eye she saw their boorish faces, imagined their cruel objectives, and trembled. But she knew she had to let these dark thoughts go.

As she returned to the kitchen, Anna narrowed her eyes. 'Contessa, you have to eat. You are too thin. You will make yourself ill and, if they come, they will see something is wrong. Please. It will do you good.'

'What's the point of it all?'

'The point is, do you want to speak German for the rest of your life? And instead of *spaghetti al pomodoro* do you want to eat frankfurters and sauerkraut?'

Sofia snorted in derision.

'I thought not,' Anna said with a wan smile.

'So, we're fighting over what food we'll eat.'

'Exactly.' Anna put a bowl of broth on the table and pulled out a chair.

'Maxine up?'

'Not yet.'

'I don't know how she can sleep so long.'

Sofia sat and forced the food down. Anna was right in a way. It *was* about preserving their culture, but it was more than that. No human wanted to be controlled by another and no country did either.

Afterwards, she went back up to her room and pressed her

cheek against the cold glass of the window where she could look out over the river Arno at the southern parts of the city. She thought of the Piazza Santo Spirito and the Basilica di Santo Spirito where Lorenzo and she would go on Sundays to sit on the steps and watch the world go by. The little square with its trees and tranquillity was one of her favourites. But then her attention was attracted by a commotion in the street below where German soldiers were dragging a young man over to one of their vehicles. *Take me*, she wanted to shout, as if that would mitigate the overwhelming feeling of guilt.

She wanted to hate the Germans, all the Germans, and she did hate Kaufmann. But Vogler? She hadn't even known him and yet he was dead. The worst thing, however, was that she had no pity left. She knew there were good, kind Germans like Wolf, who'd never wanted the war, who'd emphatically never wanted Hitler. Many Italians hadn't wanted Mussolini either and so many families on both sides only wanted to get on with living their lives. But war was making monsters of them all.

39

There was no battering down of doors, no yelling as Sofia made her way down the stairs. Anna remained upstairs tidying up the floor beneath the attic area and replacing the ladder in its cupboard. She had only just finished hiding the radio and the pistol for the umpteenth time, each time worrying it might too easily be found. Even if soldiers were to go up to the attic there was too much junk for them to find anything: boxes of clothes, curtains, bedding, crates of old toys, rocking horses, doll's houses, unwanted paintings, pottery, ornaments, kitchen and dining-room chairs, old tables and other furniture, even some cast-iron bed frames and worn mattresses. Lorenzo's parents and their parents before them had clearly never thrown anything away.

'Anna,' Sofia called up the stairs. 'The door.'

Sofia was perfectly capable of answering the door, but she wanted to alert Anna in case she hadn't heard.

'Everything is done,' Anna whispered as she hurried down. 'Go to the salon. I'll answer.'

'Your apron. Look.'

Her white apron was streaked with black. She tore it off and handed it to Sofia. 'Take it to the washroom. There's already a tub full of dirty things soaking. Add it to them. I'll show them to the salon. When you come up, say you were in the garden.'

A little later Sofia entered the salon to see Kaufmann standing by the window, gazing down at the Lungarno, the street that ran along the riverbank. He spun round the moment he heard her and then walked towards her briskly. She tried for a smile.

'Major Kaufmann,' she said as warmly as she could manage. 'I've been expecting you.'

'Expecting me?'

'Don't you remember? In the Bardini gardens. You said you might drop by.'

'Ah, yes.'

'Sorry I was so long coming up. I was in the garden.'

He frowned and his steely blue eyes narrowed very slightly. 'Hardly the weather for gardening.'

She waved his comment away. 'I don't usually garden. We have people for that. I like to listen to the birds.'

'I thought I overheard you calling the servant to answer the door.'

She thought quickly as she inclined her head. 'Indeed, you did. I was on my way to the garden in case there were any early flowers. I do like fresh flowers in a home, don't you? I didn't know it was you at the door.'

'And were there any?'

'Any?'

'Flowers.'

She assumed a look of disappointment. 'I didn't really get that far. I came up to the salon when Anna called me. But we usually see crocus, maybe some violets and hyacinths at this time of year. I must admit I haven't been feeling too well so haven't been outside as much as usual.'

He raised his brows as he studied her face. 'You do look pale. Nothing serious, I hope.'

She shrugged.

His stare was imperious and, as she gazed back at him, it was clear from his stance he believed himself invincible.

'To what do I owe the pleasure? You haven't told me why you're here.'

'I was simply passing.'

'Ah.'

A shaft of sunlight brightened the room and Sofia walked over to the window. She looked out to see his men smoking as

226

they waited. 'The sun has come out,' she said as an idea came into her mind. 'How lovely.'

'You are aware of the murder of two of our officers?'

She still had her back to him, thank goodness, and fought not to tense up her shoulders. There was a horrible moment when she thought she was about to let every detail escape her lips without her permission. That she would tell him about the blood and the ragged cut. Tell him how they had lain in wait. Tell him how she could hardly breathe.

'Yes, I am aware,' she said eventually. 'The rumours are rife.'

'We have made several arrests.'

She had no option but to face him and, knowing there would be reprisals for what they had done, she suddenly couldn't swallow.

'I take it you were at home two days ago? We are questioning everyone.'

'I rarely leave the house in the evening, so yes.'

'I didn't ask you about the evening.'

She forced a little laugh. 'I assume something like that wouldn't happen in broad daylight, Major.'

His eyes remained expressionless. 'Something like that?'

'A murder . . . of an officer . . . or two, didn't you say?'

He gave her a formal nod. 'And who else is here?'

'My friend, Massima, and Anna, who is here to cook for us.'

'Your husband?'

'No. Sadly not. We live in difficult times. Actually, Major, I already mentioned I haven't been too well so I wonder if you might be able to do something for me?'

'Oh?'

Soon after dawn, three days later, Sofia splashed her face at the washstand and then hurried to the bathroom where she'd already laid out her clothes. Since Kaufmann's visit she'd been shakier than ever but at least they were getting out of Florence, and by the official route. She had requested permission from

Kaufmann, pleading her waning health as a pressing reason to be going and, thank God, he had agreed to help.

In the golden morning light, Florence looked beautiful once more, as if it might one day throw off the unforgiving shroud of grey cast over it from the first day of the German occupation. Despite the gentle sunlight, they were all in a state of nervous exhilaration. Grave one minute, excited the next, their mood underpinned by fear that somehow they might be forced to turn back.

Maxine had managed to wire the pistol to one of the wheels of the car, concealing it behind the hub cap. Admittedly, it was dangerous to take the pistol with them, but Maxine had felt sure they ought. As they crawled out of the city and approached their first checkpoint, the two soldiers looked sleepy and Sofia's bet was they'd been up all night and were just marking time as they waited for replacements.

She was wrong. The shorter of the two men demanded to see their papers and travel pass and then, despite those being in order, demanded they get out of the car at gunpoint while the other opened the boot and removed their cases, which he tossed roughly on to the ground. After the first man had finished with their papers, Sofia looked at the distant hills and felt detached, as if none of it was happening to her. As the man scrutinized her, she froze, stranded between two worlds – on the one side, comparative safety, on the other, the exact opposite.

They were ordered to open their cases, which they did kneeling beside them on the damp grass. When the men found nothing but clothing, they lost interest and started examining the car, poking about under the seats and tapping for hidden compartments. Sofia felt her life slipping through her fingers, certain they would undo the hub caps and they would all be shot on the spot. As they bent to look under the bonnet, Maxine cleared her throat and fired her a warning look.

Remain calm.

Sofia held her breath.

One of the men lay on his back on the gravel beside the car and poked about beneath it. It felt like a pantomime. The two men were bored and in need of entertainment.

After he scrambled up again and brushed himself down, he shrugged then signalled it was over. As they loaded their cases, he stamped their travel pass document and waved them on. Sofia felt lightheaded with relief. As she accelerated away, barely able to keep the car in a straight line, they were, at last, heading for home.

40.

Castello de' Corsi

On a sparkling day of sunshine and showers, Sofia, Carla and Gabriella sat on a bench in the kitchen garden, watching over little Alberto playing with a ball and a stick. He ran along the paths between the beds, squealing, while the dogs followed him barking excitedly. Although the day was bright and the earthy smell of the garden soothed her after their nerve-wracking escape from Florence, Sofia shivered from the cold.

The house had felt strange since their return, watchful, a little bit dark. Sofia kept her wits about her as the ghosts circled, their shadows close but never seen. She sensed their judgement, their pity, but also their despair. And sometimes, along with these strange feelings, she felt as if her reason was leaving her.

'Contessa,' Carla said, 'would you stay while I ask Gabriella a few questions?'

'If you're sure you want me here.'

Carla nodded and turned to her daughter, who was now wandering along the path. 'So how are you feeling today, Gabriella?' she called out.

'A bit sick,' Gabriella muttered.

'It will pass. I was terrible with your brother. It doesn't last.'

Gabriella didn't reply but ran to the bottom of the garden. Sofia remembered the girl's birth, a tricky one, but when Carla had passed the infant to be cradled in her arms, Sofia had marvelled at the beauty of the little girl. A few days later she'd breathed in the milky smell of her and felt the sadness of her own childlessness. It had been a shock to come home to the news that Gabriella was now expecting.

Accustomed to the girl's odd little ways, Sofia was not too perturbed by her sudden disappearance to the bottom of the garden. She knew Carla would be feeling the shame of having a pregnant unmarried daughter and felt for her. But with Gabriella old enough to marry, at least with parental consent, that really would be the best option. If only they could find out who the father was. So far, Gabriella had remained stubbornly mute.

Carla got up and, with the fork she'd propped against the wall, began to dig for any remaining potatoes. 'A few potatoes with a fried egg will make a fine lunch for us all,' she murmured.

In her mind Sofia went over all the wonderful dishes Carla used to cook. Everyone loved her roasted potatoes. She could picture Carla cutting them up while humming to herself, then tossing them into her favourite mixing bowl before adding oil, wine, garlic, salt and pepper. Last to go in would be rosemary and sage, or sometimes fennel. Then into the oven with them. Delicious with meat. Sofia's mouth watered. When the potatoes were plentiful, Carla still made this dish, minus the meat. She had secret recipes too, the ones she'd learnt at her grandmother's side.

They still had squash to use up, green winter ones piled up in the larder alongside strings of onion, garlic and peppers. Nothing quite like roasted squash when the skin was blackened and blistered, and the flesh would be eaten with Carla's own garlic focaccia. As Carla worked, Sofia kept an eye on Alberto, who had trailed after Gabriella. What a pity a sweet child like Alberto had to grow up without a father and, now Aldo was gone, no man in his life at all. As she was thinking this, Alberto cried out.

'*Nonna*, come. *Nonna*.'

As Carla ran, Beni began barking madly and Sofia followed them with her own dogs coming up behind. Her stomach churned as a prickle of fear took hold. If anything should happen to little Alberto . . . but when she reached Carla and the little boy, he was pointing at the open door of the small potting shed where they kept the tools. Carla marched in while Sofia stood in the doorway, staring in. Suddenly she could not breathe. Everything stopped as she made out Gabriella sitting in the gloom, cross-legged on the floor, clutching a serrated knife.

'*Oh mio Dio!*' Carla shrieked. 'What are you doing, child?'

She rushed forward, grabbing hold of the knife, and Sofia instantly saw Gabriella was bleeding.

'You stupid, stupid girl!' Carla cried. 'What have you done?'

Sofia watched as Carla clasped her daughter's wrist and found a cut, not deep and not life-threatening, but oozing blood.

'Why?' Carla demanded. 'What do you think this will achieve?'

Gabriella hung her head and began to sob.

Sofia stepped forward to place a hand on Carla's in the hope of calming her. But too late, Carla's anger had won. 'Oh, for God's sake!' The words burst from her as she lashed out and slapped her daughter's face.

Sofia could see Carla's instant regret.

'I'm . . . I'm sorry,' she whispered in a halting voice and held out a trembling hand.

Gabriella said nothing and did not reach for the proffered hand.

Carla bit her lip before she spoke again. 'Please, no more crying. We must be practical. I need to wash your cut.'

A muffled reply came from Gabriella, but neither Sofia nor Carla could hear her words.

'What was that?' Carla demanded. 'What was that?'

Gabriella gave a fierce shake of her head and looked up at Carla, her eyes pleading and hollowed with misery. 'You don't understand.'

'Well, tell me then. How can I understand when you tell me nothing?'

'Aldo. His death,' Gabriella moaned. 'It was all my fault,' and she began to rock back and forth, weeping inconsolably.

* * *

A little later they were in the kitchen, Sofia and Carla sitting at the table and Gabriella standing near the bread oven. They had pacified Gabriella with sweet grain coffee and a slice of toast with honey. And by not immediately pressing her to explain what she'd meant, they managed to calm the girl still more, although they really did need to get to the bottom of this.

'So,' Sofia said gently. 'Can you tell us now? Nobody is going to be angry with you but why did you say it was your fault?'

Gabriella wound her body round, the look of anguish back on her face.

'*Tesoro*, it can't be so very bad, can it?' Carla asked and smiled at her daughter, trying to keep her tone light, Sofia thought.

Gabriella stared at the floor and scratched the back of her head but didn't speak. Sofia glanced at Carla, who shook her head. She took it to mean Carla would go about this in a round-about way.

'Come here,' Carla said. 'Is it the lice again? I'll comb them out.'

Gabriella still didn't look up.

'Well, can you check how the soup is doing?'

Gabriella didn't move. 'I told Maria,' she whispered, and as she raised her head, her face creased up in misery.

At the mention of Maria, Sofia could smell oncoming danger, but she took a breath and swallowed it down. 'Told her what?' she asked.

Gabriella wouldn't meet her eyes.

'Gabriella?'

'About the plan to blow up the railway tracks.'

'Don't be silly,' Sofia said. 'You couldn't have known anything about it.'

'I did know. I went for a walk in the woods and heard Aldo and another man talking. Lodo, he was called.'

Carla frowned. 'This doesn't make sense. You told Maria?'

Gabriella nodded miserably.

'Why?'

'I wanted to impress her.'

'But why?'

'Because of Paolo, Maria's grandson. You know. I wanted him to love me and I thought if I told her, she'd tell him and then . . .' She paused and gulped back a sob. 'And then he'd come back.'

'So, you told Maria about the plans?'

Gabriella looked down, her eyes glued to the floor again.

As the consequences of this revelation sank in, Sofia watched Carla clap a hand across her mouth and groan. Sofia bowed her head for a moment before glancing at the girl again. No. Surely it couldn't be true.

Gabriella was gazing at her mother. 'I love him.'

Sofia's heart throbbed and she struggled against the tightness developing in her chest. 'You know we don't really trust Maria, or the Blackshirts?' she said.

Gabriella did not reply.

Sofia wrestled with herself. The girl must be making it up. She would never have betrayed her own brother like that.

'Gabriella, is this the truth?' Carla demanded. 'Tell me honestly.'

Gabriella's eyes flicked towards her mother and then away.

Sofia was thinking hard. There was no way of knowing if Maria had told Paolo, was there? Maybe she hadn't. She said she rarely saw him. Maybe she should ask Maria about it herself. But what if the woman lied . . . what then?

'Oh, Gabriella,' she said. 'I don't know what to say to you.'

Carla clenched her jaw and got to her feet. Sofia knew Carla's fierce love for Aldo was equalled by her love for both her daughters and this awful news must be splitting her into two.

'I'm sorry,' the girl said, wincing at the fury on her mother's face.

Carla placed her hands firmly on her daughter's shoulders, as if she was about to shake her.

'I'm sorry,' the girl repeated as tears slid down her cheeks.

This was worse than unimaginable. This daughter of Carla's

234

may have caused the death of her only brother – Carla's only son. The image of Aldo's broken body, hanging in Buonconvento, flashed into Sofia's mind.

As Carla raised her hand, Gabriella shrank back. Carla gazed at her own hand but did not strike, nor did she shake the girl. How much she must have wanted to, Sofia thought.

She felt like striking Gabriella herself, for her stupidity. But they had to pull themselves together. This would never go away. Not ever. She thought rapidly, considering it from every angle. 'Anna can't know,' she said eventually. 'She adored Aldo.'

'And always criticized me for overindulging Gabriella,' Carla added. 'She'll kill Gabriella if she finds out.'

Sofia knew she was right.

'Now you listen to me,' Carla said, and stared grimly at her daughter. 'You must never, ever, tell anyone else about this. Not a single soul. Never. Do you understand?'

Gabriella remained silent.

'You will have to live with what you did for the rest of your life. But listen to me. Maria might not have told Paolo. The Germans might have known anyway. Maybe they found out from someone else. It may not have been because of you.'

Gabriella gave her a weak smile.

'This Paolo,' Carla went on. 'He is definitely the father of the baby? Yes?'

Gabriella gave a slight nod.

'And it happened the night they came to your sister's door when we were knitting upstairs?'

Another nod.

'Oh, my girl, what am I to do with you?' Carla shook her head. After a moment or two she spoke again. 'Well, things are as they are so we will just have to make the best of it, won't we? Like we always do.'

41.

Buonconvento

As Maxine entered the café in Buonconvento, she glanced about to ensure it was safe. A couple of old biddies were gossiping in the corner, oblivious to everything, and at a table by the steamy window, a young mother was trying to persuade her reluctant toddler to eat a biscuit. Anna had managed to get a message to Marco, who was due any moment. The three women had made a pact never to speak about what had happened in Florence again, but Maxine knew Marco would have been informed about the armaments raid.

When he arrived, he flashed her a warm, engaging smile and her heart immediately melted. 'So, you've been a busy girl. Congratulations.'

Insanely happy to hear his praise, she made a face as if to imply it was nothing. They both knew it was not.

He gazed at her with calm, candid eyes. 'You've shown self-reliance, courage and resourcefulness. Take the compliment.'

'Thank you, Marco. It means a lot.'

'You've let the Allies know about the successful raid?' he asked.

'Yes, James assisted me last night. He's back in the nearby farmhouse now. The roof caved in on the one higher up the hill. The radio was being used there but now it's hidden in the tunnels under Sofia's house.'

'Do you know what happened to the GAP courier?'

'Irma?'

He nodded.

'I hope she made it to the mountains with the men.'

'She knew who you all were?' He was alert, his tone now brisk, businesslike.

'What do you mean?'

'Names, places.'

'Nope. You want coffee?'

He ignored her offer. 'She could identify you?'

'Maybe, but I looked very plain, headscarf, no make-up. She wouldn't have a clue where we were headed after the raid.'

'Not that muck,' he now said, pointing at her cup. 'And you could never look plain.'

She pulled a face.

He scraped back his chair. 'Coming?'

'Sure.'

'Are you on your bike?'

She said she was. The woman with the child focused adoring eyes on Marco as she got up to leave the café. Maxine noticed Marco looking back at the woman with a mixture of concern and affection as she walked away, and she experienced an embarrassing stab of jealousy.

'She's very young,' she said, trying to keep a lid on her emotions.

'Yes.'

'A girlfriend of yours?' She scowled, failing to hide her feelings, and he laughed at her.

'Jealous?'

'Don't be ridiculous.'

'Well, the less you know . . .'

She sighed, unconvinced. How convenient.

'Do you want to come back to mine?'

He had tossed the question out rather too nonchalantly for her liking and she scoffed at his suggestion. 'Your stinking old farmhouse?'

He raised his brows. 'I have somewhere closer now. And a little more comfortable. A bed with a real mattress and only a couple of rats for company, plus the resident cockroaches, of course.'

She gazed at his angular face, thinner than before, and poked him in the ribs. 'You sure know how to impress a girl. Anyway, I can't stay. I'm going to Santa Cecilia first thing tomorrow with Sofia.'

'Then we have the rest of the day. I'll cook for you.'

'You can cook?'

He gave her the sweetest smile and took her arm. 'Lead me to your motorcycle.'

At Marco's new lodgings Maxine was pleasantly surprised. Just one room, but at least there was a bed, a small kitchen and an old sofa.

'I don't understand why you aren't in the mountains or woods with the rest of the men.'

'My job is to keep my ear to the ground, to liaise with you and to grow the network. I'm not a leader of a fighting unit, I'm a co-ordinator. My leg –' He glanced down.

If Maxine was honest, she'd forgotten about his leg injury despite the limp and the walking stick he carried. 'You really do have an injury?'

He nodded. 'I thought you'd never ask. Though you will have noticed that when in private it does seem to recover somewhat.'

She laughed. 'So, what are you going to cook for me?'

'*Spaghetti al pomodoro*. I thought we'd do it together. Here,' he passed her a brown paper bag. 'You can chop the tomatoes. Unless you'd rather crush the garlic?'

'No, that's fine.'

He handed her a knife and they both bent over a small wooden table that wobbled constantly.

'You like cooking?' he asked her.

She shook her head. 'Not my thing.'

He gasped in mock horror. 'Better keep that quiet or everyone will know you are not a true Italian woman.'

'And you? Do you think I'm a true Italian woman?'

He put down his knife, then leant across the table to kiss her, the table wobbling frantically.

'I'll show you what kind of Italian woman I think you are.'

She laughed and pulled back, despite the fact her legs had turned to jelly. 'Let's cook. I'm starving.'

'Yes, ma'am.'

They finished chopping and he put on a pot of water to boil, then heated the oil in a pan. 'It's important not to let it bubble or smoke,' he said as he added the crushed garlic cloves followed by the tomatoes and salt. 'It will take about twelve minutes.'

'Twelve minutes. How exact you are.'

'Indeed. Now make yourself useful and pass those herbs,' he said, pointing at another brown paper bag.

She passed the bag and he took out five basil leaves.

'And the spaghetti?'

He salted the large pot of now boiling water and added the pasta. While it was cooking, he came over to stand behind her, then he kissed the back of her neck while running a palm over her breasts. She felt her nipples harden and pushed against him as he continued to tease her.

He laughed and went back to the stove. 'Right, it's *al dente*.' He removed the pasta from the water and added it to the pan to finish cooking in the warm sauce along with the basil leaves.

'Smells wonderful,' she said, although now she was itching to tear his clothes off and forget about the food.

'Really, the sauce should be milled,' he said. 'But I don't have a mill.'

By the time they'd finished eating, sitting on the sofa with plates on their laps, she was grinning at him, her turn to tease. 'Maybe I should go now?'

'Don't you dare.'

He took their plates to the sink, then held out his hand and led her to the bed where he first undressed her and then himself.

The sex just got better and better and Maxine could not imagine a time when this wonderful man would not be in her life. After they were done, they lay wrapped in each other's arms.

'What was the best time of your life, Marco?' she asked, her eyes unfocused and sleepy.

'Apart from just now?' He nibbled her ear and she felt a stirring in her body all over again.

'Seriously.'

'I think the most magical time was when my little nephew was born.'

'I didn't know you liked kids so much.'

He pulled a face. 'I'm not sure if I do or if I don't. I like *that* kid.'

'But you want children of your own?'

He sighed. 'I know I once said I did. I don't know though. When you lose someone you love – I mean really love – you lose not only them, but the part of yourself that loved them. There's a hole.'

'You're talking about your brother?'

He nodded. 'I think I might be too scared of feeling like that again if I had children. What about you?'

'Children?'

'No, when was the best time of your life?'

'I had an amazing time in London before I came here.'

'And the worst?'

'When I found out my father was hitting my mother.' Suddenly she felt her eyes heat up and the tears beginning to form as she recalled the sudden shocking loss of the man she'd thought her father had been. She tried to stop the tears, embarrassed to be crying in front of him, but they just fell faster and faster until she was sobbing, gulping, trembling. He held her close, murmuring soothing words and stroking her cheeks until the tears began to ebb.

'Oh, my love,' he said as he handed her a handkerchief. 'Don't worry, it's clean.'

A few minutes passed then she sniffed, wiped her eyes and face and smiled, feeling a lot lighter for letting go of the sadness she'd been holding on to far too long. She felt warmer inside too, especially now that he had called her *his love*. The connection between them had become more intimate than ever and the spontaneous ease between them made her feel as if there was no war beyond these four walls.

'Guess what?' she said. 'You smell of garlic and basil.'

'I do?'

'But I don't care because you, *signore*, are a damn fine cook.'

He kissed her eyelids then made love to her again.

Afterwards, she told him more about her family.

'My mother was brought up, like most women, to serve her man. She brought me up the same way and I sometimes wonder, if I hadn't found out what was really going on between them, would I have turned out like her?'

'Somehow I doubt it.'

'It was never my thing to defer to men or to rely on charming them to get what I wanted. Of course, I can do all that but, if I'm honest, I've always been too outspoken.'

'Not to mention bold, brave, courageous, as I said before.'

She smiled. 'It got me into trouble at school though, and out of school for that matter. Some men seem to hate a determined woman. They just want to hush you up, make you smaller.'

'They're scared. Determined women threaten them.'

'And you? Do I threaten you?'

He laughed. 'As if . . . No, my dear, dear Maxine, never change. I like you just the way you are.'

42.

March 1944

Sofia was clinging on for dear life as Maxine bumped along the dirt roads all the way to her parents' village in the region of Rapolano Terme. When they stopped at the foot of the hill, she took out a flask of water and a sandwich to share. Despite all her worries, Carla, bless her, had managed to squirrel away a few slices of salami for them. As she took a bite, she glanced around at the stunningly beautiful day. With spring coming up fast, the fields were emerald green and a few low-lying silvery clouds floated in the sapphire sky. Winter had done with them. At last. The light today was crystal-clear and everything shone. As the sun gently warmed her arms and fresh air filled her lungs, Sofia felt hopeful. The final section of the tree-lined track up to the village of Santa Cecilia was heavily potholed so they decided to walk, glancing back at the views over the surrounding land now and then, and finally reaching an imposing gate set into a stone wall, topped by a coat of arms.

Maxine was unusually quiet, and Sofia understood that for her this was one of those special moments in life when words would be an intrusion. The gate wasn't locked and as they entered the tiny village and cautiously started to look around it felt uncannily silent. All they could hear were the birds.

'Do you think the Germans have gone?' Maxine asked eventually.

'I don't know. You'd expect to see their vehicles, wouldn't you?'

They walked on under stone arches and along narrow streets

and into shady alleys. When they arrived at the manor house, Sofia couldn't help herself and whispered that she wanted to peek through the ground-floor windows, arched in a row along one wall.

As they drew closer, the place looked deserted. Sofia put her nose to the filthy glass, glimpsing damp walls, broken plaster, piles of rubbish and upended furniture. The many marble pillars looked as if they needed a good scrub and the frescoed walls were in poor health. Turning round, she saw the gate to the formal garden was hanging off its hinges and, as they slipped into the garden, they found the weeds had taken over. Plants had run rampant and the stone pathways were green with moss and lichen. It felt like an enchanted garden in which you might catch sight of nymphs dancing in the sunlight. The Germans could only have arrived here last September, so not long enough for this amount of damage, but then Sofia remembered the family had by then already decamped to Siena, which also explained the neglect.

They were starting to make their way out to head back towards the centre of the village when they heard an imperious voice.

'Exactly *what* do you think you're doing in my garden? You do realize you are trespassing?'

They turned to see an elderly, silver-haired woman, dressed head to toe in black, who stood, hands on hips, by the broken gate.

Sofia walked towards the woman. 'I'm so sorry. The gate was open. I used to come here before . . . Oh, it's you.'

'Are we acquainted?' the woman said, shading her eyes from the sun and squinting at Sofia.

'I'm Sofia de' Corsi . . . from Castello de' Corsi. I'm so sorry, I didn't recognize you at first, but you must be Valentina.'

The woman gave a half-smile. 'I am, but what are you doing here?'

Sofia indicated her companion. 'This is my friend, Maxine.

She's come to see the village where her family came from. They had to move away.'

'She is Italian?'

'Yes, I am,' Maxine piped up.

'Your accent is a little different,' Valentina said with a frown. 'What is your family name?'

'Caprioni.'

Valentina smiled now. 'How lovely. Was your father the one who looked after the goats? You know, with that name. We used to have such a wonderful herd.'

'He was a farmer, actually. My grandfather might well have been a goatherd though. My mother worked here at the house.'

'And her name?'

'Luisa.'

'My memory is not so good these days, but the name sounds familiar. Something happened, I think . . . Why not go to the little café in the square. Someone may remember.'

'It's open?' Maxine asked. 'The café?'

'We thought the Germans were here,' Sofia added.

The old lady pulled a scornful face. 'They've only just gone . . . left the place a wreck. People keep to themselves, those who stayed, and some are still lying low. We did not enjoy sharing our beautiful Santa Cecilia with those foreigners. Best speak to Greta at the café. Try knocking if she isn't open.'

'Thank you. I'm so sorry to intrude.'

'I would invite you in, but this is the first time I've stepped inside since they left. I'm living in a village house now.'

'Will your family return from Siena?'

'Not until after the war.'

'Is the estate manager around?'

'He fled when the Germans came. He had been very outspoken against the Fascists, joined the Communists, I understand, so it wasn't safe for him here.'

'And what about you? Have you been safe?' It was a loaded

question and Sofia wondered whether the old lady would even reply.

Valentina paused then gave her a dry look. 'If you are asking if I support the Fascists, the answer is I do not. But I do know how to keep my mouth shut.'

Sofia smiled at her and they took their leave to head for the main square.

'What do you think she meant by *something happened*?' Maxine asked.

Sofia didn't know what to say, so opted for silence.

The only indication that the place they found was a café was a single wrought-iron table with two mismatched chairs sitting outside it. When Maxine tried the door it was locked, so they did as Valentina advised and knocked. For a few moments nothing happened, but then the door swung open and a diminutive woman of about forty, wearing an enormous apron, stepped out.

'You want home-made beer? Or grain coffee?'

'Do you have lemonade?'

She shook her head.

'Two grain coffees, please.'

She pointed at the table. 'Sit.'

They sat and waited, glancing around at the square. The villagers must have decided there was nothing to fear from Sofia and Maxine for the place was no longer deserted. Three ancient women in black had huddled together for a gossip in one corner, and on one of four iron benches in the middle a white-haired old man snoozed, his chin on his chest, while a child who, Sofia reckoned, had to be his grandson, played around his ankles.

When the Greta woman brought out the coffee, Maxine asked if she knew anything about a family called Caprioni who had left in 1910.

The woman frowned. 'I was only a child. You need to ask him.' She pointed at the old man.

Maxine was all set to get up right away.

'Let's finish our coffees, pay and then go over and ask him.'

But Maxine still stood up, impatiently. 'You finish yours. I'm going to speak to him now.'

Sofia watched her walk over and sit on the bench. As the old man didn't stir Maxine began to play peek-a-boo with the little boy. The child's giggles woke the grandfather, and he raised a deeply wrinkled, nut-brown face to look at Maxine. Sofia paid Greta and walked over to join them.

Surprised to see someone else on the bench with him, the old man narrowed his eyes and then spoke with a strong guttural accent, a countryman through and through. 'Who are you?'

'I'm sorry to disturb you. My name is Maxine and I'm trying to find anyone who might have known my parents.'

'Speak up, girl,' he said. 'You want to find your parents, you say?'

'No. I'm trying to find anyone who may have known my parents. They left here in 1910.'

'Well, why didn't you say?'

Maxine scratched her ear, clearly wondering if she'd get any sense out of him.

'Their name?' he asked.

'Caprioni.'

The old boy visibly paled as he gazed at her. 'You are Alessandro's daughter?'

She gave him a warm smile. 'I am.'

The old boy clutched hold of her hand. 'Your father was my dearest friend. I never expected to hear of him again.'

'You knew him?'

'Oh yes, I was older than he was, but we always got on. I worked on his father's farm and also when it became his farm too. Oh, my dear, the way they left . . . such a bad business.'

Maxine looked perplexed. 'What happened? I assumed they

left because the family had grown too big and the land could not support so many.'

'They told you that?'

'Yes.'

'You know about little Matteo?'

Maxine frowned. 'Who?'

'He was a little boy, their firstborn.'

Maxine looked puzzled. 'I think you must be mistaken. They never had a child called Matteo.'

'Before you were born. Curly blond hair. A cherub. They worshipped that boy.' His voice deepened and Sofia noticed the catch in it that signified the holding of pain.

'What happened to him?' she asked, and he looked at her as if he'd only just noticed that she was also there.

'Shot dead.'

Maxine gasped. 'I had a brother who was shot? How? Why? Was it an accident?'

'He said it was an accident. We all knew it was not.'

'Someone meant to kill him?' Maxine asked, wide-eyed with shock.

The old boy shrugged. 'Who knows. Maybe he meant to wound him. Only three years old, little Matteo. A tragedy.'

'Why did it happen? Who shot him?'

'All in good time. It happened behind the barn on your father's farm. The man claimed he was out to shoot a hare and at the wrong moment the boy ran out.'

'The man raised the alarm?'

He shook his head. 'Bastard should have done. No. It was your mother heard the shot and found your brother.'

'Dead?'

'Died a little later. Loss of blood.'

'And that's why they left?'

'It broke them. She wept for weeks. Inconsolable she was and it became impossible for them to stay. Your mother knew

Alessandro would kill the man if they did, so they set off for America instead.'

'But, if it really *was* intentional, why would the man want to shoot a child?'

'Revenge.'

'*Dio santo*, revenge for what?'

'A family feud. Got out of hand. Not sure what. Something to do with an argument over cattle. Who stole what I cannot say but afterwards the trouble began.'

'And this man killed a child for that?'

The old man shrugged again.

Maxine stared at the ground for a moment, then gazed up at Sofia with such sorrow in her eyes, Sofia's eyes watered too. It was as if the energy had drained out of Maxine, and Sofia saw a very different woman from the one she had grown to know so well.

'Let's go,' Sofia said, and gently took her hand.

Maxine rose to her feet and thanked the old man, then very slowly they made their way towards the gates.

'Give my regards to Alessandro,' he called after them.

Maxine didn't reply, so Sofia turned and gave him a little wave.

They walked through the old gates and down the hill in silence until they reached the motorcycle.

'None of it was true,' Maxine said, looking back up to the isolated little village. 'The wonderful life they told me they'd had here. None of it was true.'

'It may have been . . . before.'

'They never said a word. Not a word.'

'It would have been devastating. Maybe they wanted to leave such a terrible tragedy in the past.'

'It explains a lot about how they are.'

'Do you want to tell me?'

Maxine looked torn, then said, 'My father could be violent. I never really knew why.'

Sofia gazed at the view around them, at the rolling hills and then up at the blue sky. 'I'm so sorry.'

'Shall we get back on the boneshaker?' Maxine said after a few moments. 'We've been lucky so far. No machine-gunning, no bombs.'

Sofia smiled. 'A good day then! Let's enjoy it while we can.'

43

The sudden storm hadn't quite blown itself out but half an hour earlier they wouldn't have heard a thing in the howling wind circling the tower. Now, at the sound of a vehicle arriving, Sofia and James exchanged anxious glances. It couldn't be Maxine. It sounded more like a car than a motorcycle and, in any case, Maxine had already gone to meet Marco, despite the weather. She'd left the moment they'd finished sending her latest report to the Allies.

James began to pack up rapidly. They heard a clattering sound like someone kicking a pail and then the dogs began barking excitedly.

'Carla must have let the dogs out,' Sofia said.

'At this hour?'

'Best way to warn us.'

Recently the radio had been kept in the tunnels and now, with the weather so unreliable, they'd needed to transmit from a higher point so had brought the equipment back to the top of the tower. It felt like an age as James neatly arranged everything to ensure the case would close properly, and Sofia watched helplessly as he fumbled with something that didn't quite fit.

'Quickly. Go downstairs and get into the concealed passage,' he whispered. 'Leave me.'

'Not without you.'

Only moments later they heard Carla making even more noise as she argued with somebody outside in the square, right beneath the tower. Sofia was about to take the equipment down the stairs and into the passage, but at that moment James dropped a radio plug.

'Shit!' He cursed under his breath and began to search for it, scrambling on hands and knees under the table.

'I think it rolled. Leave it.'

'Can't. If it's Germans out there, they'll find it when they come up and then they'll know. You'll be arrested.'

'It's dark. They won't see to find it.'

'They'll have torches.'

'Could it be refugees?' she said. 'Escaped British prisoners, Italian soldiers?'

'Who've managed to get hold of a car?'

As he continued to search, she knew there was not a chance they'd have time to carry everything downstairs, even if he did find the plug. As she waited for him in an agony of suspense, the seconds passed too quickly.

'*Per Dio*,' she hissed as he finally located it. 'Quick! Up the stairs to the roof.'

The ancient staircase, uneven and incredibly narrow, hadn't been altered since the tower was built. James carried the heavier box while Sofia took the other and they squeezed into the opening, hardly daring to breathe as they crept up to the place where the stairs curved round towards the roof. The door at the top was locked so all they could do was huddle together at the top of the steps. James hadn't really needed her there, only Maxine, but she'd been looking forward to seeing him again. She told herself it was because Lorenzo hadn't been home since January and she was so lonely it consumed her, right through to the bone.

She heard the outer door being unlocked and Carla speaking loudly as she climbed the stairs and then reached the now empty room.

'There,' they heard her say. 'I told you she wasn't here. Like I said, I must have left the light on when I was cleaning.'

Driven by the fear of discovery, James and Sofia were pressed even more tightly together with the two boxes wedged on the final step above them. Had the blackout fabric slipped? Hadn't she tacked it up properly? Was that how they'd spotted the light? She could feel his heart beating as furiously as her own. As he wrapped an arm around her, she leant in.

They heard muttering and then very clearly: 'Where does that opening lead?'

Kaufmann! Sofia's chest constricted, terrified he would decide to climb up after them. In a flash she grasped that she might not be able to contain her rising terror and that a groan was about to escape her lips. She pressed them together as hard as she could. James held her rigidly still and clamped a hand over her mouth.

'It goes to the roof,' they heard Carla say. 'The door at the top is always locked and I don't have a key. No one goes up there for fear of being bombed.'

'All the same, I shall investigate when I've finished in here,' Kaufmann said.

Apart from the sound of the German poking about, it was silent for a moment. Sofia bit the inside of her cheek and focused on the taste of blood.

'Does she spend much time up here?' Kaufmann was saying. 'Too cold to paint, I'd have thought.'

'My daughter knitted her some fingerless gloves.'

Sofia felt as if her soul would spring from her chest as they waited. Was that what a heart attack would be like? The same lack of control. The feeling of being stranded and helpless as your pulse hit the roof and your fate sped inexorably closer. They were doomed. She knew it. James must know it too. And yet, despite the fear, she noticed a smouldering, trembling rage rising inside her.

'Is there a light on those stairs to the roof?' Kaufmann said.

She held her breath and counted inside her head. *One, two, three, four, five.* This was it.

'No,' Carla said.

A moment later they heard the sound of a motorcycle arriving, followed by a car horn hooting repeatedly. Sofia prayed the motorcycle wasn't Maxine's and that she'd kept to her plan not to return until morning.

'*Verdammt noch mal!*' Kaufmann cursed. 'Lead the way down. I don't want to break my neck in the dark.'

'I wish you *would* break your neck,' Sofia muttered inaudibly, and then held her breath. A few moments later, as they heard the tower door being locked, she felt lightheaded with the kind of reprieve she'd never experienced before. As she let out her breath, a powerful release swept throughout her body: a tidal wave let loose inside her.

'Phew,' he said. 'A bit too close for comfort.'

She swallowed several times before she could even speak.

They hugged each other for a long while as their hearts gradually slowed and the elation of having got away with it took over. His breath was warm on her face and as his lips brushed her forehead, he kissed her gently. Then he paused and bent his head as if he was about to kiss her lips. She reluctantly averted her head, feeling a yearning for something she really ought not to be feeling.

44

A week later Sofia was surprised by the arrival of Schmidt, who was shown into their main drawing room by Anna.

'Contessa . . . Sofia, I do hope you won't mind the informality of me calling you by your name.' He came forward, holding out his hand.

She shook it. 'Of course not. Is there something I can do for you?'

He walked to the window and gazed out before turning back to her with such a defeated look in his eyes it caught her off guard. He looked beaten, and it baffled her.

'Actually, this time, it's more about what I can do for you.'

'Really?' she said, probably sounding as surprised as she felt.

'It is rather delicate.'

'Oh?'

He began to circle the room and while he remained silent she noticed how incredibly strained he seemed. It showed in his hands, his shoulders, his preoccupied stance.

'Commandant Schmidt. Is something the matter?'

He looked at his feet for a moment. 'Klaus. My name is Klaus. My wife is Hilda.'

She inclined her head. 'I see.' Except of course that she didn't see at all. Why had he come and what on earth was going on?

'You have a very fine view here,' he said, then stared at her with an intense, disconcerting gaze. 'I regret you have been troubled by our being here.'

It was her turn to remain silent.

'But I know of what they are capable. Do you see?'

He seemed to be balanced on a fine line, so she tried to hide her puzzlement. 'They?'

He gave a slight shake of the head as if doubting himself. 'We. Us.'

This was strange. This was a man forlorn and fragile. She had never seen him looking so insubstantial.

'Look, I do not know for certain, and I have no details. I am just here to tell you it is possible you might find yourselves "persons of interest". For observation purposes.'

She stepped back, feeling a rush of heat and thinking of Florence. 'Me? Why me?'

'No, no,' he jumped in. 'Let me clarify. It is not so much you, but your family. Perhaps.'

Her hand flew to her heart. 'I don't understand. What do you mean? Is it Lorenzo? My father? My mother?'

'Believe me, I regret I cannot be more specific. Nothing is certain and I am not saying *you* are in danger. But, of course, it is conceivable they may . . .'

There was that word *they* again. Was he distancing himself from the Nazis?

'I wanted to caution you and say –'

'What? Say what?' she interrupted.

'If there is anything, anything at all, that you may wish . . . Ah, I don't quite know how to phrase this . . . If there is anything going on, as it were, at the Castello. Do you see? Anything unfitting, I mean. You must take care.'

Her mind was spinning. 'Of course,' she managed to say.

'And now I must take my leave. I am returning to Berlin, so this is goodbye.'

'Oh, I see. When do you leave?'

'Tomorrow. I wanted to speak with you first but now I must go.'

She took a breath and regained her equilibrium as much as she was able, although her heart was still thumping. 'Well, thank you, Commandant Schmidt.'

'Klaus.'

She nodded. 'But truly there is nothing to worry about here.'

They gazed at one another.

'I'm glad to hear it. I wish I could have met you and the Count at a happier time.' He clicked his heels together and made for the door, then twisted back to look at her. 'My wife and I are a family, you see. A small one, but a family. Like you and your husband.'

And he gave her a slight nod before closing the door behind him.

'I'm grateful to you,' she called out, not knowing if he had heard, 'for coming.'

During the second week of March Sofia opened the back door to find Marco and James leaning against the walls of the narrow porch.

She beckoned them in. 'Quickly. Thanks for coming.'

James smiled at her. 'We kept a lookout. Nobody saw me.'

'That's fine. Will you stay for lunch?' She glanced at Marco, who was staring at his feet. 'You too, Marco, if you'd like to.'

He shook his head and moved his weight from foot to foot. 'Actually, I'd like to find Maxine.'

'She's around somewhere. You could tell her lunch is ready.'

'I'll go and look.'

'Before you go, I wanted to let you know that a friend of ours phoned with news.'

'And?'

'The Allies are bombing Rome heavily. Florence too, again. Apparently, the Germans won't be defending Rome; he got it from a member of the government.'

'But they'll continue their defences all around Rome?' Marco asked.

'They'll block the roads, but the intelligence says they plan to eventually form a strong defence line north of Florence across the Apennine mountains.'

'Which means they believe Rome and Florence *will* be liberated,' Marco said.

'Bloody hurrah,' James said. 'I'm sorry about the bombing, really I am. But I guess there's no other way.'

Sofia wasn't sure what to say to this and turned to speak to Marco. 'Maxine's outside somewhere, I think. There's nobody much around. Tell her I'll save her some soup.'

Marco nodded and left them to it.

'Soup okay for you, James?'

He smiled in that warm, open way of his and she beamed at him. Then, suddenly assailed by a feeling of discomfort at his presence, she marched across the hall, barely waiting for him to follow.

All through lunch, which they ate in the kitchen with Carla – Gabriella was having hers in her room – Sofia could hardly speak. Carla looked puzzled by the strained atmosphere and Sofia felt so torn it hurt. Lorenzo hadn't been in touch for weeks and she was terribly worried, especially since Schmidt's strange visit. She didn't understand why Lorenzo had been unable to contact her at all and although she'd known he would be away for longer, this was longer than she'd expected. And now, here was James gazing at her with his face clouding over and concern in his eyes. She wanted to weep.

Carla was looking at her too, but she was frowning. 'You have hardly eaten.'

Sofia glanced down at her bowl of bread and garlic soup. 'I think I've lost my appetite.'

Carla tutted.

James drew back his chair. 'Well, I'd better be off. Thank you so much for lunch.'

Sofia glanced at him as he rose and felt herself redden as she spoke. 'Don't go. Keep me company in the garden for a bit.'

He accepted and Carla cleared the table.

'Actually, would you rather walk in the woods?' she said, not wanting to encourage gossip in the village. 'It's quite safe if we keep to the tracks that circle close to the walls.'

'Good idea.' He glanced out of the window. 'Although it does look like rain might be on the way.'

'Grab one of our spare macs on our way out. I like walking in the rain. Don't you?'

As they left the walls and headed along the path they walked in silence.

The damp woods were green and leafy with an eerie light that created a mysterious feeling of timelessness. In these ancient woods you could almost believe in wood sprites or elves living in the tree hollows. She liked to think of other worlds going on around her, but when she heard birds shifting in the trees and scurrying creatures in the undergrowth, she laughed at herself. Those *were* the other worlds.

He had a puzzled look as he watched her. 'What's so funny?'

'Sorry. It's nothing much. I was just imagining the wood sprites.'

His eyes lit up as he smiled. 'I like that. You could almost believe we're not at war.'

'Will it be over soon, do you think?'

He puffed out his cheeks then blew out the breath. 'I hope so. Once we drive them out of Florence, the war won't be over, but it will be over for you.'

'For me?'

'For everyone hereabouts, I mean.'

'Schmidt came to warn me, you know, before he left. At least, I think it was a warning. He implied my family might be under observation. And now I haven't heard from any of them, not my mother, my father or Lorenzo.'

James paused for a moment and they both stopped walking. He reached for her hand and as her eyes filled with tears she didn't pull away.

'I can't bear not knowing if they are hurt . . . or . . . worse.' Her voice shook and a few tears began to fall.

'Try not to think the worst. I know it's hard.'

He held her for a moment, but she manged to control herself and stepped back, her tears subsiding.

'Better now?' he said.

She brushed the wetness from her cheeks with her palms and nodded.

'Look, I wanted to apologize for the other night. Heat of the moment . . .'

'You don't need to.'

He started to speak again but she interrupted.

'James.' She gazed at his beautiful blue eyes. 'I am a married woman who loves her husband very much and right now I feel like hell.'

There was a short silence as the air between them thickened and, as she continued to look into his eyes and he into hers, she saw the good, decent man he was. Lonely, like her. But then she turned away. It was too close. *He* was too close.

'I understand,' he said eventually.

She swallowed the lump developing in her throat and glanced back at him.

'I want you to know one thing –' he began.

She held up her hand and stepped back. 'Don't. Please don't.'

There was a short, uncomfortable silence.

'Let me just say you are the most beautiful and kindest woman I've ever known. If things were different –'

'*If* is far too big a word.'

'You're right.'

They walked on a short way and she sighed deeply.

'That sounded heartfelt,' he said.

'I don't know. Everything is heartfelt these days, isn't it?' She paused, wondering how to put it. 'I don't know how to think any more. What do *you* do when you've had enough?'

'Enough of what? Not life, surely. You don't mean that?'

'No. I don't think I do. War, I mean. When I think about winning, I wonder if it even matters when so many are gone.'

He frowned. 'You can't think like that.'

'Why not?'

'It doesn't achieve anything.'

'Must thoughts always achieve something?'

There was a sudden thunderclap and she smiled weakly as the rain began. 'That's God telling me to go home,' she said.

'I guess I'd better head back to my place.'

'Yes.' And then she touched his hands lightly and took to her heels.

Back at the house, Maxine was waiting, her face anxious and drawn. She urged Sofia to come into the salon with her.

'What's happened?' Sofia asked. 'I thought you'd be with Marco. He came to see you.'

'Marco's gone. There was a phone call.'

'Oh?'

'From your mother. I told her you wouldn't be long, but she said she'd find it difficult to call again.'

A dreadful presentiment gripped Sofia. 'Is it my father?'

Maxine paused for a second.

'Tell me.'

'It's Lorenzo.'

'Lorenzo.' Sofia gasped as her head began to spin. 'Dead?'

Maxine reached out. 'No, not dead. No. He's missing.'

Sofia stared at her, aghast. What did that even mean?

'He had planned to check in on your parents, your mother said, told them exactly when, but never appeared. They waited and waited but eventually had to move on. Nobody has seen him for nearly a month. His office doesn't know where he is. Nobody does.'

'He must be travelling for his job, tracking the movement of food supplies, checking grain silos, warehouses and so on.' Although Sofia wanted to believe it, she knew she was grasping at straws. If that was what he'd been doing, he'd have been able to call her.

'His office said not,' Maxine continued. 'He has simply vanished. The German officer he travels with has disappeared too.'

There was a short silence during which Sofia stared at Maxine.

After a few moments Maxine said, 'Are you thinking what I'm thinking?'

Sofia fell back on to the sofa. She had told Maxine about Schmidt's strange visit. This had to have something to do with what he had told her. 'You mean Schmidt's warning?'

Maxine nodded then joined her on the sofa. Wrapping an arm around Sofia's shoulders, she held her tight. Suddenly, the tears Sofia had been holding back began to fall and this time they did not stop. The sadness over Aldo, the terror of what had happened in Florence, her nascent feelings for James, but above all, her utter devastation and grief over her beloved husband. Like a bolt of lightning, it hit her. What he meant to her. And she thanked God nothing more had happened with James. Silently, she made a pact with the Almighty to never let anyone down again and then she whispered, 'Keep my husband safe. Let him be alive. Please don't punish him for what I had only fleetingly wanted to do. Let Lorenzo come back to me. Please.'

45

Sofia dreamt of flying, swooping high above the mountains to the south, fixing her eyes on the fields, the hilltop villages and the farms below. Then plunging down only to soar once more, high into the sky above the clouds where everything shone, blue and peaceful. And where she drifted in the breeze. Floating free. Unburdened. Weightless. Divested of everything. When she woke, her cheeks were wet.

'Lorenzo,' she whispered. 'You made me feel happy with myself, with my whole life really, and now I feel cut adrift. Not floating free as I was in my dream. Instead there's a terrible feeling of being in limbo and utterly alone. Without you this emptiness sits in my very soul.'

It had been a week. She had contacted all the hospitals, constantly made a nuisance of herself with friends and acquaintances, done everything she could think of to find him. And none of it had been easy. Aware that phonelines were often tapped, they used a strange kind of code. But there was no news. Could he be lying dead in a ditch, killed by Allied strafing? Or was it something even worse? In the still of night, she heard herself howling his name, even if it was only in her head.

She sat up in bed and then, after a few minutes, went over to the window, where she threw open the shutters on to a beautiful early-spring day. But the lovely weather did not suit her state of mind. She turned from the window when she heard Maxine enter her room. She had been an angel through this dark time, encouraging Sofia to eat, to wash, and always thinking up ways to look for Lorenzo.

'I've brought coffee,' Maxine said, and, touched by her

compassion, Sofia bowed her head for a second to blink back tears before looking up again.

The room was silent, but Maxine's eyes were full of pity and understanding. She didn't need to say a word.

Sofia took the proffered coffee and they both sat by the window.

'I'm going to have to go,' Sofia said. 'To Rome.'

Maxine took her hand. 'I've been thinking about that. Let me go instead. Let me see if I can find Lorenzo. To be honest, you're in no fit state.'

'It should be me.'

'Your mother gave me the password to use.'

'What, over the phone?'

Maxine shook her head. 'Yesterday. You were asleep. She gave me clues and I kind of had to guess, but she seemed to think I was on the right track. She doesn't want you to go, Sofia.'

'You'll see her? Make sure everything is all right?'

'Sure, I'll see your parents and do everything I can to find out what's happened to Lorenzo.'

Sofia squeezed her hand. 'You will keep safe?'

Maxine nodded. 'I've spoken to Marco about it already. He'll come too. He has contacts in Rome. If anyone can help, Marco can.'

Sofia looked into her eyes and saw the moisture there. 'Thank you, Maxine, for everything.'

'That's what friends are for. You'd do the same . . . Now, enough of all this. Let's see if Carla has anything for us to eat. I'm ravenous.'

Sofia smiled. 'You always are.'

'And *you* need fattening up. Come on.'

'I'll follow. I just need a moment.'

As she left, Sofia realized she didn't know how she'd have coped without her. Carla was there, of course, kind, generous, nurturing, but there was still the difference in their relative status which could get in the way even now. She felt profoundly grateful for Maxine's company.

46.

Rome

Maxine could see that the bombing of the 'Eternal City' of Rome had already been extensive and she soon found out the air raids continued every night. People were saying the Americans had been critical of the destruction of Rome, but it was becoming very clear the British War Cabinet had not agreed. Now a terrifying place to be, she had chosen to arrive right in the middle of intense bombing, widespread deprivation and increasing brutality. Old and young were continually snatched under Hitler's 'Night and Fog' decree, which meant anyone thought to be endangering German security could be arrested and shot or secretly abducted under cover of night. Plus, all fit males under sixty were being seized for forced labour. The air in the city was oily, infused with smoke, and gritty in her nostrils. Damp too, even in March, and danger prowled the streets day and night. Maxine had journeyed right into the heart of hell.

German regiments continued to march; bombs continued to fall. Steel-helmeted soldiers armed with rifles stood guarding every cordoned-off corner and building. The previous July the Allies had targeted the San Lorenzo freight yard and steel factory, but the heavily populated residential district had been destroyed too and thousands of ordinary people had died. Now it was happening again.

She and Marco had travelled by train where they could and managed to walk where they could not.

Now she was on her way to the most recent address she had for Sofia's parents, Elsa and Roberto Romano. As she walked, she thought of her own family, of what had happened to the brother she'd never known about and how it must have affected her parents. Apart from his violent outbursts, her father had never shown strong emotion or feeling, and she realized he must have simply been going through the motions of living. How could anyone live normally after losing a child so tragically? Her mother's cantankerous streak had always been there, as if some hidden resentment was powering her. Maxine had had no idea what it was, but her mother had never been able to stop sticking pins into her daughter, figuratively speaking. Sometimes Maxine hadn't even noticed it happening until the moment had passed, and by then it was too late to question or retaliate. She had learnt to pick out the barbs and not to smart for too long. The awful circumstances of their first son's death explained a lot, but she wished her parents had told her the truth.

She sighed deeply and carried on. In a city brimming with homeless and starving people, Marco would be making contact with a squad of local partisans in the hope of finding somewhere safe to stay. Maxine and Marco's first refuge had been raided on the second night of their stay, a few minutes before they'd got there, so they'd slept in an unused outbuilding near the main railway station along with the tramps and beggars from bombed-out villages. Even some of those with homes had deserted them from fear of identification and arrest, which was hardly surprising given the chilling Nazi propaganda posters plastered everywhere. People now lived in the air-raid shelters or the vile basements of governmental buildings close to the sewers or, if they were lucky, in cold, abandoned homes. By day she saw them huddled on the steps of churches, grey, ghostly folk whose hope had died along with their families.

She and Marco were to meet in a small local café later, a 'standing' bar like the Caffè dei Ritti in Florence, he said. He'd also jokingly suggested they ought to meet at the Caffè Greco on Via dei Condotti, the oldest bar in Rome, but she'd snorted, picturing all the German officers there. The days of brazening it out were over.

Her shoulders drooped with exhaustion but, determined not to succumb, she scurried across Rome, keeping her eyes peeled. Very few people roamed the silent, debris-strewn streets, although long queues formed around the public fountains. When she asked, she was told private houses had no water, but you could buy it at inflated prices from the handcarts in the streets. There was no gas and no coal either, nor were there any buses, though a few trams still ran. She spotted queues outside one or two grocers' shops but the extortionate prices for the mere scraps you could still buy were hardly worth the trouble. 'You can get soup from the Vatican,' someone said. But soup was the last thing on her mind. She made her way past a group of swollen-bellied kids dressed in little more than rags and her heart ached for them. Tucking her hair behind her ears, she pulled the drab headscarf tighter round her head and knotted it beneath her chin. It wouldn't do to stick out. Rome was far more frightening now than in November when she'd last been here.

When she felt satisfied she'd finally identified the correct building, a three-storey apartment block, she wavered. Surely people weren't living here? Peeling paint, cracks zigzagging up to the roof and one partially demolished section confirmed it had been struck by an Allied bomb. An interior staircase crawling up one wall was now obscenely open to the air. She picked her way over the rubble, entered through an open door, found flat six and knocked. The sound of an argument greeted her, a shrill woman's voice answered by a gruff and increasingly irate man. She waited and eventually the door was thrown open by a large red-faced woman with wild frizzy hair.

'What?' she growled and took a step back to yell at the man again.

Maxine stiffened in frustration. 'I'm looking for Elsa and Roberto.'

'No one of that name here.'

'An older man and woman. Used to live on Via del Biscione.'

'Ah.' The red-faced woman paused. 'But why should I tell you? Who are you?'

'I am to say *I have news about Gabriella*.'

The woman narrowed her eyes as if trying to decide. 'Very well. They have gone south of the city to Trastevere.'

'Do you have an address?'

The woman shrugged. 'How should I know? Ask at the Basilica di Santa Cecilia.'

Maxine gave her thanks and then retraced her steps before heading for the west bank of the Tiber. She crossed the river by the Ponte Garibaldo and on the bridge twisted round to look at the synagogue. What had happened in the Jewish ghetto horrified her afresh. It had been October, the day after she'd arrived. She'd watched in wide-eyed horror as men, women and children had been forced from the cobbled labyrinth of the overcrowded Jewish ghetto and herded into waiting lorries, as if they were cattle. Vermin, the Nazis had called them. Rumours were rife but God knows where they'd been taken. Now, the houses with walled-up windows were possibly even more terrifying than before. These were the makeshift torture chambers of the Gestapo where souls were destroyed before bodies were slaughtered.

She soon found her way to the centuries-old, working-class district of Trastevere and walked the narrow cobbled streets, surprised by the still-colourful buildings where, despite the war, ivy climbed the walls and balconies showed signs of early cascading geraniums. After asking once or twice, she easily found the Piazza di Santa Cecilia and the Catholic church the woman had mentioned. An elderly priest sat just inside the door talking to a poorly dressed, and clearly hungry, young girl. Once he'd found a hunk of bread for her and the girl had stuffed it into her mouth and fled, Maxine approached him directly and spoke the sentence Elsa had promised would work.

'I have news of Gabriella.'

He rose slowly to his feet. 'And you are looking for?'

'An older couple, Elsa and Roberto.'

'I may know who you mean. Try Via Giulio Cesare Santini. It isn't far.' And he pointed her in the right direction. 'Go left and left again. Try the house before the corner with Via Zanazzo Giggi.'

Maxine did as she'd been instructed and found the house within minutes. It had been painted a rich terracotta sometime in its history but now, with paintwork peeling and the front door buckled and bleached dry, it looked very down at heel. She knocked and waited. After a few moments a stooped old man with an anxious expression opened the door a crack and peered at her.

'Yes?'

'The priest sent me.'

'And you are?'

'I'm Massima. I'm looking for Elsa and Roberto.'

He shook his head.

'I have news of Gabriella.'

He opened the door more fully. 'You are alone?'

'Of course.'

He looked her up and down. 'You are a doctor?' he added more in hope than expectation.

She shook her head.

He raised his brows and puffed out his cheeks, then indicated she should follow him through the rabbit warren behind the house. They eventually reached the back door of another house which he opened and then pushed her ahead of him.

'Second door on the right,' he said and left her to it.

She reached the drab brown door and knocked gently.

A woman opened it cautiously. 'Yes?'

'I have news of Gabriella,' Maxine whispered.

'Don't say anything more. Come in.'

With the curtains closed, the room was gloomy, and the air

smelt rancid. At first Maxine didn't see Roberto lying on a bed in the corner, under a thin blanket, but when she did, she took a step back in surprise.

'Oh, I'm so sorry. I didn't realize.'

He didn't speak but coughed intermittently.

'He has a chest infection, is all,' Elsa explained, looking at Maxine's stricken face. But Maxine could tell such a hacking cough, along with his appalling pallor, suggested something more serious.

'He looks awfully thin. Pale too.'

'I *am* here,' he said, then spluttered.

Elsa ignored his comment. 'This is Maxine. You remember her?'

'Of course,' he grumbled. 'Nothing wrong with my brain *or* my eyes.'

Elsa raised her brows then smiled sadly. 'He gets a little tetchy.'

'But why are you here . . . living like this?' Maxine glanced around her. There was a cracked sink in the corner, the floorboards remained bare and a small pile of threadbare bedding lay on the one wooden chair leaning against the wall.

'It's not so bad . . . we have an oil lamp.' She waved vaguely at a lamp beside the sink. 'The thing is, Roberto's name has been leaked. We don't know by whom, but the Nazis know he is one of the men responsible for hiding the printing press. They've been searching for him. We dare not stay in one place for more than a couple of days.'

'How do you manage to move? I heard there were snipers on the lookout.'

'It's difficult. Fascist, Nazi or partisan. We never know which. And German reprisals all the time for anything, no matter how small. They shoot you as soon as look at you.'

'Dear God, we have to get you out of Rome. Do you have fake documents?'

'The priest has promised us. They should be here later today.

But you don't need to worry, we are all right. People are helping us. Now please tell me, how is Sofia?'

Maxine bowed her head for a moment before speaking. 'Distraught at Lorenzo's disappearance.'

'We have had no news of him, but I fear the worst.'

'You have reason?'

She shook her head. 'Not really, but when anyone vanishes so suddenly and without trace, we always fear the worst.'

'Look, I have to meet up with a friend soon. I really want to help you both get to safety. Sofia would never forgive me if I abandoned you here. So, I'll leave now and bring food later, hopefully with a plan.'

The look on Elsa's face was intense. 'You're very kind, but there's no need . . . Just one thing . . . please don't tell Sofia about this, not where we are, or anything about Roberto's illness.'

'She'd want to know.'

'If she knows she'll come and more than anything in the world I want her to remain safely at the Castello.'

Maxine understood, deciding to say nothing about Sofia's activities in Florence. She was beginning to realize that all families had secrets of one kind or another.

47

Just before dawn the next morning Maxine and Marco listened to the sound of engines rumbling in the sky, growing louder and louder as wave after wave of Allied planes flew low. The shrill air-raid warning was followed by the high-pitched whistle of bombs shrieking and then exploding like claps of unforgiving thunder, as if the gods themselves were intent on blasting and shattering the earth below. Then came the staccato sound of machine-gun fire repeating and repeating. Maxine covered her ears as screams echoed from somewhere in the street and carried on ringing in her head. When it was over, they heard the whine of the all-clear siren. She crawled out of bed and went outside where the clouds of dust and smoke had cleared just enough to make out German patrol cars racing down the street.

Soon they would try to spirit Elsa and Roberto out of the city. She and Marco had talked late into the night devising their plan. They would pose as a family taking a train as far as they could into the hilly villages north-east of Rome. Marco had a grandmother who still lived in a mountain hamlet south of Rome, which would have been better, but the southern exits were much too heavily guarded. And, at least, it would be closer for Maxine and Marco to get back to the Castello from the north-east.

She came back inside, slipped into bed and curled up beside Marco. He murmured in his sleep and then reached for her.

'I love you,' she whispered. 'I love you.'

She remembered her mother's words: *When you love someone, you love them, no matter what.*

He rolled over to face her and gently stroked the hair away from her face.

'When the war is over –' she said, but he put a finger to his lips to shush her.

Not to be deterred, she began again. 'When the war –'

This time he checked her by covering her mouth with his. The kiss, there on the mattress on the floor in the foul-smelling room he'd found for them, was long and complicated. Its meaning, the unspoken words and its intensity, a result of the impossibility of looking ahead. She wanted him in her life forever, but there *was* no forever. Not any more.

They made love urgently, taking comfort from each other in the only way they could. The charm of him, the daring, the passion, the fortitude, she loved every part of him, every thrust of his body, and in every gasp the sensations forced from her. Prised open by him, her carefully constructed barriers had fallen away. She did love him. It was true, and never more than now when they were as close as it was possible to be. This, the Nazis could not destroy. This God-given miracle was far stronger than all the fear and hate. This was hope and life itself and she exalted in it. And when it was over, her eyes burnt with unshed tears. His lips moved silently but she understood what he was saying. *Ti amo anch'io.* With every particle of her being she knew he was saying he loved her too.

'I'm tired,' she said after a while.

He raised himself up on one elbow, then kissed her forehead. 'We are all tired, *tesoro.* Tired and afraid.'

'And yet we do what we do.'

His sigh was sorrowful. 'What else is there?'

'Find somewhere far away to hide.'

'Until it is all over?'

She nodded.

'You don't mean it?'

'No, obviously not.' But in the far reaches of herself she did mean it. She wanted to wrap him up and keep him safe. 'But don't you ever want to run?'

'What difference does it make? We're all already running from something.'

'What are you running from, Marco?'

He sniffed rather derisively. 'The fear of a mundane life, maybe.'

'But isn't it what we all want now? For our lives to be normal again.'

He laughed. 'If normal was what you wanted you would never have come to Italy. Are you saying you regret it?'

She shook her head. She did not regret coming; she just wanted it to be over.

'Just one thing,' he said. 'In case you ever need it, I want you to know my surname.'

'Why would I ever need it?'

'To practise how it sounds. What do you think of Maxine Vallone?'

'Are you asking me . . .?'

'What do you think?'

48.

23 March 1944

With a great deal of vigilance, Marco and Maxine warily made their way to the place where he'd previously met with the partisans of the *Gruppi di Azione Patriottica*. Precautions were taken to maintain the group members' anonymity as the pair of them were escorted blindfold to meet with a British officer who was in hiding in one of the city's cellars. When Maxine quizzed the man about Lorenzo, the officer said he was certain that Lorenzo had been arrested. They'd had a meeting arranged but Lorenzo had never turned up.

'So, when was this?'

'About a month ago.'

'And had you met him before?'

'Twice.'

Marco asked the officer to describe the man and was given a very clear indication he may well be right: grey eyes, greying hair, tall.

'He was cultured, educated,' the officer added. 'Clearly from a privileged background. Spoke very good English. I called him the Conte, and he did say he came from Tuscany.'

'So why do you think the Germans arrested him?'

The British officer gave him a look. 'They must have cottoned on to the fact he was helping us.'

'He wasn't at the ministry any longer?'

'No. Definitely not. He had gone way beyond that.'

After thanking the man, they arranged to meet up later, but in the meantime Marco would check out their new lodgings while Maxine waited in the water queue.

* * *

Three hours later, Maxine was scanning the street. With a feeling of intense relief, she eventually caught sight of Marco; she hadn't expected him to take so long and had been feeling anxious. It wasn't good news that he now found himself tangled up in a column of German SS Police who had been marching and singing their way through the Piazza di Spagna towards the narrow Via Rasella where Maxine was a little ahead of them. Everyone hated these shows of German might, aimed at daunting the citizens and undermining the resistance. Ordinary people did their best to ignore them while silently smouldering with resentment or drowning in apathy. None of the marching men were looking at Marco. He was brilliant at becoming invisible, just another limping, hopeless man hugging the walls. The Nazis were not interested in the weak, only the strong; to them, he did not even exist.

After a few moments she could see that Marco had managed to sidle past the Germans and had spotted her standing on Via Rasella about a hundred metres away. She held up her can of water to show she'd seen him.

As Marco started to walk towards her, Maxine noticed a street cleaner pushing a rubbish cart. She would remember this moment afterwards: the street cleaner suddenly, and inexplicably, running away and Marco heading towards her. And then the enormous flash of an explosion and the sound of it ripping through the air. Clouds of smoke billowed up, and in the intense heat, Maxine dropped the water and clutched her chest. She tried to see but could not. Where was Marco? Where was he? Around her people had dived to the ground in panic. Or they had run. The acrid smell sickened her, and she tasted the sourness in her mouth. When the smoke began to clear she saw bodies lying randomly and inert. Dozens of SS bodies: dismembered bodies, headless bodies, and the blood from them pooling everywhere. Those still standing were shaking and supporting each other as they desperately tried to get away. Maxine saw a man whose chest had been blown open, and another with no legs. Another was struggling to his feet, blood pouring from his head. Glass had flown everywhere. Debris too. An officer hobbled off, one of the lucky ones, and the people who'd happened to be in the street were hurrying, screaming at each other to run. She kept looking for Marco and then she saw him stumbling towards her. Relief flooded her body. Thank God. She was so sure he'd been caught in the blast, but there he was. Then the gunfire began, and she glanced around her – was it the SS firing in response? She turned back to Marco and watched in horror as he clutched his chest. In slow motion his eyes met hers, his face registered surprise, his knees buckled and then he crumpled to the ground. It had been a matter of moments but to Maxine the world had stopped spinning. Frozen in disbelief, she hesitated. *No, no, no*, she whispered. *Not Marco.* Her paralysis lasted for only a second or two. Then she ran, staggering and tripping over glass and debris, praying out loud, screaming for him to wait for her, her breath ragged, but when she reached him, Marco was already dead. She dropped to his side, placed her palm on the injury to his chest as if to stem the blood, then cradled him to her and wrapped herself around his lifeless body.

'My love,' she whispered. 'My love.'

But the German police were now shooting in earnest. She had to get out of there but how could she leave Marco? She clung to his body, her clothes soaking up his blood, and resisted the order to leave, but in the end she was pushed out of the way by a soldier thrusting at her with the butt of his rifle. She begged him to shoot her too and for a moment she hoped he might but then he sniggered and found someone else to harass.

How she reached the priest she'd met before in Trastevere she didn't remember, but she hadn't known where else to go. He placed her in the care of some nuns. The priest, whose name was Father Filippo, visited her daily, and over the next few days he found out the whole story behind the bombing and the terrible reprisals that followed. Maxine listened blankly as he shook his head and told how the Germans had decided that for every one of the thirty-five soldiers killed, ten would be executed in return. It was awful, Maxine recognized, it was truly awful, but for now all she could think of was Marco.

It transpired, the priest said a couple of days later, that a nun had bicycled after the trucks taking the victims to the rural area beyond the city centre where, inside the tunnels of the disused quarries of *pozzolana*, near the Via Ardeatina, the massacre had taken place. The nun had hidden behind some rocks and reported that the soldiers chosen to do the killing were given long draughts of cognac before the shooting. Then they were instructed to lead the prisoners into the caves with their hands tied behind their backs. She hadn't been able to see inside the caves, but she had counted each man going in – 335 of them. She would never forget the brutality and horror until the day she died.

The priest went on to say that the Germans wanted to keep the location of the massacre secret, so for her own safety it would be best to not share what she now knew. Maxine came back to herself when she understood the men they murdered had come from the prisons. Over three hundred random men. Oh God! Lorenzo. Had he been one of them? As for the bombing, it was now known to have been carried out by at least sixteen partisans of the Communist-led resistance organization *Gruppi di Azione Patriottica*, the very people Marco had met with. The improvised bomb had consisted of the chemical compound TNT packed in a steel case inside a bag and placed in the rubbish bin pushed into position by one of the partisans disguised as a street cleaner. Apparently, the fuse had been lit when the SS were forty seconds from the bomb. Thirty-five had been killed in total, though not all outright. Some had died later from their injuries. All the partisans involved, some of whom also fired on the German column – and may even have been the ones who had killed Marco – disappeared into the crowd and reached safety. The irony was not lost on Maxine.

In her stronger moments she made plans to leave, for she still had Elsa and Roberto to take care of, but sometimes she felt she would never be truly strong again. She had not been able to cry for the only man she had ever loved but spent hours sitting and thinking of him. Why had she not been able to cry? The moment he had died went around and around in her head, as if she might somehow be able to change the ending with willpower alone. Of course, she never could. Marco could never escape that bullet. And, in the end, she had to reluctantly accept he was gone. At last, it came to her. She would never be Maxine Vallone, not now, but she had to honour Marco's memory by standing up for what he believed in and continuing the fight. Despite everything, of one thing she was certain: Marco would live inside her forever and would always be the one true love of her life. He had been a brave and wonderful man, and she would need to be brave too. She couldn't let him down with her weakness and so she dug deep inside herself and found the strength to organize. She would take Elsa and Roberto to Sofia's Castello in Tuscany instead of to one of the closer hill villages.

49

Two days later Maxine had collected Roberto and Elsa along with their new papers and they were now settling into the waiting train. A loud whistle sounded followed by a hiss of steam as the train clanged and clattered into life. It moved slowly, shuddering and stuttering and almost coming to a stop but eventually gathered momentum and picked up speed. Elsa held tight to a basket where a loaf of bread was wrapped in a blue-and-white chequered cloth. Roberto, sitting, leant against Maxine, who stood next to him by the wooden bench, guarding the older couple's suitcase. There was an unhealthy sheen to Roberto's pale face now and Maxine worried he might not reach the Castello alive. She was aware of Elsa's troubled eyes and sensed the shame the older woman must be feeling. No one wants to steal away from their beloved city like a thief in the night, and her despair over Roberto's worsening health was visible. Roberto himself remained brave. Nothing would get the better of him if he could help it.

The train – full of nuns, soldiers and people fleeing the city – smelt of stale tobacco and urine. Maxine and Elsa both wore drab skirts, blouses and peasant-style shawls. A young mother with a crying baby crouched on the floor, ignored by two German soldiers who might have offered her a seat. Monsters. But then a much younger soldier, not much more than a boy, rose to his feet and gave up his seat for the woman. Maxine smiled at him as he caught her eye and he blushed. So, so young, she thought, his humanity not yet hardened by war. Nearby a couple of little boys, their grimy faces streaked with the signs of recent tears, their arms and legs dotted with open sores, clung to their grandmother's skirts.

'Their house was bombed,' the old lady said to no one in particular. 'I have to take them. There is nobody else.'

Elsa murmured a response, but the old lady simply repeated what she'd already said.

Once they'd left the city, the trees, bushes, agricultural lands and lone farms flew past the window. Conversation remained muted, the people too exhausted and beaten to have anything new to say. Maxine rested her eyes, the rhythmic clattering and clanking noise of the train fading into the background as her mind drifted. Everyone was on the move, one way or another, and nothing stood still, but she longed for calm and the chance of an uninterrupted sleep. Perhaps at the Castello. And now she focused on Sofia. So far all they'd found out was that a man who answered Lorenzo's description had most likely been arrested. How could she tell Sofia that, on top of the news of Roberto's failing health? She had spoken to Elsa about it, who agreed that Lorenzo's arrest sounded feasible.

She was almost falling asleep an hour or so later when the squeal of brakes and the train's sudden screeching halt sent them tumbling over each other and clutching for something to grab on to. She glanced at Elsa, who raised her brows. Then came the menacing shouts, *'Aufstehen, Aufstehen!' Get up, get up*, over and over.

After waiting a few moments while she worked out what to do, Maxine said, 'I'll go.' She struggled to reach the door but was able to push her way through. Outside, she saw a stream of armed SS officers dragging pleading women and crying children from the train and brutally shoving them to the ground. Remembering Marco, the hatred burnt in her heart and she could hardly bear to look at them. She managed to exchange a few words with an older woman who was already preparing to slip away.

'They are taking the men into the woods,' the woman said. 'And you know what that means. They'll be shot in retribution.'

Maxine listened a little longer, heard what else was going on and then hurried back to the carriage.

'The tracks are badly damaged. The engine has been derailed,' she said to the carriage in general, and then added for Elsa only, 'We have to get off. The German SS are on the train already, tearing it apart, checking papers and forcing us all to get out at gunpoint. They're sending everyone back to Rome on the next train.'

'I don't know if Roberto can get off,' Elsa whispered.

There was a sudden burst of gunfire followed by screaming. Maxine glanced across at the old man. 'We don't have a choice.'

'Was it an Allied bomb?'

'Could have been partisans. They're well ahead in these parts now. Forming a national liberation committee, I was told.'

From the next carriage came the sound of weeping. Elsa reached for Roberto's hand and Maxine helped pull him up and together they managed to get him, stumbling and coughing, off the train.

'We'll take the road to begin with and then veer off on to the hill tracks,' Maxine said.

Elsa's eyes were huge with anxiety. 'Will he even make it up the hills?'

'He will. I think they're only low hills.'

A German truck, covered in canvas tied down by ropes to a bar on each side, hooted as it passed them heading towards the city, followed by a motorcycle with a steel-helmeted soldier sitting in the sidecar. A horse and cart filled with sacks came next and then another, both heading for Rome. Then, apart from a couple of burnt-out cars, the road emptied of traffic. They wound up and around the gentle slope, but their progress was slow, hampered by the pain Roberto was in.

'Maybe we could find a mule?' Elsa suggested. 'To carry him.'

Maxine puffed out her cheeks and sighed. 'It's possible. We'll go off-road now, where he can rest out of sight. We may be able to get another train further up the line.'

They took a muddy track to the left and soon arrived in an area of undulating gullies, woodland and streams. There they lay Roberto on a mossy bank in the shade beneath a tree, Maxine and Elsa sitting beside him. Maxine drew out a flask of water from her bag and passed it to Elsa, who held it to her husband's lips. But from the expression on her face, Maxine could see resignation had set in.

'We need to find a barn or a church, somewhere to spend the night,' she said. 'It'll be cold when the sun goes down.'

Elsa's eyes were clouded with misery, but she agreed.

Maxine squeezed Elsa's hand. 'I'll scout on ahead for a bit. See what I can find.'

Elsa looked anxious. 'A woman alone out here is at risk.'

'I'm not scared.'

Elsa shook her head. 'Well, you should be.'

Maxine rose to her feet. 'I have to go, see if there's somewhere. Don't worry.'

A few minutes after Maxine set off the hairs on her neck rose at the sound of voices. German voices in the woods – real or imagined? She held her breath, told herself there were always German voices in her head. More sounds followed, but it turned out to be a couple of refugee women searching for wild herbs to eat. They passed by without a word and after that it remained silent save for planes flying overhead.

Once she found what she was looking for, Maxine hurried back to tell Elsa. 'There's a barn, only ten minutes' walk. Been hit by a bomb. Huge hole in the roof and a crater in the floor but it's safe all around the sides. Can we manage it?'

So Elsa and Maxine supported Roberto, whose eyes were now closed, and they half carried him, half dragged him to the barn where Elsa gathered some bits of hay to fashion a bed for him on the rough stone floor. Maxine collected pieces of broken wood from what had once been animal stalls and built a small fire to warm him. The man was utterly still, showing signs of life only when a coughing fit took him; afterwards, convulsed and gasping, he was barely able to breathe at all.

That night they hardly slept. Maxine watched as, through the hole in the roof, Allied flares could be seen floating in the air, looking other-worldly as they gradually fell, illuminating the ground below. If only the Allies would come now, she muttered to herself. Why were they taking so long to win Cassino? Once that happened, Rome would be next. But all the news reports continued to say the Allies were having to fight a desperate war on the ground and the Germans were holding fast to their strongest line of defence so far. And until the British army or the Americans were able to cross the heavily guarded Rapido river there was no hope of taking Monte Cassino. Reports had filtered through that hundreds of men had attempted it already and had drowned or been shot, the river turning red with their blood. In one attempt the Americans had lost 2,000 men in twenty-four hours.

Here, the moon was so bright, like an unusually blue day, the Allies barely needed the flares. Mice scurried along the walls of the barn and outside larger animals, boar maybe, hunted for food. A little before dawn she could hear soldiers shouting nearby, thrashing at the undergrowth, their dogs barking. When it turned silent again, she tried to cast the anxieties from her mind. But it was an eerie, lonely silence that made her falter as she reached for Marco's hand. Grief slammed into her again and her eyes blurred. Marco was not there. Never would be there again.

A few moments later, as the day began to break, she could make out Elsa curled up against Roberto, protecting him with her own body. Then Maxine went cold as she worked out that something was wrong. For several hours now, Roberto had not been coughing at all.

Though pale still, the day had grown a little brighter and she watched as Elsa sat up, then knelt at Roberto's side. She touched his face and bowed her head for a second or two before glancing up at Maxine, a tear sliding down her cheek.

'Well,' she whispered. 'The Germans cannot hurt him now.'

She held his cold hand to her lips one last time before rising to her feet, standing tall and proud for a moment, then walking away.

Maxine moved to follow before she realized Elsa needed a few minutes alone.

Soon they would have to find a way to get to the Castello but over the next few hours Elsa and Maxine covered Roberto's body with branches and comforted each other as best they could. They had become two of the women who had lost, and there were so many of them, grieving for brothers, husbands, fathers, lovers and, perhaps most tragic of all, sons. All gone. Good men and bad. All victims of this terrible war. Maxine didn't know if it made her feel better or worse to be one amongst so many in the monstrous regiments of grieving women.

50

Castello de' Corsi

April 1944

Maxine still had not reappeared with news of Lorenzo, but Sofia could not allow herself to sit and mope. She felt the moment had come to talk to Gabriella again, so she had summoned the girl and her mother to her personal salon. They now sat opposite her on the little chintz sofa looking a little nervous and out of place. Families had their own way of doing things and Sofia wasn't fully convinced her intervention would help, but she had promised Carla help when she needed it. And although Carla was too proud to ask outright, she'd dropped some hints that Gabriella wasn't facing up to things.

'So,' Sofia said, gazing at the girl with what she hoped was a compassionate expression. 'Do you know when your baby is due?'

Carla spoke up. 'We think at the end of July.'

'Better to let the girl speak for herself, Carla.'

Carla nodded.

In the knowledge that talking about this might be embarrassing for Gabriella, Sofia decided to approach the subject in a gentle, encouraging tone. 'Is your mother correct?'

Gabriella shrugged and shot a barely concealed but mutinous scowl at her mother.

Sofia sighed in frustration, but carried on. 'Gabriella, you do realize we are trying to help you?'

Gabriella hung her head, but muttered, 'Don't need help.'

'My dear, you are very young. You will have a baby to look after and no husband to help you. It isn't going to be easy. Do you understand?'

It looked as if Gabriella longed to glare at Sofia but did not dare, although the way she stuck out her chin plus the obstinate narrowing of her eyes clearly revealed her thoughts.

'You are right,' Sofia said in answer to what she'd picked up. 'I've had no children of my own, but I've seen plenty who have. Being a mother is the hardest job of all.'

As Gabriella glanced up, Sofia saw that the mulish facade was giving way a little and she began to glimpse the frightened girl behind the defiance.

'Mother will help,' Gabriella said, but her voice wobbled.

Sofia shook her head. 'Your mother has her duties to see to. She won't have time to look after a baby. You alone will be responsible. I have expressly told your mother she is not to step in.'

Gabriella twisted her head to look at Carla as if she couldn't believe what she was being told. 'But –'

'No buts, I'm afraid. Naturally, you may ask for advice any time you want. We will always be here. Always willing, you see.'

Gabriella fell silent, as if needing to take this in, although Sofia knew Carla had explained it all already. Maybe hearing it from her made it more real. Sofia didn't want to scare the girl but knew, from what Carla had already said, that Gabriella viewed the baby as a toy, a doll to play with and put away when she'd had enough. But she needed to understand the significance of what she'd done. Not only because she'd had sex with the Fascist lad, which could have endangered her family and Sofia and Lorenzo too, and not only because of the shame she would cause her family by bringing an illegitimate child into the world, but far, far worse – because she had leaked information that may well have led to her own brother's death. And Sofia wanted her to understand there were always consequences to actions. Carla didn't want her burdened by guilt for the rest of her life, which was right, but there had to be genuine remorse. There had been no further sign of that since the day Gabriella had rather half-heartedly cut herself. Was she being too harsh? She didn't believe Gabriella had really wanted to kill herself, but she had needed help, had wanted the truth to come out, and that had been a start.

'Now, Gabriella,' she began again. 'I want to talk to you about what you told Maria.'

The girl didn't speak but stared out of the window, and there was still an air of insolence about the way she did it.

'I'm talking about the partisans' plans to blow up the railway tracks. You said you told Maria so she would inform her grandson, Paolo.'

Gabriella glanced across and even though she didn't meet Sofia's eyes, Sofia felt it was a move in the right direction. 'And that was because?'

The girl blinked rapidly and then came out with it. 'Because he said he loved me, but then he didn't come. I was sad and I wanted him to come back and say he loved me again.'

'Oh, my dear –'

'Why didn't he come back?' Gabriella asked with such a look of sorrow in her eyes, Sofia pitied her.

Without warning, Anna, clearly having overheard, burst into the room, glaring first at Carla and then at Gabriella. Carla and Sofia froze as Anna rushed at Gabriella, grabbed her by the hair and dragged her halfway across the room.

'You stupid, spoilt little vixen,' Anna hissed and slapped Gabriella's face so hard she fell to the ground. It happened so fast that nobody had time to intervene. Gabriella began to crawl towards Carla for safety but then Sofia realized Anna wasn't finished. She bent down, about to haul her sister up again by her arm.

Sofia rose swiftly to her feet. 'Anna, stop! Stop right now,' she commanded.

Anna stopped, glancing round, and Sofia glimpsed the agony behind the anger in her eyes.

'Don't, Anna. It won't help.'

Anna's fists were clenched, and anyone could see she longed

to hit her sister again. Punch until the pain stopped. Except it wouldn't. That kind of pain didn't stop.

She took a step towards her sister and cursed vehemently. '*La puttana!* She can't be allowed to get away with it. I'm going to smash her stupid face until she understands what she's done.'

Sofia pulled Anna away and met with no resistance.

'Contessa,' she said, and her face twisted in utter anguish.

'I know, but it won't help. You know it won't. Hurting Gabriella won't bring Aldo back.'

Anna took a deep breath and then, as Sofia let go of her arm, she hurled her anger at Carla. 'You have always spoilt her. Now look.'

Sofia stepped in. 'I know you want someone to blame but this isn't your mother's fault, Anna. What would you have us do? Give her up to the partisans?'

'Why not?'

'And what do you think they would do? She's pregnant, for heaven's sake.'

'It would serve her right.'

'No. Think about how you'd feel. She's carrying your little nephew or niece.'

'A filthy Blackshirt's bastard,' Anna hissed contemptuously. 'Mother should have taken her to the witch in Buonconvento.'

Sofia knew about the older woman who prescribed herbs for certain women's conditions. No one had ever admitted going to her and yet everyone knew of her existence.

'You know it's a crime,' Carla whispered. 'Against God.'

Anna watched in disdain as Gabriella curled up on the floor with her arms wrapped round her mother's legs. 'Stand up,' she said in a tone that brooked no argument.

As Gabriella winced and tried to make herself smaller, Carla stroked her hair.

'Stop it, Mother. This is what she always does. Pretends to be a baby and you let her get away with everything. She needs to stand up.'

Carla stopped stroking and whispered in Gabriella's ear.

'I *said* stand up,' Anna repeated.

'Please don't hit me.' Gabriella's voice was babyish, wheedling, a tried and tested tone she'd used before.

'*Per amor del cielo*. I'm not going to hit you. Stand up.'

Gabriella struggled to her feet and Sofia, believing Anna wouldn't be violent again, decided to let it run. This was family business and she considered leaving the room, but the whole situation was so finely balanced, she dared not disturb it.

Once Gabriella was standing, Anna faced her. 'Now repeat after me. *I slept with a Fascist Blackshirt.*'

'I . . . slept with a Fascist . . .' Gabriella paused.

'*Blackshirt.*'

'Blackshirt,' Gabriella repeated, her voice trembling.

'*Even though I knew it might harm my own family.*'

Gabriella's voice was now a whisper as she echoed Anna's words. 'Even though I knew it might harm my own family.'

'*I am having his baby, bringing shame on my family.*'

Gabriella repeated the words.

'*And I gave away information that led to my own brother's death.*'

Gabriella was silent and oh so vulnerable. Sofia, horrified by the brutal way Anna was handling this, felt she should avert her eyes or put a stop to it but, mesmerized, couldn't help watching the unfolding scene. Carla hadn't been able to get through to Gabriella. Maybe this would work? She held her breath.

'Say it.' Anna was roaring now. 'Say it.'

Gabriella took a long, slow, shuddering breath. 'And I gave away information . . .' She burst into tears.

'Finish the words. *I gave away information that led to my own brother's death.*'

Gabriella brushed her tears away with the back of her hand. 'I . . . gave away information . . . that led to . . .' And then, her shoulders heaving, she began to howl.

To hear the deep, agonizing pain of it was unbearable and

Sofia pressed her lips together to prevent the tears from forming. But her eyes remained moist and, instinctively wanting to wrap her arms around Gabriella, her heart broke at the sound of Carla's sobs too.

'*That led to my own brother's death,*' Anna said.

'My ... own ... brother's ... death,' Gabriella repeated between gulps of air and the sobs which kept on coming.

'Good,' Anna said, satisfied at last.

Gabriella lifted her skirt to her face and wiped it. 'I am sorry, Anna. Please believe me.'

'That's good too,' Anna said, white-faced.

Gabriella's voice shook as she continued but a different, more grown-up Gabriella had emerged. 'I know you can never forgive me and I don't expect you to.'

Anna stared at her sister and Sofia wondered what would happen next. Carla had stopped sobbing.

'But I am so sorry. Truly.'

For a few moments nobody spoke.

'I will never forgive myself,' Gabriella continued in a whisper.

Anna's face was expressionless, and you could hear a pin drop in the following silence.

'I'll go away. I don't want to shame you all. I know there's nothing I can do to make it right.'

The tension in the room had become excruciating. Sofia had no idea where things would go from there. She took a long breath and exhaled very slowly, wondering if now was the time for her to intervene. Again, she decided not and glanced at the window, longing for air.

But then Anna held out her arms. Sofia was so surprised she felt her mouth fall open and she saw Carla was staring, wide-eyed, too.

'Come here,' Anna said, and at first Gabriella just looked at her as if she didn't understand. 'Come here,' Anna repeated.

Gabriella's face suddenly lit up, realizing what Anna meant, and she ran to throw herself into her sister's arms.

'You're not going anywhere,' Anna whispered as she hugged her. 'We will deal with this as a family.'

Gabriella sniffed as she pulled away to look at Anna. 'I promise I will never let you down again.'

'I'll hold you to it.'

Gabriella nodded.

'Well now, time to dry your eyes. We can't stand here all day. There's work to be done.'

Gabriella beamed at her and her face glowed as if an enormous weight had fallen from her shoulders.

'I'm sorry for the intrusion, Contessa Sofia,' Anna said, and Sofia almost laughed at the sudden formality.

'Think nothing of it,' she said.

And then the sisters left the room, side by side, and a new era was born.

'Well,' Sofia said, gazing at Carla. 'I wasn't expecting that.'

Carla shook her head in disbelief. 'Me neither. Who would've thought it? Maybe Anna was right all along and I have been overindulging Gabriella?'

'We both know you only did your best. You were doing whatever you could to protect a vulnerable child.'

'Thank you. Today, I think Gabriella grew up.'

'It will never be easy for her to live with her part in what happened to Aldo,' Sofia said.

'No. But at least she's taken responsibility for it and can begin to . . . well . . . I'm not sure exactly what.'

'Make amends?'

Carla smiled. 'Something like that.'

51

A few nights later, just before midnight, Maxine and Elsa arrived at the Castello, filthy and worn-out. Sofia, alarmed by her mother's sunken cheeks, ran straight to her, but her mother's eyes clouded and she seemed dazed as she stood shaking with fatigue. Sofia, desperate to ask where her father was, glanced at Maxine, and with eyes full of sorrow her friend shook her head. Instantly, Sofia knew. Her father was dead. In a trembling voice she asked Carla to run them each a bath and put out nightclothes, which she did. Then she carried soup and bread to their rooms and reported that they'd both gone to bed.

During the long night, aeroplanes flew over almost incessantly but in between it was impossible to avoid hearing her mother's muffled sobs. Sofia wanted to comfort her, but something told her Elsa needed to be alone. Meanwhile, the questions went around and around in her head. She needed to know exactly what had happened to her father and to hear if there was any news of Lorenzo. Plagued by wretchedness, she did not sleep.

In the morning Sofia was in her little salon when Maxine appeared and stood in the doorway with Elsa right behind her, thin, wraith-like. Maxine looked as if she was trying to prepare for something and Sofia's throat tightened as they exchanged a glance. Sofia remained standing and pressed her palm to the wall for support but indicated they should both sit. Maxine curled up on the blue velvet sofa while Elsa sat bolt upright on a hard-backed chair, her face ashen. Sofia turned first to Maxine and gave her a pleading look.

'So?' she asked, hardly daring to hear what was bound to be an agonizing account.

Elsa began to speak in a flat, emotionless voice. 'Roberto . . .'

Sofia shoved her fist into her mouth to stop herself from crying out. When she spoke, it was almost a whisper.

'They . . . they . . . killed him?'

'Not exactly.'

Elsa gave Maxine a look and nodded, seeming to give Maxine permission to continue.

'Your father had to go into hiding, Sofia.'

She blinked rapidly, hardly able to absorb this. 'Hiding? Why?'

'Someone informed,' Elsa said, taking over but still sounding deadened. 'They found out he was one of the men behind the printing of illegal leaflets. Then he became ill and we couldn't get the treatment he needed.'

Sofia stared at one and then the other, then turned back to her mother, who shook her head hopelessly.

'We had to get your father out of Rome,' Maxine said. 'I'm so sorry. He just didn't make it and died on the way.'

'Oh, *mio signore*! No. Not my poor father. Not him.' Sofia swallowed hard, feeling the heat prickling her eyes and the lump developing in her throat.

Neither Maxine nor Elsa spoke.

'You . . . you were with him?' she asked her mother with a sob in her voice.

Elsa nodded.

'I can't bear it. Did he know? Did he suffer?'

'He was very ill. He knew he didn't have long. But the end was peaceful. He simply slipped away.'

Sofia's eyes overflowed with tears. 'Did he know how much I loved him? I never told him, Mamma. I never said.'

'Oh, my darling girl, of course he knew. You were the light of his life.'

'Who is *we*?' Sofia whispered after a moment. 'Maxine said *we*. Was it just you and Maxine?'

She glanced around the room, wringing her hands, as if expecting to find someone in the shadows, then turned to Maxine.

Maxine held her gaze, blinking rapidly and struggling to hold back tears.

'Did Marco help you with my father? Where is he now?'

Maxine swallowed visibly but her voice remained steady. 'Marco died, Sofia.'

Sofia gasped in horror. 'Dear God! Not Marco too. What happened?'

'We got caught up in Via Rasella when a bomb exploded, and he was shot trying to get away.'

'Oh no, I'm so dreadfully sorry.' She took a step forward, but Maxine lowered her gaze and shook her head.

There was a long, agonized pause.

Sofia swallowed the lump in her throat. Then, after a moment, she said softly, 'But the bomb was three weeks ago. Why didn't you come home sooner?'

Her mother replied. 'We left a week after the explosion, but it took us two weeks to get here. The train was derailed. It was a terrible, frightening journey . . . so many roadblocks . . . so many Germans heading north. And the Allied planes too. Awful.'

Sofia squeezed her eyes shut and bowed her head. There were no words for this, and she felt an overwhelming need to blame someone for her father's death. 'If my father was so ill, wouldn't it have been better to stay in Rome?'

'We had run out of places to stay. There was no water, virtually nothing to eat. You can't imagine.'

'You should have –' she began, but the lump came back in her throat. She swallowed and began again. 'You should have come here when I asked you to.'

Maxine gazed at her sympathetically. '*Should have* doesn't help. We all did what we thought was best at the time.'

Sofia nodded, knowing she was right.

'I'm afraid there's more,' her mother said hesitantly.

A stab of fear ran through Sofia. 'What more? Have you found Lorenzo?'

'We are almost certain he was imprisoned,' Maxine said then glanced at Elsa, who took over. 'We believe the Nazis found out about his work for the Allies.'

Sofia gasped and her hand flew to her mouth.

'You will need to prepare yourself, Sofia,' Maxine said. 'We don't know for sure but it's possible he might have been one of the men shot in reprisal for the partisan bomb. They took over three hundred from the prisons.'

Sofia remained standing, staring at nothing, didn't see the room at all. She didn't even know if anyone was speaking. Lights flashed before her eyes as ice surged through her body. Cold, searing heat, cold again, and behind all of this, a feeling of outrage exploding in her head. Then, all she could do was grab handfuls of her own hair and pull as hard as she could, as if by ripping her hair out by the root it might dull the excruciating emotional pain.

Her mother attempted to draw her hands away, but Sofia fought her off.

'It isn't true,' she cried. 'It can't be true.'

Then she gasped for air, doubled over and groaned as if she'd been punched in the stomach. Someone helped her sit. Despite the spring weather, a long and dreadful silence chilled the room. Sofia rocked back and forth, unable to contemplate a life without her father and . . . she could not even bear to think it . . . Lorenzo. She glanced up at the painting of San Sebastiano. 'You didn't keep him safe,' she whispered. Then, with a life of its own, a cry of anguish rose from somewhere so deep inside, and so dark, she hadn't even known it existed.

'Bastards!' she screamed. 'Bastards! Murdering bastards!'

As pain ripped her apart, she thought of Lorenzo in prison, maybe dead, and her gentle, loving father gone. It was too much. Even if they did win this vile war, what would be left? She closed her eyes and thought of her beloved husband. In her mind she watched the gentle rise and fall of his chest as he slept and couldn't believe she might never see him breathe again. She saw him gazing at her, his eyes blazing with love. How could something as powerful as that be gone? That light. That essence. He could not have been shot. He could not have been murdered. He was too good. Too honest. She refused to believe it. Would not believe it.

'He may still be in prison,' she heard her mother whisper. 'There is a chance, my love.'

'They haven't issued a list of the dead?' Sofia asked, clutching at the shred of hope.

Maxine shook her head. 'They want to hush the whole thing up.'

Then Sofia rushed from the room and escaped to her bedroom. She knew she should be comforting her mother, and she would, but right now she needed to weep alone for the two men she had loved the most. She threw herself on to the bed and, with a pillow over her head, she howled out the pain until there was no breath left inside her.

During the following week the sound of weeping echoed around the house, along the corridors and in and out of distant rooms. Sofia's eyes were constantly gritty from a combination of exhaustion and tears. Elsa's were swollen and she barely ate, grown so gaunt Sofia feared for her. Her mother slipped about the house, a shadow of her usual vibrant self, and when Sofia caught her staring into empty space, she would have given anything to make her well again. But there was nothing she could do. Her father and Lorenzo were constantly on her mind. She recalled the way her father read to her when she was young, and how she'd drift off to the sound of his beautiful voice. To be loved, no matter what, was the gift he had bequeathed her. And that was what she had found in her husband too. She lay on their bed, curling into her own arms and wishing they were Lorenzo's. She wanted to touch his skin again, see the light in his eyes and, most of all, she longed to hold him.

52

As if to taunt Sofia, spring was unbelievably beautiful. The days were longer, the gloom of winter partly gone, and sunlight brightened their world, at least some of the time. They always prepared for rain and cold at this time of year but, so far, the weather had been spectacular. Along the grassy paths between the young vines and spilling into the slopes of the olive groves, poppies raised their cheerful heads. Butterflies and bees hovered in the air. Daisies dotted the fields in yellow and white, delicate pale roses tumbled down their verges and broom and mustard carpeted the margins of the fields. While Sofia walked the dogs, she collected the wildflowers, beneath a sky so blue it felt, despite everything, that life might one day be worth living.

She placed the flowers in little vases of hope all around the house, their scent so clean and good, it helped a little. Elsa began to eat again, not quite so lost in her own silence, while Maxine came and went. She talked but not about her grief. Sofia could see it building in her, building and building until she feared Maxine would crack. Sofia didn't ask where she had been or what she was doing. James and some of the partisans had taken the radio equipment away to use elsewhere and Maxine reported that a vast amount of meticulous intelligence had been transmitted to the Allies.

There was still no list of the men shot in reprisal for the bomb in Via Rasella, but under the blue, blue sky, Sofia made the decision that unless she heard for certain Lorenzo was dead, she simply was not going to believe it.

They heard that the partisans had been looting in some areas, which was not a good sign. On the other hand, there were now over four thousand partisans in hiding at Monte Amiata. A veritable army.

Late one afternoon Maxine roared into the kitchen, her eyes alight, her clothing torn.

'What on earth?' Sofia said, alarmed.

Maxine swept her arms around the room. 'I was there. I saw it all.'

Sofia shook her head at the outrageous state she was in. 'What, for heaven's sake?'

'You don't know about the battle?'

'No,' Sofia said, but had already guessed Maxine's way of dealing with grief would be to throw herself in the path of danger again.

'It was wonderful. I just happened to be in Monticchiello . . . by chance, of course.'

'And if I believe that . . .'

Maxine grinned. 'Well, you know . . . I did hear whispers.'

'So, what happened?'

'I was behind the old walls along with the partisans. Someone passed me a rifle. A rifle, can you imagine? The Fascists were attacking from below – no Germans, just Italian Fascists. Hundreds of them and only a hundred and fifty or so of us. Some of the women helped with loading, others kept bringing food and drink. I wish you could have seen it, Sofia. It was amazing.'

'You won, I take it?'

Her eyes glittered with excitement. 'We did. Oh, the joy of killing those fucking bastards! The local partisans had held up the grain lorry and brought the contents for the villagers. The Fascists came in reprisal, but they ended up fleeing, dragging their dead behind them.'

'Did you have many losses?'

Her face fell. 'Sadly, one or two. But they lost dozens. The idiots. We gave them a taste of their own medicine . . . Look, I'm going back. There's to be a party. Low key. Well . . . not even a party really, more of a get-together to celebrate, but I want something nice to wear.'

'I hope you know what you're doing. Are they not concerned about further reprisals?'

Maxine winked. 'Don't you worry about that.'

Sofia couldn't help smiling, seeing her so buoyant. 'You can borrow something of mine if you like.'

'Thank you. Some earrings and a shawl might be nice.'

Upstairs, they spent a few minutes gazing into the wardrobe, and then Maxine began to pull out delicate silk blouses which she fingered longingly but deemed too small. Soon brightly coloured clothes lay strewn across the bed, but none would do. Then Sofia opened the drawer where she kept her scarves.

'Have a look at this.' She held up a rich crimson silk, fringed with gold tassels.

'Oh,' Maxine said and held it against her face. 'It's so soft. You'd let me borrow this?'

'Just try to bring it back.'

As she continued to admire it, Sofia remembered the day she and Lorenzo had found it in a tiny shop in Montmartre, perched at the top of a cobbled street. She'd fallen in love with the village atmosphere and, if it was possible, fallen even more deeply in love with Lorenzo.

She smiled at Maxine. 'But if you happen to lose it, we'll simply have to return to Paris and buy another.'

'You bought this with Lorenzo?'

'Yes.'

'And you're sure it's all right?'

Sofia gave her a hug and felt her heart thumping. This girl had been so good to Elsa and had come to mean such a lot to them both. 'Wear it and enjoy it. We all deserve some fun now and then, don't we, and I reckon if anyone has earnt it you have. Now, let's look for some earrings.'

When they found the perfect pair of gold hoops, Maxine put

them on, slipped into a black dress that had belonged to Loren-zo's sister, let loose her curling chestnut hair and wrapped the crimson scarf around her shoulders.

'Like a gorgeous gypsy dancer,' Sofia said.

'Not too bold?'

'Could anything ever be too bold on you?'

Maxine laughed and Sofia laughed with her.

'Can I borrow a red lipstick?'

'Of course.'

'Thank you,' she said and kissed Sofia's cheek. 'You're a true friend. I'll be back soon.'

53

The celebration was held in the biggest square and all the towns-people joined in. No lamps were lit because of air raids and there was no visible moon, but there was local wine and someone played the fiddle quietly. It wasn't long before all the young people were up on their feet. A strange kind of dancing it was, each bumping into the other in the dark, trying not to make too much noise, but somehow even more special. And no one would ever forget the night the ghosts came out to kick up their heels. Because in a way they'd all become ghosts, shadows of who they'd been before, even by daylight.

Right from the start Maxine hooked up with a local woman, Adriana, who'd lost her husband early in the war while fighting on the German side.

'It was hard,' she said in a lull from the dancing during which they sat together to catch their breath. 'When we switched sides, I mean. The Allies killed my Gianni and I hated them. I didn't want them to win but later, when I saw what the Germans were doing to us, I realized it was the only way.'

It was true, Maxine thought as she listened to the melancholy tune the fiddler was now playing. The sadness of it altered the mood and she imagined everyone would be thinking of people they'd lost or were still afraid of losing.

'I saw you loading the guns earlier,' Maxine said.

'Wasn't it great?' Adriana's eyes lit up.

There was a moment of silence between them.

'Did you lose somebody?' Adriana asked. 'Is it why you're here?'

Maxine looked at the ground.

'You did, didn't you? Don't talk about it if you don't want to.'

'It's all right.' There was a pause before Maxine continued. 'He was a partisan. He died after a bomb exploded.'

'What was his name?'

'Marco. Marco Vallone.'

The woman's eyes widened. 'Really? My maiden name was Vallone, but my brother is Luciano.'

'I only heard his surname at the very end when he . . .' She swallowed hard, remembering the moment. 'He never really spoke of his family; said he didn't want to put them in danger. He never even told me where he came from.'

'And where are you from? You don't sound local.'

'New York, but my parents were from Tuscany.'

'What did he look like, your Marco? Was he handsome?'

Maxine smiled as she recalled the brilliance of his eyes. 'Very. With a wicked side to him.'

'Luciano is handsome too,' Adriana said. 'Come, I'll show you a photograph.'

They went into her small village house and as soon as Maxine glanced at the framed photograph on Adriana's sideboard, her mind went into a spin. She picked the picture up and stared at it, her eyes swimming with tears. How could she tell Adriana the truth now? After a moment she brushed the tears away with the back of her hand.

'Your Marco?' Adriana whispered, her face ashen, already guessing what Maxine had seen. 'He is my Luciano.'

Distraught to be inadvertently bringing such terrible news, Maxine gazed at her. 'I'm so sorry.'

Adriana blinked rapidly, took the photograph from Maxine and kissed it repeatedly, her face awash with tears. 'My poor, poor brother. Can you tell me what happened? The details of how he died.'

And after Maxine had unburdened herself of everything she had not wanted to talk about, had not until now been able to find the words, the two women held each other and wept openly.

'He was the only man I've ever loved,' Maxine said as she eventually dried her eyes.

Adriana nodded. 'Same with Gianni . . . It hurts so much but it does get better after a while.'

Maxine gazed at her. 'Does it?'

'Well, maybe it's more like we get used to it. My brother was such a good man. I'm glad he had you to love him before he died. I've missed him so much, but I think I knew he wouldn't be coming back. I was always waiting for the moment when I'd hear. It was his fate.'

Maxine didn't say she didn't believe in fate. 'Are your parents alive?'

'There's only me and my little boy, Emilio. My older brother is gone too, taken by Fascists before the war. I was only young at the time.'

Maxine remembered Marco telling her about his brother. 'I'm so sorry. It must have been awful. You've lost so many.'

'I have my son.' Adriana's face blossomed as she spoke of her child. 'He's the spitting image of Luciano.'

'So, where is your boy now?'

'He's with a friend of mine in Montepulciano. I knew there'd be trouble for a day or two after our local partisans held up the grain lorry and brought the food here. I didn't want him to be around when the reprisals happened.'

'Do you think there will be more reprisals?'

'Let me put it this way. I wouldn't want to be sleeping too soundly tonight.'

Maxine gazed at Adriana, admiring the resilience and courage she saw in her eyes.

'I'll make you up a bed here on the sofa and lend you some of my clothes. You don't want them to see you dressed like that. It'd be like rubbing salt in their wounds.'

Early the next morning Maxine woke to a thunderous battering at Adriana's front door. She jumped out of bed and smoothed her hair inside a scarf, which she knotted at her throat. Adriana rushed down the stairs and they both listened to the sound of other doors being battered further down the street.

Adriana took a deep breath. 'Ready?'

Maxine said she was, and Adriana opened the door. Two steel-helmeted, pitiless German soldiers stormed in and turned the house upside down, leaving it in disarray, but finding nothing. There had been no physical abuse, just the threat of beatings if they did not comply. This scene was repeated in every house in the town.

'You knew they'd find nothing,' Maxine said, impressed.

Adriana nodded. 'To protect us the partisans took everything to the woods and hid it.'

Afterwards it went quiet, then the news came that a lorryload of Fascists had attempted to wipe out the partisans in the woods but had failed miserably and ended up fighting among themselves. As for the partisans and their weapons, they had melted away. At least that attempted Fascist reprisal had failed, and although the Germans had come to search the village, that's all they were likely to do. Their fight was heavily focused on the Allies now and they were not too bothered about supporting the Italian Fascists any more.

54.

May 1944

On the third of May they heard the awful news that there had been intense bombing over Florence again. With a heavy feeling, Sofia wondered if their ancient palazzo would still be standing. Then, soon after dawn a week later, a bomb fell so close it shook the villa at the Castello. Sofia rushed to her mother's bedroom and found Elsa staring out of the window. 'It could so easily have been us,' she said. 'It's the luck of the draw, isn't it?'

Later they found out it had destroyed a neighbouring hamlet where women and children now lay dead among the rubble. This apparently indiscriminate Allied bombing incited the villagers to anger. *Why do they bomb our villages?* they demanded, and Sofia had no answer, except to say the Allies needed to halt all German traffic and block their routes north. Sometimes they were not so accurate. Secretly, people wondered if the Allies trusted them or cared about them at all. They had changed sides. They had once fought for Germany. Maybe the Allies didn't forgive them for that. Did it make them careless when they threw their bombs? Again, Sofia didn't have an answer but, knowing how much the Allied armies were suffering, she forgave them.

They heard rumours of German SS spies infiltrating local partisan groups and also that denunciations in Florence were leading to the arrest of anti-Fascists. To save their own skins, neighbours with old grievances were informing on those they knew the Germans would consider traitors; even relatives would denounce their own families if someone was evading a draft or hiding a Jew.

She hadn't seen much of James but knew from Maxine that he'd been working with the partisans, still receiving and transmitting information. She worried he might be staying away because of her.

But then came absolute joy on the nineteenth of May, when they were listening to the news on their illegal radio. All of them there in the kitchen – Sofia, Maxine, Elsa, Carla, Anna and Gabriella, their house full of women. They whooped and shrieked and then cried tears of hope and relief. At long last Cassino has fallen. The Gustav Line had been breached and the Allies were advancing towards the Adolf Hitler Line. Carla uncorked two bottles of the best red wine and poured everyone a generous glass. 'To the future,' she said, and Sofia silently prayed the Allies would reach Rome quickly and release Lorenzo. In her mind, he simply was not dead. Gabriella did a little dance, jumping up and down like a marionette, and they all drank and laughed as hope swelled and swelled until it filled the entire room. They were light and bright and happy.

Even Sofia's mother was more cheerful after this news so the next day they decided to take a walk together, the first time Elsa had ventured beyond the walls of the Castello. Sofia whistled for the dogs, but they were getting older and sometimes favoured sleeping in the kitchen.

Sofia always kept her gun close, and today it was in her pocket. She calculated that if they took the track that circled the Castello they'd be safe from any bombs, although the sky was mercifully empty of planes. When they reached the woods Elsa sat on a fallen tree trunk and beckoned Sofia to join her. 'I don't have the energy I had any more,' Elsa said.

'I think you'll outlast me, Mother.'

Elsa just smiled and looked up at the sky.

Sofia stared down at a line of ants making their way round her foot. 'Do you really think they arrested Lorenzo because they found out what he was up to?'

'Yes. We think so.'

'Did somebody betray him?' It hurt Sofia to say it and she groaned when her mother nodded.

'How can people do that?'

'It happens. It happened to your father too. They have their reasons sometimes, I suppose. Maybe to save their own skin.'

There was a long silence but for the sound of the warblers and jays who sang all day at that time of year.

Eventually Sofia stood and reached out a hand. 'Shall we walk?'

Elsa took the proffered hand, getting to her feet, and they began to wander through the woods where sunlight was dancing a pattern through the branches overhead.

As they walked, Sofia could smell the wild mint, one of her favourite herbs, and pointed it out to her mother. 'I love the taste of it in a fresh fruit salad, don't you?'

'Do you remember when you were little and we cooked together?' Elsa asked.

Sofia smiled at the memories. 'Of course.'

'Sugar in the pasta!' Elsa said, and dug Sofia in the ribs.

'Oh my goodness. You told me to add a tablespoon of salt to the water in the pan.'

'I did.'

'And I added sugar. It was such an awful mistake. Remember Father's face? He was horrified.'

Elsa patted her hand. 'I do.'

'And I was so utterly mortified, I hid under my bed.'

'And then Roberto came to find you.'

'He told me it didn't matter, and mistakes were important because that's how we learn.'

Her mother sighed. 'Full of little sayings, he was.'

They fell silent for a moment and then Sofia thought of other meals they'd made together and eaten with her father at their dining-room table. She could smell the lemony polish her mother used and his favourite beans with wild mushrooms and garlic.

'Remember shelling peas on the balcony?' her mother asked.

'Yes, and deep-frying zucchini flowers. I always seemed to burn them.'

'The kitchen too! Or very nearly.'

'Oh God! It wasn't my fault the drying-up cloth was too close to the flame.'

'No, it must have been the drying-up fairy.'

Sofia laughed. 'Oh, won't it be lovely when we can have good food again?'

'I'd love some chicken liver bruschetta.'

'Yes. Or rabbit in anchovy sauce. Although Carla served that not long ago. Rabbit one hundred ways.'

'Where did she get the anchovies?'

'Tinned ones she'd hidden.' Sofia smiled, remembering the day Carla, Aldo and she had hidden the food.

'She's been very loyal, hasn't she?'

'It hasn't been easy, especially since Aldo . . .'

'No. And now this young daughter pregnant. How will she cope?'

Sofia decided not to tell her mother anything much about that. 'Gabriella has grown up a lot recently. She'll cope, or at least she'll learn to.'

At the edge of the woods they walked out into a small field where the crops were growing so lush and green it filled Sofia with optimism.

'Will it be the Americans who come this way, do you think?' she said. 'Or the British?'

'The Americans will have chocolate.'

'Let's hope it's them then.' They both laughed and Sofia's mouth watered.

They slowly made their way around the perimeter of the field.

'It's hot,' Elsa said. 'I should have brought my hat.'

'We can turn back.'

There was a short silence and then Sofia asked how she was feeling.

Her mother's eyes clouded. 'I miss Roberto with every beat of my heart. Every minute of every day.'

'I know.'

'And yet life goes on. Somehow. I don't think we ever understand how it possibly can. Yet it does.'

'I don't believe Lorenzo is dead. I think I'd feel it.'

Her mother gave her such a sympathetic look, Sofia put an arm round her and held her close, her clever, sad little mother.

'We'll be all right, won't we, Mamma? We'll pull through.'

And when they got home, they heard the wonderful news: the Allies had broken through the Hitler Line. They hugged each other and Sofia glanced at the painting of San Sebastiano. Maybe he had been protecting them after all.

55

June 1944

There had been fierce fighting south of Rome and, despite her recent optimism, Sofia couldn't shift the feeling something awful was about to happen. Their local roads were being bombed so relentlessly now that none dared travel anywhere or even go for a walk. Day and night, in their dogged determination to halt the Germans, small groups of Allied fighter planes flew terribly low, targeting every moving thing. Such dangerous work – her heart went out to the pilots. And then, early on the fifth of June, she saw James again. She'd been expecting him at some point as the partisans had recently brought back the radio and transmitter to hide in the tunnels once more.

But she *was* surprised to see him in the kitchen at eight thirty in the morning. He looked as if he'd just tumbled out of bed, hair tousled, eyes still sleepy. He gave her the biggest, broadest smile before he spoke. 'Haven't you heard? I came right away.'

'Heard what? My radio isn't working properly.'

'The Allies have entered Rome.'

'No! Can it be true?' Relief rushed through her as he nodded, and tears swamped her eyes. 'Oh, thank God. Thank God. But how do you know?'

'I have a small hidden radio of my own now.'

He was so animated and full of it he seemed unable to stop. 'I was sure you'd want to know. The partisan units are ready.'

Sofia took a deep breath in and exhaled slowly, still hardly able to take in the news.

'Mark my words. We're after the bastards now.'

'At last. I couldn't sleep last night because of the sound of lorry after lorry heading north.'

'German lorries. Retreating. They're on the run. And we are right behind them. We've turned the tide.'

She gazed at him, suddenly aware of still being in her dressing gown. 'Look, I'm sure you'd like some breakfast. We have eggs.'

'Sounds perfect.'

'Give me five minutes and I'll join you. We can take it in the garden.'

'And watch the falling bombs?'

She smiled. Even that seemed funny today though, really, it wasn't. 'I'll ask Carla to serve breakfast outside.'

When she came back down, she found James already sitting at the table in the garden, nursing a boiling hot grain coffee.

'Will the Americans bring real coffee?' she asked.

'I think they'll be coming up west of here, but you never know. We're more likely to be bringing tea!'

She laughed then glanced across at him as he sipped his brew. 'You'll be leaving when the British arrive?'

'Yep, we'll take the equipment further north.'

'You won't be able to go home first?'

He pulled a face. 'I doubt it. But maybe. For a short break.'

'I'll miss you,' she said, and really meant it.

There was a long silence during which she thought about the friendship between them and how much she had valued it.

'I'm so sorry if I gave you the wrong impression,' she added, feeling a little awkward. 'It's been . . . well, I guess it's been difficult this last year.'

'I know.'

'I still love my husband very much and I feel sure he's alive. I think I'd know it if he weren't.'

'Don't apologize. There's no need. I have my fiancée at home to think about too, but war brings people together in unexpected ways.'

'Or drives them apart.'

'Either way, emotions become –'

'Heightened? Tangled?'

'Raw, I think. None of us know how we'll respond when our backs are up against the wall.'

She smiled, thinking of that night hiding on the staircase. 'In our case, almost literally.'

'You were lonely and I was too.'

She gazed at his warm eyes. 'Can we just let it go?'

'Absolutely. My dear woman, I'm a man of my word. I hope you know that above all I'm your friend and will be your friend for as long as you need me to be.'

He took both her hands and enclosed them within his own.

'Do *you* believe Lorenzo could still be alive?' she asked.

'Anything is possible.'

'With the Allies now in Rome, will we know soon?'

'I imagine it may be a bit chaotic at first, but yes.'

There was a pause after which he gave her back her hands and they sat in silence for a few minutes more.

'Thank you . . . for everything,' she said.

'No, thank you.'

They both took deep, long breaths, bringing that part of their conversation to a close.

'Now,' he said. 'On to practical matters.'

'I know, it's time. No more soul-searching today.'

'We need to send the Allies detailed information about the German situation hereabouts,' he said.

'The radio transmitter?'

'At the top of the tower again, if you don't mind. It transmits so much more reliably from there.'

She told him it was fine and, after he'd gone, she saw the light had changed, with a different more optimistic atmosphere in the air. She felt changed too, the lightness of her step as she walked through the garden reflecting the anticipation she was beginning to feel. Everything *was* going to be all right. The sense of something awful being about to happen had vanished. She felt liberated from the gloom of the war and from her fear for Lorenzo. He *would* be all right. June the fifth, the memorable day the Allies entered Rome – the beginning of the liberation of the city and the day she began to look to the future.

56

From the top floor of the house, Sofia and Carla watched the Allied bombers swooping low over the German convoys heading north, cheering when the bombs dropped and the planes arced away unscathed. They were brave those pilots who dared to fly so low over an area now crawling with German troops and trucks. Sofia felt a new and stronger determination, and with it the expectation she would hear news of Lorenzo soon. For her, hope was a shadow that daren't quite come out to show itself fully, but it was there, and it was edging closer.

During the previous few weeks the Fascist cause had finally collapsed. To the south of the Castello hundreds of partisans waited to ambush German vehicles as they retreated. At the Castello the talk was of bridges exploding, railways being destroyed and roads becoming impassable. This intense partisan action had followed a broadcast by General Alexander urging everyone to play their part in halting the Germans. For people under occupation, as they had been, it was their country and their homes they were desperate to protect.

From the south the fighting was heading their way and Sofia held her breath when, one morning at dawn, she heard planes circling their small village followed by cannon fire and shelling. As the house shook, two perfume bottles crashed from her dressing table and her Arpège shattered. A spicy, sensual scent rose to fill the room with hints of rose, jasmine and lily of the valley. She instantly felt Lorenzo's arms around her, his head nuzzling her neck where she'd dabbed the perfume. The gorgeous scent, so completely at odds with the sound of bombs falling, seemed almost improper. But her mind flooded with memories of Lorenzo handing her the first exquisitely packaged parcel back in 1927. Ever since then the perfume had been an absolute favourite. Now, as she wiped tears away and bent to pick up the fragments of black glass, she spotted she'd cut herself. As the blood dripped from her finger she stood still, watching it in a daze. She had not been without one of those little black bottles for seventeen years and, now the last one was gone, it felt like an ill omen.

They were all under intense stress, day and night, so Sofia asked Anna to knock on doors to tell the villagers the Castello manor house cellars were available as a refuge for anyone who might feel safer underground. For several hours Sofia, Anna and Carla lugged blankets, pillows, even old mattresses down to the cellars. They carried down pitchers of water, the few loaves they had, some bottled fruit and an oil lamp. Sofia feared it wouldn't be enough. Before nightfall, Sofia and Anna, aware of looters, checked all the windows and found only a single broken one, two floors up. No one could get in there, so they left it as it was.

In the evening the villagers streamed in. Sofia settled the dogs then took the villagers through the large basement, past a warren of dark passageways, alcoves and secret rooms to the deepest cellar. The temperature dropped as they descended. From the cellar they could access the escape tunnels, but she didn't show them those. She looked at their thin, exhausted faces and prayed they would all be safe. Sara was there and Federica with her little boy. Some came only to steal a peek at the cellars and one or two wouldn't come at all, Maria among them. When Carla asked why not, she said she'd rather not be buried alive. The rest of the old, the young, even two babies, settled themselves in, although the babies screamed and screamed until Sofia felt she'd rather take her chance outside. The other children slept or played games and she worried about how they would feed them all. She was worried about Maxine too. She hadn't been there at all, not for days, and she tried to remember when she'd last seen her. Was it after the Monticchiello victory? No, it must have been the day Cassino had fallen.

Despite the blankets, it was not only cold in the cellar but damp too. When two of the children, a tall boy of about thirteen and a smaller boy, headed down towards the door to one of the tunnels, Sofia called them back and ordered them not to go down there again. The tunnels formed a network, a labyrinth spreading under the village, and if you didn't know where you were going, you could be lost forever.

When they heard the first bomb exploding, the younger children started to cry and the adults trembled and clutched each other. Sofia heard Carla praying, probably to San Sebastiano, and felt a growing apprehension about the tower. Would it be destroyed that night? Hilltop towns such as theirs were the most at risk.

The frightening moments passed as one of the old men pulled out a mouth organ and played to try to cover the sound of further bombs ripping through the sky. Some attempted to sing along, Carla louder and longer than anyone, but the crash and thunder was painfully close. Sofia clapped her hands over her ears, trying to sink into the silence of her mind, hoping and praying their homes wouldn't be wrecked by bombs or fire. And yet Carla still sang for courage, for hope and for their survival. One of the old women took out her knitting and by the light of the lamp clicked and clacked for hours. The noise in the cellar, adding to the sweat and fear, mildew and earth, became too strong for Sofia and, in what she hoped might be a lull, she made her way upstairs with a small torch to light the way. She longed for air but when another bomb exploded in the distance, she crossed herself and headed back down where a commotion greeted her.

Her dogs were barking wildly and a woman was shrieking and waving her arms. 'My sons, they have gone. My boys. I must have fallen asleep. Did anyone see them?'

Sofia held up the torch and scanned the startled, drawn faces, but it was clear the two boys she'd spotted earlier were nowhere to be seen.

'Did they go upstairs?' she asked.

A woman sitting cross-legged by the stairs spoke up. 'No, I'd have seen them.'

The mother, beside herself, began to wail, and Sofia walked over to Carla and whispered that they needed to look for the boys.

'But, Contessa,' she said, 'what if the oil in the lamp runs out? It is already low.'

But more loss was the last thing any of them needed so Sofia took her torch and entered one of the tunnels herself.

57

Maxine had gone back to Monticchiello to spend some time staying with Adriana and playing with her little boy, who was home now and so resembled his uncle Marco. She saw it in the way he smiled, the way he laughed and the way he could suddenly become so serious. Marco was always in her mind. She remembered what he had been to her, how much he had meant, and the legacy with which he had left her: a capacity to love she'd never known could be hers. She'd laboured tirelessly with the local women helping the partisans and now, along with many of them, she was bursting with excitement as she waited at the top of Montepulciano. Her cousin, Davide, was there too and his wife, Lara.

A cheer went up as the first British foot soldiers crawled along the narrow streets of the ancient hilltop town and then a little later their tanks rolled into the square at the top. Maxine stood jubilantly with a rifle Davide had obtained for her slung across her shoulder, relieved the roar and smoke of battle was over, at least here. Old women wept openly as children chased each other, shrieking with the kind of joy that had been missing for so long as they caught sweets the soldiers were flinging into the crowd. The younger women embraced the soldiers, kissing them on their cheeks and plying them with glasses of wine, their eyes dancing with joy. Old men clapped each other on the back and there was not a single Fascist to be found. Maxine had spent the last hour seeking them out, but with the approach of the Allies, every single one had fled or suddenly switched sides. That wasn't going to help them in the days ahead. In the late afternoon one of the British soldiers told her the Nazis had looted everything from every single place they'd passed through: blankets, clothing, books, poultry, anything edible, plus precious works of art. Maxine realized she needed to get back to the Castello to warn Sofia before it happened there. Anything they couldn't take with them, the Nazis burnt or destroyed. So, with Sofia's beautiful family home firmly in mind, she retrieved her motorcycle and headed downhill, waving at the soldiers as she did. The Castello, north-west of Montepulciano, was about twenty-five miles away if she took the main road, but as she faced the risk of being gunned down, she decided to go for the hidden tracks. She might not have long before the Germans began doing their worst so would just have to hope she didn't get lost.

58

In the morning Sofia made her way to the tower to check that it hadn't been damaged the night before. The air reeked with the acrid smell of smoke and God only knew what else. She thought again about the two boys they'd been unable to find. Half the village were now out looking for them in case they'd made it to the further woods, while Anna and two of her friends explored the tunnels with oil lamps, torches and chalk to mark their way back.

By the evening they still hadn't been found and Carla was at their mother's house taking care of the poor woman, who was beside herself with worry. As it was quiet, Sofia dared hope there might be a lull in the bombing and that they might still find the boys. She made her way to her lamp-lit private salon, and there, she picked up a book. But try as she might, she couldn't concentrate; after every sentence her mind strayed, and she needed to reread it. It was impossible to get lost in a story when you were constantly on alert as you waited for the next planes to fly over. She picked up her knitting instead. Sometimes it helped to do something with her hands, but she was even too restless for that. She thought a lot about the past and what the future might or might not hold. She had closed the windows to keep out the smoke but it was warm, really warm, so she stuffed her knitting back in the basket on the small table by her wing-backed chair, then opened a window to lean out and listen to the hum of mating cicadas. The air was softer now, reminding her of walking with Lorenzo on those June evenings when it hadn't quite cooled and they'd spend an hour or two before twilight, batting away the flies but nevertheless enjoying being outside.

A man's cough interrupted her reverie. Her heart swelled

with relief as she whirled round, thinking it must be Lorenzo. At long last.

It was not Lorenzo.

It was Major Kaufmann, leaning nonchalantly against the door frame.

'Oh,' she said, fazed by his unexpected arrival. 'Have you been watching me? I didn't hear a car. Where's your driver?'

He straightened up and gave her a stiff little bow. 'Do forgive the intrusion. I did knock.'

'Carla isn't here.'

'I let myself in.'

She frowned, taking in his myopic blue eyes which looked out icily from behind the horn-rimmed spectacles. 'She should have locked the door.'

'Lucky for me, then. My car is a little way down the hill. I'm here on a private matter – at least, it should be if all goes well.'

'I assumed you'd be gone. Surely you are retreating by now?'

'That is not a word I choose to use. We will be taking up alternative defences, when we're ready, that is all. I have a few loose ends to tie up here first.'

'Loose ends here?' she asked, trying for indifference but, completely bewildered by what he had meant, her throat dried.

'Indeed.' He smiled, a smile so chilling it had no hope of reaching his eyes.

'The Allies will be here soon.'

'You may be right but, understand this: they cannot fight the might of the Reich and win.' He laughed. 'It is impossible, you see.'

They locked eyes and a shiver ran down her spine. She wondered if he was mad. If they were all mad in their unswerving belief in Hitler and the Reich. She steeled herself to speak. 'So, may I ask what it is you want?'

'Ah. I had hoped for a little civility before getting down to business, but since you ask . . . My superior officer is certain the radio the partisans have been using is here and has tasked me

322

with locating it before we leave. The triangulation pinpoints this location.'

A beat or two passed and she noticed he didn't seem quite so well built without his greatcoat. 'I have no idea to what you're referring.'

'Come now, Contessa. No need to be so haughty. We both know that isn't true.'

Sofia commanded her skin not to reveal her guilt but, certain her cheeks had coloured, she could feel the heat rising. She took a slow breath to cover her initial response. It didn't work. Instead, the apprehension she'd felt before grew stronger, tightening the muscles of her throat until she felt she might be about to choke.

He tilted his head and took a step forward. He now stood behind the chintz sofa and was trailing his fingers along the back of it. His nails were clean, perfectly manicured. 'There, you see,' he said. 'I can always tell when someone is lying. I think *you* have been lying. And on more than one occasion.'

'How ridiculous,' she managed to mutter. 'What would I know about radios and transmitters?'

'Did I mention a transmitter?' He frowned. 'No . . . I do not think so.'

'You mentioned partisans using a radio. Naturally, they would have a transmitter.'

'Perhaps you are right,' he said.

'Where are your men?'

He ignored her question and walked over to the painting of San Sebastiano. 'A fine piece,' he said as he twisted round to study her face. 'So beautiful.'

This time she couldn't stop herself flinching under his cold appraisal. Was he referring to her or to the painting?

He laughed, mocking her. 'The painting, I mean, of course. You didn't think I meant you?'

'No.'

'You are looking rather drawn if you don't mind me saying.

Lost your bloom a little, I think.' He gave another short laugh. 'But I'm sure we agree this picture is quite wonderful and it never ages, unlike a beautiful woman. Well, well, here's the deal.' He took a few steps away but then went quiet, staring at the intricate patterns of the encaustic floor tiles.

A short silence followed, leaving her confused, not at all sure what was going on.

'Now, where was I?' He raised his head, glanced at her.

'You were talking about a deal.'

He smiled disdainfully. 'I feel these matters of business are somewhat beneath me. But of course. Of course. The deal is, you gift me this little painting and I report back that the radio is simply not here.'

She stifled a laugh. Surely, he was joking? It wasn't as if she could stop him from just taking the painting if he wanted.

'You don't like my idea? You think it's funny?'

Just for a moment, his face darkened in anger. He hid it quickly, but she had glimpsed it. Oh yes.

'No. It isn't funny; I simply don't believe you.' She looked him right in the eye and his brows shot up.

'What kind of talk is this? I am a man of my word.'

'So, I give you the painting and then off you go? Just like that?' He shrugged.

She wasn't sure what else to say as he took a few steps closer to her. 'It's an excellent offer . . . You will all be shot otherwise. On suspicion, you see. I do not enjoy shooting women.'

'Suspicion?'

He came right up to her and lifted her chin to look into her eyes. Then he pushed the hair from her forehead, and she fought the impulse to spit in his face.

'You are not a stupid woman.'

'This is crazy,' she said, backing away and bumping into the side table. 'You can't waltz in here and demand to take a painting. My husband would have a fit if he knew.'

He shook his head and walked back to finger the frame of the painting lovingly. She tried to remember where she'd put the gun. She knew, of course she knew . . . every day, she knew, every hour of every day, but then, right then, her mind had gone completely blank.

'No,' she said, desperately needing to buy herself time while she worked out what to do. He would take it whatever she did, and after all, it was only a painting. And yet . . . not even sure why, she persevered. Pride maybe, or pig-headedness, or maybe just so fed up with them taking whatever they fancied, she wanted to dig her heels in for once. He'd probably shoot her whatever she did. 'Unquestionably, you cannot take it. Lorenzo would never forgive me if I allowed it.'

He looked back over his shoulder at her. 'Ah, now. I am afraid your husband is not in any position to forgive you or otherwise.'

Her heart lurched. 'What do you mean?'

In the moment of silence, during which he turned to face her, she felt her knees beginning to buckle. Just in time, she stiffened and managed to resist.

'Your husband, my dear lady, has been working for the enemy. Terrible shame really.'

She stared at him.

'I'll throw in another offer.'

She gulped back the tears pricking the back of her eyelids and, in a flash, she remembered exactly where she'd hidden the gun.

'Not only will I report that the radio is not here, I'll also give my men the order *not* to destroy the Castello . . . and not to touch anything in it. We'll leave you all in peace. There now, it's an offer you can't refuse.'

'What has happened to my husband?' she hissed, hardly able to get the words out.

He smiled. 'Oh, my dear lady, how he danced. They dance, you know, on the end of the rope. Jerk their legs about. A little jig is all. It's rather entertaining . . . I take it you agree to my offer?'

He had his back to her again and was removing the painting from the wall. She stepped backwards and, as he murmured his appreciation of the picture, she silently retrieved her gun from the knitting basket and held it behind her back. She wondered for a moment if he was goading her, provoking her, to see how far he could go.

'Major,' she said quite clearly, 'about your offer,' and he turned with the picture under his arm, perfectly confident of her compliance, and nonchalantly scratching the back of his neck. He was so delighted to have the painting, his face looked a little less cruel, but she couldn't let anything deter her, could she? And then he smiled.

Up until the moment she saw that twisted smile, the one that wasn't really a smile at all, she had not been certain she could go through with it. As she willed her courage, her whole life gathered in front of her as if it were she who might be the one about to die. She glanced at the window and the moment stretched on and on, and yet it could only have been for a split second. The heat rose, igniting such a fury in her that she knew this was it.

Before he had time to register what she was about to do, she whipped the gun round from behind her back, took aim and shot him twice in the chest. It had to be twice. One for Aldo and one for Lorenzo. He stepped back, forced by the momentum, still on his feet, his eyes widening in surprise. She imagined she might have been the one to collapse on the floor, the aftershock making it impossible to breathe, but it was he who twitched grotesquely, groaned as he fell and then slumped back against the wall, his chin dropping to his blood-soaked chest. *The wall will be a terrible mess*, she thought. After a moment or two he was completely still. '*A little jig is all*,' she whispered, '*so entertaining*,' and then she closed her eyes. For a moment she dared not look for fear he wasn't dead and might still rise up and throttle her. That apart, she felt nothing. Then she opened her eyes again to watch the blood spreading on the floor and she still felt nothing. She stared down at the gun in her hand, unsure what to do. It was easy to kill a man, far easier than you'd think. And then she was gripped by a strange unshakeable feeling: she was not the person she'd believed she was. The word for this did not exist. This being but not being. When she looked up, the light in the room had softened even further, a lovely golden light falling on the wall behind Kaufmann, quite beautiful, but she noticed their gorgeous gold painting was now turning crimson with his blood. The room shrank inwards, dizzyingly.

As if her will had deserted her, she sank into a kind of torpor. It drained her strength, her soul . . . everything, and she was lost as if in a trance. She kept thinking she should do something, act, clean up the mess, the blood, the bits of flesh she could see sticking to the wall, but felt paralysed in those moments of total silence. Then two voices from her past started whispering in her head, beckoning her, insisting she listen to what they had to say. And so, she did. First to her father and then Lorenzo. It was vital she heard them, but their voices became indistinct, and she couldn't work out what they wanted. She reached for Lorenzo, wanting to touch his skin, look in his eyes, but was met with only air. She glanced at her empty arms and saw the gun again. The two men merged into one. The two men she had loved the most. Both gone. And when their voices ceased, she felt as if she'd failed them unforgivably and the pain was unbearable. No one could understand what loss really meant until they'd lost the most precious, most loved person in their world. Now she heard someone else calling her name, although it was coming from very far away. There was a sound of whimpering and she realized it was her. She was the one who was whimpering.

59

By the time Maxine arrived back at the Castello from Montepulciano it was already evening. Feeling grateful and more
than a little relieved not to have come under fire, she parked
her motorcycle and spotted Carla walking wearily across the
square.

'I thought I heard gunshots as I came up,' she said. 'They
sounded close. Did you hear them?'

Carla shrugged. 'There's always gunfire. Tell me when
there isn't.'

'So, what's been happening here? I saw a German vehicle
parked part way down the hill. Not a soul in it.'

They reached the back door and found it slightly ajar. Carla
frowned. 'I couldn't have locked it.'

Maxine raised her brows. 'Careless of you.'

'I've been a bit distracted,' Carla grumbled. 'Two boys went
missing. One has turned up but not the other. His brother thinks
he's still hiding in the woods.'

They went into the shadowy hall and Maxine called out.
'Sofia, Elsa?'

There was no reply, but Maxine caught the sound of gentle
sobbing coming from the salon. She and Carla exchanged worried glances then headed for the door. As she opened it, Maxine
gasped in disbelief.

'Dear God,' she whispered, numb with shock as she took in
the carnage before her.

Elsa brushed at her tears to stem the flow and rose to her feet
shakily. 'She won't speak. Stands there trembling and whimpering and clutching the gun. I can't get it away from her.'

Maxine shuddered but forced herself to edge closer to Kaufmann's body. 'Jesus, the blood.'

Elsa glanced across at the body. 'I already checked. He's definitely dead.'

Maxine looked at Carla, saw the panic in her eyes.

For a moment they froze in indecision, then Carla blinked rapidly, recovered, and went straight to Sofia. Maxine watched as she put an arm round her mistress and led her to a sofa, gently helped her to sit and then silently peeled away Sofia's fingers, safely removing the gun from her grasp. Elsa went to sit beside her daughter.

'Do you think he attacked her?' Carla asked, her face a picture of anguish. 'I'll never forgive myself. I should have been here.'

Elsa shook her head. 'I don't know. See the painting on the floor? He may have come for that.'

Carla looked baffled. 'She wouldn't have killed him over a painting.'

'Right,' Maxine said, suddenly focusing and taking charge. 'Never mind what happened. We need to get rid of his body and fast. The vehicle I saw was empty so it's possible he may have come alone, but I wouldn't bank on it.'

Carla glanced at her. 'They don't usually.'

'Have you seen any others?'

Carla shook her head.

Maxine shrugged. 'Either way, we need to be quick.'

Despite Maxine's insistence, Carla was still staring in Kaufmann's direction. 'But why *is* that painting on the floor? His blood is all over it.'

'Never mind that now. Come on,' Maxine insisted. 'Help me roll him up in this rug.'

After they had twisted and tugged at the rug to fully envelop him, the two of them tried to lift his rolled-up body, one at the shoulders, one at the ankles, but it instantly drooped in the middle and dragged on the floor.

'Put him down,' Maxine hissed, practical as ever despite the shockwaves still ricocheting through her. 'We need more help. We'll trail blood through the whole house like this. It'll take three of us to carry him.'

'I'll help,' Elsa said, beginning to rise from the sofa.

'No,' Carla said. 'I'll fetch Anna. You need to stay with the mistress.'

'Hurry then.'

While Carla was gone Maxine asked Elsa if Sofia had said anything at all about what had happened.

'All she said was they had hanged him.'

'Who? You don't think she meant Lorenzo?'

Elsa slowly let out her breath. 'Maybe.'

'I'm not surprised she shot him then.'

'She has blood on her blouse.'

'Maybe she checked to see if he was dead. She'll need to change.' Maxine glanced down at herself. 'We'll all need to change.'

A few minutes later Carla was back with Anna, who stared, dumbstruck, first at the blood on the wall and the floor, then at the sight of Kaufmann's booted feet hanging out of the rolled-up rug, and finally at Sofia. She crossed herself and whispered over and over, '*Madonna santa.*'

'All right?' Maxine asked after a moment.

Anna blinked rapidly and shook herself out of it. 'To the tunnels then?' she said. 'I can't be long. I've left Alberto on his own.'

Carla patted her daughter's hand. 'He'll be fine, but we need to hurry anyway. Once the bombing starts the whole village will be sheltering down there.'

'The village have been taking refuge there?' Maxine asked as they began to lift the rolled-up form. 'God, but he's heavier than you'd think.'

'A dead weight,' Anna said, and guffawed at her own joke.

'Shush,' Carla scolded and shook her head at her daughter.

Maxine glanced across at Elsa, who was gently stroking Sofia's hand. 'Will *they* be all right?'

'For now,' said Carla. 'I'll clean this mess up when we get back and you hide the gun, Anna.'

'Let's hope the Allies get here before the Germans realize Kaufmann is missing. I'll need to move his car, dump it somewhere,' Maxine said.

'What about the keys?'

They all realized the same thing at the same time and Maxine rolled her eyes. 'Jesus! We can't keep picking him up and putting him down again. He's not a damn handbag.'

'Have you got a better idea?' Anna muttered back.

'Put him down then.' Maxine grimaced as she unrolled the rug and recoiled at the sight of Kaufmann's lifeless eyes. Then she forced herself to hunt for the key in his pockets.

'Aren't you scared? You're getting covered in blood.'

'I'll burn my clothes, after.'

'Before or after you move the car?' Anna said.

'All right. You burn the clothes. I'll put on clean clothes and then move the car. Now come on! I've got the keys. Roll this bastard up again.' She smirked, her black humour rising at the insanity of it all. 'I'd love to have seen his face when she pulled the trigger.'

There was a sudden noise. Was it someone knocking at the door or a branch brushing against a window in the wind? Wide-eyed, they exchanged glances, their shock and distress still uppermost, and fear making them imagine the worst. Could it be the Germans? Already?

'Did I lock the door?' Carla winced at the possibility that she might not have locked up after she fetched Anna.

'Too late. Ignore it,' Maxine ordered.

'You did lock it,' Anna said. 'Don't worry.'

Carla pulled a face and hesitated before she spoke. 'Sorry, but there's something else. We're going to need a lamp.'

'Oh, for Christ's sake, why don't we bake a cake while we're at it?' Maxine looked over to Elsa in frustration. 'Would you mind coming with us, after all? We need someone to carry a lamp.'

'There's one in the kitchen, matches on the shelf,' Carla added.

Elsa ran to the kitchen and came back carrying the lit lamp. After that, they made their way across the room.

'He's dripping,' Maxine muttered, glancing at the floor. 'The rug's not thick enough.'

Carla groaned. 'Too late to worry about that now.'

Finally, they made their way to the cellars and then into the tunnels. Carla knew exactly where to go, and they carried him, rather awkwardly, thumping and bumping him along the tunnel as far from the house as they could manage.

'We only need to hide him until the Allies come. They can deal with the body then,' Maxine said. 'They're already in Montepulciano, so it won't be long.'

Carla gave a little cheer.

'Wonder if the little boy is still down here?' Anna said. 'Should we look?'

'His mother's in an awful state but his brother insists he's in the woods. Anyway, we can't look now. There's too much to do.'

They traipsed back to the house, ready to go their separate ways: Anna to hide the gun, Carla to clean up the mess, Maxine to dump Kaufmann's car and Elsa to comfort her daughter. Except, when they returned to the salon, Sofia was gone.

60

While Carla fetched a bucket of water, a mop, some old rags and a scrubbing brush, she worried about her mistress. Before leaving, Anna had searched the house but had found no sign of her. Sofia's studio door was locked so they assumed she had to be in there. Carla wanted to check again, but they all had urgent tasks to complete before the bombing began, so Elsa began the search on her own, in case Sofia wasn't in the studio. As Carla entered the little salon, she glanced back over her shoulder, fearful a German officer might walk in and discover her about to mop up Kaufmann's blood. The Allies had not yet arrived, and the Germans were *definitely* still there, so it was possible. What's more, if Maxine didn't get the car away quickly enough, she might get caught in machine-gun fire.

Carla started at the sound of a distant explosion, crossed herself and began to scrub. Had to get it done before the villagers came to shelter in the cellars. But, my Lord, she had never seen so much blood. The sweet, sickly animal stink of it filled her nostrils as she worked. It had saturated the rug and seeped through on to the floor, so she mopped there first, running to fetch clean water every few minutes, but still a faint stain of pink coloured the patterned tiles. She got rid of the mop then ran to find a rug from another room to cover the stain. Next, she dealt with the wall where the blood was most extensive. She kept wiping and wiping but needed to pick out the pieces of flesh with her fingers. She'd never get the blood out of her fingernails. When it was done, she fetched a clean cloth and clean water to wipe the painting, dabbing at it gingerly so as not to damage the gold by rubbing too hard. Her beloved San Sebastiano. She found

Kaufmann's horn-rimmed spectacles and pocketed them to dispose of later. Then she checked and wiped clean the bloody trail they'd made when they carried him through the house. Maxine was right, the rug hadn't been thick enough and blood had dripped all the way. Finally, she scrubbed her hands until they were raw, took off her stained apron and rushed to the boiler house where Maxine's clothing was already burning. She stood motionless, hearing the aeroplanes flying over and the first bombs exploding, though not yet too close, thank goodness. The villagers would be knocking at the door at any minute.

The night that came was the worst yet. Still nobody could be sure where Sofia was, and they had to force Elsa to stop searching and come down to the cellars. She had repeatedly knocked on the studio door to no avail and had gone into the garden to look through the windows but found the shutters closed. Anna caught up with her wandering about outside, calling her daughter's name and weeping.

The bombing was intense but seemed to be moving a little north of them. The Allies must be doing everything they could to halt the German retreat. There was no singing, only prayers. No one slept. The mother of the missing boy wanted to search the tunnels for him, but Carla told her there was no oil left in any lamp and without one she wouldn't be able to see a thing. She felt bad, because it wasn't quite true, but they couldn't risk her stumbling across Kaufmann's body. She would look for the child herself in the morning, take the dogs with her and go through all the tunnels once the villagers had left. She'd check the woods too. She'd grown up here and knew every nook and cranny of those woods, every hollow tree, all the best places for a young, frightened child to hide.

61.

29 June 1944

In the morning a pink glow cast its light over the land but there was still no reply when Carla knocked on the studio door. On a hunch she headed for the tower and, finding it unlocked, went up. She hadn't thought of it before; after all, who would choose to go to the top of a tower during an air raid? The room at the top was empty but she climbed the narrow steps and there she found Sofia on the roof, curled up on the hard flagstones. Carla froze. Her tension was only slightly relieved at finding her mistress, because of Sofia's unnatural stillness. Fearing the worst, Carla held her breath and reached out to gently shake her. Sofia murmured and waved her away, so she went back down to the house to fetch a blanket and a pillow and then returned with a glass and a jug of fresh water too. She helped Sofia to drink a little then wrapped the blanket around her shoulders.

'Once the sun climbs higher it will be too hot up here. Won't you come down to your studio?'

Sofia allowed Carla to take her by the hand and lead her down the steps.

'Did you stay up there all night?'

'I wanted them to hit the tower.'

'Oh, my dearest Contessa, you mustn't think like that.'

'They hanged him,' Sofia said in a broken voice. 'They hanged my Lorenzo.'

Carla's heart plummeted. So, it was true. She had to stay strong if she was to help Sofia, though this was enough to destroy the strongest, let alone their gentle mistress. 'Come now,' she said, helping a stumbling Sofia to a chair. 'Sit here and I'll wrap you up. Do you think you might be able to eat something?'

Sofia shook her head. 'Just leave me here.'

'On your own? You shouldn't be on your own.'

'Please. Don't let anyone come up. Don't tell them I'm here. Tell them I'm fine and say I'm resting.'

'What about your mother and Maxine?'

'Tell them I'm all right.' She paused. 'I killed a man, Carla. In cold blood I killed him. I need to be alone.'

'You did the right thing.'

'He wanted the painting.'

'San Sebastiano?'

'It didn't really matter. I'd have let him take it. In fact, he could have just taken anything he wanted, but . . . it was when he told me they had hanged Lorenzo.'

Carla stood in horrified silence, but Sofia didn't speak again.

'Well, you come down later when you're ready,' Carla finally said, speaking softly as if to a child. 'I'll leave the water and make you a nice supper this evening, a special one. Now sleep, sleep for as long as you can.'

Sofia nodded.

And Carla held the horrible wrenching pain inside herself, hurried down the stairs and ran to her kitchen. She wanted to be somewhere else. Be someone else. Someone who wasn't on the verge of panic. She took a long, slow breath to calm herself, then sat down, laid her head on her folded arms and wept hard and long. She hated to see her beloved mistress like this, but Lorenzo . . . she had known him since he was a baby. If she had been the one standing before Kaufmann with a gun in her hand, she'd have shot him too. In fact, shooting was too good for him. She pictured Sofia, all alone up there, hollow-eyed and broken. It didn't feel right.

Later she crept up the stairs to the tower and found Sofia fast asleep. She wouldn't risk interrupting her slumber again but would do exactly what she'd said. Try to find something tempting to cook for her and hope she'd come down by the evening. Grief took people in different ways. Some needed to be with people. Others need to be alone. She would reassure Elsa. She'd say her daughter would be all right and then she'd spend some time looking for the missing child.

But by the early evening, with no luck at finding the boy, Carla alerted Maxine; not only was she worried about the child, but about the Contessa too, because Sofia still hadn't come down. Maxine had been asleep much of the day but, hearing this from Carla, she grabbed a robe and threw it on.

62

Even at the end of the day the smell of smoke still lingered in the air. It crept into their hair, clothes, even their skin, so most of the villagers had stayed inside, either sleeping or resting after their wakeful night in the cellars. The evening grew heavy and still. In the distance, the sound of gunfire continued but, in the piazza, the only voices you could hear were those of the tiny swallows. Yet when a large black-winged crow took flight from the top of the tower, an ear-splitting screeching began. Another crow followed. Then another. 'Three crows,' Maria whispered. Three. Hadn't they had enough death? She stifled a yawn and, despite the warmth of the evening, wrapped her frayed woollen shawl around her shoulders.

In the azure sky, the sun, at present still a huge yellow ball, would soon be sinking. Despite the bombs that had fallen so close by, the ancient stone buildings surrounding the square were still intact, gleaming as if transformed into pure gold by the sunlight. It had been such a beautiful, peaceful place to live until the war.

A sudden shout echoed around the square. After a moment a dark shutter flew open and Anna's startled face appeared in the window, her sleepy eyes turned towards the sound. *What now?* Surely there could be no more. Weren't the Allies almost there? Maria glanced up as if she might already know *what now* but there was nothing save for a few pigeons fluttering to the cistern in the centre.

A fresh breeze rustled the flat leaves of a fig tree and you could hear the air beginning to sing.

There was another shout as young Alberto raced through the

main archway chasing after Gabriella's three-legged dog, the child's crust of bread clamped between its jaws. As he circled the cistern and slipped on an unripe fig, Anna called to her boy and the dog escaped.

Maxine, wearing a navy-blue robe Sofia had lent her, left the house and went into the square where she spoke to Carla. 'She has been alone too long. Go. Be gentle with her.' She pointed to her right, knowing Carla would take the hidden passage. 'I've got the spare tower key in case she's locked it. Either way, she really needs to come back to the house now.' After Carla had slipped through a doorway into the darkness, Maxine strode towards the tower. At the noise of an engine, some distance away, she paused. Surely not the Germans, not now? She took a moment to cross her fingers and then hurried on.

But at that very moment, a moment that might go on forever in her memory, she heard a strangled cry coming from the top of the tower. She stared up, shading her eyes with her hand, disbelief flooding her whole being. There, on the crenellated battlement at the top of the tower, Sofia was sitting right on the edge with her back to the square. She was just sitting, not moving, not looking round, her head bowed as if in prayer. Maxine's throat dried as she called to Sofia to be careful then she squinted into the light in puzzlement. A few seconds passed, although for Maxine time had now completely stopped. It looked as if someone else was up there with Sofia, but then the light changed, and she could see her friend was alone. It had been just a shadow, a trick of the light. And then something fell, billowing, drifting, floating in the breeze. She saw it was a scarf and as Sofia moved slightly and then tipped back a little further, Maxine began to run.

63.

Two hours later

Lorenzo sat in the British army jeep as it climbed the track to gradually encircle the Castello. Lightheaded with relief and expectation, and loving the scents of home – the rosemary, the lemons, the earth itself – he couldn't avoid the smell of smoke still hanging heavily in the air. But after the subterfuge, the danger, the running, the hiding and the imprisonment, he felt overjoyed to be home.

The jeep came to a halt outside the grand archway into the Castello. The British were travelling northwards but they'd agreed to bring him here, even though it had been a little out of their way. Of course, he'd have walked the two hundred or so kilometres to get home, but the offer of a lift saved time and now he couldn't wait. Out of politeness he asked if they'd like to see something of the Castello and the three men readily climbed out, happy to stretch their legs. After they passed through the archway and the familiar stone walls that had kept Lorenzo's family safe for generations, they entered the piazza. In air teeming with flying insects, they gazed in awe and batted the mosquitoes away with their hands.

'Don't get these in Yorkshire,' one of them joked.

Lorenzo loved the twilight, the absence of shadows, the beautiful buildings silhouetted against the sweet, still sky, and the way, apart from the insects, it was all so tranquil. Too still maybe? But it would be dark soon so anyone out for an evening stroll would probably have headed inside. He was thrilled as he imagined Sofia's beautiful face wreathed in smiles as she ran to greet him. It had been far too long, so he gave the British lads the briefest of tours and then bid them farewell, clapping each one on the back and wishing them good luck.

They took one final look at the ancient buildings and the view across the Val d'Orcia, now fading with the last of the light.

'Gorgeous place, mate,' another one of them said, and the others nodded.

He was delighted to hear it and, happy that nothing too bad appeared to have happened there, he glanced around again, just in case. All the buildings were intact – a blessing indeed. Then he strode towards the front door, heart thumping with inexpressible longing for Sofia. Her eyes, her smile, her long dark hair. And that way she had of looking at him, right in the middle of doing something else, so that only he knew how much she cared. But then he felt a slight stab of apprehension, which could sometimes happen after a prolonged separation. He chided himself and chuckled at his idiocy. Sofia would be as excited to see him as he was to see her.

He took out his key, unlocked the door and stepped inside the house, calling out for Sofia in his eagerness. There was no reply, and with a sudden sickening feeling in his gut he sensed that something was wrong. As he moved closer to Sofia's little salon, he heard urgent whispers. Carla came out of the room in answer to his call, her face blotchy, wiping red, swollen eyes with her apron.

'Carla?'

But Carla's mouth had fallen open.

'Carla,' he said again.

She still didn't speak but as she pointed at Sofia's room, an icy chill swept through him. What the hell was going on here?

He strode into the room where he saw Maxine kneeling beside somebody lying on the sofa.

'Maxine?' he said. She didn't seem to hear at first then lifted her face and looked at him, wide-eyed, as if astonished that he should be there.

He gulped at the air and moved closer, and then he saw his darling girl lying on the sofa, her face entirely devoid of colour. Fear formed a lump in his throat so large he could not swallow and he could feel the pain crushing his chest.

Maxine rose to her feet and held out her palm as if to stop him. 'No. It's not . . . she's not,' she said.

And then Sofia's eyes flew open and she stared at him as if in utter disbelief. In a split second she was on her feet, her trembling hand covering her mouth, audibly gasping for breath, and then her whole body seemed to freeze as if in shock. She swayed, he ran, and then he caught her in his arms as she passed out.

He carried her back to the sofa. She was so light, so fragile, and when she came to, he held her close, wanting never to let go of her again. Never, ever. He kissed her lips, her cheeks, her forehead, but her skin was cold and tinged with blue. She was still gazing at him with such a look of wonder, he could not understand her bewilderment.

'For a minute I thought you were gone,' he said. 'Oh God, I could not have borne it.'

She reached out to stroke his face, shaking her head and drinking him in. 'Is it really you?'

He smiled. 'Of course it's me. Why are you looking as if you've seen a ghost?'

'Because you are a ghost.' She blinked rapidly. 'Because this is impossible. They told me . . .' She bit her lip as she took a shuddering breath and her voice choked as she said the awful words. 'They told me you'd been hanged.'

As they sat side by side, staring at each other, he wanted to howl out his rage at the anguish she must have gone through.

Tears moistened her eyes but did not fall. My God, she was strong, he thought. His adored girl. There was so much to say but now the rising emotions of love and overwhelming joy stopped his voice. He took her hands and placed them in his lap, stroking them, lifting them again, kissing them, allowing them to fall once more. Then he began to weep, swallowing at air, his shoulders juddering. He could see and feel his own tears falling on their linked hands, hot, furious tears. She drew up his hand and kissed away the tears and they continued to sit close until the darkness came.

Maxine entered the room with a coffee for both of them and it was only then he realized they hadn't been alone. Sofia's mother, Elsa, was sitting quietly in the corner, her eyes puffy, the silent grief etched into every line of her face. Sofia got up and went over to Elsa. They held each other, rocking back and forth for a few minutes.

Then his wife came back to him, held out her arms, and together they walked upstairs to their bedroom.

Once there, he gently laid Sofia on top of the eiderdown, now able to find his voice and whisper all that he wanted to say, had dreamt of saying, would go on saying for the rest of his life. Those few seconds during which he'd thought she was gone had cut very deep indeed. He told her how profoundly he loved her, how much he'd missed her, repeating over and over, 'You are the love of my life. The only love of my life.' Then, after a while, when there were no more words, they simply held hands and stared into the mystery of each other's eyes, from time to time shaking their heads, still overcome both by relief and disbelief. She wrapped her arms around him, comforting him, luminous, her eyes alive with light.

'You're warmer now,' he said. 'You were so cold.'

'I spent too long in the tower.'

'Why?'

She shook her head and put a finger to his lips.

She was right, he thought, there'd be plenty of time to hear about everything later. Now all they needed was there in that room. The feeling in both their hearts was so immense it could never be described or ever told. Release. Reprieve. Liberty. A second chance. All those things but, most of all, the deep abiding gratitude that they were both alive.

Suddenly, out of the blue, she said, 'Do you remember the day we first met?'

'I remember how your face lit up at some silly joke I'd made and the way the laughter bubbled out of you.'

And in that moment of remembering he felt it again as the same infectious, joyous laughter took hold of them both.

64.

September 1945

On the eighth of May, 1945, the Allies accepted Germany's surrender. As one of those who had lived through the war in Italy, Sofia had seen its brutality at close hand, as had all the villagers of the Castello. They'd suffered the deepest sorrows and yet they hadn't given up or given in. With resourcefulness and determination, those in the resistance and those supporting the resistance had held out against home-grown fascism and the fascism from abroad. Sofia felt proud to have been part of it, although Lorenzo had been astonished when she'd told him everything she'd done. His eyes had widened, and he'd gazed at her with such a depth of admiration and love it made her heart falter.

They now knew that when the last of the German soldiers left Florence, the partisans had walked through the deserted streets ahead of just a few Allied soldiers coming up behind. They'd glimpsed hundreds of eyes silently staring out at them from the bottom half of otherwise shuttered windows, then slowly at first, eventually rising in a crescendo, hundreds of hands began to clap. The partisans were in tears, the soldiers were in tears and, Sofia felt sure, most of the citizens must have been too.

And now, on a beautiful, shiny September day, Sofia was sitting outside in the garden next to the pomegranate tree as she pondered these things, thanking God it really was all over. At the sound of the back door opening, she turned her head.

'Maxine!' She rose to her feet, smiling broadly, and ran to her friend. 'I'm so happy to see you again.'

The two women embraced, hugging each other for the longest time.

Sofia stepped back first, held Maxine by the hands and scrutinized her face. 'You've been gone so long. More than a year.'

'I know. I had to go home. The British were fantastic, arranged my flights and everything.'

Sofia reached out a hand to touch her. 'Your hair is shorter.'

Maxine smiled and turned her head from side to side so that her bobbed hair swung. 'Do you like it?'

'It's gorgeous.'

'Thanks.' She paused for a moment. 'You look well, Sofia.'

'Carla has been fattening me up. Now tell me about you.'

'Well, I've been back in Italy for a short time now, looking up relatives and people my parents once knew in Santa Cecilia.'

'You talked to your parents about Matteo?'

'A little. It was pretty tense, I can tell you. And I've just been visiting with Marco's sister before coming here.'

'How was she, and his little nephew, of course?'

'Absolutely wonderful . . . But how are you, Sofia, really?'

'I'm good. Honestly, I am. Shall we sit?' And then she gazed at her friend with serious eyes as she drew up a chair.

'What is it?' Maxine asked as they both sat.

'We never talked, did we? You left so quickly . . . after Lorenzo returned.'

'I know. It felt like the right thing to do. You and Lorenzo needed the time together.'

Sofia's brow furrowed as she looked down at the ground and then up again at Maxine. 'It's a terribly hard thing to say, but I had intended to do it, you know.'

Maxine nodded. 'Yes. I think I know that too.'

'I couldn't bear that after everything we'd gone through, I was going to have to live my life without Lorenzo. I think I went a little bit crazy after killing Kaufmann.'

Maxine held out her hand. Sofia took it and squeezed.

346

'I was absolutely bloody terrified,' Maxine said. 'I've never run so fast, and my heart was pounding so damn hard I thought it was going to stop. And then, there you were, calmly coming down the stairs.'

'And you barged straight into me, sent me flying.'

They both laughed.

'Your face. You were absolutely scarlet from running up the stairs.'

Maxine shook her head. 'You gave me the fright of my life, lady. Look,' and she pointed at her hair. 'Grey!'

Sofia peered closely. 'Not even one,' she scoffed.

'I can't tell you how unbelievably glad I am that you changed your mind.' Maxine paused to look down before glancing sideways at Sofia. 'I never had the chance to ask you why. When we came back inside the house you were so ashen and so cold, I couldn't begin to interrogate you then. Do you mind if I ask you now?'

'It's fine.' Sofia let out a long, slow breath. Thinking back to the worst day of her life was painful and she keenly felt the shame of what she'd almost done, but she knew Maxine deserved an answer. 'It was several things,' she said. 'I didn't want to live, and that's the truth, but I thought of my mother and that brought me back from the brink. What it would have done to her after the loss of my father. I thought of you too. I couldn't let you down, nor Carla, or Anna, or the villagers. People had died who'd wanted so much to live.'

Maxine's eyes filled with tears. 'Marco.'

'Yes. How could I have done that to him? Or Aldo, or anyone who had fought so bravely. No. I had to honour the ones who died by living my life, not escaping it.'

'Didn't you choose to stay alive for yourself too?'

Sofia nodded slowly. 'Yes. That too, in the end. I did choose life. But I can't deny I felt the pull of such an overpowering urge to jump, to fall into oblivion, to let it all go.'

There was a long silence as Maxine brushed her tears away. 'Thank you for telling me,' she said eventually as she rose to her feet. 'Shall we walk a little now?'

They wandered through the village, and then stood looking out across the Val d'Orcia at the sunshine after rain. The trees dripping with moisture, their leaves sparkling. The summer coming to an end, the light less harsh. The vineyards bursting with perfumed grapes. And they both knew it was an ending of sorts.

'One thing is certain,' Maxine said as she gazed up into the distant, shimmering hills. 'I will never forgive Kaufmann for the lie he told you. Of all the terrible things that happened, that was one of the cruellest. Thank God you had time to reflect.'

'I thank God for that all the time. But you know there is a price to pay for killing a person.'

'And that is?'

'I'm not sure I know yet. It's internal. Hard to put your finger on.'

'What does Lorenzo think about it?'

'I haven't told him how I feel. It will take a while. For now, I think we both just want to forget. He doesn't talk about his imprisonment either, but there are marks on his body that weren't there before.'

'Oh, Sofia.'

Sofia gave a slight shake of her head. 'I didn't have to kill Kaufmann, you know. I could have just let him take the painting.'

'He may well have had you shot anyway.'

'Well, there it is. I did it. I never thought I'd be capable of such a thing.' There were a few moments of silence, then Sofia spoke again. 'And you, Maxine, what about you?'

'How do you mean?'

'You're changed too, aren't you? You seem, I don't know, softer maybe?'

Maxine smiled. 'I don't know either, but I do feel as if I have a more definite identity now. Does that sound silly?'

'Of course not.'

'I didn't know who I was when I came here. Now at least I'm halfway to finding out.'

Sofia smiled. 'I think I've always known who you were, even if you didn't. You are the most courageous, vital person I've ever met, and I will miss you *so* much more than I can say. But, Maxine, you'll always be welcome at the Castello.'

'Thank you.'

'And until you come back, I'll think of you often and pray for you every day.'

'You pray now?'

Sofia laughed. 'Better late than never.'

'Well, I will miss you too.' Maxine sniffed and blinked away a tear.

Sofia took her hand. 'At least things are looking up now. My mother is showing signs of slowly coming back to life, beginning to come through the darkest time.'

'Gabriella had her baby?' Maxine asked.

'Oh yes. A boy. Carla and Maria compete over who is the best grandmother, or great-grandmother in Maria's case, and they quarrel about whose turn it is to mind little Aldo.'

Sofia thought back to the day they discovered Maria had not passed on the information Gabriella gave her; it had been such a relief to know the girl was not to blame. They never did find out who had betrayed them. People had wondered about Giulia, the maid who had left so suddenly, but nothing could ever be proven, even if they did suspect her. The missing boy had turned up, thankfully, none the worse for wear, although starving hungry. He'd been hiding in a hollow tree all the time.

'Did you ever finish the painting of Aldo?' Maxine asked.

'Of course. Carla has it in her bedroom now.'

'It must bring her comfort.'

'I hope.' Sofia sighed. 'So, when do you go back to America?'

'I'm sailing in a week's time. Sorry it's such a short visit but my poor long-suffering parents. We did talk about Matteo, as I said, but there's still so much more to say. I'll come back here though, maybe even next year, or the one after. And that's a promise. I have to earn some money first.'

'Journalism again?'

Maxine nodded. 'I've had a few offers, even wrote a few pieces when I first arrived home.'

'Good for you. And, whenever it is, we'll be happy to see you. This is where you belong, at least a part of you, and where you always *will* belong.'

As they walked back to the house, arm in arm, Sofia knew neither of them would ever forget that day at the end of June: the heat, the bright light, the Allies arriving and the sun about to fall from the sky. The day that Lorenzo had come home, and she had chosen to live. She wondered if future generations, future visitors even, would have any sense of what had happened there as they gazed at the rolling hills and valleys, and at the avenues of cypress trees. When they saw the brilliance of spring – the fields carpeted with vivid red poppies, the verges teeming with wildflowers and the air alive with butterflies – what would they think?

And when they smelt freshly baked bread and strolled in the gardens where the scent of rosemary and sweet jasmine lingered, would their hearts sing as hers did? Or in their mind's eye would they see German tanks and steel-helmeted soldiers? Would they envy the simplicity of country life or would they wonder how the people had survived?

As they drove through this breathtaking landscape, would it be peace they felt? Peace – such a small word for something so huge, and something they took so much for granted, until it was gone.

Maybe it was best they didn't know about the past.

Maybe it was vital that they did.

Author's Note

My Inspiration for the Setting

Castello di Gargonza

I envisaged my primary location as a beautiful, relatively isolated and self-contained community where, at first, the villagers might imagine that the war had passed them by. The truth turned out to be different, and many such Tuscan villages and towns became embroiled in some of the fiercest fighting of World War II.

My fictional village, Castello de' Corsi, was inspired by and is based on the fortified hilltop settlement of Castello di Gargonza, although I combined elements from other remote medieval villages and hamlets I found as I ventured off the beaten track on to a network of unmetalled roads in our hired four-wheel drive.

For the purposes of the narrative I relocated my village further south than Gargonza's actual location. I chose a section on the hills north of the Val d'Orcia, south of the Crete Senesi and west of the Val di Chiana. My aim was to bring the narrative closer to a major front of the fighting that took place in Tuscany during World War II.

Gargonza itself is situated a few miles outside Monte San Savino in the province of Arezzo. You turn off the road towards Siena and follow a winding narrow track through the forest until this walled village looms in front of you. Exactly as it is in my book, one single archway allows access to the village, once home to the 110 people who served the network of farms belonging to the estate. Enter and you feel as if you've arrived in a mythical past. Walk the narrow alleyways and cobbled lanes and you might never want to leave the seductive feeling of peace you find. I was there in November when the early-morning mists enveloped the ancient walls, adding to the already overwhelming atmosphere of inaccessibility. However, once the sun burns off the mist, the views are captivating. Rising over the small square, an ancient tower is set into the buttressed walls – the tower of my story.

I have to thank Neri Guicciardini, the owner, who showed us around and explained the history. Relaxed and informal, he gave no hint that his was a family of counts and marquises with a lineage going back to the Medicis except, maybe, for the gracious and attentive way he greeted us.

The village passed into the hands of Neri's family, the Guicciardini Corsi Salviati, in 1696. It was the centre of administration and support for the surrounding farms until the end of World War II when a rural exodus led to the abandonment of the village. By the early 1970s it had been deserted and became one of Italy's fabled ghost towns. The skilled carpenters, blacksmiths, mechanics, builders and others who supported the peasant farming community were gone.

The Castello is now surrounded by forest, where game and truffle hunting continues, but previously the land was cleared to produce wheat, olives and vines. Gargonza has a wonderful restaurant where their own olive oil is served, and where fresh truffles gathered in the morning are used in a dish of wild boar ragù with handmade tagliatelle.

Neri's father, Roberto Guicciardini Corsi Salviati, made it his ambition to restore the village and create something that echoed its former glory, and thus began its evolution from ghost town to guest town. Though *castello* can mean 'castle' it can also mean any fortified dwellings such as those found around a manor house or village. The olive mills, communal oven and blacksmiths' workshops clustered around the small square, and the village boasted both a church and a chapel. The latter was deconsecrated and is now used for wine-tasting sessions. The small yet frescoed church is still consecrated and used for weddings as well as regular masses.

The houses of the various workers and officials of the village have been turned into apartments or rooms where guests can stay. Although it looks like a normal village, the whole place is now a hotel with a conference centre where musical performances are held, and where meetings of leading academic bodies come together. Down near the restaurant there's a magnificent swimming pool. There are no televisions, although Wi-Fi is installed. We simply slowed down, enjoyed the wonderful food and soaked up the incredible atmosphere in this unique and inspirational place. If you'd like to read more and see photos, their website is: http://www.gargonza.it/

San Gimignano

The tower in *The Tuscan Contessa* was also inspired by the months I spent as an au pair looking after two children at La Rocca in San Gimignano, for the family of Roberto Guicciardini Strozzi. It was 1967, long before the town became the tourist destination it is today, but its many towers always haunted me. I couldn't help imagining how terrible it would be to fall from one, so you see the seed for this book was sown many years ago.

Lucignano d'Asso

I fell in love with this little hamlet and it became further inspiration for the spot I created for my peaceful fictional village overlooking rolling hills and surrounded by cypress trees. I first came across it on a trip out from Montalcino when the valley beyond Lucignano was wreathed in mists, so I just had to return in May when all the spring flowers were blooming. We stayed in what had been a village house, now transformed into a holiday rental. Like Gargonza, many of the houses are now part of the hotel, one of the most magical places I've ever stayed. Their website is https://www.borgolucignanello.com/en/

Buonconvento

This marvellous red-brick medieval town had to be included so I settled on this as a larger town in the book. It's absolutely gorgeous and bursting with moody atmosphere.

Research Trips

I went on four wonderful trips to Tuscany at varying times of year and one specifically to Florence where we stayed in the palazzo that inspired Sofia's own home in Florence. Although I lived in Tuscany in 1967, I hadn't been back until 2018 and 2019. I loved every moment of being there again and can't wait to return.

Research

I read a multitude of books about Italy during World War II, including:

The Other Italy: The Italian Resistance in World War II, Maria de Blasio Wilhelm, Ishi Press International, 2013
Gargonza, the Castle, the People: Memoirs of a Landowner, Roberto Guicciardini Corsi Salviati, Edifir Edizioni Firenze, 2014

Italy's Sorrow: A Year of War 1944–45, James Holland,
    HarperPress, 2009
War in Val d'Orcia: An Italian War Diary 1943–1944, Iris
    Origo, Pushkin Press, 2017

Two films were particularly useful:

Rome, Open City, Roberto Rossellini, 1945
Tea with Mussolini, Franco Zeffirelli, 1999

Acknowledgements

I continue to be massively grateful for all the support I get from the magnificent team at Penguin and especially Venetia Butterfield, who really does have the magic touch. Huge thanks to my agent, Caroline Hardman, who I trust implicitly and who is always there when I need her, sharp and bright as a pin. My readers? I thank every single one; I can't tell you how grateful I am that you enjoy my books. And I mustn't forget the book bloggers who have been staunch supporters of my novels – thank you so much, it really means a lot.

In the autumn of 2019, I went on a course to 'Unleash My Potential' and I want to thank Bertie Ekperigin and Philippa Gray, plus my entire RASA family, for changing my life and giving me the confidence to sail through some very tricky edits and the courage to believe I can try something different.

As for my family – well, you are my inspiration, the reason I get up in the morning and why I want to go on writing. You are my everything. Here's to all our futures and lots more wonderful adventures.

Dinah Jefferies

He just wanted a decent book to read ...

Not too much to ask, is it? It was in 1935 when Allen Lane, Managing Director of Bodley Head Publishers, stood on a platform at Exeter railway station looking for something good to read on his journey back to London. His choice was limited to popular magazines and poor-quality paperbacks – the same choice faced every day by the vast majority of readers, few of whom could afford hardbacks. Lane's disappointment and subsequent anger at the range of books generally available led him to found a company – and change the world.

'We believed in the existence in this country of a vast reading public for intelligent books at a low price, and staked everything on it'
Sir Allen Lane, 1902–1970, founder of Penguin Books

The quality paperback had arrived – and not just in bookshops. Lane was adamant that his Penguins should appear in chain stores and tobacconists, and should cost no more than a packet of cigarettes.

Reading habits (and cigarette prices) have changed since 1935, but Penguin still believes in publishing the best books for everybody to enjoy. We still believe that good design costs no more than bad design, and we still believe that quality books published passionately and responsibly make the world a better place.

So wherever you see the little bird – whether it's on a piece of prize-winning literary fiction or a celebrity autobiography, political tour de force or historical masterpiece, a serial-killer thriller, reference book, world classic or a piece of pure escapism – you can bet that it represents the very best that the genre has to offer.

Whatever you like to read – trust Penguin.